LOST RINGS AND OTHER THINGS

LOST RINGS AND OTHER THINGS

Vanessa Raccio

This book is a work of fiction. Names, characters, places, and incidents are the product of the author's imagination or are used fictitiously. Any resemblance to actual events, locales, or persons, living or dead, is coincidental.

Cover Design | Formatting
Enchanted Ink Publishing

ISBN: 978-1-7778630-0-5 (eBook)
ISBN: 978-1-7778630-1-2 (Paperback)
ISBN: 978-1-7778630-2-9 (Hardcover)

Printed in the United States of America

For me,

and the anxiety that thought it

was stronger than my will —

not this time, jerk.

CHAPTER ONE

Chasing Shadows

IT'S TOO QUIET.

Neglect had a way of making noise and adding unwanted weight. After a lifetime of prowling streets littered with trash, being kept awake by the fury of empty stomachs, and hiding behind cracked windows, a person's ears and shoulders ached from the heft of it. But neglect reminded Emily why she was the only one still awake when the rest of her fellow orphans huddled deep in their beds, asleep—it was an enemy to fight. And fighting was better than staying still.

Cold snaked its way through Emily's threadbare blanket and she shivered into her thin, warped mattress. It was impossible to get comfortable, but that was all right. Her bed wasn't supposed to be comfortable—none of the beds she'd slept in ever were. And there had been many. Thankfully, the Commons weren't designed for comfort, so her expectations were appropriately low whenever she outgrew one home before jumping to the next.

Crumbling walls boxed her into her own little prison, the cracks in the stone crying tears of condensation that would turn to ice by morning. This bedroom was larger than her last, at least. With walls of exposed and rotting timber instead of stone, her previous residence shook and rattled with the slightest breeze. Her straw cot was laced with splinters as well as rat droppings, the solitary window empty and crooked. Here, in her thin bed, she was dry, her hands and feet numb from the draft. But there was glass in her window and cats to keep the rats at bay.

She flexed her fingers, willing the blood to keep moving.

She always had to keep moving.

"Molly?"

No response from the bed beside hers.

Should she stay?

Not unless you like eating stale bread for three days. Emily wrinkled her nose, and her stomach rumbled, a dull tug in the pit of her gut. She had to leave.

Maybe the quiet's a good thing. No complications.

Her legs twitched under the blanket, ready to run, ready to *go*. Saint Barth's was heavy with sleep, the street it sat on empty as the homeless and the merchants escaped from the unexpected cold. Frost crept across the deep-blue glass like a delicate spider's web, and she traced the crystal filigree with hooded eyes. She forced each muscle to relax, the tension moving from her neck to her shoulders, arms, stomach, and she counted the cracks in the ceiling as she completed her assessment. A rogue spring in the old cot dug into her back and she winced, abandoning her half-hearted attempt to relax.

Comfort was a myth.

Quiet was a trap.

Everything was a trap.

See? This is why you're alone. No one likes a downer. The voice crept up from the dark, muddy place in her mind, so she rolled onto her side, the creaking mattress springs chasing the voice away. She ran through the plan again, closing her eyes to let the familiar mantra sweep over her: *Hide, listen, hurt, run.*

Sliding the blanket off her legs, Emily's life cleaved in two; a small part of her stayed behind, watching over Molly in the next bed, while a much bigger part itched for freedom that was at her fingertips. She ghosted across the cold wood floor to the window in her thickest woollen socks. A pair of leather boots waited for her under the barred window, and she pulled them on, wriggling her toes into the grooves.

Her black braid coiled into the hood of her sweater, and Emily pulled the thin cotton low over her eyes to keep out the night. Her hands were steady, her focus on the patchy rooftops giving off a thin blanket of mist—heat escaping into the night. Tongue trapped between her teeth, she snaked her thin fingers between the bars and forced the latch on the window open. She held her breath, like she did every time, waiting for someone to wake, to catch her and tell her to stay.

"You're going again, aren't you?"

Right on cue. Behold, the complication. Emily turned away from the cold and sighed. "Go back to sleep."

Molly's face was blue in the faint moonlight, her hair

like ribbons of blood against her pillow. "You're going to get caught."

"Pretty sure I won't." Emily leaned against the windowsill and crossed her arms into a tight knot over her chest. "I'm only going for a walk, remember?"

Molly's delicate features melted into a frown. Small hands pulled her blanket higher, so a pair of large eyes and blue fingernails were the only things visible. She shuddered against the icy air. "I still don't like this."

"You don't have to." Emily released one of her hands and ran her palm over the rough steel bars decorating their window, ignoring the prickle of rust against her callused skin. Her nails were broken and gnawed down to half moons—not pretty, but they didn't have to be. If someone got close enough to see them, she was doing something wrong.

"You know you can get back to bed anytime, right?" Molly's voice lilted, whined. Young. So young. "Just come back to bed, Emily. You can sleep here with me, if you're lonely."

"I will in a bit. Promise." Emily reached for the necklace sitting above her breastbone, twisting her fingers around the warm, soft gold, and her heartbeat slowed. A talisman, a comfort, a constant. The trinket was her only true friend in the world. But instead of being overwhelmed by sadness and self-pity, she was at peace—loneliness was part of the job.

"I don't like it when you're gone." Molly's voice quivered. Small. So small. "My stomach hurts. If they find you, they'll take you away and I won't see you again."

Emily shrank away from the sadness forming invisible hands to claw her back to bed. "I'll be back before you even wake up."

Molly wiggled her toes under her thin blanket. "Whatever you're doing, I can be your backup."

Not this again. "Molly—" Emily began, but it was no use. It never was.

"Come *on*, Emily!" Her voice barely registered above a whisper, but the words screamed panic. "I promise, if you give me a chance—"

"No," Emily said, and Molly shrank into her mattress. "One more year, maybe two, and Chancellor Pascale will send you off to some initiate up at the castle. You can get out of this place, be more than an orphan with no magic. If you get caught helping me, you'll never get out of here. You understand that, right?"

Molly was stubborn, even in her brief bouts of silence. "But what if you get caught? People get caught, and you're not supposed to be out after hours. They'll lock you up."

There it was again: a familiar question Emily never wanted to answer. She focused instead on the solid weight of her necklace and breathed. In and out, in and out. "I never get caught. It's just a walk, kid. Come on, why don't you go back to sleep?"

"I'm not tired." Molly stifled a yawn.

"Uh-huh." *Poor girl. Please go to sleep.*

"It's true."

"Oh, I believe you." Emily longed to cross the careful distance between them, to wrap her arms around Molly's shoulders, so thin and fragile. To reassure instead of disappoint. But she couldn't. Distance was safety—for them both.

A cry pierced the bitter night, and Emily turned back to the window, glaring out at the dark pinpricks circling the stars. The sky spread over the realm like a navy dome, tiny shadows streaking across the heavens like a fiery storm of arrows. They were only spots of brightness, too far to make out against the backdrop of the heavens, but the hatred boiling up inside told Emily everything she needed to know.

Dragons.

Molly's large eyes were fixed and unblinking. "I hate that sound. Gives me nightmares."

Me too, kid. "The dragons would never come down here."

Molly sniffed. "Thank Elders for that."

The surge of anger took Emily by surprise, and her hate bubbled over. She turned, voice sharpened to a point. "The Elders are the reason you're here half-frozen and starving and *they're* up there living in fancy castles. Don't mention the Elders to me."

"I just meant—"

"I know what you meant." Molly's eyes swam and Emily's heart sank, and the cycle repeated itself, yet again. *Oh, perfect. Way to go, Roth.*

Dragons circled the distant city, towering over the rest of the realm, and Emily tracked their blazing movements just as she had done day after day. Large part hate . . . tiny part envy. She steadied her breath, following the bursts of fire in the distance with practiced eyes. "Listen, I'm sorry," she said when she was certain there wouldn't be any lingering bitterness in her voice. "The dragons stay around magic—around *their* kind. They won't travel so far away from the castle. So don't worry about it, okay?"

Silence.

"Molly?"

The sheet covering Molly's chest moved up and down in an even, predictable rhythm. Sadness, bitter and unexpected, kept Emily rooted there for a moment longer than necessary. The tiny folds between the sleeping girl's eyebrows smoothed into the flat plane of easy dreams, all the prying questions dissolving on her chapped, parted lips. So peaceful.

Loneliness sucked.

Sweet dreams, kid. Emily grasped the bars on their window with tight fists and closed her eyes against the onslaught of doubt. Her breathing slowed; her mind cleared. There was no Molly, no dragons in the distance, or weight from her necklace. There was only the cold under her fingers, the rusted hardness of the metal caging her in.

Gone. She urged her shoulders to relax enough to let the millions of tiny insects travel through her veins at their own will, acutely aware of every shift in her body.

The steel wasn't trapped by the brick and rust of the prison she had no choice but to call home. No . . . it was rubber, so flexible and light.

Gone.

The rubber shrank under her hands. Fragile. But breaking anything would make too much noise, and she needed it to be . . . *Gone.*

Emily exhaled, the insects prickling her skin fading to a light whisper across her palms, twisting into the sharp sparks of fire. Her blood was flame, but her hands ran cold. Empty. She opened her eyes, and a small smile played across her face.

Widely considered a runt by the other orphans of Saint Barth's who were no bigger than runts themselves, she should have minded the way clothes hung off her, the way her wild, dark hair and large, black eyes overwhelmed her sharp cheekbones and jutting bones, always making her appear slightly out of balance. But she didn't mind much. Small meant agility. Speed. The ability to move like a shadow, an invisible plague among the eternally invisible.

She squeezed through the remaining gap in the bars, a shadow.

The rest was simple muscle memory: the narrow ledge, the gutter dripping with black sludge snaking its way to the ground, cracked but solid enough to support her shifting weight. Freedom. Exposure.

Her soul flew faster than her feet. The shadows were allies racing her along narrow paths, over rubble, rocks, rats scratching and soon gone on their own hunt for survival. Rotting vegetables piled into blackened corners, low-hanging trees, the sorrow of the village calling her back, calling her home. She pounded the pavement, reveling in the burn tearing at her leg muscles, her lungs. The burn of the hunt. Of leaving it all behind.

Hide, listen, hurt, run.

Hide, listen, hurt, run.

The silent command played in her mind as she chased Coven Hill up a road of gravel. She sprinted for a patch of maples, eager to return to the safety of the dark. Chest heaving, eyes sharp, her thin sweater clinging to her back in a pool of sweat, she ran without breaking stride. It's what she was born for.

Old forests were always her favorite. As a child, she would pretend the ancient trees were ogres, monsters with two heads, teeth dripping with hunger, and she would slay them all. Attack those monsters, one by one, until the day had run out and she was too tired to hear her growling stomach. In the woods, a thousand thick, gnarled branches with broad trunks concealed her with ease, their shadows the perfect cloak. And on raid nights, those trunks—those monsters—were her allies. Emily crouched low behind the line of trees and pressed her fingers against the flaking bark, using the solid weight for support as she hunkered down.

Hide. Listen.

The road was still empty, which meant either she was too late, or her timing was perfect. As soon as the wayward thought crossed her mind, the steady crunch of rock pounded in the distance, and she grinned into her hood. Emily's heart stuttered, her muscles bunched tight, and her fingertips tingled in anticipation. Large wheels crunched the ground, and an *S* scrawled in shimmering gold cursive pulled into view on the side of a large cara-van. Calling her, begging to be defiled.

Right on time. She nestled into the darkness, letting it consume her just a little longer.

Two shadows hunched behind the massive purebreds disturbing the rubble-encrusted path, breathing smoke and chatting low over the hoofbeats. But Emily could only see the horses with their twin pairs of dark, shiny eyes set in chestnut coats, fixed on the road ahead. Their powerful flanks worked to pull the heavy cargo, those eyes searching the darkness for danger. For monsters. For her.

Closer now, enough to notice the white curls peeking out from one rider's hood, hear the exasperated mutter-ings of a female. She sat straighter than her companion. A brooch glittered under her chin, pulling the embroi-dered edges of her cloak closed. *She's the boss. Good to know.* Emily's fingers dragged through the wet earth, leaves slithering under her palms. She turned the stone around in her hand, testing its weight, the sharp edges perfect for causing pain.

Hurt.

The caravan drew level, the heavy musk of manure and sweet wine mingling with the wintry bluster. No matter how often she practiced, timing went hand in hand with pure luck. She gripped the stone and pulled her elbow back, trapping her lower lip between her teeth. The stone whispered through the air, a silent arrow.

The horse whinnied, bucked. Both riders cried out in the night. Hooves gouged the earth, and the caravan came to a shuddering stop.

"Shhh, now! It's all right, girl. What's gotcha so spooked?" Boots landed on the ground and stomped uncertain circles around the animals. The driver's cloak swept a path around him, feathering the loose gravel into fan-like rubble.

Run.

The forest collapsed behind Emily like a tower of cards. She bolted for the back of the caravan, its canvas thick and broad enough to hide behind. The even mumbles from the other end never changed, never stopped or spiralled into protests of alarm.

No one had spotted her. At least not yet.

"You see a spirit in these trees, girl?" The driver's words were hushed and soft. A caress.

"Don't be silly." The woman sighed. "Spirits haven't haunted these woods for centuries. Besides, she has some sort of welt on her side. It looks like she was hit with something."

Oh no, stay where you are, don't go looking around. The canvas was thick and well protected. Emily's frantic fingers ran over the heavy ropes set in stubborn knots, crossing like diamonds over the caravan. The last barrier between her and her goal. Emily closed her eyes.

"Vengeful ghosts!" he cried out.

"Oh, for Elders' sake. Have you ever met a ghost that enjoys flinging rocks at animals?"

He grunted. "No, but I never met a ghost before, so I can't really say nothin' for sure, now, can I?"

Emily suppressed the urge to laugh and refocused on the caravan—the things she needed *inside* it, begging for a well-deserved relocation.

The knots were flowers in her mind, budding in the spring, delicate and fragile. Sweetness filled her senses, the leathery petals thin and supple. They weren't ropes but pretty vines decorating the cargo like ivy filigree twisting across a castle wall.

Loose. Her fingers moved with gentle ease, the coarse fibers growing soft. Every pump of her heart filled her hands with calm, with certainty. With fire.

A peek through hooded lids, and she exhaled in a silent huff. Not a rope in sight. She shook off her hands, willing them to stop trembling, and slithered inside.

The thick, warm smell of success assaulted her. Crate after crate of berries, apples, the ripest melon she'd ever come across, sat brimming with possibility in the belly of the wagon. Emily's mouth watered, the yeasty warmth of rolls fresh from a wood stove battling with the spice of warm cider for her attention. Both could win, for all she was concerned. There was enough of her appetite to go around.

The female rider cried out in the distance. "Honestly, Marcus, the horse is fine!"

"Hurtin' don't always happen on the outside, now, does it, Magdale? Or do all ya Elementals not believe in what ya can't see?"

First went the strawberries. Emily popped the firm, red fruit into her mouth with unsteady fingers while the other hand caressed the barrel, urging the fire through her arms and into her fingers, eager for it to do its job.

This shouldn't be so easy.

She ignored the nagging thoughts, moving to the peaches next. The flesh tore with a light snap over her teeth, the nectar sliding down her chin and throat with the burn of sweetness.

Why aren't they nailing these crates shut?

A cold sheen of sweat beaded on her forehead, trickling down her temples. Her fingers slid from crate to crate, slower and slower. It was harder to breathe. As the caravan emptied, so did her reserves, her energy draining away into the slatted cargo bed.

"Lemme check the back, Maggie. Don't wanna give no initiate some bruised apples. You know how they get, am I right?" The man chuckled, his voice closer now. *Not yet. No, not yet!* The footsteps stopped. "What the Elder is this?"

The canvas flap peeled open as a grey hand with nails caked in mud sliced through the blackness, spilling light across her feet. Emily retreated to a corner, her breathing shallow and fast. She clutched the lid, grateful for the solid weight between her fingers.

"Hey, Maggie!" the man cried. "C'mere!"

"What now?"

A shiny head with ears boasting an alarming number of wiry grey hairs popped into view. Eyes covered in milky-white film roved around the corners of the caravan, and Emily willed herself to become as small as possible, her shoulder brushing against the side of a barrel of wine. The darkness was thick but still not deep enough to make her disappear. The forest was a collection of monsters she knew. Getting caught was another beast altogether.

"Stuff is missin' in here!"

Concern now. "What are you talking about?"

The lid was bulky, hard to grasp with slick and guilty fingers. The wood scratched against the slatted floor as the wizened face pivoted toward her, the crack of arthritic bone locking her location in his crosshairs. His eyes widened, two moons lighting her small hiding place.

Go. C'mon, move!

"What the 'ell do you think you're—*oumf*!"

Emily didn't stop to see the extent of the damage. Her foot slid on a puddle of something dark, but her legs pumped without faltering, her recovery immediate. A heavy *thud* made her heart stutter. He fell—more darkness, this time spilling from the man's head as he crumpled to the ground. She jumped, and the lid clattered to the earth while cold air slapped her face, raking through her hair as the trees called her back. Her necklace bounced under the moonlight with every step, glinting and flailing with every beat of her frantic footfalls.

Ancient maples swallowed her whole, but she couldn't hide from the eyes on her, seeing her, the blood on his head, the man on the floor. Too much colour washed past in blinding streaks, and she missed the grey. Her muscles ached, her heart screamed in her ears, drowning the sounds of the night with its even beat.

Get away.

Just get far away.

From all the monsters. From everything.

Dawn broke as soon as Emily shut her eyes. The morning filled with shuffles and grunts, pillows still warm compared to the frosty shiver of the air in the halls. But she had no desire to return to her dreams. Images poked at her thoughts, and she pushed them aside, gripping the edges of her cot. With heavy eyes, she counted the bars in the window, then again for good measure. The complete set of vertical lines were intact and keeping her safe from whatever lurked outside. And there was too much waiting for her.

"You're finally up." Molly peered at Emily from her bed with eyes as round as teacups. "So? How'd it go? I guess if something *had* gone wrong, you wouldn't be back, right?" She twisted her hair around her finger, over and over, red on cream.

"Too early," Emily grunted. She squinted against the daylight, the knife in her stomach twisting with slow precision. "And if you talk any louder, you might as well hand me over to the Guard yourself."

Molly fidgeted, mattress springs creaking under her slight form. "Right. Sorry. But . . . did you get it?"

Emily grinned, the eagerness on Molly's face enough to distract her from her worries. Distractions meant lowered defenses, but they were also useful. Distractions kept Emily from looking too hard at everything around her, and the Commons weren't a place to linger too long. Keep moving. "Nothing like success to make kitchen duty less annoying." Lying was a regrettable necessity. She couldn't burden anyone with the life she chose.

Molly grinned. "That's a relief. I was worried about you, you know."

"You shouldn't." She pulled her fingers through the tangles in her hair into some semblance of a braid and wiped her face clean with the corner of a bedsheet. "Let the others know they can come in twos and threes after lunch when I've had a chance to ration it all. I'll be back right after I'm done scrubbing the pots." She stretched, winced. Her legs screamed, the muscles in her calves pulling as her feet hit the ground.

"Right," Molly said, her toothy smile contagious. She set to straightening her skirt, smoothing her palms over the box pleats. More wrinkles creased the old cotton, so she stopped, setting to taming her mane of fire instead.

Emily dressed with nimble fingers, hoping busy hands would be enough to ease her nagging worries. In her experience, though, hope never panned out.

The crash of knees hitting the floor echoed from her memory, the deep pool of burgundy spreading across a worn, wooden floor, *drip, drip, dripping* between the slats onto the gravel . . .

Emily shook her head. "Stop."

Molly's hairbrush stopped midway through her locks. She looked up. "I didn't say anything."

"Sorry. I was talking to myself." She forced her feet to move, hoping to outrun the images crowding her mind. The door handle was cold in her sweaty palm. "You ready to go?"

A blue bow flew onto Molly's bed, abandoned for an emerald ribbon, frayed, but still the perfect shade of green. She raced past, the ghost of a flush colouring her milky cheeks. "You got the rolls I like, right?"

"'Course. I set a few aside for you already." She grinned, and Molly beamed back. One last smile, so sweet and trusting.

When the girl disappeared around the corner, panic overcame Emily like a storm, fast and overwhelming. Her stomach turned and her hands shook, the ground unsteady under her aching feet. A few days at most was all she needed to forget it ever happened, to be sure no one had followed her. It would all be a lesson, a cautionary tale. She'd had close calls before, unexpected meetings in the halls or bed checks that made it necessary to pile on the lies. But it had never been as close as the night before. Not by a mile. She'd get through this, too, and the fear would stop gripping her chest so tight. One day.

Until then, she'd have to wait.

"Close the door, please, Emily dear."

Emily's stomach dropped. Her legs turned to lead, anchors refusing to move. Numb. Forgetting to blink, she turned toward the new yet familiar voice, the door still ajar.

"On second thought, allow me."

A light *click* and they were alone. Trapped together.

"Who are you?" Emily asked, her mouth dry.

The short, heavy-set woman shifted on Emily's bed, jabbing the pillow with a forefinger. "This bed really is uncomfortable. My back would be in agony if I had to sleep on this." Her hair glowed silver under the weak sun filtering in through the windows, her eyes a deep sapphire. Her voice . . . the silver curls a true pearly shade of white…

"You." Emily's tongue was scratchy, uncomfortable against the ribbed roof of her mouth.

"Hello, Emily." The rider from the supply caravan gestured to Molly's bed. "We should chat."

Chapter Two

Ghosts of Present's Past

The air clung to Emily's lungs like dirty water to a dry rag. The sun climbed higher through her window, chasing away the chill in her room and brightening the rooftops until they gleamed like blank ponds. Outside her door, the children of Saint Barth's Common trudged off to their individual days, word of a long-awaited treat soon to be making its way from Molly's mouth to every ear. Staring at the woman perched on her bed, Emily doubted she would ever experience excitement again.

"Randall—*no*—Randall! Give that here. What is that in your mouth, Randall?" Chancellor Pascale cackled down the hall, eager to ruin poor Randall Leeman's day with her reprimands filtering through closed doors and stone walls alike. Emily pressed her back against the door, feeling the Chancellor's shrill voice vibrate against the wood.

"Poor boy." The woman pondered the door and sighed. "Why put a wooden toy in your mouth at all?"

"You'd do funny things, too, if you were hungry." There was no doubt left in her mind; Emily had been seen, and punishment was sure to follow. If someone from the city had found her, the Council Guard wasn't far behind. What would they do to her? Were dungeons still in use, or did they banish lawbreakers and leave them to their own defenses outside the city walls? If punishment was around the corner, there was no time to be polite. And if directness failed, there was always escape.

Uh-huh. Did you hit your head in that caravan? Blood on the floor, *drip, drip, drip,* the man sprawled at her feet, because of her, her fault, her fault. *All my fault.* Emily cringed away from the memory.

The stranger considered her carefully as though Emily's inner thoughts screamed across the room. "I suppose you're right," she said. "He seems rather attached to that small toy horse."

Emily shrugged, shoulders stiff. "I've never heard him speak, so I can't tell for sure what his deal is with the horse." Her tone was even, but her heart stuttered. "He showed up with it a few years ago and never let it go since."

The woman nodded. "Poor boy."

"So you said." The silence was deafening, and Emily was sure her chest would explode if things didn't move along. "So..."

"Yes?" Wide, blue eyes, clear of anger and absent of explanation, bored into hers. The stranger waited, hands clasped across her lap.

Emily shifted her weight and fiddled with her necklace. "Are you really going to make me say it?"

She smiled. "I'm sorry. I don't mean to make this more difficult for you. I thought giving you your space to settle was best. But I see you prefer getting straight to business."

"I might stand a chance of surviving that way, yeah." *But for how long?* Were they already waiting outside her door? What was the penalty for theft? Funny, she never thought to ask.

"Very well," the woman said, voice kind. Too kind. "So, you took some things that don't belong to you."

Quick and painless. Although, waiting for the guillotine blade to drop was anything but.

Nothing to lose if you lie. Emily peered out the window and allowed her eyes to relax, the edges of the world blurring. "I don't know what you're talking about."

"Are you certain you wish to begin this way?" The woman motioned for her to sit on Molly's bed, the picture of patience.

Emily ground her teeth but obeyed. No sense in irritating the woman more than she had to. The room was small, but it took an eternity to navigate the tight space. She lowered herself onto the uneven mattress, the invitation to sit in her own room mildly irritating. "Fine. I was out last night, and I found your caravan. You were at a stop and seemed to be having some trouble with your horses, so I thought I'd take a look."

"Try again, please."

Emily blinked. "What?"

"I'd like the truth if you'd be so kind." Calm. Peaceful. A request and not a command. "You weren't simply taking a stroll, dear. It was cold enough to freeze dragon fire last night. I should know—I was sitting outside that Elder-forsaken caravan."

Stall. Just stall her. "I hadn't noticed. I don't usually mind the cold."

"But more to the point," she continued, "you were out for another reason, were you not?"

Emily focused on her breathing, willing it to slow down. Torture. "I know where the caravans come in from the city and that there's food in them. I was hungry, and my door was unlocked, so I slipped out to find something to eat. No harm, no foul."

"Except my companion ended up with a gash on his forehead and a new, unhealthy fear of forest spirits." She rolled her eyes to the ceiling, her thoughts on the idea of forest spirits obvious. "So, there was some harm done. Especially to my patience."

Emily's cheeks heated. "I didn't mean to hurt anyone."

Surprise flashed across the woman's face. "You didn't, dear! I had to knock the poor man unconscious before he got a good enough look at you! By the time I realized what was happening, he was already inside the caravan, so I'm not sure it worked. At least he didn't run straight to the Guard. Yet."

"Wait." It was impossible. The rosy-cheeked, polished woman before her was without a doubt a resident of Gildenveil City, lover of order, of division. Of power. "*You* knocked him out?"

"No choice, I'm afraid." Her face sagged. "I hope you don't think less of me for it. I don't condone violence, but desperate times and all that."

Emily's ears buzzed, her body taking on a foreign lightness. "You . . . you're scared *I'm* judging *you?*" The concept left her with a mild headache. It was a trick, a way to get her to confess, a tactic she hadn't anticipated. "What's your play here, exactly?"

The woman blinked, her eyebrows disappearing into her hair. "Play, dear?"

"Yeah, your game! If everything you're saying is true, then you knew what I was doing last night, and you helped me."

"Yes."

"That makes absolutely no sense."

The woman smiled. "I can see how it looks that way."

I did *hit my head, then.* "That's exactly how it is."

Blue eyes, twin sapphires set in iridescent opal, drank her in. Colour in a world of grey. "I can see we've gotten off to a less than desirable start. I'm Magdale Toth, Master Elemental at Selwyn castle. And you're Emily Roth, yes?"

An invisible force swung out and hit Emily between the eyes, throwing her off guard. "Master Elemental?"

"Yes, I work with the initiates at the castle to hone their various abilities—"

"I know what a Master does." Karma, some cosmic joke. Years of work, dozens of close calls, never a mess this big. This *damaging.*

"Of course," Magdale allowed. "How long have you known you're an Elemental, too?"

The room shrank around her like a cold prison cell, and Emily froze. This wasn't a discussion she'd ever had with anyone, and the idea of being thrown into it without warning brought a thin sheen of sweat to her forehead. "I've lived in the Commons my whole life. I'm pretty sure if I was an Elemental, I wouldn't have stuck around here."

"Perhaps." Silence. Waiting.

Emily frowned. "You think I'd *want* to stay here? Look at this place. It's no Selwyn's."

"Yes, I've seen it, unfortunately." A shadow flickered across her face, the light in her eyes dimming. "Granted, I haven't been here in quite some time. I'd rather hoped it would have changed or that my memory didn't do it justice." She sighed. "Regardless, it's understandable why you'd choose to stay. Someone with an ability can help others who cannot help themselves and keep their magic relatively quiet. It's commendable."

"This wasn't a choice," Emily spat. "People like us have no choices."

"I disagree," Magdale countered. "You chose to leave this room after hours, track a supply caravan, use a planned disturbance to magic your way past secure bindings, and take an impressive amount of food. Those all point to some purposeful choices."

For once, Emily was grateful her stomach was empty. *Lie.* "How would I have done any of that on my own? Don't you think you would have noticed that much cargo leaving your caravan?"

"Not if you used your abilities." Magdale peered at her, making it impossible for Emily to look away. "My theory is that you're quite good at transferring matter from one space to another, but you have to have physical contact with the items you're transferring for it to work. That's why you had to be there *in* the caravan instead of here in this awful room."

"Nice theory." *Keep it simple. Admit nothing.*

Magdale lifted Emily's pillow with the flick of a finger, rotating it before her nose. The dim sunlight made the stiff material translucent, patchy and yellowed in the places sweat had eaten away at it during hot summer months, or tears had pooled in the darkness. "That's quite advanced for someone who hasn't had any formal training. Your peers must be very grateful to you for your sacrifice."

Emily bristled. "What do you know about sacrifice?"

"A fair bit. And I would be careful about assuming otherwise, dear." Magdale's tone bit Emily's protests down to ineffective pieces, demanding immediate respect. "Reports of disappearing supplies to the Commons—food, blankets, things of that sort—have been circulating for years. It *has* been you all this time, has it not?"

When in doubt, silence was preferable and much less dangerous. The ice was thin under her feet, and Emily sat quite still, willing the fragile web underneath her to hold.

She can't do anything to you if you say nothing. So, she pressed her teeth together and made sure never to break eye contact.

Magdale smiled. "I've known the truth about you for years, so your own admission is a formality."

Surprise again, disarming and disorienting. "You knew?"

"Oh yes."

Emily laughed. "Then why didn't you stop me?" A joke. It had to be. "What you're accusing me of is illegal. It's *treason.*"

"That's true, and you pose a fair question." Magdale straightened her periwinkle skirt around her ample hips, the fabric shimmering in the hazy light. "You are not the only one who has had to make difficult choices, Emily. I've known about you for a long time, watched you come dangerously close to discovery on many occasions. But seeing you operate and how it gave you purpose . . . well, I thought it best to let you be. For as long as I could, at least. It made you happy, and those around you were taken care of because of you. There was no harm done."

"Seeing me operate?" The idea of unseen eyes on her made her stomach churn and her fingertips hum with ill-suppressed anger. "You were spying on me?"

"You've been stealing supplies that don't belong to you and getting away with it. Do you really want to discuss injustices and breaches of privacy?" An even stare, void of anger but brimming with truth. "At any rate, I've kept you safe from discovery up until now, but last night changes things."

And here we go. Emily peeked up through her lashes, half expecting a hammer to be hovering right over her head, but found the peeling, water-stained ceiling instead. "I don't care what you do to me. Just leave everyone else out of it. I acted alone, and that food I took . . . it's hidden where no one but me can find it." She squared her shoulders, jaw flexed. "It belongs to them now."

"I'm not here to punish you," Magdale said, eyes wide and earnest. "Or interrupt your plans for the supplies you took. The food is quite safe under your floorboards, I assure you." She stomped a heeled foot once, twice, and the hollow thump of rubber on wood echoed like a guilty heartbeat in the tiny room.

Emily closed her eyes and took a steadying breath. "Is there even a point asking how you know that?"

"Not a single one." Magdale smiled. "The others will come and take their share, as intended. The hiccup, as it were, is with regards to you."

Emily studied her own fingers, the dirt under her nails still fresh from the night before. "He saw me. That man you were with."

Magdale nodded. "And my partner's story of ghosts in the woods might be absurd, but it's enough to earn a second look by the Guard when paired with the vanishing stock. They've already noted the missing cargo and are waiting for orders to investigate further."

Her throat was much too tight, her windpipe shrinking to a pinprick, suffocating her inch by agonizing inch. "So, they're going to find me."

"Yes," Magdale said. "It might take some time, but the more immediate issue is that security will be tighter on the caravans. Spot checks will be happening more frequently, escorts for bigger transports put in place. It's already in the works."

Emily nodded as understanding dawned. "I won't be able to get away with it anymore." The truth hit her harder than the danger of being discovered. "But everyone here will starve. The supplies we get from the city aren't enough! They'll be dead by spring."

"I'm so very sorry." That much sounded sincere, at the very least.

"What if I stay and fight this?"

"Stubborn." Magdale sighed. "A family trait, it seems."

The sentence was short, spoken without hesitation or one blink too many. But it hit Emily like a fist to the gut. The ice cracked, the fragile layer between control and emotional abandon tore apart, and Emily floundered, searching for a raft in the ocean storm. "What do you know about my family?"

"Emily, dear, I understand this must all be overwhelming, but you need to focus. I cannot stay long, and this is important." Every word was clear, every breath urgent. "You won't be able to move as easily as you once did. And I might not be able to intervene every time one of your expeditions goes sideways, especially now that things will be so closely monitored. You need to leave."

Leave. Leave the Commons. Huh. "I want to know about my family," she blurted out. "Are they alive?" She didn't so much ask the question to know more about them, to fill some gap in her heart. The question weighing on her since childhood had nothing to do with missing them and everything to do with worry—how much of the ice in their veins ran in her own?

Magdale shook her head. "We can discuss your family later, but for now, you're not safe here."

No. Not again.

"I don't want to go to another Common and learn everything all over again! I like it here, and I can handle myself when they come for me."

She frowned. "I'm afraid you've misunderstood. I meant that you needed to leave the Commons behind completely. For good."

Another blow. Another unexpected hit. Her legs kicked out, trying to keep her head above water and finding nothing but roiling, merciless riptides. "What are you talking about? Where do you expect me to go?"

"You can come with me."

The laugh bubbling up her throat was unexpected and even somewhat unhinged. "What—you don't mean to the *city*? With all you fancy people?"

"I was thinking about Selwyn's, specifically."

She's joking. "You're joking."

Magdale pursed her lips. "This can't be so absurd to you, Emily. It's in your blood—where you belong. The

Guard will be searching the Commons for a local thief, and they *will* find you unless you leave. They'll never be looking for you at the castle."

Emily grimaced. "But it's in the city."

"It's not a dirty word, Emily," Magdale countered, shoulders pulled back in a huff. "Honestly, consider what you could do, what kind of *difference* you could make if you actually spent some time around others like you. Isn't that better than spending your life living from one theft to the next?"

Gildenveil City, Selwyn castle, the *others*. Those places, those ideas—they were the problem, never the solution.

Say no. Why can't you say no?

Emily floundered, mind working fast, but still too slow for comfort. "But I stole from you," she said. "I stole, and I did it a *lot,* and you're offering to . . . what? Reward me?"

"I'm offering you the opportunity you are owed by birthright."

Emily's thoughts snapped back into focus. Her eyes hardened to coal, the embers in her belly stoked to a bright burn. "Being born with an ability doesn't make you better—it just makes you lucky."

Magdale's face was impassive. "That's very true."

The fire licked at her stomach now, a true, overwhelming flame. Heat in her chest, anger in her throat, fingers sparking. "I'm part of the Commons no matter what I can do and what ability I have. They'll never accept me up there, and I don't want to leave everyone I love behind. I think I'll pass and take my chances here."

"Do you truly love anyone here?"

The fire consumed her. "That's not your business."

Magdale cleared her throat. "I imagine you're right. As I've said, this is your choice. I'm simply laying out the reality of your . . . situation. I don't need to be an Empath to see into your mind and know you thirst for more. Why else would you continue to steal and risk exposure? A part of you wants to make a bigger difference. It's noble of you to stand by your peers, but holding yourself back helps no one. Especially not you."

"You'd be a terrible Empath." She'd found her footing, but it was unsteady, at best. "If you knew me at all, you'd know I don't run."

Magdale stood, one swift, fluid motion rippling her skirts in an invisible windstorm. "I'm heading back to Gildenveil City today. That awful woman who runs this place is attending to a rather severe outbreak of the stomach flu in the kitchens that should resolve itself in about an hour. She'll be quite preoccupied until then. I'll be walking the first leg of the journey—I'd like to take in the sights around your neighbourhood."

Emily snorted. "There's a pretty big cat living in the trash heap out back. I'd say that's a highlight you shouldn't miss."

Magdale smiled and the world brightened, just a little. "I think you'd be surprised how many interesting things one discovers here if they know where to look." Her eyes were dancing gems, glittering. "Good luck, Emily."

"That's it?" she blurted, knuckles throbbing with how hard she was clinging to the mattress. "You're just leaving?"

"I've said what was needed, and the rest is up to you. I'm certain you'll make the best decision for yourself."

This is probably what it feels like to have parents. I hate it. "But you're not going to punish me or anything?"

"My dear," Magdale said, so sweet, so warm, "haven't you punished yourself enough?"

The air shimmered, the outline of cracked stones quivering around her, and there was no more air. It was harder to breathe, to think, to move. Flicker. Swirl. A blink.

Magdale was gone, and Emily was alone.

Again.

Forever.

Chapter Three

A Pitchfork in the Road

"MAGDALE?"

It was a wonder her legs were still able to bear her weight. Her lungs expanded, contracted; her heart beat its steady rhythm. The room was the same one she had longed to escape for months. But now, with the chance to escape so close, she stood rooted to the ground, tracing the cracks in the wall and counting the chips in the flooring with new appreciation for her life.

"Magdale!" Emily peered out the window for any sign of the woman: a swish of blue skirt, a flicker of a jewel-bright eye. The world stared back at her in its usual tones of grey and brown. Clouds trudged low, away from the sun as though eager to put distance between themselves and the cheer of daylight, while the bins littering the sidewalks continued to fester. Trash. Trash all around, surrounding her, closing in.

She could leave. She *wanted* to leave.

Could it be that easy?

The bed.

Her head was heavy, and her legs dragged as she worked, pushed, moved. One floorboard stood out from the rest, worn and crooked, the nails holding it in place long gone. She pulled up the slab of wood and tossed it to the side, hands already rifling through the small pile of her belongings.

Okay. Clothes. You need clothes.

What are you doing? You can't just leave.

And socks. Doesn't everyone need extra socks?

Two heavy sweaters, one to throw on top of her thin cotton shirt and the other to tie into a makeshift pack for the rest of her things. She already wore her only pair of pants and shoes. *Light is better. Take only what you need.*

Mind ablaze, she sank into the hidden spot under the ground and shovelled half a dozen rolls, a few figs, and a handful of grapes into the spare sweater. An old leather pouch clinked faintly as it landed on top of the pile. Her necklace dangled around her neck, still safe.

The sun had already crawled to another position in the sky.

An hour. She had an hour before Magdale disappeared, taking Emily's way out of the Commons with her. *Okay, move.*

Both sleeves looped through a weathered hole at the bottom of the sweater. The makeshift basket would hold for a time, but her luck wouldn't. Refusing to look at

Molly's empty bed, she replaced the wood slat, jumped to her feet, and struck out for freedom.

Down the long corridor, condensation dripping ashen sludge down moss-covered walls, *what am I doing,* empty faces with matching faraway gazes, down a steep set of stairs, more faces. More emptiness.

"Oh," she breathed, coming to a stuttering stop. The door loomed ahead, so close. "Hey, Randall."

Randall Leeman sat beside the entrance like a silent guardian. Grey eyes, large as moons, met hers. The horse Chancellor Pascale had chastised him for hiding in his mouth marched over his knees in light, muffled thumps. Left to right to left, over and over.

Emily smiled, the muscles in her face tight. "I was just . . . uh . . . going for a walk."

Silence.

Right. "So . . . I'll see you later. You stay out of Pascale's way, okay?" Her voice caught, and she could say no more. Her smile flickered and went out like a flame in the wind with those clear eyes on her. She pulled open the portal to freedom while Randall's chubby fingers popped the wooden horse back into his mouth. He waved goodbye as she breached the threshold.

She didn't wave back.

And then came the pain.

She was alone. Unwanted. She had parents, sure she did. A mother and a father and baby make three. A small, happy family. Except she was—

Alone. Abandoned. Unworthy.

Emily's stomach twisted. The sun shone too low, too bright overhead. Randall's steady gaze wavered behind her eyelids with every blink, and she couldn't keep her eyes open long enough to forget the boy's accusatory eyes, his small, angry face with the thin, puckered lips. He hated her—they all did.

She would go back inside. Inside was home, was safe, was everything she needed. She was alive, wasn't she? No thanks to her mother and father; they'd left her in the slums, in the grime and starvation of the Commons. They knew the life they condemned her to, and yet, there she stood. On a broken doorstep with the sun in her eyes and a quiet boy disapproving of her darkest shame.

It wasn't enough to have a way out. Magdale was lying; there was no place for her anywhere but here at Saint Barth's, with Molly sleeping, smiling, braiding her long hair by her knee. A sister, that's what Molly was. She didn't have parents because they didn't love her enough to keep her, but Molly . . . Molly was family. If she left, wasn't she just abandoning the small girl, too?

"What are you doing?"

Whiplash. "Molly?" Emily's breath came in heavy pulls as the world focused.

Skin, milky and translucent, hugged her narrow frame like fine silk pulled tight over a coat hanger. "Why are you standing outside like that?" Molly's flat green eyes travelled to Emily's shoulder. "Are you going somewhere? Can I come?"

No, never. Let's go back inside, kid. "I—I'm not sure." Emily's stomach clenched at the thought of leaving her behind. Molly needed her. And where would she even go? A castle? Ridiculous. "I'm just getting some fresh air."

"With all your stuff?" she asked. "You're leaving." Not a question. Molly's voice trembled, and she pulled her fingers through her hair, twisting a strand into a tight cord.

Down the road, a woman rifled through mouldy crates of discarded bones picked clean of their meat and apple cores chewed into nubs—food for the rats, both human and animal. Emily recoiled at the thought of stepping off the stoop, of passing the woman eating trash on her way to find Magdale. It was safer inside. "It's not like that, Molly. I thought I could do it, but I don't think I should. We should get back inside."

Molly frowned, eyebrows so pale they glowed like a thin brush of gold across her brow. "You know where you want to go?"

The truth would hurt her. But so would a lie. "I got offered a way out of the Commons," Emily said, settling on a vague compromise. "But I don't think I'll take it."

Molly shook her head, the quick motion setting her head aflame in the doorway. "Is it better than here? I mean, it has to be, right?"

No, she thought at once. "I'm not sure. It could be." What was she even saying? She was late for her chores. Chancellor Pascale would take away all outdoor privileges for a month if she knew what Emily was doing. What was Magdale thinking, dangling Selwyn castle in front of her like that?

Molly nodded. "You should go, then."

"What?"

"You should go." Molly's eyes were wide and shiny, the sun overhead not quite touching her eyes or the dark, musky hallway behind her. "If you can leave, you need to do that."

Emily faltered, heart thudding behind her ribs. The street was not her friend. There was the hallway behind

Saint Barth's front door, her bedroom with the grey coverlet stained black in some places from years of dropped, stolen food. "It's okay. Let's go back inside."

"No." Molly's chin quivered, dimples forming under her bottom lip, but she stood firm. "You're going. It feels right, Emily."

Agony. "Come with me, then."

The slight creases on Molly's forehead softened. "I can't go anywhere. I'm useless. But you . . . you're special. I always knew that." She sighed, twisting her fingers around a strand of red hair so it curled around her pale skin. "No one's ever left before."

Because it's insane. "I know."

"Be careful, 'kay?" Molly's voice cracked, and Emily's soul shattered.

Emily stumbled backward with a small grunt. Everything inside her screamed, told her to run to the girl and wrap her arms around her shoulders, to calm the turmoil twisting Molly's face. "I don't want to leave you," she said. And it was true. The dam around her heart was cracking, leaking blood and pain. Saint Barth's tugged her closer, and the memory of Magdale slipped further away. "Who's going to make sure you eat?"

Molly glanced at her toes, wiggling them in the thin cotton slippers with the bow made of twisted hay. "I won't starve, Emily. Plus, it's time I learned to be a fighter without you." She smiled. "Will you visit?"

"I'll try."

She nodded as though the thought reassured her. "Will you be okay?"

There was somewhere she needed to be, wasn't there? Someone was waiting for her . . . Magdale? Was that her name? "I'll be great. Promise." Chancellor Pascale's orders echoed from the basement, jarring Emily from the haze fogging her mind. "I don't have much time, kid. The food is under the floorboards. You remember which one, right?"

"Yes."

Emily hiked her crude bag higher on her shoulder, and a flash of pain stabbed her between the eyes. Her knees buckled, and she fought to straighten herself, to meet Molly's gaze without swaying on her feet. A migraine pulsed between her temples. A big one.

Molly frowned and took a step closer, the concern immediate and pure, but Emily held out her hand to stop her. She cleared her throat and pushed the pain down. "Stay out of Pascale's way as much as you can," she said, her voice gruff. "The other girls are greedy, so stash some extra food under your mattress for yourself, even if you decide to share things equally. And try to get kitchen duty as much as you can. I know you like gardening because you get to stay outside longer, but you have a better chance at some leftovers that way."

Molly brushed a stray tear from her cheek, silver tracks spilling down her pale face. "Got it."

"Good." It wasn't much, but it was enough. Her bag was getting heavy. "Take care of yourself, okay?"

A sniffle, too many tears, and her hands rubbed her arms, up and down, scratching the old fabric. Molly didn't move closer. "I'll miss you."

Miss you too.

I'm so sorry.

"You should get inside." *Before I change my mind.* Another shock of pain lanced through her skull, and she pressed her eyes closed, longing for her bed. It was so close…

"Bye, Emily. Love you." Molly tucked her chin into her chest and turned on her heel, racing back into the house before Emily could answer. Maybe she knew she wouldn't hear those very words returned to her. Maybe she didn't need to hear it. Either way, Emily swallowed hard and hurried away, leaving the girl and a piece of herself behind.

It was a direct route to Coven Hill Road once the narrow streets were behind her. Leaning, cracked, mildewing stone gave way to towering firs and maples boasting crowns of red and orange and rich ochre. The pavement was soft and unmarked. The higher stretch of Coven Hill Road was reserved for transport caravans and official travel, two things that were scarcely seen so low down in the Commons. That's where she needed to go because that's where Magdale was likely headed.

Her stomach heaved, burned, molten lava lapping at her insides with every step. Instead of beautiful leaves and clear skies, she saw claws made of old tree branches swiping at the path, pushing her back. Emily willed herself on . . . to what? She couldn't remember. There was only Saint Barth's, warm and safe and solid.

A few more paces, the sky was a dark green, oozing and heavy. She couldn't breathe. Under her, the earth turned to mud, to sludge sucking her deeper into the ground, dragging her back. A tree root slithered across her path and swiped at her legs, but she was stuck to the ground and couldn't escape it. The pain in her head was blinding, and the ground swayed under her unsteady feet. With a sob, Emily crumbled to her knees, gasping.

A hand—a *claw*—fell from the sky, ready to end her life if she didn't turn back . . . if she didn't go home.

Emily screamed as cold fingers caressed her head, twisting in her hair.

The pain stopped.

"She seemed sweet." The voice was soft and light, like the down of a swan. A gentle arm wrapped around Emily's waist, pulling her upright.

Emily exhaled, relief washing over her like warm bathwater. "Magdale?"

"Yes, yes." Concern radiated from Magdale's face, her eyes travelling over every inch of Emily's body. "Are you all right?"

No. "Yes. What happened?"

"I forgot about the curse around this place." Magdale reached over to retrieve Emily's bag from the ground and offered it to her with a look of deep apology. "I'm truly sorry about that. I've heard it's quite terrifying."

Emily's voice stuck in her throat. "I don't understand. One second I was running out to catch up with you, and as soon as I stepped out of Saint Barth's, all I wanted to do was run back inside!" A shiver crept down her arms despite the growing heat. "I was forgetting you. How could I forget you?"

Magdale sighed. "The Commons are meant to keep anyone born without an ability safe. The rest of the realm is much too volatile, you see. Dangerous. The High Council thought it best to use their best Empaths to discourage anyone who sincerely considered leaving from actually doing so."

Emily blinked fast. "You're saying that there's some kind of spell someone put in my brain to keep me trapped in the Commons?"

"Not trapped, dear," Magdale said at once. "Safe. Outside the protection of the Commons, there are all sorts of Empaths and Elementals, not to mention beasts with terrible abilities that could pose a threat to someone without any magic to protect themselves."

The speech came hurried and even, as though Magdale had practiced it before. "So, we're kept here against our will," Emily said, heat radiating from her hands. "As soon as we want to leave, we're tortured into staying?"

"Merely *encouraged* to stay," Magdale said. "I really am sorry, Emily. No one has ever tried to leave the Commons in quite some time, so I completely forgot that would happen."

"This place is a trash heap," Emily said, straightening herself to better look Magdale in the eye. "I'm sure I'm not the first one to want to break out of here." Molly's face flickered in the trees by the path—an illusion, a cursory memory—and Emily frowned. "What about the ones who go on to become assistants up in Gildenveil?"

"Oh, people can leave!" Magdale's eyebrows jumped. "As long as they're accompanied by a resident of Gildenveil City, they can travel freely in and out of the Commons. Since I didn't personally escort you out of Saint Barth's, the moment you stepped outside with the intention of never returning, the curse took hold and drove you back. I hadn't even considered that would happen when I wanted to give you the space to decide on your own."

A prisoner, all this time. The choice was never hers, not in any real way. Until now. She had always assumed every Elemental and Empath in the city thought themselves superior to anyone stuck in the Commons. The curse was the proof of their hate and fear. *They're in for a surprise when they see me, then.* "How do we get to the city?" she asked, voice stiff with betrayal. "Magic?"

Magdale smiled, her gaze moving to Emily's shoulder. "For some of the journey, yes." She swatted the sweater bulging with stolen food, so it swung back and forth. "You pack light."

Emily clutched her bag to her side. "It's all I need. Are you sure I'll be able to really make a difference where you're taking me?"

Magdale's eyes softened. "I believe you're making the right decision by giving yourself a chance. But, ultimately, whether or not you make a difference is up to you."

Emily could picture it: Molly shuffling down the hall and back to their now-empty room, peeling up floorboards to find the last influx of food she would ever get. Chancellor Pascale would interrogate her, but with a history of popping from one orphanage to the next, no one would question Emily's absence further. After all, it's not like anyone could leave the Commons completely. They were just recycled somewhere else. She pushed the image aside, blinking the warm sting from her eyes. No weakness. "I can't do anything more for them back there. I know that."

"You're probably right." Magdale turned back to the road, moving at a surprising speed. "Come on, then. Lots to do."

"We're going on foot?" Emily jogged to keep up pace.

"Not the whole way. Like I said, there will be some magic. Just not yet." Magdale crested the hill where, less than a day before, she had entered the Commons by caravan.

Emily brightened, eager to burn off the adrenaline pooling in her limbs. The more distance she put between herself and the Commons, the less the chance of changing her mind. "Do we go through the Void to get there?"

Magdale laughed. "What do you know about the Void?"

"Not much, really." And it was true. "I've heard stories about how people could travel to other lands through it. That there are monsters worse than dragons there."

A delicate laugh. "And that's where you seem so eager to go?"

Emily shrugged. "I figured if it could take you to other realms, it could take us to Selwyn's quicker than walking."

She considered for a moment. "Well, firstly, it seems we need to correct your impression of dragons."

"What's to correct?" Emily suppressed a shudder. "They're massive monsters with huge teeth and deadly breath. Sounds pretty black and white to me." Years of waking in the dark to inhuman cries rattling her window, fire blazing in the distant skies, and children crying for lost mothers had left a bitter taste on her tongue, impossible to wash off in one conversation.

Magdale waved her hand, swatting the notion away like an annoying gnat. "It's easy to think a creature with such strong magic can be destructive, but they're rather docile if you know how to communicate with them."

"Docile? Maybe if you're an Empath and you can control them," Emily argued. She peeked up into the sky, relieved to find a significant absence of fire.

"That certainly helps, yes." She meandered across the empty road, weaving left and right, inspecting a patch of daisies, then the bare branches of a low-hanging tree. "Most members of the Guard are Empaths since they have an easier time communicating with their dragon. It makes the bond unmatched by anything, but it is not a requirement for the job. You never know—you could find yourself taking a liking to one of the dragons at the castle." She peered at Emily from the corner of her eye. "More than one Elemental has been known to show a knack for it."

"If you say so." Emily's braid was heavy down her back, a familiar weight. She allowed the soft breeze to cool her heated cheeks and considered what Molly would think of the Selwyn dragons if she had to see one up close.

That won't ever happen, she reminded herself.

They trudged up the road, past farmhouses and rows of cornstalks that she had raided in her early days when her magic would appear at the worst times—a tantrum, a day where the supplies hadn't made it through the snow, a fight with another kid for the last apple—and moving targets were too complex. Caravans were difficult to pin down, but the corn and fruit stayed still enough.

The pack swung under her arm, the thick smell of fresh bread making her stomach clench, her mouth flood, her tongue itch.

Magdale ran a hand over the tall stalks. "I should tell you, then, that the Void is completely off-limits to anyone who isn't authorized to use it. To get permission to do so is difficult enough, and those gateways are closely monitored. Dear, please eat something from your sweater-bag."

Heat prickled Emily's cheeks, and she looked up from the path at once. "What?"

"You're hungry."

She stared up at Magdale, distrust freezing her heart. "You sure you're not an Empath?"

Magdale rolled her eyes. "It doesn't take an Empath to hear your stomach from across the road. Go on—old bread tastes awful."

Permission had never been a consideration in the past—forgiveness was much easier to come by. However, Magdale's words unblocked her reservations. Her hands flew to her pack. She pulled a piece of bread off a large roll, popped it into her mouth, and a moan of pleasure slipped from her lips before she could stop it.

Magdale turned her head toward the homes passing by the road. "The Void isn't a place as much as a . . . doorway. We have Empaths and Elementals working to guard the entrances and navigate the chaos inside. But, even so, it's a quick in and out, no lingering of any kind. Traveling to other realms requires a substantial amount of energy, so unless one has enormous power, we require the Void."

A fig came next, tender on the outside, grainy with sweetness and ripe with nectar. Another piece of bread, softer now, closer to the fluffy white center of the roll. "Gatekeepers, right?" Emily asked, her words muffled.

"Officials who work for the High Council," Magdale said. "They're charged with guarding the entrances and exits to the Void. Only they know where they are located since the gates between realms change every so often. It's quite a prestigious position."

Emily nodded, helping herself to another fig. "Okay, so dragons are good, Gatekeepers are important, and the Void is off-limits. Anything else?"

"Plenty, but nothing you need to know right now." The crunch of fine, loose stones gave way to larger cobblestones pressed in level with the mud, and Magdale led the way with her head high. "Here we are. That didn't take as long as I'd remembered."

Emily stopped beside Magdale and peered down at the path where the uneven stones dropped out ahead of them. A wide gap in the earth carved its way across their toes, blocking their passage with an infinite drop into sharp rock and darkness. "I've never been this far out of the Commons. I guess this is where we need magic to leave." Emily took a step back, her brows drawn tight.

Magdale frowned. "What's wrong, dear?"

"I had no idea how hard it was to leave." For so many years, staying in the Commons was a point of pride. In her mind, there was no doubt she could have left at any time. Her decision to stay had given her control and the desire to keep fighting. But all along, there had only been the illusion of choice. Of control. In the end, there were only curses and more lies and chasms in the ground. "Let's get this over with."

The frown never left Magdale's face, but something in Emily's expression must have demanded the conversation to end. "Of course." Magdale stretched out a hand to her. "Grab on, dear."

Emily took the old Elemental's hand without another word, suppressing her guilt. The gesture should have been a lifeline. But instead of a lifeline, a chance to start new, she could only swim in the overwhelming waves of her betrayal. Red hair swam in the wind while wooden horses pounded the mud, their eyes hollow and their mouths screaming.

Magdale closed her eyes. Yellows and greens, blues and browns shimmered and dissolved, each hue blurring into the next. The air pressed in on Emily's ears until there was nothing but an uncomfortable hum squeezing her bones. The ground lurched, pitched, tipping her over the dark chasm into the vast nothing. Every speck of colour shattered, and oblivion spun out from under her.

She was weightless. She didn't exist.

And that was fine.

Chapter Four

Gildenveil

EMILY SWAM IN DEEP, FATHOMLESS nothing. But swimming wasn't the right word. *Drifted* was more like it. The current moved her, pulling and pushing her until up and down was the same beast. Magdale's fingers still gripped her own, but Emily couldn't see her. Black and white rushed past, blocking out all sound. *What happens if I scream?* The thought came to her like a flickering candle, but she couldn't feel her mouth or anything outside herself except for Magdale's warm hand.

The current shifted, and she was falling. With a gasp of surprise, her lungs expanded, taking in air and driving her heartbeat into a raging gallop. She flew through the abyss, through the light-speckled black. There was wind and sound somewhere beneath her—ahead of her? —and her legs crumbled as she landed.

Hard.

Emily's fingers clawed at the wonderful, solid ground filling her vision with jade and brown, and she swallowed air mixed with bitter grass and dirt in big, delicious gulps. Her head swam, and she blinked fast, the world materializing around her.

"I should probably have told you to look out for anything green coming your way." Magdale's voice was thick with suppressed laughter as she stared down at Emily, the bright sun illuminating her silver hair.

There was too much green; it was in her hair, her mouth, blocking the sun above her head. Leaves from bushes and low-hanging trees, pines littering the soft earth under her cheek like emerald snow, all clouded her view.

"That . . . was . . . terrible," Emily choked, pushing up from the ground with trembling arms. She spat once, twice, brown saliva peppered with grass, and tested her legs gingerly. "I don't think I broke anything."

"You seem fine to me, dear." Magdale brushed her hands over Emily's shoulders, patting away the dust and leaves clinging to her dingy clothes. "And *that* was called Transference. These kinds of physical spells come easier for Elementals like us since we're better connected to the material world."

"That's the first time I can honestly say I'm jealous of Empaths." Emily shook out her hair, and green bristles floated around her feet. Her pack lay on the ground, and she snatched it up at once.

"Empaths can do it, too." Magdale dusted off her skirts and flexed her fingers, her knuckles giving off a satisfying pop. "They must learn to lead with their mind. It's simple to do once you know what you're looking for."

Emily snorted. "Oh yeah, sounds as easy as breathing." She frowned into the tangle of weeds and twisted branches blocking out the rest of the world. "Did we land in a tree?"

Magdale laughed. "We're in the forest outside the city, actually. I thought it might be nice to see Gildenveil from a distance the first time. I don't want you to be more impressed with transference magic than with your new home."

"Beating Transference won't be hard, Magdale." She took an unsteady step and waited for the pain, but her legs worked fine. "Good news is my head isn't spinning and nothing hurts."

"Wonderful!"

"But," Emily continued, pushing past Magdale with a look of warning, "if you need to take me somewhere again, I think I'll take my chances with a dragon first."

Magdale chuckled and stepped aside. "I thought you would appreciate the surprise. Clearly I still have much to learn." She stepped beside Emily until they were shoulder to shoulder and inhaled deep as the last branches peeled away from them like a living, breathing curtain. "Welcome to Gildenveil City."

The ground sloped away from them, down a steep hill of tall, wild grass. Beneath her feet, a wall of ivory marble carved its way through the unmarked earth, travelling out to the east and west for as far as Emily could see with only one small gap in its barrier. Sunlight hit the stone, sending flecks of diamond light dancing up to greet them.

"It's very . . . tall," Emily said.

Magdale laughed with pure happiness. "That city wall protects most Empaths and Elementals in the realm. Look, you can see some of the shops from here."

Emily squinted past the impressive wall to the city cradled within at Magdale's request. Sure enough, the peaks and thatched roofs of several buildings peeked out from behind the glittering edges of the city border, thick clouds of purple, onyx, and crimson smoke spilling from brick chimneys. "Am I going to live in one of those?" she asked. If she was being honest with herself, she would have much preferred staying where she was, safe behind a few humble trees and far from anyone who could speak to her.

A light hand ushered Emily down the hill with a gentle push. "No point wasting time talking about our plans yet, dear," Magdale said. "Now, when we get inside the city, keep close to me and don't speak to anyone carrying a large bag or crate of any kind."

"What?"

"Just a warning is all. Nothing good comes from an Empath or Elemental with a strange sack or box." Magdale looked up at the sky and smiled as they approached the boundary of the wall, its tall shadow towering over them. "Do you understand the rules?"

"Sure. Don't get lost or kidnapped. I lived in the Commons my whole life. I know how to stay alive." Despite her confidence, Emily stepped closer to Magdale and hurried after her. From a distance the opening in the marble was a simple gap. Now, up close, Emily marvelled at the vast archway where two curved, scaled beasts carved out of solid marble arched in a furious embrace to form the entrance. Their teeth gnashed, claws reaching for one another in frozen battle. "Are those dragons real?"

Magdale marched under the archway, never slowing. "Not today," she said over her shoulder. "Remember, keep up!"

Emily's insides squirmed. With a sharp pang, she longed to be back in her small room with Molly, eating their stolen food and complaining about the stench rising from the trash piles in the streets. Instead, she pushed herself forward, clutching every belonging she had, and followed Magdale under the arching dragons. For a moment, there was a beautiful silence echoing in the dark marble passage.

And then there was pure chaos.

Emily ran to catch up with Magdale, who was already disappearing in a sea of brown and grey clothes. Men in robes, women in tailored coats and trim suits towing a horse or a wagon filled with cages of unseen cargo zoomed by without so much as a glance at their surroundings. Children huddled over a stack of levitating cards shuffling itself to shrieks of pleasure while shop owners called their daily specials and new arrivals at the top of their voices. The cobblestone spiralled and sprouted every which way, carving through the city like a living maze. Emily's ears rang as screams and laughter, chirps and clangs, joined one another to form a storm of noise. Sure, despair had a way of being heard—but life, as it turned out, was so much louder.

"Are we going far?" Emily shouted, leaning into the safety of Magdale's arm. Unfamiliar faces passed in a blur of rushed panic or businesslike determination. The scent of ripe melon, burning leaves, and dark chocolate assaulted her while well-fed children argued over the last candy melting in their hands. It was sickening. "I think I need to sit down."

Magdale patted Emily's arm and steered her down a narrower street to their right where every building leaned to one side or another and bricks the colour of beet juice gave off waves of heat. "I know it must be overwhelming. But it won't be much longer. I'm taking you to one of my favourite places in the city for food and rest."

Emily pushed a dark lock of damp hair out of her eyes. "So, this place of yours probably won't be empty, then."

"Probably not," Magdale said. "But don't worry. You'll have plenty of time to gather yourself before we head back out. And Cattails is rather low-key, considering its popularity." Down another wider road lined with outdoor cafés offering seasonal juice, fresh bread, and old books for sale. A tall woman towed her toddler by the arm, the little boy's screams of 'but I want a *llama*, not a cat!' shattering every glass cup they passed. They walked for a minute or an hour, Emily couldn't tell, until they stopped under a crooked, bronze street sign. Magdale flicked the hanging panel with a finger so that it glinted under the smiling sun. "Court Avenue and Pickering Road. This is the cornerstone of Gildenveil. And this," she said, nodding beside her, "is Cattail Inn."

Emily had expected something ridiculous and opulent for the city's best haunt for food and rest. Instead, Cattails was a plain shop of chipped, violet brick set with black windows in bronze frames. The door was heavy, solid oak with no hinges, handle, or obvious way to get past it. Above the doorframe, a cat carved of the same oak sat, its empty, wooden eyes following the passersby.

"*This* is where we're going?" Emily asked, relief flooding her. "It looks so . . . plain."

"I beg your pardon?"

Emily backtracked at once. "I mean, I *like* plain! I always figured Gildenveil was fancy, but this feels . . . homey. I think that's the right word."

Magdale unruffled her feathers and gestured to the door. "Cattails is an institution. You can't live off a couple of figs and day-old bread forever, and this place has the best food you can find. Come on, let's get you inside."

At her words, Cattail Inn let out a low, even groan. The wooden cat pawed its way across the top of the door and stretched, its tail curling over and then under it like a fine, sturdy lasso. An eyeless face turned to them and, with another rumble of shifting brick, the cat's tail swept across the door front. Emily blinked, and the way into Cattails stood wide open, the thick wooden door nowhere to be found.

"I'm guessing the person who owns this place is an Elemental." Nerves twisted Emily's stomach into a heavy ball weighing her down.

"He is, but the cat was his father's touch. It's a skill that came in handy when tourists looked for a bit of flair in the taverns they frequented. Ernie owns it now and has a way with speeding up time for smaller objects but kept the cat as a tribute to his father."

Emily glanced up at Magdale. "What does that mean? He can control time?"

Magdale placed a hand on Emily's back and steered her inside. "I'll explain as soon as we're seated."

A bar carved out of rich cherry wood stretched around the far side of the inn. Hundreds of tall, wide, oval, and spiralling bottles perched on uneven shelves, their contents swirling, smoking, or buzzing with insects. Magdale approached the bar, and the noise in the room muted to a low hum as dark, curious gazes tracking their arrival. Emily lowered her eyes, shaking a thin veil of loose hair across her face.

"Good morning, Ernie," Magdale said, voice low. "We'll be needing a table, please."

"Maggie! Nice to see ya, lovely!" The old bartender tipped an invisible hat in greeting, smiling with too much gum and not enough tooth. Thin wisps of hair protruded from a liver-spotted scalp, his eyes black as pitch as they locked onto Emily's. "Welcome to Cattails, little miss."

"Thank you." She smiled a beat too late, but if Ernie noticed, he didn't let on.

A man by the door wore a magenta smoking jacket and had a distinct bald patch in his silver beard. The stranger at the table beside him wore unremarkable black travelling clothes and had a scar running through his right eyebrow, shining white in the low light. One exit, three closed doors between multiple fireplaces, their grates veiled in steel bars. Emily smiled at Ernie, and the old barman grinned back, oblivious.

"Travelin' with Maggie then," Ernie said with a good-natured chuckle. "Good company to have. Are ya new to the city?"

Magdale looped an arm around Emily's shoulders. "She's a new initiate at the castle. That table, Ernie?"

"In a hurry, eh?" He chuckled and shuffled down the bar, waving them over with a gnarled hand. "I understand. I won' be botherin' ya."

"We've had a long journey." Magdale nodded to a few faces shrouded in shadow. Weathered wooden chairs creaked as strangers shifted in their seats, their amber-filled glasses leaving deep brown rings on the dull tables.

"Ernie!" A small man wearing red leather and a scowl stood up on his chair as they passed, his ruddy face dripping with foam. His voice slurred. "You gonna get us ano'er round, or do we have to take off our clothes te get yer attention?" His companions exploded into an appreciative round of laughter, their voices booming in the compact room.

"I'll be with ya in a sec!" Ernie puttered between tables, grumbling his way to one in a far corner with two high-backed chairs. "Here ya go, lovelies. What can I start ya with?"

"I said more ale!" The man smacked a thick-bottomed pint against the table and toppled onto the floor to another explosion of laughter.

Ernie shook his head and let out a guttural sigh. "Freggin' dwarves. They're in here every day drinkin' me best stuff and makin' a mess o' the place."

Emily took her seat across from Magdale. "Why don't you throw them out?"

"Can't." He shrugged, one shoulder resting higher than the other. "They're a pain, but they be payin' me good coin…'cept fer that one under the table. Not sure if he knows what year t'is, to be honest." He looped both crooked thumbs into the waist of his trousers and tugged them up to his ribcage to reveal a few inches of bony ankle. "Anywho, what'll ya have?"

"Whatever food you have on hand is fine," Magdale said with a wink.

Ernie turned deep scarlet. "Right away, ma'am!" After another wide smile, he puttered off to the bar. As he strolled down the row of shelves, bottles and vials slid around one another in a silent, intricate dance like puzzle pieces sliding in and out of placement. As a spot vacated, it filled instead with a steaming dish, a ceramic bowl with a self-stirring spoon, or a goblet dusted with a sheen of condensation. With one flip of his wrist, Ernie directed the new dishes to their table, the scent of broiled meat and sweet cider making Emily's mouth fill with saliva.

"That was quick." Magdale dodged a slopping goblet before it clipped her ear. Dishes clattered onto their table, and she shook her head with a deep sigh. "Thank Elders the man makes up for his lack of decorum with good food. Here." She slid a basket of buns and a butter dish over to Emily and set to filling her own plate. "Eat."

The slumbering beast in Emily's gut woke with a vengeance. She reached for her goblet first, downing the cold cider in three large swallows. She ate and ate with no regard for saving anything for anyone else, something she'd never done before. Before long, the surrounding chatter became background noise, and when her appetite was satisfied, she put her utensils down with a small sigh.

"Good?" Magdale asked.

"Mmm." Emily took another sip, smaller now, and her stomach purred. "So, what did you mean when you said Ernie can speed up time?"

"Ah." Magdale's eyes twinkled, and she set her fork down on her empty dish. "He can make organic objects run the course of their lives in a fraction of the time. See this apple cobbler?" She spooned a generous helping of the warm pie into Emily's dish and handed her a clean fork. "It was just apples and flour and sugar. But they were always intended to be cobbler."

"So . . . what? He blinks, and the apples cut themselves and turn into cobbler?" Emily poked at her dessert, unsure whether or not she was still hungry enough to eat possessed pie.

"It's slightly more complicated than that, but essentially that's exactly what he does. The apples are fine, dear. Have a bite."

Emily took a forkful and moved the warm morsel around in her mouth, absorbing the sweet taste of fruit with an appreciative groan. "It's good. Does his ability only work on food?" She took another bite.

"It took years for it to get to this point." Magdale leaned in and lowered her voice. "For a while, all he could do was kill poultry. Scared his parents straight until he learned to apply his skills to other, more practical things. Hasn't touched a pheasant since."

"Right." Emily pushed her half-finished dish aside. With her belly full and the Commons far behind her, her mind was clear, leaving space for logic. And panic. "I can't pay."

"What?"

"The food. I can't pay for it." With frantic fingers, she clutched her sweater-bag to her chest and scanned the exit. How had she never considered the issue of money before now? The way out was clear, but would Magdale let her go before Ernie threw her out?

"The food is taken care of, dear." Magdale frowned. "I didn't expect you to pay."

"But what about Selwyn's? That can't be free."

"Well, no, but—"

"So, I can't pay for it!" She had come all this way for nothing. There was no other choice but to head back. With any luck, Chancellor Pascale wouldn't have noticed her disappearance yet, and she could slip back in after nightfall when the others were asleep. No harm, no foul.

Magdale's eyes grew wide with understanding. "I see. There are exceptions for cases like yours, Emily. You're not obliged to pay a thing."

"But I should. I want to." The table of drunk men with thick beards and matching eyebrows struck out in song, the lines of the chorus so muddled, Emily couldn't tell if they were singing the same tune. With any luck, the terror in her voice wouldn't carry over the noise.

"Right. Well, you could always work at the castle in exchange for room and board. There are Masters and older initiates always looking to delegate minor tasks and maintenance that no one wants to do." She nodded as though the idea was beginning to make much more sense. "You would be paying your way, so to speak, and learning a few things in the process."

Emily's heart rate slowed. "Work in exchange for living there," she said, nausea subsiding. "Is that enough?"

"There is a reason no one wants to perform certain tasks." Magdale laughed. "I'll arrange for an initiate to take you in and show you around. Give you the tasks as they come up. Yes?"

"Yes." Emily slumped back into her seat as the front door vanished once again. Two girls about her age marched over to a booth, arm in arm, and slid over the velvet seats in a flurry of skirts and ruffles. One had long auburn hair and a pretty smile with a smattering of freckles under honey-coloured eyes while the other girl stood tall, her mane of wild, brown curls, square jaw, and thick glasses giving her the look of a well-dressed fighter. "Who are they?"

Magdale peered over to the booth. "I believe the one on the left is Camilla Kirby, and the curly-haired girl in glasses tossing balls of paper into that poor man's hair is

Catherine Bonner." She frowned at the pair as the girls set to work creating more paper balls out of a sheet of parchment and flinging them into the frizzy hair of an unsuspecting neighbour.

"They look . . . nice." *Not really.*

"I'll admit it's not the best first impression you could have of your future friends, but they're mostly harmless."

"Future friends?" Emily groaned, her appetite a thing of the past. "They live at Selwyn's?"

Magdale nodded. "Brand new, too, so I expect you'll be seeing a lot of them."

"Perfect." She wasn't surprised the girls were about as friendly as two hungry dragons, but before then, she at least had the hope of finding something redeeming about the initiates at Selwyn castle. Two coffees zoomed to the girls' table and the one named Catherine proceeded to dunk her paper balls in the steaming mug before flinging them across the room.

"Girls!" Magdale called. The two newcomers stopped at once, arms still outstretched in mid-fling. "A little respect, please? Emily here is new to the city, and we don't want to give her the impression you're rude, do we?"

Emily's cheeks blazed, and she hid her face in her hands, hoping to dissolve into the ground. However, she had no such luck. Both girls stifled another round of giggles, and the one with the wild curls and angular jaw spoke up first. "Sorry, Master Toth. I didn't see you there."

"Yeah," her friend chimed in while tears of laughter shimmered in her eyes. "Sorry." They leaned in close and began chatting under their breath, coffees forgotten.

"There," Magdale said with a wide smile. "Now you have some new friends!"

"Oh, sure." Emily closed her eyes with a pained expression. "We're going to be braiding each other's hair in no time."

Willow Court was a circular road lined with shops framed in walls of glass. Green, lavender, yellow-tinted panes connected by silver and gold beams reached up to the sky. Clothes for every occasion called to her from displays, and a dragon registry sat in a far corner, the High Council reception centre beside it. At the centre, in a spot of its own, a building made of emerald glass with bronze-trimmed arches brushed the clouds, a stream of people coming and going through a pair of double doors.

"What's that?" Emily asked, walking toward the building as though pulled by an invisible hand. Above the front door, a brass sign glittered with three interlocking *W*s scrawled in gold letters "*Wick, Wax, and Wane—binding spells since TGD*," she said. "What's '*TGD*'?"

"The Great Divide." Magdale's voice thrummed with reverence. "Gildenveil was part of another realm many years ago. After some difficulties, the realms split into two very separate, very opposite entities. The Dwalind realm and Gildenveil."

"So Gildenveil didn't always exist as its own realm?" Emily asked, the idea sounding foreign on her tongue. "Why didn't I know about this?"

"It happened a long time ago, dear. Nothing to worry about yet. Oh." Magdale peered over Emily's shoulder and bit her lip. "We'd better step inside."

Emily turned, but there was nothing in the crowd mingling on the street to warrant such a scared look. Then came the voice.

"Ozzy! Darling, why don't you wait for me? We haven't finished picking up your clothes!" A tall, thin woman wearing a bright, canary-yellow dress scanned the faces of everyone she passed, spinning a girl with an orange tunic around with unapologetic force. "Ozzy? No, sorry. Have you seen my boy?" The girl ran off without answering, and the woman stretched her long neck over the shoppers, finding Magdale before they could dip into Wick, Wax, and Wane. "Master Toth! How absolutely lovely to see you!"

"Oh, Elders help me." Magdale closed her eyes for a second, opening them with an instant smile that spread a touch too wide. "Hello, Penelope! Yes, yes, lovely. I was about to send this new initiate in for some books." She dipped her head and whispered into Emily's ear with an urgency demanding no argument. "Dear, why don't you get a head start and wait for me inside?"

Emily pulled open the green glass doors and ducked inside, eager to escape the commotion. Breaching the threshold, silence clapped on her ears with immediate force. Stacks of cluttered shelves and rows of books bound in leather and faded cloth stretched from the entrance all the way to the back of the store in hundreds of individual shelves running their own course. A fine sprinkle of dust blanketed every surface, muting the vibrant colours to a soft haze of rainbow colours and pastels divided by polished wood displays. Jewels glittered from different covers, swirls of silver and gold lettering twisted down the length of spines, and every so often, a vellum-bound book would whizz around a bend or fall into waiting hands with a mind of its own.

"Can I help you?" A man with warm, brown eyes smiled down at her, salt and pepper hair split in a neat part down the centre of his head.

"Just looking, thanks." Emily smiled back and chose the nearest aisle to disappear into. The silence was a welcome relief from the constant chatter on the streets and at Cattails. She inhaled deep, the scent of old parchment mingling with the sweetness of burning candles. Her feet took off on their own until she hit the end of the passage, where a sudden glare stopped her short.

The room opened to a glass-domed ceiling with a golden stairwell twisting up to the sky. Books orbited the stairs like thousands of small planets, each with its own path and speed. Emily made her way to the bottom of the stairs in a daze and peered up at the burnished rails snaking away from her.

"Excuse me." The man who had greeted her at the door edged past her with a book hugged tight to his chest. Emily stepped aside as he took the steps two at a time, winding his way higher while the other strange books swarmed around him. Once he arrived at a narrow landing, he peeled the book away from his body and muttered something she couldn't quite make out. With a final brush of its cover with trembling fingertips, he released the leather-bound volume into the air, where it zoomed a quick circuit around the room. Emily had enough time to make out the title, *Migellus and the Quest for the Lost Ring,* before it took off among its brothers and sisters.

The man hurried down the stairs, and Emily edged into his path before he could disappear into the stacks.

"Sorry, I'm new to the city. What are all these books doing?"

His smile was too wide, his eyes blinking too fast. "Private collection." He steered her to the nearest aisle by the elbow and released her beside a collection of furry pink journals. "Nothing flashy or fun. Just some old texts no one reads anymore that shouldn't take up proper shelf space. Here—the girls your age all love these journals. Have a look and let me know if you'd like me to store any of them behind the counter for you."

"Uh . . . thanks." She wrinkled her nose at the display, grateful he'd already hurried away before turning away from the nauseating books. "Who wants their journal to look like earmuffs?"

A soft laugh interrupted the quiet, and Emily's head swivelled around, searching for its source. The aisle was empty save for a small, husky boy sitting cross-legged on the ground with his back against the shelves. A large book sat propped open on his lap, the illustrations painted in navy ink across the pages. Patchy facial hair and cheeks with a hint of roundness put him around her age, but his hunched shoulders and easy flush at her sudden attention reminded her of children with wooden horses.

"Was something funny?" An honest question—she hadn't meant to make any sort of joke. Something in the way the boy hunched in deeper, his cheeks turning a vivid magenta, made her wonder if her question had been rude.

He lifted his book until only the top of his chestnut mushroom cut was visible. No eye contact. No answer.

Right. "I guess you *like* furry pink books, then," she muttered. He shifted his body, turning his back to her. The air between them was thick, uncomfortable. Emily rocked back on her heels, waiting for any sort of response from the silent boy in the lumpy orange sweater-vest. "Okay, nice chat," she said, annoyance mounting. First there were the two girls at Cattails who were as pleasant as two slugs, and now this rude boy with the eavesdropping issues. She had never longed for the Commons more.

The front of the shop was as good a place to regroup as any. She marched past the silent boy and headed toward the entrance to choose another, much friendlier aisle.

"Sorry, but have you seen my son?" A wall of yellow appeared around the nearest corner, the woman named Penelope pursing her bright red lips as she scanned the bookstore, gesturing to anyone who would cross her path. "Honestly, how far could he have gone!" She turned and spotted Emily, her eyes narrowing with recognition.

Not this lady again, Emily thought with an internal groan. *Perfect.*

"Sorry, have you seen my son? Tiny chub-muffin of a boy, cute as a button?" She wrung her fingers, large teeth speckled with lipstick.

"I don't think so." Emily tried stepping around her, but the woman cut her off at once.

"Are you sure?" she persisted. "He was wearing a gorgeous tangerine sweater, hard to miss. He usually comes to hide in here, Elder knows why." Penelope laughed, the sound like out-of-tune piano keys, and Emily cringed.

The antisocial kid with the book. "No tangerine sweaters in here as far as I can tell," Emily said, the lie forming without effort. "I wish I could help, but Magdale is waiting for me."

Penelope's eyes widened. "That's right! You're the girl who was with Magdale outside. She told me she was escorting a new initiate personally." The statement was more of a question. Her smile polite. Invasive. "You must be something special to get a Selwyn Master's attention. Whose are you?"

Emily frowned. "What do you mean?"

"Well, I didn't catch your name." She leaned in for a closer look. "Maybe I know who you belong to. Your parents, dear."

Emily blinked and her stomach rolled. "I doubt it since I've never even met them. And I don't belong to anyone."

Confusion flickered across Penelope's face. "What a sad thing to say."

She sighed. "I have to go. Good luck finding your son." She marched past Penelope, clipping her arm with a firm shoulder as she went, and took cover down the next empty row.

A deep breath, then another. Gildenveil had never been a friendly place in her mind, but it was all her imagination back then. Prejudice and speculation. Now she *knew* her instincts had been right. The people of the city were awful.

"Why'd you do that?" a voice asked.

Emily glanced down one side of the aisle, then the other. Still empty. Still alone.

"Over here." The voice was low and muffled, as though coming through a thin wall.

Emily ran her fingers across the spines of the books across from her, unsure what to expect. She was an Elemental, good with physical objects she could touch and move and hold. Hearing voices was more of an Empath's skill, so it was unlikely she was hearing the books talk. Still . . . the voice had been so real.

"What are you doing?" Another question, closer now.

Emily leaned into the stacks and turned her ear to the nearest book. "Trying to hear better." There was no answer, no muffled voice or hint of a whisper. She frowned and waited for it to return.

"Hear what?"

Emily gasped and twisted around, elbow pulled back and ready to strike.

"Hey there, that's not how we say hello!" The boy from the stacks stepped away from her, his book tucked under his arm.

"Ugh, it's you." She dropped her fist, and her shoulders relaxed, sending the flickers and tongues of flame under her palms back up her arm.

"You were expecting a talking atlas?" He spoke with a slight lisp, his eyes a clear hazel up close. "Why'd you lie to my mother?"

"Was that your mother?" Emily asked with a smirk. "I had no idea."

He snorted. "Show me someone else wearing a *tangerine sweater*, and I'll eat it. You had to know she was talking about me, and even though you think books here can talk, you don't look stupid." He wrinkled his nose in distaste. "Scary woman, isn't she?"

Despite herself, Emily smiled. "I've seen worse."

"You'll have to tell me where, so I know to avoid that place." He shook his head and sighed. "She means well, but honestly, it's like having a really annoying parrot on your shoulder all the time—if parrots could shop for weird clothes and feed you unsalted food. And, uh, to be clear, birds can't buy clothes here, either."

To her own surprise, she laughed. Her shoulders were lighter, a small hole in her heart she didn't know existed no longer throbbing. "Good thing you cleared that up for me."

"I'm Oswald Shinkle, by the way. But I like Ozzy better."

"Nice to meet you." She reached out and shook his hand, returning it at once to the necklace around her neck, toying with the gold, the familiar weight. Old habits. "I'm Emily Roth."

"Huh. Never heard of any Roths around here. Are you new to the city?"

She nodded. "It's my first day."

Ozzy's eyes brightened. "I've never met anyone from outside the city! Did you see the new foreign transport booth over on—" His eyes drifted to Emily's neck where she twisted her necklace around her fingers, rotating the pendant on its axis. What was in his eyes? Fear? Surprise?

She lowered her hands and folded her arms across her chest. "Uh, no. I've been to Cattail Inn, but that wasn't interesting or anything."

"Roth? Are you . . . I mean, are you *sure?*"

Where is Magdale? "Why wouldn't I be sure of my own name?"

Ozzy's ears turned pink. "Sorry, it's just your necklace."

"What about it?"

"Where did you get it?"

A familiar fire burned in Emily's chest. "What's it to you?"

He frowned. "It's just that . . . well, it looks really familiar. I could be wrong. I mean, anything is possible. But Roth sounds close to . . . are you *really* sure?" He bit his lip and took another step back as though expecting her to hit him.

Emily took a steadying breath. "It can't be familiar because this necklace is a family heirloom. My father gave it to my mother, and she left it to me."

"Stupid. I'm being stupid. Can we start over?" Worry pinched his eyes as he waited for an answer, the tension making him appear smaller.

With a heavy sigh, Emily relaxed her arms to her side. "Sure," she said with a tight smile. Might as well; there was no point making an enemy of everyone she met. "So how long are you planning on hiding in here?"

"I figure about ten minutes before she calls the Guard." He shuddered.

"That sounds fun."

"It's actually my worst nightmare," he said. "I hate dragons. They're the *worst*. And every member of the Guard has to have his dragon close by. It's an obsession with them."

Emily nodded, understanding the need to avoid dragons at once. "You'd better head out, then."

A red velvet book swooped down the aisle, twisting around a corner before sliding in the empty space on a far-off shelf. Ozzy grinned. "This is my favourite place. I tried asking Mister Gregory for a look at the exclusive collection, but he scares me blind."

"Who's Mister Gregory?"

"The shop owner." Ozzy pointed to the man with the parted black and silver hair who had added a strange book to the revolving collection in the air. "He can talk to books. Hears them, or they hear him or . . . maybe both? I'm not sure."

"And I guess the exclusive collection is anything not attached to a shelf?"

Ozzy brushed the hair from his eyes for a better look at the display over their heads. "I'd give anything to go up there and see what he has. This store has a copy of almost every spell book ever written, and the rarest ones go up around that staircase. He's the only one who can get a book down once it's locked up."

"Rare or . . . dangerous?"

"Don't say that." Ozzy's voice lowered to a whisper. "My father is on the High Council. He told me someone tried taking one of Mister Gregory's more priceless items a few weeks ago. Scared him, too. He's been going up and down those stairs, double-checking his inventory and taking things in and out of rotation like he's scared to leave them there."

"Emily, there you are!" Magdale puffed down the aisle, eyes wild with worry. "I thought I lost you!"

"Sorry, Magdale," Emily said, disappointed at the interruption. "I got caught up talking to Ozzy."

"Ah, yes, Mister Shinkle!" Magdale inclined her head in polite greeting. "I believe your mother was looking for you."

Ozzy's shoulders sagged. "I heard. I'd better go, then. It was really nice meeting you, Emily."

"You too." And she meant it.

He hesitated, fingers drumming on the book he refused to put down. "Look, I don't know when you were scheduled to Skytrain it up to the castle, but I'm going tomorrow afternoon. If you want, I can save you a seat."

Thanks, that's okay.

That's nice, but I can find my own seat.

What's a Skytrain?

Each thought flew through her mind, but her lips wouldn't form the words.

Sensing her hesitation, Magdale chimed in. "That sounds like a lovely idea! I was going to escort her myself, but she should get the experience with other initiates her own age."

Ozzy beamed. "Great, okay. So, I'll see you tomorrow, then!"

"Apparently." Anxiety, crippling and unfamiliar, overwhelmed Emily. Breaking the law and roaming the Commons alone at night was peaceful. Making friends, however, was a disaster.

Ozzy lifted the book over his head, and it slipped from his fingers, zooming through stacks and displays as it headed home. "I'm not the best flier, so if I get sick or have a panic attack, ignore me, okay?"

Emily nodded despite having no idea what he meant. "Fair deal."

"Well, see you!" With a final wave, Ozzy ran to the door, his *tangerine* sweater catching the daylight and sharing its warmth with the rest of the shop.

Magdale sighed as he exited the store. "Sweet boy . . . horrible mother."

Emily stood rooted to the spot, her fingers and toes numb, and said the only thing she could think of: "What's a Skytrain?"

CHAPTER FIVE

Once Upon a Nightmare

"ARE YOU SURE THIS IS the place?" Emily asked for the second time. She stared up at the faded purple brick and crimson window frames set in the lopsided shop front. Thick rivulets of purple smoke wafted out of an equally crooked chimney, sending amethyst clouds over the city.

"Blintwoods," Magdale announced. "Most secure place in the entire realm. The owner is an Empath who can bend the perception of anyone within a stone's throw of her."

"Right," Emily said, her thoughts knitting together one at a time. "So, if she doesn't want you to find something…"

"Then you're out of luck," Magdale finished. "Not

many people are insane enough to attempt robbing her. It just never happens."

Emily stared at the brick and smoke with new eyes. "What do people keep here?"

"Some of the most powerful and valuable magical items in the realm are stored here," Magdale said with reverence. "Some for sale, some for safekeeping. Come on, let's get this over with."

The oak door vanished, and streams of sand and brick rained down the storefront at the sudden shift in weight.

"Well, that's ominous." Emily followed Magdale inside where there was no light or sound. Long, thin whisps of purple mist prowled toward them, twisting in a tight orbit around their ankles, and Emily took an involuntary step back. A child crying, a rustle of dead leaves, cold steel on warm flesh. "Magdale, I'm not sure I like this."

"Follow my voice, dear. Remember, it's a shop like any other. You're seeing what Zaphira wants you to see." Magdale moved deeper into the black.

The air was too thick. No one was comforting the child. She cried louder, harder, salt and tears, the damp reek of pine needles decaying over old, discarded bones from a long-forgotten meal.

"That's enough, Zaphira. Can't you see she's just a child?" The smoke shifted in response to Magdale's command, taking with it the horrible stench clogging Emily's senses.

A small, hunched man materialized before them, his orange hair a perfect match to the eyebrows framing two watery brown eyes. "I'm so sorry, Master Toth!" he blubbered, his face shining with sweat. "I didn't know it was you, or I wouldn't have made things so . . . so . . . scary." He shuddered, dipping his head in an exaggerated bow.

"Hello, Mason. Emily, this is Mason Ball. He's an Empath with similar talents to Zaphira's except with a tad less control." Mason blushed deep crimson, but Magdale didn't seem to notice. "Is Zaphira here? I need a few things for my new initiate."

"She's still on vacation." Mason trembled. "I'm sorry, I thought you knew."

"Still?" Magdale frowned, peering around the wall of purple mist swirling around them. "She's never taken so much time to herself. She deserves it, but it's quite out of character." She waited, rocking on the balls of her feet. "Mason, could you please clear out this fog for me? It's quite stuffy in here."

Emily suppressed a laugh as Mason tripped over his feet before even moving. "Of course, Master Toth, of course!" He sneezed, and the purple filigree flew back into the floorboards, filling the room with sudden air and clarity.

Blintwoods was a long, narrow room with tall ceilings and one large window embedded into the old brick front. Dust floated through the air like glitter, and cobwebs curled around every corner of the room. But the astounding part was the walls; doors, both large and tiny, square, round, and everything in between, covered the walls from floor to ceiling. Each individual shape was set with a unique keyhole trimmed in either brass, silver, or gold and layered in a thick film of grime.

"What's all that?" Emily asked, pointing at the overwhelming number of shapes.

"Each of those doors is a security box," Magdale explained. "Treasures and objects of incredible importance sit within these walls, Emily. It's a wonder Zaphira let Mason take over for her at all."

Mason lowered his eyes but did not protest. His brows pulled together as his gaze settled on Emily's neck, and the urge to hide her own face overwhelmed her. "Do you need a key to get inside any of these boxes?" Emily asked. She shifted so Mason had a better view of the back of her head, his gaze a burning flame between her shoulders.

"Oh no, that wouldn't be very secure," Magdale said. "The keys are purely ornamental. Old tradition, I suppose. Each box is protected by its own enchantment and its own curse should someone try to access it who should not be there. Isn't that right, Mason?" She raised a brow, her voice hard, but he ignored the question.

Her necklace.

He recognized her necklace, same as Ozzy.

"That's all right, Mason, you just stand there and join us when you're ready." Magdale pushed further into the shop, and the clumsy man followed, his wide eyes moving between Emily's neck and her face, lower lip trembling. "We don't have anything valuable to pick up, but I thought it would be interesting for you to see firsthand how Blintwoods works."

"It's . . . impressive." Emily's hand moved to her neck, hiding the pendant. "Uh, Mason? Is something wrong?"

He jumped as though pricked with a hot iron. "M-Me?"

"Mason's fine." Magdale threw her arm around Emily's shoulders and steered her to a row of triangular doors nearby. "His mother always pushed him too far as a child, and he hasn't been the same since. He sees things. Unfortunate. Come on, Emily, let's get to it."

Before Emily could agree, the front door dissolved, and a young couple darted inside, making a dash for a tiny security box across the room. Magdale faced one of the wooden triangles and placed her index finger on the keyhole. The door crumbled, the splinters turning to droplets of a waterfall, and a drawer slid out of the wall.

"Are you . . . Rathburn?" Mason asked. Sweat beaded on his large forehead like dew, and his fingers clutched at his chest above his heart.

Emily scanned the room, but the couple was still busy by their box, out of earshot. "What? Magdale, what does that mean?"

"These security boxes belong to Selwyn's," Magdale continued as pink tinged her cheeks. She pulled out a piece of parchment and unrolled it, running one pale finger down the row of scribbled words. "Every initiate in the castle needs to be registered and documented here."

"So, are you?" Mason asked again. "I mean, I recognize the initial on your necklace. It's your daddy's, isn't it?"

"My father?" Emily asked, Magdale's box forgotten. "This was his, but I never knew him. I'm sorry, what was the name you just said?"

"I'm going to put your name down, then," Magdale spluttered, a quill already in hand, shaking its way across the page.

The *R* on her necklace stood for Roth, not *Rathburn*. The room was too quiet, a faint ringing in her ears accompanied by the rapid beating of her heart. "Sorry, I think you're making a mistake." On the other side of the shop, the couple stood still, their backs hunched.

"It's a mistake, Mason." Magdale's smile was too wide, a high note of warning colouring her usual easy manner. "Jewellery can look similar."

"No, I'm positive that's old Baxter's necklace," Mason continued, finger waggling in the air. "He used to wear that all the time. You're his daughter?" He shuddered, fear and curiosity warring across his overblown features.

The couple peered over their shoulders at them.

"Magdale?" The room was spinning.

"This isn't the right time to discuss it, dear." Magdale replaced the list, rummaged through the box, and withdrew a velvet purse. "I'll go ahead and get your room information going, too, shall we?" She pulled out a small brass number 9 and tucked it into her sleeve.

"Magdale!" Emily cried with unintentional force. The hair at the back of her neck stood on end, and her fingers pulsed with an energy she longed to unleash. "I left my life to be here! It might not have been much, but it was *my* life, and I trusted you with it. So, if you know something I don't, you need to tell me."

Magdale's shoulders sagged. "Well done, Mason. Can you give us a moment?" Mason nodded and shuffled to the back of the shop while the couple stood beside their open box with a ruby gleaming in the man's palm. Unmoving. "I wanted to wait a little while longer before burdening you with this." Her hands trembled at her side, her eyes a distant ocean of secrets. "Do you remember what I told you about our realm? About where we came from?"

Emily frowned. "You mean that we split off from another realm? You called it The Great Divide."

Magdale nodded. "Empaths and Elementals haven't always existed. There was no magic, no Gildenveil. The dragons were a thing of the distant future. It was all very . . . simple. And when we were discovered, it wasn't received kindly."

Emily crossed her arms. "People don't like different."

"It was more than that." Magdale moved to another box: square, the size of an egg, and a pale, bleached wood. "That hate destroyed the first Elemental ever born, and that persecution continued until our kind learned to keep our abilities to ourselves and control them. Needless to say, that way of life didn't always go over well with our kind. There were rebellions, attacks, bloodshed on both sides."

"They killed each other all because of a bit of magic?" Emily asked.

Magdale nodded, put her finger through the keyhole, and summoned another row of miniature books, offering three to Emily. "The High Council was formed in the hopes of calming the constant war, and eventually, the decision was made to split the realm in half so both sides could live in peace."

"I'm guessing some people didn't go quietly."

"Hold these for me please, dear." Magdale opened another door in another row and placed each book in a different slot in the tray before moving on to the next. "Mordred was the leader of the rebellion," she said, face hard. "He had many supporters, and Empaths and Elementals were happy to follow him. That is, until the violence started again, magic on magic violence that needed to stop. Mordred and his followers were captured, one by one, but his ideals stoked a fire much harder to stop."

Emily shivered. In the Commons, there were those without magic who dreamed of those who had it. There was no violence she could remember, no Commoners turning against their own over jealousy and competition. There were only dreams and those too powerless to make them reality. "Sounds like a waste. Anyone with magic should be grateful for their luck."

"Yes, well, those who are fortunate find it difficult to revel in their luck," Magdale said, eyes distant. "They always want more."

"So, Mordred was caught, but his ideas must have been popular outside of his circle, too, right?" Emily leaned against a column of doors while Magdale opened slot after slot, rearranging things until she was satisfied. The couple had closed their security box and made their way to Mason's desk, where the three were huddled in quiet discussion.

Magdale peered over at them and sighed. "For a long time, there was peace, even though ideas of rebellion were always thrown about. But twenty years ago, something shifted. Your parents were newlyweds, and your father was a highly respected Gatekeeper, a naturally talented Empath."

The story had an ending, and Emily knew what it was. Still, she fiddled with her necklace, willing it to tell her a different story with a much different ending than the one she imagined to be true.

Magdale's hands paused over the strange wooden doors containing riches and secrets Emily couldn't begin to understand. And suddenly didn't want to. "It was raining that day," Magdale said, her voice trembling. "And cold—unusual for late spring. I was giving a lecture when I felt a jolt in my heart as though it had forgotten to beat. Large tragedies tend to vibrate in our very souls, it seems."

No.

Tears dripped down Magdale's round, pale cheeks. "Your father didn't arrive for duty that day, but he was so respected that no one thought anything of it."

There was a reason an Elemental like her lived in the Commons, abandoned. And no one wanted her.

No, no, no.

The couple stormed past them, sneers etched on their young faces. Before they exited the shop, the woman turned, her beautiful blonde waves a drop of sunshine in the musty shop. "Traitor," she spat, and allowed herself to be towed out into the busy street by her husband.

NO.

Magdale glared after them. "I'm so sorry, dear. That was inexcusable of them. Please don't take it to heart."

"Tell me." Emily's voice cracked. "Tell me exactly what he did."

Mason lingered by his desk at the back of the shop and fiddled with a book for far too long. Magdale's face fell. "Baxter Rathburn led a dozen or so rebels through the Void to the Dwalind realm and mounted an attack."

Emily nodded, not trusting herself to meet Magdale's eyes. "How many?" she asked.

Magdale's face was ashen. "Over three hundred lives were lost that day," she said, her voice no higher than a whisper.

Emily's necklace burned against her skin, and she slashed her sleeve across her face to erase the traitorous tears. "What happened to him?"

"The Guard found him moments too late. We were told he was the only one left alive on the road. As soon as the Guard closed in, he ran straight into the Void, and no one has seen him since."

So that was her story. That was her legacy. *That* was what she left Molly for. "Baxter Rathburn," Emily repeated, the words like acid.

"I could be wrong. I mean, anything is possible, but Roth sounds really close to…"

"Ozzy recognized my necklace, but I don't think he knows for sure who I am." All her life, being a thief was the worst crime attached to her name. She had never considered a worse label existed. "What about my mother?"

Magdale took a deep breath and locked her final box: a diamond with a square-shaped keyhole. "She insisted she was innocent, of course. But she wouldn't leave your side to come in for questioning, so the Guard put her under surveillance while she settled her affairs."

"She could have been telling the truth," Emily said, hurt and betrayal colouring the world black.

Magdale shook her head. "They waited outside your home, but there was horrible screaming coming from your room. By the time they got inside, you and your mother were gone. We searched, but it was no use." She reached out a hand to comfort Emily, retracting it at once when Emily shrank away from her touch.

"So how did you know I was alive?"

"I had always hoped, of course. But when I heard reports of missing cargo on transport caravans in the Commons a few years ago, I knew for certain it was you. There was no way someone without a magical ability could have gotten past the safeguards protecting those transports. When I found you, I thought it best to leave you alone. For as long as I could, at least." Magdale steeled herself and rested her hand on Emily's shoulder. "I am so very sorry, Emily."

Rage at her traitor father, rage at her weak mother, rage at Magdale for her pity, swarmed like bees inside Emily's skull. "What are you bringing me to Selwyn's for, then?" she spat. "I went with you thinking I was a wanted criminal in the Commons, but it turns out I'm the daughter of a murderer instead! They're going to riot when they find out who I am, and I'll never get what I came for."

Magdale's eyes grew hard, stern. "Some things are predetermined in this life, but your actions need not be," she said, enunciating every word. "It would be a shame to squander your talents because of who your parents were. You deserved a chance."

Emily fought the coil of energy threatening to tear her apart. "Who else knows my real name?"

Magdale's answering smile was tight and sad. "I am the only other person who knows your identity at Selwyn castle, Emily. You are a Rathburn but, tomorrow, you can choose to hide your necklace forever and be Emily Roth. I can head off any rumours circulating around the city, and this will never haunt you again."

"Or I can fight. Just like always." The thought had no heat. She wanted to sleep, to retreat into unconsciousness and never surface again. She wanted to throw her necklace into the Void, to run, to cry, to be unburdened and reckless and violent. Invisible.

Magdale dusted off her sleeves. "You don't have to decide yet. What do you say we head back to Cattails? I'll get the rest of your things for you, but I think some quiet time might be in order right now."

Emily didn't argue. She couldn't.

Outside, the day was too bright. Emily moved through the sea of bodies on weak legs, all her desire to prove herself, to help the Commons, gone. The piece of jewellery branding her a threat to the realm hung, lifeless, under her sweater. It had betrayed her, too.

Across the road, a mother and father crouched over a small child. The little girl's blonde curls and wide, blue eyes danced as she laughed in the glow of the beautiful afternoon light. Her full lips formed a perfect O as she blew iridescent bubbles from the tips of her fingers. Mom and Dad laughed, applauding their daughter with each shiny new orb materializing from nothing. Emily turned away, wishing the pang in her chest would go numb. Sadness was unwanted.

There was only room for shame.

CHAPTER SIX

Happy Accidents

SMILING FACES CHATTERED WITH EXCITEMENT as Elemental and Empath initiates strolled through Willow Court like a massive school of fish moving downstream. Emily stood on the wide walkway, letting the happiness wash over her, hoping it would be enough to quench some of the anxiety clawing at her stomach. But it wasn't.

The tall buildings of rainbow glass, so beautiful and mesmerizing the day before, leered down at her, menacing. There was nothing beautiful about a place riddled with threats and people who hated her on every corner for something out of her control. Still, the crowd moved forward, their shortened shadows ticking the time away at a dangerous speed.

"Are you sure I shouldn't be bringing anything?" Emily asked. "I feel a little . . . light."

Magdale rested her hand on Emily's shoulder. "All your things have been sent directly to the castle for you. I have to check you in before heading to the train. Are you all right to wait for me here?"

Not really, Emily thought, her nerves twisting her heart ever tighter. "'Course," she said without feeling.

There had been no simple choice, no obvious decision she could make to erase the sense of doom hovering over her. While Selwyn castle opened the door to a past she couldn't begin to accept, the Commons promised more of the same: misery, hunger, a helplessness she couldn't escape.

Roth or Rathburn?

Anonymity or infamy?

She paced the walkway, kicking the joints between the uneven stones and wishing the choice was as obvious as it sounded.

"What are you doing?"

"Arg!" She kicked the ground too hard, crushing her big toe against an uneven paving stone jutting out from the rest.

"Sorry, sorry!" the girl chirped. She tossed her neat ponytail of strawberry-blonde hair over her shoulder, large green eyes peering up at her with unguarded curiosity under a fan of honey-blonde lashes.

Emily ignored the throbbing in her foot. "Where did you come from?"

The girl shifted a large book from one arm to the other and smiled. "I'm heading to catch the Skytrain." She shrugged her delicate shoulders with difficulty under the weight of her enormous bag. "Isn't that where you're going, too? You look about my age—I'm sixteen. Are you sixteen? I haven't seen you around here, so maybe you're not going to Selwyn's at all. And you have no bags or books . . . " She frowned. "Well . . . *are* you headed there? I can't be sure now. It's a bit embarrassing."

"You don't look embarrassed," Emily muttered, her toe thumping with a heartbeat of its own. "Yeah, I'm going to Selwyn's, too. I'm sorry, but who are you? Except for being a *really* bad omen because I think I broke my foot." She flexed her toes and grimaced at the pain lancing up her ankle.

"You're funny. Weird, kicking at sidewalks like that, but I like you." She bobbed her head with vigorous determination, as though deciding they would be best friends right then. "I'm Willow Colray. It's nice to meet another initiate who doesn't try hiding from me. Mom and Dad let me come up on my own today, which was a relief, you know, because they're pretty overwhelming when they get excited. I'm adopted, by the way. Did I mention that?"

"Uh." Emily shifted her weight from foot to foot and peered into the shop behind her. Why was Magdale taking so long? "No, you didn't say. That sounds tough, though."

"Oh no, my parents are great," she said, ponytail swishing behind her. "I was born in the Commons, but I had an ability when my birth parents didn't. They were pretty stunned when I started talking to lettuce heads, and they had no choice but to give me up to the city."

"You hear lettuce?" Emily repeated. "So, you're an Empath?"

Willow nodded and let out a tinkling laugh. "It would be pretty strange to hear lettuce if I *wasn't* an Empath, don't you think?"

"Oh, I think lots of things are strange around here, Willow." Despite the awkward conversation, Emily found herself relaxing, the tension in her shoulders easing. "Your birth parents lived in the Commons. Do you ever talk to them?" *Maybe I know them?*

"I'm not allowed to." Willow shrugged. "Empaths and Elementals aren't supposed to have anything to do with the Commons. I thought everyone knew that."

Of course. Emily's jaw clenched as she bit back her words. So, anyone born with magic was banned from crossing the line over to the Commons, as though they carried an incurable disease. "That doesn't seem fair," was all Emily could manage, not trusting herself to say more.

Willow frowned. "It's the way it is. Anyway, enough about me. What can *you* do? You look like an Elemental. I can't put my finger on it, but you definitely have that look."

Breathing did not seem to be a priority for Willow Colray. "I'm . . . Emily. Yeah, I'm an Elemental."

"Oh good! That's a relief. I thought I was making a horrible first impression for a second there. Hello, Master Fogg!" Willow waved, and Emily wished the ground would swallow her whole.

"Hello, children," Master Fogg called over the noise on the street. Her voice was high, her hair a long, frazzled mess of brown tangles and her fingers thick around a plain black bag. "Best not temp the Fates and linger. You may miss your train and rewrite the book of time all because you could not be punctual!"

"The Fates?" Emily asked in a whisper.

"Who knows?" Willow sighed. "Fogg is the first Empath to claim to speak to time itself. Not sure how that works, but who can prove her wrong, eh?"

"Right," Emily said, unsure what else to add as Fogg ghosted away.

"Bit weird that she's taking the train, though."

"Why's that?"

Willow fiddled with the ends of her hair. "The only adults on the Skytrain are the chaperones so that nothing bad happens on the ride. Most of the Masters live up at the castle already or can Transfer directly up there."

"What could possibly happen?" Emily asked, afraid of the answer.

Willow smiled. "Two years ago, some new Elemental was showing off how she could sneeze fiery sparks at the exact same time Christopher Vicars was pouring his friend a glass of water across from her. Well, their magic mixed, and fire and water aren't the best of friends, you know. It was a disaster—would have been worse if Master Grey hadn't jumped in." Willow shuddered.

Sunshine bounced off the glass shops, and Emily shielded her eyes from the glare. "I'm guessing Grey's one of the powerful ones if she has to take care of a bunch of initiates by herself."

"Oh, she is. Terrifying, but useful when people are trying to blow themselves up. You know what I mean."

Not even a little. "Oh sure."

Willow stepped aside as a group of young children charged up the walkway. She waved at them as they disappeared with the rest of the crowd. "Grey usually chaperones because no one dares get into trouble with her around. Wonder why they replaced her with Fogg—she doesn't seem to be in touch with reality at all, poor woman."

Emily wished Magdale would forget something, find another way to the castle. "What happened to those initiates?"

"Oh, don't worry, no one died," Willow said, correctly reading Emily's expression. "But it was pretty touch and go for a minute. They could have taken the whole thing down."

"Down?" What kind of train *was* this?

"Oh, yeah, I heard about that!" The new voice belonged to a short, round boy with light brown hair, his tweed jacket pulling at the straining buttons. His physical opposite trailed close behind: tall, gangly, pale as oatmeal with a shock of black hair over an expression of perfect terror.

"Who are you?" Emily blurted.

"Rude." The shorter boy frowned at Emily, nose scrunched as though he smelled something unpleasant coming from his kitchen. "Who're *you*?"

"That's just Fitzpatrick." Willow waved a thin hand over her head.

"It's Fitzgibbons, actually," he said, face falling. "Elliott Fitzgibbons, charming Elemental. Willow, I've known you since we were five."

Willow was content ignoring him, moving on to his companion. "And that's Finn Dashwood. He's our age, but he's been at Selwyn's a whole year already. They still haven't managed to get him to do much more than light a candle, but fingers crossed this year is *the* year!"

Finn turned a dark shade of magenta. "My ability is fire. I'm afraid of fire. It's not easy to be motivated to do something terrifying. Magic really does have a cruel sense of humour."

Elliott snorted. "You scare yourself when you cough, man."

"You'd be scared too if every time you got sick, your parents had to lock you in a special room to keep the house from going up in flames." He withered in embarrassment as Emily and Willow erupted into a fit of giggles.

"Anyway, I'm hoping they can do more with me than they did with Finn," Elliott said. "I can change my shape. I'm sure you noticed I look a bit . . . healthy around the middle." He grimaced, pulling at the lapels of his jacket. "I can make myself shorter or taller or slimmer, even, but I can't hold it for long. Anyway, Dad has high hopes for me. Honestly, I'll be happy if I can just find myself a girlfriend." He glanced at Emily, appraising. "I have a good memory for pretty girls and haven't seen you around here. Are you new?"

Emily shrank away from their watchful eyes. "I got in yesterday with . . . um . . . Master Toth. I'm Emily." She remembered to smile, the muscles of her face working hard.

"Master Toth brought you in personally?" Finn asked, his attention diverted from the passing crowd. "You must be something special to get a Selwyn Master's attention. What's your ability?"

She shifted her weight from one foot to the other. Resentment should have left a bitter taste on her tongue, disgust at having to prove herself, to have her worth measured by her magic. Instead, the challenge bolstered her, shaking her loose from the bonds keeping her silent.

"I can make objects disappear and go somewhere else if I want to." On an impulse, she marched up to Elliott and placed a hand on the duffel bag resting at his feet. She closed her eyes and let the fire blaze through her fingers, so close to the surface over the course of the last day. The rough canvas under her fingers grew warm, bright white in the sun. Nothing but air.

"Wow," Elliott muttered, head swivelling in search of his bag. "Not many Elementals have that kind of control when they start off. That's pretty impressive!"

"Thanks." Emily smiled, hating the surge of pride welling up inside her.

"So, where did you send my stuff?"

Emily winked. "It's a surprise."

He burst out laughing. "Hey, you're all right! I hope they put us together for lessons."

"As long as she doesn't touch *my* stuff." Finn squeezed his leather carry-on closer to his chest. "It was my Uncle Mick's, and he'd hang me if I lost it."

At last, Magdale glided out of the shop behind them, Elliott's heavy duffle in tow behind her in mid-air. "Emily, dear, do you know why this large bag full of coffee cake landed on my toes?"

"That's awesome." Elliott grabbed the bag out of the air with an open mouth.

"Mister Fitzgibbery! Mister Dashwood! It's nice to see you both." Magdale grinned, joining Emily with a glittery smile.

Elliott frowned. "It's *Fitzgibbons*, ma'am."

"Isn't that what I said?" Magdale shrugged.

Emily stifled a laugh as Elliott bit back his protests. For a second, a fraction of time, she wasn't a blank face from the Commons, a thief, an orphan, an outcast on the run. She was a girl, and she could imagine what it would be like to feel . . . equal.

Willow bounced on the balls of her feet, elated at having a new face to talk to. "Hi, Master Toth! I came over here because Emily was kicking the sidewalk."

"Ah, yes, Miss Colray. I was wondering when you were going to make your way up the hill. It's nice to see Emily is in good hands. You all can head up together and save me the climb."

Emily frowned. "Climb? Seriously, where is this train?"

"It's a bit of a pain to get there," Willow explained. "The train needs to leave from the highest ground possible to avoid destroying any of the buildings."

"You'll love it." Elliott nodded, face beaming. "But I'm sure you've heard about it already? You'd have to be living under a rock not to know about the Skytrain."

"I do like rocks," Emily said. "Sorry, I've never heard of it before."

"It's completely terrifying and dangerous, and I'm shocked no one's found a better way to get us up there," Finn interjected. "Mother almost had a myocardial infarction halfway up the climb last year."

"A what?" Elliott asked.

"You know, a heart attack." Finn waved a hand and then yanked it back with a look of disgust as a tall girl carrying an orange lizard grazed his elbow. He checked the sleeve of his jacket for damage and muttered something that sounded like *'completely unsanitary.'*

"Why didn't you *say* heart attack, then?" Elliott protested.

Finn shrugged. "Mother says it's best to use the proper terms."

"Heart attack's proper," Elliott scoffed. "No one's going to understand you if you—"

"Right!" Magdale interjected, clapping her hands over the squabble. "You four had better move fast."

Willow looped her arm through Emily's and steered her down the sidewalk. Her first instinct was to brush off Willow's hand, but she resisted. "Thanks, Magdale!" Emily called over her shoulder.

"You have a safe ride!" Magdale waved over the crowd. "And remember to avoid the head!"

Emily faltered. "The what?"

"We should hurry," Willow said, her voice low and her hair swinging with every step. "It's a big hike, and I'm pretty sure Fitzgobbers and Dashwood are going to have trouble keeping up."

Elliott threw his arms up in the air. "Honestly, why can't anyone remember my name?"

The trek out of the main city was quick and effortless with the right company. Their group fell into an easy rhythm, and conversation flowed uninterrupted, never circling back to Emily or her past. Elliott and Willow contented themselves with chatting about the crowds and shops and the hopes they had for the upcoming year. All the while, Emily was part of them, an easy fit in the conversation, and the vise gripping her stomach relinquished its hold.

The city was growing familiar with the rows of coloured brick stacked in a predictable way, the notable shop signs and weaving roads taking the initiates and their families away from Willow Court up the same shopping route she and Magdale had followed the day before. Their footsteps navigated the crowd with care until an unexpected wave of dense smoke choked off their view. Emily peered through the moving bodies and slowed as onlookers clogged the street. The air was a deep plum, thick and warm and suffocating while necks craned around for a better look at Blintwoods.

"Is that supposed to happen?" Emily asked.

"Zaphira's place?" Willow glanced at the crowd and frowned. "I've never seen it look like that."

"Maybe there was some kind of explosion." Elliott stood on his toes, eyes bright with excitement. "Not the best thing to happen when you're in the business of protecting people's valuables. That Mason helper of hers really did it this time."

Emily frowned. Smoke poured from the windows and underneath the front door in steady streams. Concerned muttering flitted over their heads, and Emily pulled at her necklace, fiddling with the familiar grooves. "An explosion sounds serious," she said. "But, I mean, this sort of thing must happen."

"This isn't the Commons, Emily," Elliott said with a mild snort, and Emily fought the urge to punch him. "Fires and disasters don't happen every day here. There aren't criminals running around picking locks and blowing up shops."

Yeah, 'cause that's what happens in the Commons. Emily ground her teeth. She wasn't expecting Gildenveil City to be perfect, but if accidents were as rare as Elliott made it sound, then something was seriously wrong in Zaphira's shop. The commotion inside the old shop might have been an accident, but, in Emily's experience, accidents were rarely true accidents at all.

"Hey, could you give me a few minutes?" Emily asked, already peeling herself away from their group. "I promise I'll be right back."

"Sure, we'll wait for you here," Willow agreed at once.

Finn, however, paled as Emily broke off into the crowd. "You've got five minutes, or we're leaving without you! I won't miss this train!"

As usual, Emily's small size was perfect for getting somewhere quick without being seen; it was easy to navigate tight spaces, weave in and out and avoid the majority of prying eyes. She moved through the gaps like water trickling through a bucket of rocks, finding the easiest and quickest path to the other side.

"Did you see a face? Anything at all?" A man in a navy uniform, a badge affixed to the shoulder of his right arm in the shape of a silver star—was he a Guard official?—struggled to question Mason, a quill and parchment in hand. Observers shook their heads, and when Mason simply shrugged, the man's face fell. "You don't remember who was in the shop with you at the time of the explosion?"

Mason coughed and dusted ash off his starched pants. "It's dark in there, you know." Tears pooled in his red eyes. "That's the whole point of the smoke. You know how Zaphira likes things."

"And have you contacted Zaphira at all to inform her of the incident?" The Guard official arched a brow as though already expecting the answer to be one he'd disapprove of.

"She's away, I told you!" Mason said, flustered. "She isn't easy to reach! Oh, I can't believe this happened. I'll be fired. I need the money! I have three children—do you know how much three children *eat*?"

Emily edged behind a woman wearing a long, flowery gown closer to the front of the group. Blintwoods was covered in dust, and the top corner of the solitary window had shattered clear away from its frame. But there was a door Emily hadn't seen the day before at the side of the shop. And it stood open, leaking heat and ash into the street.

"And the clothes!" Mason continued with a sob. "They need new ones every other month, and Zaphira's cheap, you know. The most valuable items in the realm are in this place, and yet I can barely afford shoes." He took a deep breath and glanced over his shoulder at the smoking shop. "Why aren't you trying to put out the fire instead of questioning me?"

"Elementals are on the way." The official's eyes scanned his parchment, words clipped.

In the space of a breath, Emily tucked her chin into her chest and dashed over to the open door. Pools of purple smoke formed a wall of heat around the entrance, and she covered her face with her hands while her mind cried out for clean air. A small fire burned inside, the orange flames giving the interior of the shop a soft glow through the murky haze. Her eyes streamed tears, and she coughed, struggling to breathe, struggling to see.

Blintwoods was choking. Another wave of heat slammed into Emily's face as she took a step closer. Soon enough, she would run out of breathable air, and she would have to leave. Until then, a soft shuffling inside the building like feet scuffling across the ground begged her to stay.

Someone's inside. Did the Guard official know? Where was his dragon? Should she tell him, or would he send her off as soon as he learned who she was? So many questions, and no answers in sight for any of them.

She inched ever closer until the smoke hugged her like an old, bitter friend.

The soft swish of fabric against the rough floorboards accompanied the pop of the fire inside the building. *Someone's still in there.*

No sooner had the thought flitted through her mind than the darkness shifted. A shoulder slammed hard into her chest, and Emily fell back onto the cobblestone, the wind knocked out of her lungs before she hit the paving stones.

An angry cry. An unfamiliar voice. A snarl of anger. "Watch it!"

Emily stared up at the sky, searching for the source of the sound, and found only smoke and shadows. With a grunt, she pushed herself to her feet, chest burning, head reeling. She stumbled forward, lungs pulling dirty air into her body while her ribs ached, and her hands searched and searched. "Are you okay? Do you need help?" she asked.

The woman coughed inches away from her. Strange hands grabbed both of Emily's wrists and pulled her forward with surprising strength. "Who are you? What are you doing here?"

The control in the stranger's voice was too perfect for someone caught off guard by a sudden explosion. "I'm Emily. Who are *you*?"

"Emily?" the shadow repeated, fingernails pressing deeper into the soft flesh at Emily's wrists. The smoke was dissipating, and the woman's outline became clearer. Slanted eyes the colour of frozen steel cut through the murky air. "Rathburn?" Without waiting for a response, one hand released Emily's wrist and dug with greedy force around her neck for the chain resting against her skin.

"Let go of me," Emily demanded, bile rising in her throat.

"You shouldn't be here. Get out!" The grainy voice boomed with hate, her fingers twisting to claws around the necklace as though to tear it off her skin.

"I think you're the one who shouldn't be here," Emily said, fighting another cough. "Did you do this? Why are you—?"

A vise clamped down on Emily's windpipe. Stars erupted like sparks across her vision, her lungs suffocating on the smoke she'd inhaled. But the woman's hands were visible, one around the chain at her throat and the other still gripping her wrist. Still, the edges of her throat pressed together. Emily's vision flickered, and her mouth worked to make words, but no sound escaped her.

"You're in no position to ask questions, Rathburn." The invisible grip tightened, and Emily kicked out with frantic force, finding nothing but air. "Always getting in the way. Like father, like daughter." Just as the edges of the world turned black and Emily's limbs grew heavy, the woman backed away, the strange pressure constricting her throat evaporating.

The stars faded as blood rushed to her head. Emily stumbled forward in a fit of coughs, her lungs pulling greedy breaths and finding thick, dirty air. Any longer, and she would lose consciousness. With shaky legs, she traced her fingers along the stone wall, blind in the thick smoke until the brick cut out and the air cleared. Where was the cloaked woman with the silver eyes? Wouldn't someone notice her running off?

A black cloak flipped out of the corner of Emily's eye, and the hooded woman hurried into the crowd. Emily followed, humiliation and pain fuelling her need to face her attacker in the daylight.

"Is that Emily Rathburn?" the woman called, jabbing a thumb over her shoulder.

Emily's heart hammered against her ribs, and she stopped before the group. Eyes moved from the Guard official to Emily's spot on the road, her necklace laid bare for the world to see. *I can't deal with this now.* She ducked her head and gave the crowd a wide berth as the whispers hissed on the wind.

Someone cursed at her.

Someone else told her she deserved to be dead like her father.

Emily forced her feet to move and searched Willow Court for the hooded stranger.

Move.

This wasn't the Commons. And while Emily hadn't known what to expect from the city, a large part of her had never anticipated crossing paths with a criminal. A criminal who knew her father well.

Every accident was no accident at all. And the strange woman's biggest mistake was allowing herself to be seen.

Emily hurried across the street, leaving the growing mob behind.

CHAPTER SEVEN

What's a Skytrain?

FINN'S FACE BOBBED OVER THE crowd. "Are you insane?" He didn't wait for her to apologize before his anxiety got the better of him. "The train leaves in eight minutes!"

Willow frowned. "You look awful, Emily."

The crowd across the road was growing both in size and noise. "Sorry about that. Finn's right. We should get going."

Under the pressure of time, no one thought to question the uproar across the street. Together, they rushed up the rest of Willow Court, the weight of their bags and frantic panic making the trek a silent one.

"Any chance you could do your thing and send our stuff to the train?" Elliott huffed, face purpling as they turned a corner only to face a steep incline up a road of magenta cottages.

Emily shook her head, her breath coming in shallow bursts. "I need to know where I'm sending things to be able to do it. I've never seen the Skytrain, so—"

"So we need to move faster!" Finn's forehead dripped with anxiety and effort. "Whose idea was it to put a stupid train at the top of a *stupid* hill?"

"The train needs to leave from a high spot so it doesn't damage anything when it takes off," Emily said at once. "Whatever that means."

Willow beamed up at her. "I knew I liked you. So, see anything good over at Blintwoods?"

Emily pushed her legs to move faster and stared straight ahead, half blinded by the white sunlight. "Not really." Her mind was too consumed with the silver-eyed woman to allow for any unwanted guilt at the lie. In truth, she'd seen more than she'd cared to.

The path blossomed into a wide, circular clearing of flat rock and wild grass. She lifted her hand over her eyes, the back of her shirt sticking to her skin, and listened to the distant hum of happy goodbyes and Finn's rasping breath.

"We made it!" Willow declared, letting her bags drop to shake out her arms. "See, Finn? You worry for nothing. Come on!"

"Give me a minute, will you?" Elliott muttered, finding a bright green patch of grass and lowering himself to the ground with as much grace as a falling tree. Finn threw his hands in the air and towered over his friend, letting his fury fly.

"Come on, before Finn kills him," Willow said under her breath. She grabbed her bags and danced across the clearing, fearless, into the hundreds of initiates swarming the . . .

No . . . not possible...

Emily planted her feet on the ground, and her tongue turned to sand in her mouth. "Willow, that's a—"

"Dragon!" she said, beaming. "Have you ever seen one so beautiful before?"

"Remember to avoid the head!"

Emily took an involuntary step back. "No, Willow, not up close."

A dozen navy carts were strapped with thick iron supports to the back of a very large, very glossy, black dragon like a second set of ribs. Scales the length of Emily's leg covered its entire body in inky armour, its golden underbelly flat against the soft ground. With every breath, the string of carts arched into the sky, sending those on board into peals of excited laughter. One yellow eye moved over the crowd and settled on a young girl standing nearby, who was eyeing the beast with a mixture of fascination and pure terror.

"I thought we were taking a train," Emily said, her tone flat.

"You mean, like one that runs on the *ground*?" Willow giggled. "I know you're not from the city, but honestly, you should know Selwyn's is *way* too remote to be accessed by land. It's way up on the top of a cliff at the edge of the city. There's no way a regular train would get us there."

"Right, my mistake." Her heart hammered in her ears, and her palms turned slick. "That . . . *thing* doesn't look safe." As though hearing her, the dragon sniffed, sending a spray of sparks into a nearby patch of weeds, turning them to ash.

Willow rolled her eyes. "That *thing* is called Naglar. He's been flying the Skytrain for as long as I can remember. He's as safe as dragons get. Plus, we'll all get to ride our own soon, so you should get used to it. Come on, or we really are going to miss it!"

Emily's necklace hung heavy around her neck, no longer a delicate string of gold but a noose. She hesitated, more uncertain than she had ever been in her life before hurrying to catch up with the girl, the air growing warmer with every step she took. Up close, she could see the steps buckling with every one of Naglar's breaths, lifting off from the ground and threatening to dislodge the unfortunate initiates climbing into their wagon.

Willow stepped aside. "Go ahead, Emily. You look like you're going to be sick, and this dress is new. Can't risk getting any vomit on the back."

Emily shook her head. "I'm fine, Willow. You first."

"For Elders' sake, *I'll* go if you two crones can't make up your minds." A pair of strong hands shoved them aside, and two girls edged past them, their laughter enough to pull Emily from her cloud of fear.

The girls from Cattail Inn, the ones who assaulted others with balls of coffee-soaked paper for fun. Emily groaned. "Not you again."

"You remember me! I'm flattered." Catherine Bonner climbed onto the first step with a flip of her curly hair. Her lime-green skirt swayed in the low breeze, matching the headband sitting like a crown atop her head. "What happened to your chaperone? Is she off finding you a safety blanket for the flight?"

Emily ground her teeth and forced her face to remain impassive. "Are you always this nice?"

Camilla stood beside her friend and ignored the question, leering down at them like a gargoyle. "Are you planning on joining the kitchen staff when we get to the castle, or did your parents think to pack you some nicer clothes?"

Emily's fingers prickled, but Willow smiled at both girls with oblivious kindness. "It's so nice that you all know each other already! I hope we can be friends. Maybe even roommates."

Catherine wrinkled her nose. "Doubtful."

Willow shrugged. "That's fair. C'mon Emily, Naglar won't bite; his teeth are all the way over there."

"Ugh!" Catherine's friend observed Willow as though she were a tarantula. "Why is she still talking?"

"Doesn't matter, Cammy." Catherine grabbed Camilla's arm and pulled her up the rest of the steps. "Let's go before we're stuck sharing a row with them."

Willow nudged Emily up into the cart, and Emily forgot about the deadly set of teeth at the other end of the dragon long enough to seethe at the girls' backs as they slid into seats in the middle of the wagon. The compartment was cool and smelled of lavender and sweet vanilla. Despite the new faces in every row and the bucking of the aisle as she and Willow picked their way past happy faces and luggage being packed away, she was surprised to note that the Skytrain was beautiful.

Minus the dragon, of course.

Seats of thick, soft velvet in the darkest shade of navy lined each side of the cart, clusters of four chairs making up a section. Bronze rails ran the length of the cart where heavy blue curtains draped down to the cream runner. Some sections were curtained off for privacy, but more stood open and ready to welcome newcomers.

"Emily! Over here!" Ozzy popped his head over the back of his seat at the end of the aisle and waved over the heads of two girls giving him a look of disgust. Emily waved back with a smile of relief, and Willow thrust her things in his arms by way of greeting.

"Hi, Ozzy." Willow's smile was warm as she lowered herself into an aisle seat. "Be careful with the small one. My collectibles are in there."

"Er . . . hi there, Willow." Ozzy resigned himself to the duffel bags now weighing him down. "You haven't changed over the summer, then." With a few awkward heaves, he stowed the luggage away and took his chair by the window, glaring at the clouds.

"Nice seats," Emily said. *Nice seats? Sure, why not ask about the weather or how his mother's doing.* She resented how nervous she was, longing for the days where the fewer friends she had, the better off she was.

Ozzy smiled warmly. "These are some of the best seats on the train. Less bucking during the flight the closer you are to the ribs."

Emily slumped down opposite him, grateful for the chance to breathe. "You could have mentioned the Skytrain was a massive dragon carrying a wagon on its back."

"I don't like to think about it too much." He shuddered. "Flying isn't my favourite thing in the world."

"If it's anything like Transference, I'm right there with you," Emily agreed. "So, you two already know each other?"

"Oh, yes," Willow said. "But I'm surprised he made another friend already. It's not easy for him, you know. He's shy, and as soon as they meet his mother, it's all over."

"Thanks for that, Willow," he muttered.

"Oh, it's no problem." Willow beamed. "Anyhow, I like you, too, and I'm a pretty good judge of character."

Emily muffled a laugh behind her fist as Ozzy's jaw went slack. "Hear that, Ozzy? You passed her standards."

Willow peered around the cart. "I thought for sure we'd be late. Any idea if we're taking off soon?"

Ozzy wrinkled his nose. "I hope so. Better to get it over with." He yanked the velvet curtain of their compartment closed and sighed. "Hope you don't mind. I'd rather no one else see me break down during takeoff."

"It's perfect, actually," Emily reassured him. "I could use a few minutes of peace."

"Good, because my brother and his friends are right outside, and I don't want to talk to them. Or hear them."

"Which one's your brother?" Emily asked, looking around a gap in the curtain.

"The big one with the ugly face." Ozzy scowled. "His name is Brady, and he's an absolute nightmare."

"He's top of the class, and he's really handsome!" Willow added, feet swinging above the ground. "Brady bonded with a dragon after only six months at Selwyn's. Finora and him are absolutely in sync. That's the quickest any Empath has made a link with a dragon in over—"

"Three centuries," Ozzy finished with a pained expression. "I'll never hear the end of it. Mom and Dad were so proud they could have died right there and been happy about it."

Naglar got to his feet, sending Emily lurching back into her chair while Ozzy scrambled to attach his safety belt to avoid falling forward. "Making us fly," Ozzy muttered darkly. "All the magic in the realm and they strap us to a monster with wings."

Emily clicked her own belt into place and leaned in closer to Willow. "People can't actually get thrown out of this thing, can they?"

"I don't think so," Willow said. "Although, I did hear that, one time, a boy forgot to tighten his belt, and he flew all the way to the back of the train and hit his head on the far wall. He was okay, though," she continued, curling her legs underneath her. "He only spent a month or so in the Selwyn clinic."

Ozzy moaned. "Will . . . you . . . stop . . . talking?"

The wagon bucked, rattling the windows and sending Ozzy into a loud burst of curses. They clutched their armrests, screams of panic and laughter exploding around them.

"This is so exciting!" Willow announced, green eyes flashing.

Ozzy closed his eyes, his face draining of all colour. "Really? You're excited to be launched thousands of feet into the air on the back of a murderous lizard?"

"Oh sure! Shame I'll have to take a nap, though."

"*Nap?*" he exclaimed. "How can you think of sleep?"

Willow shrugged. "I'm tired. Plus, Mom says I can get a bit annoying if I'm not well rested, and I want to make a good first impression."

Emily waited as Ozzy struggled to find his words. Naglar gave a giant snort of effort, and the window clouded over with tar-like smoke. Giant wings beat at the haze, clearing it away so Emily could admire their smooth texture shining in the daylight, delicate gold veins forming a living, moving web. The dragon reared up to the sky, and Emily was pressed deeper into the velvet cushion.

"Oh, sweet, bleeding Elders," Ozzy moaned, fingers turning white against the seat.

Naglar was running now. Trees and clouds rushed past, great booms making their teeth clatter as he took long, tremendous strides. With one final lunge, the ground gave way to clouds whirring past their window in a mass of white and grey.

"Are we dead?" Ozzy moaned.

"We are very much alive," Emily breathed. Her worries were back on the ground, behind her, small and insignificant, leaving her with the steady beat of the ancient beast's wings and the vast expanse of blue stretching on forever.

"I don't believe it," Ozzy breathed, face tinged with green. "She's already asleep!"

Emily grinned at Willow's peaceful face. "You sure you're going to be okay, Ozzy?"

"I'll be fine. Takeoff is the worst of it. Sorry," he added with an apologetic look.

She laughed. "Don't worry about it."

They banked right, and Emily was flying. They launched headfirst into the wind, and as Naglar picked up speed, all the worries bogging Emily down fell away like broken shackles.

"So, are you nervous?" Ozzy asked.

"I'm actually enjoying this," she admitted.

"Insane." He shook his head. "I mean, about your first day at the castle. I'm terrified."

The peaceful trance cracked, and thoughts like acid

ate into her mind. "Oh. I guess I try not to think about it much." It was as close to the truth as she dared go.

"It's okay, I think. I don't know much about controlling my own power, but neither does anyone else. And even when I get it to work, I can't do it for long."

"What can you do?"

"I'm an Empath," he explained. "I can . . . well…" He squinted, an odd glint flashing behind his eyes. "Will you let me show you?"

Emily shrugged. "Why not?"

A mischievous look crossed Ozzy's face. His irises expanded, painting his eyes black, and Emily fell into them. Her mind unraveled until there was nothing except Ozzy and those eyes, that black pool she just wanted to dive into. Somewhere in the distance, a voice spoke: "Oh, Willow, wake up! You missed the whole year, and they decided to send you back home!"

Willow's eyes flew open, and she clutched convulsively at her armrests. "Wha? What's happened?"

The black pools disappeared, and Ozzy's eyes returned to warm shades of brown and gold with flecks of green. As the world rushed back to her, Emily clamped her hands over her mouth—a mouth that had formed words without her permission. "Was that me?"

"Nothing, Willow," Ozzy said, suppressing a grin. "Go back to sleep."

"What . . . what did you do?" Emily asked, as the small girl curled into a tight ball and dropped back to sleep.

Ozzy shrugged, cheeks turning deep pink. "Bit of a creepy talent, if you think about it. I can control what people say by getting in their heads. Isn't that terrible?"

Yes. Don't ever do that again. Do that again. "I mean,

it's not turning rocks to gold or anything, but it's pretty cool."

"My parents say I'm advanced for my age. That Selwyn's will get me to learn how to manipulate a whole room of conversation without breaking a sweat." Ozzy gnawed on his bottom lip. "I'm not sure how I feel about being able to get into people's heads."

"Well, when you put it that way, it does sound a *bit* creepy," Emily agreed with a grin.

Ozzy groaned. "See? And because of how strong my ability can get, the Masters are going to be watching everything I do. The High Council has really strict rules about stuff like this. I'm not technically allowed to use my ability on anyone unless I get their permission."

"But a power is only as good or as bad as the person who has it. You shouldn't beat yourself up because of who you are."

"I guess so. Still doesn't beat turning rocks to gold, though," he said with a small smile.

Heavy footsteps thumped down the aisle and, with a violent swish of velvet, their privacy curtain jerked open. Catherine and her friend loomed over them, wearing identical sneers while an older boy with wavy black hair towered behind. He stared down the aisle, dark brown eyes slanting over pronounced cheekbones and a muscle in his angular jaw flexing visibly under pale skin. With a wide yawn, he leaned a broad shoulder against the edge of their compartment and crossed his arms over his chest.

"Would you two keep the bonding thing down?" Catherine said. "It's hard enough to ride this stupid dragon without having to hear you gush over each other, too."

"You can move if you don't like it," Emily pointed out.

Camilla smirked, bright eyes flashing. "No, I don't think so. If anyone should move, it's you."

"Any reason why, or do you just like telling people what to do?" Emily brushed her hair from her face and offered a serene smile.

"Because you have no right to be here."

The necklace hidden under Emily's sweater came alive with her mounting panic. "I disagree."

Camilla leaned over Willow and lowered her voice. "Unless Selwyn's is doing some outreach program, letting trash outside the city in, you have no business playing in the big leagues."

Emily frowned at Ozzy with mock confusion. "Do you know what she's talking about?"

Fire gathered behind Camilla's eyes. "Don't even try to deny it. I know everyone who is anyone around Gild-enveil, and I have *never* seen you and your second-hand sweatshirts around here. I'll bet you're from some little town outside the walls, which means you're no more gifted than a Commoner."

A wave of resentment brought the blood rushing to Emily's face. "It's possible for some people from the Commons to turn up with magic. And even if they don't, there's nothing wrong with it."

"That rarely happens," Ozzy said, eyes bright with apology. "But only the really stuck-up people bring it up like being a Commoner is a bad thing."

Emily locked eyes with Camilla. "Huh. Makes sense I'd hear it from these two, then. I didn't expect much before when I saw them acting like kids at Cattails, but I guess I have to lower my standards." She turned to

Catherine, face impassive. "You should run along before I contaminate you with my lack of magical talent."

The boy's eyes flickered to her for the first time, alight with interest. A small smile crept across his face, but Catherine's lips pressed together, her knuckles turning white. "Don't talk to me or my friend like that," Catherine said, a hard edge in her voice.

Emily sighed. "Then put a little more effort into entertaining her. If she wasn't so bored with you, she might not need to come bother *us*."

The metal bolts holding the curtains in place screeched, wiggling in their rusted loops. "I could strangle you with your own necklace and make it look like an accident," Camilla whispered. As though needing to emphasize her point, she flicked her fingers, and Emily's necklace quivered.

"Leave her alone," Ozzy blurted. "Please."

"Look at that! She's got a boyfriend." Camilla laughed. "You're Brady's brother, aren't you?"

Ozzy didn't answer, but Emily's fingers itched. She forced the power in her hands down, willed it to obey. "Go. Away," she said.

"Honestly, Shinkle, you should know better by now who to hang around with and who to avoid," Camilla said with a wicked grin.

"Emily's my friend," Ozzy said. "I don't care what Brady thinks."

"This is social suicide, you know. But I guess you deserve what you get, hanging around this disgusting Commoner. She looks like trash, like she—*gah*!" Camilla's eyes went blank, her body rigid. Emily and Ozzy gaped in mutual horror as the girl tipped to the ground, face frozen in a mask of disgust.

The boy sighed and brushed off his hands, staring down at Camilla with a pained expression. "She never shuts up, does she?"

"Victor!" Catherine shrieked, dropping to the ground. "What did you do that for?"

"What?" he asked, his face the picture of innocence. "Come on, don't tell me it doesn't feel good to have *quiet* again."

"It doesn't!"

"Well, what choice did I have?" Victor shrugged. "She's irritating. And *rude*."

"She's your friend!" Catherine hissed.

"Actually, she's *your* friend. I just stick around because she thinks everything I say is gold." Victor turned to Emily, his angular features brightening, warm eyes boring into hers. "I'm Victor Graven, by the way. I apologize for Camilla being so . . . well, Camilla. She won't be bothering you again if I can help it. Just because she hasn't seen you in Gildenveil doesn't make you a Commoner. That was a pretty horrible thing to say."

Just as Emily had begun to feel somewhat grateful toward the dark-haired boy, her stomach clenched at his words, and her fingers turned cold. "What's wrong with being a Commoner?"

He laughed, a husky, short sound. "Nothing, really. Every magical prodigy needs an assistant."

"An assistant. You mean a *servant*."

"No, I'm pretty sure I meant an assistant. I could think of worse things to happen to a Commoner in this realm than being stuck carrying my reference books, can't you?"

Emily faltered. "Yes, but—"

"Well, then, can't we agree that since none of us are true Commoners here in the sense that we all possess an ability, we can drop the sociological debate and you can accept our apology for Camilla's actions?"

"*Our* apology?" Catherine squeaked.

Emily's mind was a blank. His request was polite enough, and yet she was overwhelmed with the urge to plant her fist in his jaw. "You're used to getting what you want."

His eyes widened a fraction. "I wouldn't say that I—"

"Nope, that wasn't a question." Emily met his stare with a challenge of her own. "But I'll accept your apology because I'm tired of this conversation and it seems like that's the only way to end it. You can go now."

His eyes narrowed and his teeth flashed. "Okay, then. Let's go, Catherine."

"What about Camilla?" Catherine asked, still trying to shake some movement into the girl on the ground.

Victor shrugged. "You can drag her back with us, if you want. I would personally leave her here for someone else to sort out. Teach her a lesson she really needs."

A muscle in Catherine's jaw twitched, but she grabbed hold of Camilla's feet and, with considerable effort, pulled her off until they disappeared into a cabin.

Victor regarded Emily once more. Earnest. Kind. *Deceptive.* "I really am sorry for what Camilla said. I hope I didn't offend you. Honestly, the last thing I wanted was to make a bad impression on the new girl."

Emily frowned. "I've heard worse, so don't lose any sleep over it."

He bowed his head. *Mocking.* "Okay, I'll stop apologizing." The wagon lurched, and Emily was dragged forward, her hips straining against the restraints as they plummeted to the ground. Victor held on to the edge of their compartment and stood his ground with ease. "We're landing. I'll see you around, then? It was great to meet you, Emily. Look sharp, Shinkle!" He winked and loped out of sight.

"He knows your name already," Ozzy observed. "Plus, that's the longest conversation I've had with Graven in all the years I've known him."

"Count yourself lucky you've been spared up until now," Emily scoffed.

"I don't know. He's super powerful and gets everything he wants. Not a bad friend to have."

"I don't care how nice he was," Emily said at once. "If he can turn against his friend like that over someone he's never met before, then he's an ass." She smirked at Ozzy's look of silent shock. "Anyway, let's wake Willow up before she really does get turned around and sent back home." She reached over and nudged the girl's shoulder. "Willow! Wake up, we're landing!"

"Wha?" Willow blinked fast. "We're there already? That was fast."

Emily shook her head, and the dragon took another sharp nosedive, sending Ozzy into another round of hysterics. She turned to the window where the ground was racing up to greet them.

"Don't worry, Willow," Emily said into the glass. "You didn't miss much."

CHAPTER EIGHT

Home Is Where the Anxiety Is

TWILIGHT HAD COME AND GONE. Wobbly-legged, they disembarked into an empty clearing surrounded by ancient trees, their trunks twisted and cracked, and the blossoming canvas of stars overhead. Crickets sang their lonely song as the leaves rustled in the cool wind. Emily followed the quiet snaps of twigs breaking underfoot as the initiates wound their way through the darkness. Ozzy huffed at her side while Willow's shiny ponytail pulled ahead of them, the girl already disappearing down the path out of the woods.

"Who lands a dragon inside a forest?" Ozzy protested. "Couldn't they drop us off at the castle, or do they want to burn half the realm down?"

"I guess they'd rather have a dragon damage a bunch

of bushes than smash the castle to pieces," Emily replied, squinting into the trees.

"Bushes!" Ozzy scoffed. "It's so dark in here I can barely see my own feet."

Emily inhaled the cool air and smiled. "I think it's kind of nice."

A boy strode up to Ozzy and dropped a heavy arm around his shoulders. "I agree. But you'll want to keep your eyes open for this next bit because *that's* spectacular."

"Hi, Brady," Ozzy mumbled.

Emily smiled. "Oh, you're Ozzy's brother." The boys had similar smiles, similar hair colour, but Brady lacked a certain warmth Emily couldn't quite pinpoint. Her nerves were raw, exposed, and Brady's unexpected appearance set her teeth on edge.

"The one and only." Brady ruffled Ozzy's hair. "You must be Emily. Oswald told me he made a friend, but I didn't believe him up to now. He didn't mention you were sort of pretty."

Charming. "Ozzy's been a good friend."

The canopy of leaves shattered apart as their path came to an end. A castle jutted out into the blue-black above, its bulk sitting on hundreds of feet of razor-sharp rock. Waves crashed and water gurgled somewhere below them, the edge of the realm noisier than Emily had ever imagined. The outlines of cottages littered the grey rock like patches of moss. Behind the turrets and peaks, the jagged edge of a mountain wrapped itself around the castle, a thin layer of fog blurring the place between the stone castle and the dark peaks.

"Finally," Brady said. "It's bad enough we have to ride a crowded train without having to hike for an hour. I could have flown up on my own."

"Yeah, except Mom still won't let you get your own dragon after what you did last year." Ozzy smirked.

"What happened last year?" Emily asked, enjoying the dark flush blooming on Brady's cheeks.

"The genius decided to take his dragon out after dark for a romantic tour of the grounds." Ozzy grinned with nostalgia as they climbed, and Brady fumed. "Master Fenstorm caught them making out near Black Mountain. The dragon was so scared of the telling-off Fenstorm gave them that she burned down half the trees in the area."

Brady raised his voice over Emily's laughter. "That was blown way out of proportion, Oswald!" he said, the tips of his ears turning a deep pink.

"He got a permanent note on his record, plus the Guard sent him a reprimand letter about it and everything." Ozzy's eyes glistened with happy tears. "Mom turned purple. Dad didn't talk to him for a month. It was beautiful."

"I'm done with this." Brady climbed faster, leaving them behind in a huff. "If you're in North Tower, you'd better not embarrass me by being this dumb." With a stream of curses Emily couldn't quite hear, Brady took the steps two at a time, pulling away from them with rigid shoulders.

"Bye, Brady!" Ozzy waved, his arm swinging over his head. "I'm so happy right now."

"Well," Emily said, looking at Ozzy from the corner of her eye, "he seems great."

Ozzy snorted. "He's a nightmare and he deserves it. Trust me."

"Well, if it makes you feel better, he didn't seem too proud of himself, either." They hit the main landing, chests heaving and legs burning. The double doors stood wide open to reveal a large entrance hall with black granite floors and wooden panelling on the high walls. Beside another set of open doors to their right, where most of the noise and activity was coming from, was a line of initiates with pinched, anxious looks on their faces.

"That's the line to check in." Ozzy pointed to the back of the queue. "I hope we're in the same wing of the castle. I'd hate to be alone in North Tower with Brady."

Emily wrapped her fingers around her necklace and tucked it under her shirt. She stood on the edge of a high cliff with nowhere to go but down into the belly of the beast. However, with the familiar crown of white curls waiting for her at the top of the line, the smile radiant in Magdale's round face, the jump was a little bit less terrifying. "Look! I think Magdale's checking people in." Relief at recognizing a familiar face overwhelmed Emily. "Do you think we should wait for Willow?"

Ozzy shook his head. "You haven't known her long, have you?"

"Emily!" Magdale called, waving them over. "Come, I'll check you in before the meal is served. Once the dining begins, there are no more changes to the list." Her smile was radiant even in the low light of the hall, and a long sheaf of parchment hung from her pale fingers. "And you found Mister Shinkle! I trust you two had a nice flight?"

"The dragon was a shock," Emily said.

Magdale winked. "Another surprise for you."

"I *hate* surprises." More initiates filtered in, the line weaving around an intricate wooden staircase up to the higher levels, and Emily was aware of their eyes. So many eyes boring a hole in her back, waiting for her to get out of line or wondering why she was speaking with Magdale for so long.

Magdale cleared her throat. "So, Oswald Shinkle, first year initiate. You're in North Tower with your brother."

Ozzy groaned. "That's just perfect."

"*You are a Rathburn but, tomorrow, you can choose to hide your necklace forever and be Emily Roth.*" Magdale's words echoed in her mind, adding weight to the pendant around her neck until it dug into her skin. But the necklace didn't have to be a noose—not unless she wanted it to be.

"Emily, you're in North Tower as well. Good news, isn't it?" Magdale's eyes were warm, the chatter in the hall no longer menacing but a soothing lullaby.

"What name am I registered under?"

Magdale blinked and cleared her throat. "I put you down as Emily Roth, of course."

Emily smiled, a strange calm settling over her. "It's Rathburn, actually. Emily Rathburn."

Two girls behind her stopped speaking. An older boy jogging down the stairs stopped in his tracks, his left foot dangling in midair. A hush rippled through the hall, and still, Emily smiled. She turned to Ozzy, ready for the worst. What would she see on his face? Horror? Disgust?

Emily untucked her necklace, setting it on top of her sweater. "So?" she asked, shoulders braced for a harsh blow. "Did you hear what I said?"

He stared back as though she had grown a second head. "Of course I heard you. I told you I recognized that necklace the moment I saw it."

Now there's *a surprise.* Emily frowned, unsure of what he was saying. "So, you knew all this time I'm a Rathburn? That my father is a murderer and a traitor?"

Ozzy shrugged. "Well, sure."

"Why didn't you say anything, then?" Emily asked. "You let me go on all this time thinking I had this big secret I was terrified of telling you."

"I figured you had your reasons for keeping it to yourself and you'd talk about it when you were ready." The blush was creeping above his collar, but his voice never wavered. "Anyway, your dad doesn't have anything to do with you. Plus, you don't *look* insane, and my mother is her own brand of crazy, so I'm not going to judge."

"Excellent!" Magdale grabbed Emily's elbow and steered her and Ozzy out of the line toward the next set of doors. "Knew you'd make the right decision, dear. Now, you should go on inside the Gallery and find a seat. I'll . . . eh . . . take care of things out here."

At Magdale's words, Emily broadened her mind to the rest of the hall. The line was a snake of hostile looks and pointed fingers Emily was only too happy to leave behind. "Are you ready for this?" she asked Ozzy as they passed under the arched doorway. "You stick with me, and they'll hate you too."

Ozzy grinned. "That's okay. I was never going to be popular, anyway."

Beyond the doorway, the entire castle crowded under the same roof. An immense, circular room, the Gallery was big enough to fit a thousand people in its belly with space to spare. Voices hummed from oval tables scattered across the flagstone floor, dotting the rock with colour and shine. Seven large hearths boasting seven roaring fires punctured the curved walls, casting dancing shadows against the light.

The walls.

Creeping around the room, curving into cracks both wide and fine, feeling and twining their way across the floor, were thick vines of bark and foamy green moss. They climbed higher, veins into arteries, until they converged into one giant knot at the apex swarming with a million tiny lights.

"Is that . . . a *tree*?" Emily asked, bewildered.

"Old Gwendolyn," Ozzy said, lights dancing in his eyes as he stared at the great tree. "She's older than this castle. The founder, Alexander Selwyn, built this place around her because she was so magical, he couldn't bear to tear her down. That's probably why the fairies swarm there."

Emily squinted at the tangle of roots and dirt hovering over their heads, the small pinpricks of white light moving with ease. Alive. "Those lights are fairies?"

He nodded. "Awful things; completely off their dragon and drunk on the dark side of magic." He pointed to a table beside the nearest fireplace and laughed. "Unbelievable! How did Willow get here so fast?"

Sure enough, Willow sat with a book on her lap and her feet swinging freely under her seat. A girl with deep, golden-brown skin and a head of short, tight curls smiled politely at her while a boy with broad shoulders and a thick mop of brown hair frowned impatiently at the table.

"Hey, you two!" Willow called as more initiates filtered past. "I saved you a seat!"

Emily exhaled in a huff, relieved at having a destination, a plan. A way to get away from the whispers and side-eyed looks darting her direction. A way to avoid standing on legs of cotton. A way to ignore Victor

Graven's not-so-discreet assessment of her from across the room.

"Hope you two don't mind," Emily said as they approached the table. The heavy scents of roast meat in gravy, buttery corn, fresh bread, and roast potatoes wove together, curling under her nose and making her stomach rumble. There wasn't a platter or bowl in sight, but Emily clung to the promise of food as a familiar way to avoid conversation.

The girl smiled, brown eyes dancing. "Not at all! We were just talking about Willow's adoption and her worst fears coming to Selwyn's."

"You know each other already?" Ozzy took the seat beside Emily and offered them a hesitant smile.

The girl stifled a grin. "Nope, we just met. Willow's a sharer, apparently."

"Everyone here's so nice," Willow said, eyes shining. "Her name's Piper, by the way. This is Emily and Ozzy, the two I was telling you about."

"Oh good, more introductions." The boy wore a glum expression, deep green eyes combing the room. "Well, if we're doing this again, then I'm Horus. And that," he continued, staring up at the ceiling, "is Big Dirty Tree."

Piper frowned. "Have some respect, Horus. She's an institution. You'll hurt her feelings."

"Then she should stop tossing bark into my food every year," Horus said, pouting. "And speaking of food, where is it?"

Piper rolled her eyes. "You know where it is, Horus. *Relax!*"

"They do this every year!" Horus glared at the table and swiped his hand over the wood top as though trying to swat a fly. "They cloak the food until every single person gets here, but you'd think they'd find a way to cloak the *smell*, too. It's torture! But hey, who's even hungry, right? I only threw up every meal from the last week because of the stupid death train."

"Well, not *everyone* needs to show up, Horus, so it won't be long." Piper nudged him with her elbow, and the corner of his mouth pulled up into the tiniest smile. "We've been here for three years already. You'd think age would bring him some self-control."

"What do you mean, not everyone needs to show up?" Emily asked, Piper's tone triggering a warning bell in her brain.

"Grey," Horus said, as though the answer were obvious. "She never joins in. Probably can't, anyway. You have to know about her."

"Isn't she an Elemental?" Willow asked.

Piper nodded. "One of the best. I mean, she's terrifying, but she knows her stuff."

"I heard she has no limit to what she can do with solid matter." Ozzy shrugged. "But that's pretty rare, isn't it?"

"Rare, but true." Horus gave an exaggerated shudder. "She's got a way with carbon—anything carbon-based. And since everything is made of carbon…"

"She can manipulate anything," Emily finished. "That must have taken her years to learn."

The noise in the hall was settling into a constant thrum of anticipation, so Piper lowered her voice. Light shifted with the pulse of energy as fairies swooped around the tree roots. "Not really. It's all-natural talent. They made her a Master here when she was twenty. That's two years older than I am."

"Yeah, but aren't all sociopathic killers some kind of prodigy?" Horus chuckled low in his throat. "Sanity's the price for being so annoyingly good with your magic."

"He's not serious." Emily turned to Ozzy, shock making her reel. "One of the Selwyn Masters is a killer? How's that even allowed?"

Piper picked up the panic on Emily's face and reached out a hand to pat her on the arm. "Don't worry about it. It happened a long time ago, and she was cleared of the charges. It's just rumour now."

"Rumours are usually true." Horus shook his head.

"Maybe," Piper continued, "but every Master in here has their eye on her, so I'm not afraid of Grey. One wrong move and they'll find a way to convict her, just like they did with her friend, Rathburn."

The room spun out, and Emily's heart hammered so loud the others would hear if they bothered to listen. There he was again—her father. Someone in the castle knew him, worked with him, *killed* with him. And got away with it. She peered around the room as sweat beaded on her forehead, each unfamiliar face a threat. "A Master here was friends with . . . *him*?" She wouldn't say his name. Not yet.

"Yeah, that's right," Horus said. "How they let her come in here and mentor us when everyone knows she helped him murder all those people is insane. If I wasn't so hungry, I'd be pissed all over again."

"Is it true she has a set of skeleton keys that can get her in and out of any room in the castle?" Willow asked.

Horus nodded, a lock of mahogany hair falling over one eye. "I mean, I never saw any keys, but I bet she does."

The information was coming too fast to digest. "Why does she need a key if she can control all matter?" Emily asked.

Piper straightened the bow around her neck, looking bored. "The Selwyn Chief Master puts protections in place even Grey can't break. That's why he runs the place and she's still where she is. But apparently she found a way around that somehow."

"Food!" Horus slammed his palms against the table in his excitement.

"What?" The world was too loud, noise jarring Emily from the dark place her thoughts cowered.

"Look at the roots." Ozzy pointed to the wall. Old Gwendolyn shuddered and came alive, her roots splitting from the stone to crawl onto the ground, around their ankles, over the backs of chairs. "I think the initiation is starting."

Emily shrank back as a twisted sliver of bark crawled up their table leg. "What's happening? What's it doing?"

"It's the first meal of the year." Horus rubbed his hands together, letting a muddy tendril caress his shoulder. "We accept our places here, but the castle has to accept you back."

"That's why Selwyn built this place around the tree," Ozzy explained. "Here, watch."

The Gallery stilled, and the light dimmed low. Every muscle in Emily's body begged her to push off from the table and run for the doors. No one had warned her about an initiation. A delicate root twined around the back of her chair and caressed her cheek, the soft stem warm against her chin, a faint heartbeat pulsing against hers. "What's it doing?"

"Just watch," Ozzy insisted.

Old Gwendolyn overcame every initiate in the room, and no one was fighting back. Faces disappeared behind a mask of brown and green, and Emily's blood thumped in her ears. A small knot of leaves, round as a button, pulled her attention from Ozzy's calm face. In the space of a blink, the bud unfolded before her nose to reveal soft petals of pure white blooming under the glow of the watching fairies. Emily couldn't remember ever having seen something so beautiful, so smooth, and yet so threatening. The Gallery erupted into a full spring bloom, low gasps punctuating the otherwise reverent stillness as each initiate was offered a blossom of their own.

"What are we supposed to do with this?" Emily leaned into the back of her seat, and the flower followed her. "Ozzy?"

Horus plucked his blossom out from under his chin and dropped it into his goblet. "Don't look so paranoid," he said. "It's symbolic. Come on, the faster we do this, the faster we eat."

Ozzy and Willow obliged at once while Horus and Piper took a swig from their own goblets. The petals were soft, translucent and veined in gold fibers reflecting light back at her. Emily pulled the flower loose and let the petals fall to the bottom of her cup. She held her breath as the fragile plant dissolved to a clear liquid, gold flecks spiralling in her drink. *Too late to go back.* With a trembling hand, Emily tipped the contents down her throat and shivered as the strange nectar seeped into her stomach, her blood, her very bones.

"That's it, we're all in!" Horus brushed crumbs of dirt off the table, and the roots retracted at once, slithering back up the walls to rest inside the cracked mortar and rough stones once more. "You're part of the castle now. Oz, you mind passing the chicken?"

Platters of roast duck in jelly sauce, tureens of gravy, silver bowls of potatoes, all shimmered into existence across from them. Ozzy reached for the chicken while Willow helped herself to a heap of peas in gravy, the clatter and scraping of forks against dishes echoing around the Gallery. Emily rubbed her palms over her arms, still sensing the flower leaching into her body, taking over. She wasn't hungry.

"What's the work like?" Ozzy looked up from a full dish and cast a wary glance at Emily's empty one. "Brady always told me how tough the Masters are."

Horus eyed him over a turkey leg dripping in butter sauce. "Shinkle's all flash and no brains. He can ride a dragon, sure, but can he spell his name?" He snorted. "You'll do fine—just make sure you show them progress. It's pretty expected to be a bit useless the first few months, but that doesn't stop the Masters from trimming the fat if they need to."

"Trim the fat?" Emily asked. "You mean they kick people out?"

"Sure," Horus said over a large bite. "Not everyone gets better with training. But I wouldn't worry. They let that Dashwood kid back, and he was pretty hopeless."

Gooseflesh erupted down Emily's arms. Since Magdale's invitation, she had never considered the idea she might not last in Gildenveil. Had she been stupid enough to think she was given a spot at the castle without having to prove herself useful?

"There aren't too many Masters to impress, but I'd focus on the big ones." Piper scrunched up her nose in concentration, abandoning her soup. "Magdale's one of the most senior people here, but you probably won't have her as a mentor for a few years."

Horus swallowed and stabbed a roast potato with glee. "Fogg's a giant loony. But I guess that's what happens when you think you're married to Father Time." His eyes went wide, and he tapped a finger on his forehead.

Piper frowned at him. "Master Fogg is a renowned Empath. Not many people in history have had her gift."

Horus rolled his eyes. "Have you ever *seen* her do anything with a pocket watch except lose it? She's insane. Anyway, I'd take Flight with Master Fenstorm seriously. Impressing that man means big things for you if you're looking at a future in the Guard."

"I thought riding dragons made you nauseous," Ozzy said, the betrayal thick in his voice.

"Naglar is old and half-blind. It's terrifying!" Horus dodged a pea Piper tossed at his head and grinned. "But the dragons *we* get to fly are smaller, more manageable. But I'm an Empath, so I'm probably biased."

"What can you do?" Willow asked.

Horus puffed his broad chest until he sat a full foot taller than before. "I hear turtles."

"Turtles?" Ozzy frowned.

"It's a decent ability," Horus said, a new edge giving his words bite. "There's plenty in the sea right by the castle, so I get to hear what's happening underwater a lot of the time. Plus, turtles are only a few steps off from dragons, so I'm hoping to get good enough to earn me a spot in the Guard."

"Turtles are good." Ozzy poured him some cider, and Horus relaxed his shoulders again. "I'm an Empath, too. How about you, Piper?"

"Elemental." Piper waved her hand over her goblet, and a stream of clear liquid spiralled out of her palm, looping in the air once before pouring into the glass. "My thing is water."

Dessert rolled in on carts manned by no one, and Ozzy sighed as the others helped themselves.

"You're not having anything?" Emily offered Ozzy a pie dish, but he pushed it aside so Willow could take a slice. "I know why I'm not hungry, but what's your excuse?"

Ozzy patted his stomach and slumped in his seat. "Mother says if I come back home any bigger, she'll have me running laps for days come summer."

"You look fine to me." Emily shrugged.

"Agreed," Horus said, mouth full of custard and strawberries. "Shinkle, you're fine. Take a pastry."

After a second's hesitation, Ozzy helped himself to a chocolate croissant. Conversation picked back up, the noise level rising with the end of their meal. Furrowed brows and accusatory glares flew like spears in Emily's direction, and she shrank away from them until Magdale cleared her throat, bringing the hostility to a crashing halt.

"Attention, please!" Magdale called. "Chief Master Millendorf was unable to be with us this evening—"

"Yeah, probably 'cause he's hiding in his office, drunk as a skunk," Horus said. "The man is a crazy good Empath and has all these cool magical items that belonged to every other Chief Master in his office. You'd think he'd be a bit cheerier."

Magdale's eyes flashed in their direction. "There have been some unpredictable storm fronts up in Black

Mountain that you should be aware of, so any combat training or tournament organization will be done on the grounds instead of up in the mountain."

"Ugh!" Horus scoffed. "It's just a bit of fog. I'll bet Millendorf is nervous about those missing persons reports from, like, a year ago. It's all media garbage."

Ozzy grew pale. "I heard about that from my father." Magdale reminded the initiates where the nearest exits were located, that the dragon eggs in the den were off limits, and tournaments were to be organized by skill level. Ozzy leaned in closer, careful not to be overheard by the nearby table. "A couple people outside Gildenveil vanished. No sign of them anywhere. Father told me the Council set up Empathic links as far across the realm as they can to help find them. That way, any Empath in the chain can share what they see with the others."

"I'm guessing that's not normal," Emily said.

Ozzy shook his head. "Not since . . . well, you know."

Another reminder of dear Dad. Emily peered down the table, counting the swirls and loops forming a fingerprint in the wood. *This year's going to be a blast.*

Magdale raised her voice over the rising chatter. "I hope you all enjoyed your meal. Your coaching schedule will be up on your beds, and I expect you all to impress us tomorrow. Good luck!"

At Magdale's words, chairs scraped the stone floor, voices lifted to a high pitch, and the initiates clambered to the exit in droves. Emily was more than ready to put the day to rest. But the day had other plans.

"That's her!"

"Rathburn? Are you sure?"

The ground lurched underneath her. The exit and the great mahogany stairwell were too far away. Unreachable. Horus, Piper, and Willow moved in slow motion while Emily ducked her head behind Ozzy. A strong hand pulled her forward to face the growing crowd. Emily tried to free herself, but it was no use; when one person backed away, another took their place.

"Let me see her!"

"I want a look!"

The voices were converging, the mob around her growing in anger and volume. "Are you really Rathburn's daughter?" Brady asked, his eyes travelling from her to Ozzy as though confused. "Did you know about this, Oswald?"

Let go of me. Emily wanted to sound strong, to be liked, to be welcome, to scream. Instead, she bowed her head and willed herself to disappear. "Please . . . stop."

Ozzy stepped between her and the *others*, but the initiates surrounding them didn't back down. They pressed in on her, eyes searching for her necklace, questions punctuated with insults flying in from all sides. She was trapped once more—except, this time, the cell was much prettier.

Emily's head was heavy, her heart splintered and hollow. There could never have been a different outcome for her; it always came down to blood, money, and status—everything she lacked. Because she was a murderer's daughter from the Commons.

Emily closed her eyes and let the mob have her.

CHAPTER NINE

You Can't Run Forever

"GO AWAY NOW, GET LOST!" Horus grabbed a smaller boy by the back of his shirt and dragged him off to the side with the ease of a bear rounding up its cubs. "Nothing to see here, let's move. Really, Dashwood, you don't need to stand on a chair." He placed a hand on the small of Emily's back and steered her and Ozzy toward the exit, Piper and Willow close behind.

"You okay?" Piper asked as they hurried out of the Gallery. "I mean, I had no idea you were . . . that you're . . . They shouldn't act like that."

"Bunch of animals!" Horus called over his shoulder as he joined them out the door. "They know how to say hello like civilized people, don't they?" Instead of heading up the stairs, he marched them down a narrow corridor off to the right. "Seriously, Emily. Are you okay? 'Cause if you're not, I can punch someone for you."

"Er, no. I mean yes, I'm fine." Emily picked up her pace. The farther they moved down the hall, the weaker the outraged voices became, until there was nothing but the sound of five sets of footsteps and her own blood rushing in her ears. "Thank you."

"Forget it." Horus pulled open a door that blended seamlessly into the wooden wall panelling and waved them inside. "No one uses this passage. It connects to all four dormitory wings, but it's supposed to be haunted, so everyone's too frightened to come this way."

"Except for Horus." Piper grinned and shook her head. The passage was empty except for the torches affixed to the walls, the brass caked in dirt and dust under bright orange flames. The air was heavy and damp, the ground covered in a worn red runner.

"Why do you come this way when the big staircase outside is so much warmer? And cleaner?" Willow wrinkled her delicate nose but bounced along without any sign of true concern.

"They don't let you take food from the kitchen between meals," Horus said with a mischievous grin. "So not getting caught with your shirt stuffed with cake is the key to staying fed." A statue of a woman holding a large bowl of water loomed over them from the end of the hall, with two dark corridors branching out on each side. "Okay, Willow, you're in the West Wing, so follow the green torches up the right side."

Piper waved goodbye as Willow's blonde hair glowed green in the strange light. "We're up this way," Piper said, motioning them down the left corridor with light the colour of ripe eggplant. "So. You're Emily Rathburn, huh?"

"Apparently." Emily wrapped her thin arms around her chest, the dank air leaching through the thin knit of her brown sweater.

"How's the old man doing?" Horus asked in the same way you'd ask for more eggs at breakfast.

Piper balked. "Horus!"

"What?"

"She doesn't want to talk about this!" Piper said, giving Emily a sideways glance. "Right?"

Emily sighed. "I never met him. Actually, I didn't know I was his daughter until yesterday. It's been . . . fun."

Piper offered a shy smile of encouragement, but Horus frowned in unabashed disappointment. "Well, that's unlucky," he said. "It would have been pretty cool getting to know him. You know, find out what makes the old guy tick."

The passageway sloped upward, and conversation ran dry as their heavy breathing chewed away any opportunity for subsequent bonding. Emily kept pace with Ozzy, who had begun to lag, relishing the break from Horus and Piper, who pulled ahead. After a minute or ten, Horus stopped and ran his fingers over the stone under a torch with one bolt missing, light flickering low. "We're here," Horus said. "I keep forgetting how hard our dorms are to get to. All right, so you have to touch the stone and wait for the tower to let you in."

Emily clenched her fists. How many conditions did this castle have?

"It's a safeguard for new initiates," Piper explained.

She placed her own hand on the stone beside Horus's and the stone began to waver as though covered in rippling water. "It's a spell that's supposed to keep out intruders who don't belong to our dorms. Go ahead, it doesn't hurt."

Ozzy peered at Emily with doubt. "You ready?"

"Does it matter?" Emily asked with a tired sigh. She raised her hand to the stone at the same time Ozzy did, expecting the rough, cool surface under her palm as the ripples spread wide.

Her skin grazed the stone, and the violet light in the dank corridor faded to darkness.

Emily blinked, disoriented by the absence of light and sound. She was alone.

"Ozzy?" Her ears popped, and she winced. The tower . . . was she in North Tower already? It didn't look like a dormitory—then again, it didn't look like anything at all. Where was . . . ?

Emily pressed her eyes shut but couldn't remember his name. She hadn't been alone, had she? Emily pressed her palms to her eyes, and coloured lights bloomed in her vision.

Footsteps vibrated the ground under her feet, making her jump. The darkness shifted, ghosts of familiar shapes washing past her, too quickly to recognize. Emily stumbled forward, and her skin erupted into a blazing, invisible flame. She screamed and shook out her arms, but there was no fire to put out. The burning was inside her.

Emily fell to her knees, willing the pain to stop.

As soon as the thought crossed her mind, the torture receded. Her hands clawed the ground, and she struggled to stand, but there was something wrong with the floor.

It was too soft, too unstable. The world came into focus little by little, edges becoming sharp, colours coming into existence.

There were bodies. So many bodies. *Where it all begins. Where it all ends.* The words were unfamiliar, and their urgency cycled over in her mind as though her world would crumble if she forgot them. And yet, her thoughts running away from her, the darkness, the confusion, did not matter.

Not as much as the little girl lying at Emily's feet with light brown hair covering her vacant face.

Pain, sharp and blazing, tore through her, having nothing to do with the fire that claimed her seconds before. It threatened to shatter her to pieces.

But there was more. Something . . . delicious.

Power.

Despite her insides pulling apart and her flesh burning, burning *hot*, she could do anything she wanted. There were no limits to her will. She was not an Elemental; she was something more, something *better*.

There were more bodies on the ground, strangers, and yet Emily knew each one in her soul. Because she was responsible for their deaths, for every ounce of pain they suffered. Undiluted power ran wild in her veins, begging to be used. But she shrank away from it, folding in on herself with the effort of controlling the need yearning to break free.

"No," Emily said, her breath coming fast. The bodies. Her palms vibrated with power. "Stop!"

With a grunt of pain, she turned away from the gore at her feet and ran back into the darkness, welcoming it. She needed to escape the empty eyes, the terror on their frozen faces. Cold crept into her blood like fog through the trees, and she shivered, refusing to slow.

Moonlight lit up the shadows now, and it filtered through the twisted fingers of ancient trees, reaching for her as she ran. Her legs pushed at the soft ground, but someone was after her and they were gaining. She tried to scream for help, but no sound escaped her dry lips.

With a crack like thunder, her foot slammed down onto a plush, even surface and a very real, very solid hand reached out to steady her.

She gasped with fatigue or fear or relief—she couldn't be sure. "What happened? What was that?"

Ozzy's eyes were wide and familiar. "Nothing happened. We passed right through, but you didn't come through with us."

"Did you see it?" Emily whirled on the spot to find the wall staring back, innocent and solid. No bodies. No trees. No chase.

Ozzy blinked. "See what?"

Emily's stomach bottomed out. "So none of you saw anything . . . weird?"

Piper shrugged. "It worked for me like it always does. One second you're in the hall, next you're standing here."

"You look like a ghost slapped you in the face." Horus frowned, the fire from a nearby hearth illuminating his large frame as he gestured to a chair beside him. "Here, why don't you sit for a minute."

"I'm fine," Emily said at once. She took a step away from them, the concern etched across their faces fuelling her embarrassment. "I think I'm just tired."

"Right." Horus hitched up his smile and moved deeper into the room. "So, this is the main lounge of

North Tower." He indicated the cozy room decorated with coffee tables, mismatched chairs, and beanbags. Fires blazed under two large stone mantels, one on each side of the lounge, while birds fluttered from window to window a hundred feet overhead. "I like to work in here because the library's way too quiet. You can use this place to study or eat or smuggle illegal species of gnomes into the castle."

"Horus," Piper warned.

He grinned. "Girls' rooms are down that hall to the left, boys' on the right." He nodded over his shoulders to indicate two long, well-lit corridors branching off on either end of the lounge. "And you can use those platforms up there to practice your spells if you want some privacy or think you'll blow someone up if you stay down here."

Ozzy squinted at the ceiling. "Those floating things are platforms?" he asked, looking more than uncertain about the square slabs of wood drifting in the air far above their heads.

"You get used to the height," Piper said with a reassuring smile.

"So that's it!" Horus cleared his throat as a large group of initiates entered the main doors at the far side of North Lounge. "You probably want to find your room before the pitchforks come out, eh?"

"Thanks, Horus," Emily said, voice still shaking. "I'll see you tomorrow." She took the left corridor at a brisk walk, eager to be alone and gather her thoughts.

Room after room rushed past her in a haze, the corridor dark and silent. Nameplates in burnished gold hung on every door, and she searched for her name with tired eyes as each one flicked past. The hall wound deeper into the tower until a large '*E. Rathburn*' etched in neat letters beside a number 9 caught her attention.

Please be empty, please be empty, she thought, pushing open the door with a squeak of hinges.

Except for the bags and boxes piled onto three twin beds, she was alone. Safe. The walls were a pale lilac, the drapes running down the large window a light cream. Each bed boasted a patchwork comforter, a uniquely carved wooden headboard, with a dresser to match.

The letters 'E. R.' in bright gold marked the tags of a set of forest-green luggage beside the window. The bed had a simple frame carved of rich mahogany, and her bedspread was a soft mint green. On the pillow, a single sheet of parchment had a message addressed to her: '*Emily—I thought bringing a bit of green indoors might remind you of the forests you love. Enjoy, M.*'

For a brief and blissful moment, Magdale's note chased away the strange vision of bodies and echoes of pain. Emily tucked the note under her mattress, the familiar act reassuring in a small way. Without bothering with her bags, she dropped onto the bed and ran her palms over the soft blanket, ready to put the day to rest.

"Ugh, it's true!" Catherine Bonner loomed in the doorway, hard face throwing daggers of displeasure at Emily. "I thought it was some kind of joke when I found out *Emily Rathburn* was sleeping in the same room as me. I wish it was."

"What are *you* doing here?" Emily asked.

"I *sleep* here!"

Emily groaned. "Well, then I guess that makes us roommates. Yay."

"What are you complaining about? I'm a gem." Catherine pursed her lips and made her way to the bed beside Emily's. "They're all talking about you, you know."

"Lucky me."

Catherine fumbled with the latch on a weathered duffel bag, her jaw set and shoulders trembling. "So, you admit it. You're Emily Rathburn." She laughed, the sound hollow. "I hope you have a ride back to wherever you came from because you won't last a week here."

Emily crossed her arms, and any thoughts of sleep moved to the back of her mind. "I'm not going anywhere. See? I have a bed and everything."

Catherine's face darkened. "You're a traitor."

"My father was." Emily kicked off her shoes with a satisfying *thump, thump.*

"Hi!" A girl with dark brown hair and kind almond eyes peered at them from the doorway. "I think this is my room." She looked between Emily and Catherine and clutched a bag to her hip. "Am I interrupting something?"

"No, no," Emily said with a wry smile. "We were bonding."

Catherine tossed a book, then another, to the ground in a growing heap. She pulled on the flap of an unmarked box, struggling with the corners until a stream of dog-eared books and half-chewed quills spilled onto the floor.

"I'm Tina Lee," the girl said, walking over to claim the bed across from Emily with a small smile. "I'm a new initiate here." She waited, the pause heavy in the room.

"I'm Emily." Her muscles tensed, and her heart exploded into an uphill gallop. *Please don't ask for my last name, please, please, please.*

Tina smiled, the first drawer of her dresser already lined with neat rows of sweaters and cotton shirts. "I figured. I've known Catherine for years, and the other girl who was supposed to be in here grew up on my street, so I know her too. You were the only stranger."

Emily frowned at the girl's bed, bags still tied up tight and bulging on all sides. "Supposed to be here? Is she okay?"

Tina stared into her duffel bag, the apples of her cheeks growing flush. "Mary asked for a room transfer," she said with an apologetic look. "I . . . I know you're Emily Rathburn."

Right. "I guess I'm not surprised she left," Emily muttered.

"Don't take it badly." Tina transferred the rest of her belongings to the foot of her bed and scrambled under the duvet. "She's scared of your dad, not you."

Emily curled up on her bedspread without bothering to get undressed or slip under the covers. Her head pounded, and the images of bodies on the ground and a moon up above were quickly fading. "You could leave too, you know. I won't be offended."

Tina yawned, her eyes bright. "I'm okay with having you as a roommate." With a snap of her fingers, the torch above her headboard flickered and disappeared.

"Are we done with all the nice-nice?" Catherine slammed unopened boxes on the ground and jumped into bed. "I'm tired."

Tina obliged by turning down the rest of the lights. In the dark, Emily could imagine she was back at Saint Barth's and the window beside her crackling with frost was the same one Molly slept beside now. Somewhere across the realm, Molly counted the same stars, listened to the same wind howl its lonely song.

Emily fiddled with her necklace, the easy breathing from Tina's side of the room lulling her into a deep state of calm.

"Why are you here?"

Catherine's voice yanked Emily from the edges of sleep, and her eyes fluttered open. "What?"

"You heard me." Catherine glared at her in the moonlight, hair spilling onto her mattress in a sea of curls. "You can't seriously think people will accept you here. Why do you even bother?"

With a low groan, Emily turned to the window once more. "Look, can we kill each other tomorrow? I was sleeping."

"We can do it now, if it's all right with you."

Emily sighed. "I didn't do anything wrong. I didn't even know who my father was until Magdale told me. Everyone has to see . . . " She clamped her jaw shut, not trusting the waver in her voice.

Catherine waited, the air thick and heavy with judgement. "See what?"

"That I'm not bad."

Silence. A heavy breath. A flick of her covers. "You're a Rathburn. That's bad enough."

CHAPTER TEN

Friends, Foes, and Something In Between

"THIS IS SO GOOD." Ozzy swallowed and reached across the table for another slice of toast. He, at least, had an appetite.

Emily stared at her own eggs on toast with regret, the yolk pooling at the bottom of her dish threatening to turn her stomach. Fairies swarmed above, Old Gwendolyn's roots dotted with delicate white lights that, any other day, might have impressed her. Sitting there at an empty table with Ozzy so composed, the lights were doing no more than giving her a migraine. "Show me your schedule again."

Ozzy groaned. "But I'm eating!"

Emily leaned in and pushed her dish across the table. "If you do, I'll give you my eggs."

Ozzy reached over for her dish and slid a sheet of

thick vanilla parchment over to her. "We both have Flight and Formation with Master Fenstorm first, at which point I'll probably end up vomiting all this food everywhere, so no one will remember you're there. And apart from one meditation class for Empaths, we have every lesson together, so you're fine."

"You sure about that?"

He upended the entire contents of his goblet into his mouth and yanked the parchment back. "I know you're nervous, but I'm right there with you."

"You're not a Rathburn." The word on her tongue did nothing to help with her nausea, and she clenched her stomach, the thought of heading outside daunting.

"That didn't seem to bother you yesterday."

"Yeah, well, call this a moment of weakness," she said. "They're going to throw stones at me when I walk out of here."

"Not stones, necessarily." Ozzy dug into his backpack, the rattling of ink bottles muffled by the piles of books hidden inside. "Maybe some really heavy books."

Emily withered in her seat. "That sounds so much better."

With a flourish, he withdrew a new, heavily creased piece of parchment and flattened it on the table. "It is, if you consider books are less sharp."

Emily stared, dumbfounded. "You get some assignment already that I don't know about?"

"This is the Scroll." His eyebrows disappeared into his hair. "How do you not know what this is?"

"I lived down in the Commons." Emily squared her shoulders. "We were lucky if we got baths."

"Outside the Gildenveil border?" he asked, eyes wide. "How'd you end up there?"

"My good looks and some parental abandonment," she said. "I hear daddy was unpopular so dragging a kid around with him was probably not the best idea. So, what's the Scroll?"

Ozzy closed his mouth at once and lowered his eyes to the page between his fingers. "It's how we get our news. All the important things happening in and around Gildenveil are recorded in here."

Emily frowned. "It's blank."

"It's blank *now*." His eyes flashed. "It resets itself every day. Here, watch." Ozzy placed his hand in the center of the page. "Today, September thirtieth." Black swirls spun out from his fingers, twisting across the page like a spider's web to form words and images. "As long as you're an Empath or Elemental, you can work one."

"Why doesn't anyone in the Commons get the news?" Emily asked, bristling. "I would have killed to have access to what was happening around the realm when I lived down there."

A light flush tinted the skin around Ozzy's ears. "I guess they figure no one in the Commons would care or need to know anything like that. I mean, they have no abilities, so what do they care?"

"*They* are still people, and *they* still live in the realm. If it affects Gildenveil City, it affects the Commons."

Ozzy's blush deepened. "I never thought of it like that. I guess that's what my dad and Brady think, so I never questioned it."

Emily's necklace burned against her skin with the force of her anger. *Us and them,* she thought. *That's what it always comes down to.*

Ozzy flicked through the titles, banishing them one after another to the backdrop until a pair of angry voices pulled him out of his reading. "Is that Magdale?" he asked.

Emily glanced over at the Gallery doors, and her heart gave an uncomfortable jolt. "Yeah, that's her." *The question is, what's* he *doing here?*

"She doesn't look happy."

And Ozzy was right. Magdale stood tall, her frown lines etched deep even from a distance while her voice hummed with rage at the man opposite her. A man in a navy suit with a silver star on one shoulder. "That's a Guard official, right?" Emily asked.

Ozzy nodded, and her heart climbed into her throat. "I wonder what they're talking about. It looks serious."

Magdale's stormy eyes flickered over to Emily. "I think I have an idea." Her blood was fire in her cheeks, and every curious face brought a fresh wave of fear. "I saw him yesterday."

"You . . . you saw a member of the Guard? On your first day? What happened?" His stream of questions petered off, and he sucked in a sharp breath. "Uh . . . they're coming over here."

Of course they were. The hooded stranger had called attention to her to escape. She had screamed her name aloud, a name that no one was expecting to hear. It was no surprise the Council Guard would jump on an opportunity to link Baxter Rathburn's daughter to a major crime in Gildenveil. Still, that didn't make it any less terrifying as he and Magdale approached their table.

"Mister Shinkle." Magdale's smile was thin, and it didn't touch her eyes. "Emily, this is Guard Officer Reinhold. He would like a word with you, if that's all right."

"I can take it from here, Magdale, thank you." Guard Officer Reinhold was young, with a trim navy suit that brought out the gold flecks in his eager eyes and the yellow in his wiry, blonde hair. He ran a large, callused hand boasting an array of raised, red scars across his soft jaw, the sound of rough skin scraping against the stubble like sandpaper. "You're Miss Emily Rathburn, correct?"

This is it. I didn't even last a day, Emily thought with a silent groan. "Yes, sir."

Reinhold took a seat beside Ozzy, hands clutching the familiar parchment and quill. "We were informed that you were at the scene of the disturbance at Blintwoods yesterday."

Emily could hear her heartbeat, but her face was controlled with years of practice. "Me and about a hundred other people, sure."

"Yes, the event was quite eye-catching." Reinhold's gaze held hers as his quill scratched over the page. "Blintwoods hasn't been attacked this brazenly since it opened centuries ago."

"Bad luck."

"Yes," Reinhold said, "it is. Either bad luck or perfect timing."

"Reinhold—" The note of warning was heavy in Magdale's voice.

"Perfect timing, sir?" Emily asked as Ozzy looked between them, bewildered. "For what?"

Officer Reinhold smirked. "Well, it can't be a coincidence that the child of Baxter Rathburn is spotted on the same day that the realm's most secure institution is attacked and almost robbed."

"Robbed?" Her composure slipped, and Emily leaned over the table, her fingertips tingling. "Blintwoods was *robbed*?"

"*Almost* robbed, dear," Magdale said. "I told you, she doesn't know anything, Reinhold."

Ozzy's brows pulled low over his eyes. "What's he talking about?"

"There was a fire at Blintwoods yesterday," Emily explained, her breathing shallow. "I saw it on the way to the Skytrain. I knew there was a fire, but I had no idea it was a robbery."

"Do you expect me to believe you had nothing to do with it?" Reinhold asked, his eyes tight.

"*Expect* you?" Emily leaned back into her seat and tapped her toe against the ground. "I don't expect any-thing." She sighed. "Look, I was with Magdale right be-fore it happened and was part of a group trying to make it to the Skytrain in time. Someone was with me all day, there are witnesses who can vouch for me. You can check that, if you want." She turned to Magdale, and her face softened, Reinhold's red face too irritating to look at. "So someone tried robbing the place? Do you have any idea what they were after?"

Before Magdale could answer, Reinhold lifted a hand to silence her. "That's Guard business, not yours, Miss Rathburn. And I will be verifying your story with your . . . *friends*."

"I can get you their names." Magdale rested a hand on Reinhold's shoulder and squeezed. "Now, if you've finished interrogating an innocent initiate, I think it's time you take your investigation back to the Council."

"One more question." Reinhold pressed the tip of his quill into the parchment. "What did you see at the side of the shop?"

Emily's stomach bottomed out. "What?"

"You were spotted coming around the side of the shop while everyone was watching from the road. Mister Graven is particularly concerned since his lock box was right beside the one that was attacked."

Yeah, this looks bad. "I was there," Emily said, "but I didn't do anything. I only wanted a closer look."

Reinhold pressed his lips together. "If you weren't involved in the assault on Blintwoods, can you perhaps tell us what you saw inside while everyone was busy getting things sorted the *proper* way?"

Three pairs of eyes fixed on her in varying states of curiosity. "I went to the side of the shop because I thought I saw someone inside."

"And was there?" Reinhold asked.

Good question. If she told them about the stranger with the unsettling eyes, her name would be cleared. She might even be seen as helpful if her information led to the capture of the person responsible. But her last name was Rathburn, and nothing she said would absolve her of that fact—the conversation with Reinhold was enough to convince her of that. And what good would telling the truth do if the real criminal behind the robbery got wind that she spoke to the Guard? She would be putting another target on her back when she was already on thin ice.

"There was too much smoke," Emily answered, her gaze level with Reinhold's. "It was probably the fire and smoke playing tricks on me. But then, people had already seen me and, well, you know the rest."

"You see? Emily's greatest crime was her curiosity." Magdale nodded, a half-smile carved into her round cheeks. "If you're satisfied, perhaps we can flesh out the details of your investigation in my office so that these two initiates can get to their Flight lesson on time."

"Oh no," Ozzy moaned. "We're going to be late!"

Magdale smiled as Guard Officer Reinhold got to his feet and tucked the parchment into his jacket pocket. "You have plenty of time, Mister Shinkle. I'm sorry for the interruption."

She ushered Reinhold out of the Gallery with not so much as a wave goodbye from him. The Gallery was emptying fast with the few stragglers eyeing them with deep frowns.

"So do you want to tell me what happened there?" Ozzy asked.

Emily swallowed hard, those cold eyes flickering before her as though they stared from across the table, her throat aching from the invisible pressure choking the air from her lungs. Would telling Ozzy what she saw put him in danger? After all, she had no idea if the woman with the silver eyes was Empath or Elemental and how far her reach went. And it was more than likely she would never see the thief again. "Maybe it's best you don't know."

He frowned. "I can't help if you don't tell me what you know. The Guard doesn't send a representative up to Selwyn's for no good reason."

Emily's heart clenched and, all at once, it was Molly in Ozzy's seat. Wide green eyes stared back at her, the small girl offering to help, needing to be included. But the chances of seeing Molly again were slim, and all the girl with the fiery hair would remember was the quiet outcast in the bed beside her who snuck out at night and shared her food. The best gift Emily could give was the gift of ignorance.

But that was Molly. And she was lost to her forever.

Emily steeled herself. "I noticed a group gathered around Blintwoods on my way to the Skytrain yesterday, so I broke off from Willow, Finn, and Elliott to see what was going on," she said.

"I got that part."

Emily sighed. "But I *did* see the woman who tried robbing the place. I mean, I'm pretty sure that's what she was doing there." *I can't be this unlucky, can I?* she thought, followed by, *Yeah, of course I can.* "She knocked me over trying to escape and tried choking me."

Ozzy's eyes widened. "You're kidding."

"I don't have that good a sense of humour." And with that, the words came tumbling into the empty space between them, building up until they were bonded together with the truth. With her trust. She confided in another soul, telling him about the crowd, the smoke, the open door. The woman with the silver eyes.

"I can't believe that something like this happens when Zaphira is away," Ozzy said, shaking his head. "Blintwoods holds some pretty dangerous, high value stuff, and is pretty impossible to rob. If that woman thought she could get away with stealing something from Zaphira, then she could do worse. You're lucky you're alive."

Emily patted his hand. "She seemed to be in a hurry to get out of there. Murder takes time she didn't have. Plus, except for her eyes, I didn't get a good look at her. So, unless I come face to face with her again or hear her talk, it's better I forget the whole thing."

Ozzy blanched. "Let's hope that doesn't happen. I'll keep an eye on the Scroll for any news about it, though. We can't be too careful." *We . . . that actually sounds nice.* "Why didn't you tell Magdale and Reinhold what you saw? That would have cleared your name with the Guard."

Emily's answering chuckle held no humour. "They'd never believe me. You saw how he spoke to me; if it wasn't for Magdale backing me up, he would have shipped me off because of my last name." She shook her head. "No, if I'm going to get more involved in this, I'll have to do it without telling anyone else here. But even then, I'd rather keep my head down."

The Gallery grew quiet. Emily piled a helping of fresh fruit onto a dish, knowing a light breakfast would be best if she was going to get up close and personal with a dragon. *Dragons.*

Oh no.

"I don't know you well yet, but I'm pretty sure you don't want to be late on your first day." Victor Graven leaned over her shoulder, eyes dancing under his unruly hair, and plucked a blackberry from her plate. Camilla and Catherine lingered behind him, brooding like two very pretty, very unhappy statues. "Especially if you caught the interest of the Council Guard. I'd love to hear *that* story."

"Elders, he's right!" Ozzy vaulted to his feet, and the table shuddered as he kicked it.

Victor looped his hand through the strap of Emily's bag and offered it to her. "I'd be happy to walk with you. Make sure you don't get lost or harassed by the law again." He winked.

"Well, that's nice." Emily yanked the bag back and shouldered it with more force than she had intended as she stood to join Ozzy. "But we're fine. Didn't you say something about being late?"

"Sure," Victor said with an easy shrug.

"Well, then, don't you have somewhere to be?"

"Free period." He stuffed his hands in his pockets, seemingly unaware that Camilla was turning a nice shade of maroon. "So, how about that walk?"

Emily pulled a frantic Ozzy away from the table and made for the exit. "Like you said," she called over her shoulder, "we don't know each other well!"

"We'll have to fix that sometime." With a grin, he looped his arm around Camilla's waist and followed them out the door from a safe distance, Catherine trailing behind. Emily could hear him laughing as she raced out of the castle.

Ozzy led the charge, tumbling out the main door and into the bright fall morning. "Come on, the courtyard's not far!"

"Right," Emily said, grumbling after him. "I can't wait to spend an hour with a dragon *and* a mob of people who want to feed me to one."

The tiny village of stone cabins lined the path down to the sea, but the courtyard sat at the back of the castle. Taking the path away from the cliffs, the salty mist from the sea chased them around the castle, down a low, stone wall protecting the west side, and over to the open expanse of land at the base of Black Mountain. Less than a dozen initiates were already huddled together on the manicured lawn, their coats pulled tight against the humid air. At Emily's approach, they grew silent and cast wary looks over their shoulders as though bracing for attack.

"Fenstorm's not here yet." Ozzy exhaled in relief. "We made it!"

The courtyard was vast, and the twisted trees and

shrubs surrounding the outer borders lent a splash of mystery to the otherwise pristine lawn. Two voices travelled to her ears from a distance, and Emily's heart dropped into her stomach. "Oh good, now my day is perfect. I guess Catherine and Camilla don't care about being late."

"Camilla's mother was on the Guard with Fenstorm when they started out," he said, following her gaze back the way they'd come, "and Catherine's father is the Chief Master's drinking buddy whenever he comes to the castle. So, they're pretty much untouchable."

Emily sighed. *That's it for me, I guess.* "Bad enemies to have."

Ozzy laughed. "Look at it this way—no one will be thinking about you while they're trying not to die by dragon fireball."

"So, I'm saved because I'm less scary than a painful, fiery death?" Emily asked. "Nice."

"Owning who you are took guts. Plus, if you survived the Commons, this should be easy."

Emily wasn't so sure.

A strange sound, like blankets beating the side of a brick wall, came from somewhere in the distance. The wind kicked up, rippling the grass and pulling their hair back over their foreheads as the temperature of the day shifted, little by little, warming Emily's cheeks and drying her eyes.

"They're getting close!" Elliott Fitzgibbons called, breaking off from the larger group to join Emily and Ozzy. Beside him, Finn Dashwood eyed the sky as though the clouds were set to rain spears of fire.

"Hey, Ozzy!" Elliott waved with a cheerful grin. "Nice day for a dragon fight, isn't it?"

"We ride the dragons. We don't fight them," Finn pointed out, turning a paler shade of ash.

"We'll see." Elliott turned to Emily. "Emily, I wanted to let you know that I had a good feeling about you yesterday, so as far as I'm concerned, you're all right. Your dad was a loony, but that's no reason to stop trusting my gut now."

"Which means he wants to date you." Finn shook his head.

"Cut it out, Finn," Elliott moaned.

Finn ignored him with the ease of years of experience. "But you're a pretty girl," he continued, "and Elliott has about fifty-three weak spots for pretty girls. So, you could be a closeted murderer or just cute."

"And you wonder why you have no luck with girls." Elliott sighed, shaking his head.

The trees across the courtyard swayed and bent as the windstorm grew all around them. A shriek ripped through the sky, and Emily's hands reached up to cover her ears. Leaning into Ozzy, she looked up to where two dark figures plummeted to the earth like twin cannonballs.

Tina Lee stood up on her toes, face turned up to the clouds. "Ooh, look! I think that's him!"

Finn cringed. "That looks so unsafe."

They weren't cannonballs; wings stretched out on either side of two massive, gleaming dragons. The larger one swooped overhead, his belly the colour of ripe pumpkin and scales a deep, molten black. The other was smaller but no less impressive, following close behind with bright, yellow eyes to match the colour of its underbelly and scales flashing crimson and navy depending on the light. Both beasts let out guttural screams and clicks, a language all their own, before landing on the ground in a flurry of fallen leaves and delicate sparks.

"Impressive, sir!" Camilla craned her neck for a better look.

"Don't be a kiss-ass, Miss Kirby." A man dismounted the larger dragon in one swift shove off its long, winding neck. Wind-burned hands pulled his collar high up over his weathered face. Lines mapped a hard life in difficult condition, his mouth a thin, straight line that showed no mercy. Only his eyes, a deep violet flecked with gold, showed any sign of warmth. "I'm Flight Master Fenstorm, retired Commander of the Coven Guard and disappointed Empath, who was pulled out of his fishing retirement for this assignment. This, here," he said, patting the black dragon's belly as though it were a puppy, "is Paffos."

"I can't believe they get *names*." Emily wrinkled her nose. "First Naglar, now Paffos?"

Finn nodded. "I'm with her. It's not like they're pets."

"Flying is *not* a joke," Fenstorm continued, his hoarse voice like pebbled leather. "Your abilities won't work on dragons. Their hide is resistant to any of that sort of manipulation, so when it's you against the dragon, the dragon usually wins. Many have died trying to tame a beast smaller than this."

"Now he tells us," Ozzy moaned.

Fenstorm's eyes flashed. "As you might have heard, most of you won't make it past this year with me. Flight isn't for everyone, and many might be wondering why you're even here if that's the case." His jaw flexed, making it clear on what side of that argument he stood. "But Chief Master Millendorf feels that everyone deserves a chance to prove themselves and, at the very least, learn a bit of respect for these magnificent creatures. So . . . here we are." He shifted, favouring one leg over the other, and Paffos moved in time with his master, the two in a close, unspoken dance.

"Sir?" Camilla's hand darted into the air, her lip twitching with a suppressed grin.

Fenstorm sighed. "Yes, Miss Kirby?"

"Is it true that mastering flight basically puts you in the running to join the Guard?"

Fenstorm considered her question with as much excitement as Ozzy showed toward dragons. "The Elders and High Council require their Guard to be experts on a dragon, yes. So," he continued, "who can tell me what— Elders help me, *yes*, Miss Kirby?"

Camilla spoke up but kept her hand in the air. "Well, I was wondering why *she's* here, then." She cast a dark, pointed look at Emily, and their group fell silent. "I don't feel comfortable with a Rathburn on a dragon around me."

The lines between Fenstorm's eyebrows grew deeper, more pronounced. "Miss Kirby, I should warn you that you are way out of bounds."

"I'm only saying what everyone here is thinking," she said with a defiant shrug.

Emily locked her jaw and focused her gaze on a faraway tree while Ozzy, Elliott, and Finn converged around her, their warmth soothing.

"Is this what you all are interested in?" Fenstorm asked. "Fine, then—let's talk about the dragon in the room. Yes, Emily Rathburn, daughter of Baxter Rathburn, is here today." He nodded in her direction, eyes hard but not unkind. "Her presence at this castle is no one's business but her own and the ones who have allowed her to be here. I'm here to teach you how to fly an Elder-forsaken dragon, not be your gossip companion. Is that clear, Miss Kirby?"

Camilla's hands balled into fists, turning her knuckles white as bone. Her eyes bubbled with hate, and she leaned over, whispering something in Catherine's ear while the girl picked at her fingernails.

Let it go, Emily told herself. *Remember why you're here.*

"Now, if I'm going to waste a perfectly good retirement being here, you lot better shut your mouths about Miss Rathburn and learn something." He marched between both dragons, arms extended on either side of him. "So, who can tell me what it takes to successfully mount and ride a dragon?" Paffos eyed them as furls of smoke clouded the crisp September day, and Fenstorm sighed at the deafening silence. "Right, a lively group. First, it takes magical blood. So, really, anyone here has the potential to walk away from an encounter with a dragon with their lives."

"Fantastic," Finn said under his breath.

"But the true key to success is unity with your mount." Fenstorm closed his eyes, and his face went blank. His shoulders vibrated with energy, sending a hum into the ground that shook the earth under their feet. He tilted his head to one side, and Paffos echoed the motion at once. "You have to truly feel and understand your dragon. Now *that* isn't easy and can't be learned—it happens through lots of talent and some dumb luck. Empaths have the most success with this, but it's not impossible for an Elemental to bond with a dragon."

"Sir?" Elliott asked, his hand raised around his ear.

"Yes, Mister . . . uh…" Fenstorm's weathered face creased, fingers flexing at his side.

"Fitzgibbons. Are you bonded with both of those dragons?" Elliott pointed to the small red dragon who raked the ground with his claws, his head swaying tall on his sinuous neck. Yellow eyes roved across their faces, and when they settled on Emily, her heart stuttered.

"This little demon here is Titan." Fenstorm patted the second dragon on the neck. "He's only a couple years old, so he hasn't bonded with anyone yet. I thought it might be good to start you off with something smaller. Easier."

Camilla snorted. "I've handled dragons bigger than these dogs."

"Shut up, Cammy," Catherine said under her breath.

"You have something to say, Miss Kirby?" Fenstorm rounded on her, one mangled brow patchy and twisted above his strange eyes.

"Just that . . . I'm excited to see how well I do, sir." Camilla had the sense to clamp her jaw shut, but her eyes brimmed with fury.

"Well, let's see right away, shall we?" Fenstorm lifted a large hand and waved Camilla over. "I say, the best way to learn is to do. And since you're so excited to follow in your mother's footsteps, you can get on Paffos here."

"*Your* dragon?" Camilla asked, turning pale. "But he won't let me ride him if he's bonded to you!"

"He will if I tell him to," Fenstorm said. "Come on, now, don't be shy. And take miss Bonner with you. She looks bored."

Like any good disaster, it was impossible to look away. Camilla straightened her spine and marched over to the front of the group, a wide-eyed Catherine following close behind. Despite Fenstorm's assurances, Paffos did not look thrilled about the arrangement; he clawed the ground, thick blasts of yellow saliva spattering onto the ground at his feet.

"This is crazy!" Ozzy hissed under his breath. "It's our first day! We shouldn't even be touching a dragon."

Despite a small part of her hoping Paffos would buck them both off midair, Emily's insides writhed the closer the girls got to the dragon. "I know, but what can we do about it? Fenstorm doesn't exactly look open to suggestions. Plus, Paffos looks sort of . . . tame."

Ozzy's eyes were wild. "Tame? That's a dragon, not a kitten!"

"We need another pair to take Titan here for a ride," Fenstorm continued. "Any takers?"

Titan beat his wings and sliced a nearby fir tree in half. No one volunteered.

"Fine." Fenstorm assessed his audience. "Let's see who we've got."

"He's not going to just *choose* someone, is he?" Finn asked.

Elliott stamped on his foot. "Would you shut it?"

"Shinkle!" White faces swivelled to the back of the group where Ozzy stood, dumbfounded. Fenstorm nodded to him. "Let's show them what you've got."

Ozzy's mouth moved in stunned silence. He cleared his throat and spoke in little more than a croak. "I—I don't think I'm ready for that, sir."

"Come on, don't be modest," Fenstorm said with a hint of impatience. "Your brother's been with me for a few years now. Impressive talent, a natural-born flier. It's in your blood."

Ozzy shook his head. "If I get on that dragon, sir, my blood's going to be all over the floor."

"So, you're saying you can't handle it." The Flight Master stepped forward, and the rest of the initiates parted to avoid Fenstorm's wrath. "Fine, Shinkle, fine. Anyone else?"

Ozzy stumbled forward, the toe of his shoe catching on a hillock of grass jutting out from the rest. He frowned, jaw flexing, and a sense of dread trickled down Emily's spine. Finally, in a small voice, Ozzy called out across the courtyard: "I changed my mind, sir. I can do it."

"Are you sure?" Emily asked. When Ozzy grew pale but nodded, she simply sighed in defeat. "Okay. Keep your head down and do whatever Fenstorm says. He won't let anything happen to you." She patted Ozzy on the shoulder and offered him an encouraging smile before he trudged to the front of the group.

Fenstorm clapped his hands. "That's the spirit, Shinkle. Go on, step up there."

"Step where?" Ozzy asked, his face a touch green as he cowered in Titan's shadow. "There's nowhere to hold on."

"Shut *up*, Oswald," Camilla said over Paffos's rumbles, her annoyance as loud as her voice. "If you make me look bad, I'll scorch you!" With an ease earned only through experience and pure talent, she mounted Paffos with one shove from the ground and jammed a foot into the joint of Paffos's wing. In another motion, she swung her other leg over the side of his neck. The dragon let out a sharp cry of complaint, but Camilla ignored him, reaching for Catherine, who wasn't as convinced about the entire thing from her safe place on the ground.

Emily's eyes locked onto Titan's. His tail swished and caught the light in a red and navy flare. *He wants to move. He wants to fly . . . but Ozzy's too nervous.* Titan's eyes slid over to her, his pupils narrowed to slits.

"One spot left!" Fenstorm called. Paffos lowered his neck to the ground, his tail swishing to the left and right in a rhythmic motion of black and orange.

Ozzy placed his foot on the dragon's side, searching for the wing joint as Camilla had done. His sneaker slid down Titan's ribs and he stumbled, cheeks turning a deep, beet red. Titan's body vibrated with energy, and while Emily could see the dragon was harmless, Ozzy wasn't so sure. He extended his arm and withdrew it at once as Titan puffed smoke into his face. Ozzy coughed, the sound provoking a low snarl. Still, Ozzy didn't back down. He cast a look over his shoulder, and his eyes met Emily's with fear dancing in their depths.

Her friend was losing his nerve. Emily pushed to the front of the group, ignoring the hisses erupting around her like water on a blazing log fire. "I think I'd like to try."

CHAPTER ELEVEN

Escape

FENSTORM'S EYES GLINTED LIKE AMETHYST as Emily marched up to Ozzy's side. "You want a shot, Rathburn?"

I want to make sure Ozzy doesn't die. Her mind was disjointed, a mess of memories and images that were hers, yet so distant, they flickered in and out of focus like a moth's wings. Nights in her room, hearing the dragon cries in the night, comforting a scared child or willing sleep to come despite the noise. Then there was the feel of Naglar weaving through the clouds and leaving the world behind. "I want to learn, sir."

"What are you doing?" Ozzy asked under his breath.

"Keeping you from riding a dragon alone," she shot back.

Fenstorm's jaw jutted out, the grey stubble on his face reminding her of the stiff brush she used to clean the Common's pots with after a heavy stew. "All right, then we're set. Get on your dragon, Shinkle. Miss Rathburn."

Too many eyes tracked her every move. Waiting for her to fall—to fail. Waiting to laugh. Emily straightened her shoulders and inhaled deep to steady her racing pulse. Titan's leathery wings flexed with excitement, but he held his body still as she searched for a good place to rest her foot. Where could she hold on? His neck? Was there a harness?

She couldn't do this. And yet, a blanket of calm settled over her, clearing the fog from her mind. Titan curled his neck around, scales dragging against the grass, until one large eye was level with Emily. Ozzy took a step back, pulling on her sweater as he went, but Emily stood firm, rooted to the spot. Calm. *Calm.* "Hi, Titan," she said.

Titan blinked, a strange clicking noise resonating from deep within his throat. Like a purr. *Hi back,* he seemed to say. She smiled and stretched her fingers out to the side of his head. Placing her palm against one of his scales was natural. Safe. His body was surprisingly cool, each individual segment a different shade of crimson or navy, each as smooth as the last. Like glass.

Emily ran her palm down his neck, searching for the best place to mount. She rested her sneaker in the horseshoe-shaped crevice where body met wing, and she leaned forward, securing herself on his back. The scales of Titan's neck shifted over one another, lifting like gills to offer him more movement. She slipped her hand under a scale to the rough skin underneath and pushed off hard with her other foot, looping her leg around his body.

She grinned. "That wasn't too bad." The scales and tough muscle fibers between Titan's shoulders made for a rough seat, and she pressed her knees together, hoping it would be enough to keep her upright.

Ozzy gaped at her. "How'd you do that?"

She glanced over at Fenstorm, Camilla, the rest of the initiates. "Do you want me to help you up?"

Ozzy nodded. "I'll get behind you, though. I don't think I can stand seeing that thing's head breathing fire right next to my face."

Emily leaned over and tugged the boy up behind her. "You okay?"

He nodded. "Did I tell you how happy I am you're here?"

"Not yet," Emily said, her laughter hollow. Nervous.

Across the courtyard, Camilla leaned over Paffos and patted him a little too hard, kicked him with her heels a little too often. "Come on, Cat." She offered her hand just as Emily had done for Ozzy and snapped her fingers as they hung there, empty.

"I'm happy on the ground, thanks," Catherine called back.

Camilla rolled her eyes and grabbed Catherine's arm with both hands. "He won't do anything to you!" She tugged.

"Let go, Cammy!" Fear flickered across Catherine's face, replacing bitterness for the first time since Emily had met her. "I don't wanna do this!"

"Jump up. I'll do the rest!"

Fenstorm marched to Catherine's side, his face screwed up in concentration. "Uh, ladies, maybe we should take a break. Paffos doesn't like this much."

"I agree, sir." Catherine braced one foot against the dragon's side and the other on the ground, trying to pull her arm free. "Paffos doesn't want me up there, either. Let go." Punctuating the point, Paffos shimmied from side to side, his restlessness digging long ditches in the ground.

Camilla, however, wouldn't be outdone. "You're embarrassing me! He's harmless, aren't you, you ugly monster?" She pulled hard on Catherine's arm once again, peeling Catherine off the ground and onto Paffos's back.

It all happened in quick bursts after that. Paffos bucked to one side in a flurry of sparks and charcoal smoke. Camilla toppled off the dragon's back, her fingers raking, pulling, grabbing. With a heavy thud, she landed on the ground, tugging Catherine onto Paffos's back in the process.

"Cammy!" Catherine's shriek was overpowered by Paffos's roar. As he writhed, rearing up on his hind legs and shaking his head, Emily spotted a hint of brown hair flailing back and forth between his shoulders, her position unsafe, even to her eyes.

"Bonner, get off of there!" Fenstorm roared. "Paffos! Enough!"

"What's happening?" Ozzy gripped onto Emily harder than he should.

"Catherine's still up there!" Emily called over the noise.

Paffos roared, and Emily ducked behind Titan's neck to avoid the sudden stream of flames blazing through the air.

Fenstorm waved his hands over his head, his eyes wide and focused. "Stand down! Paffos, *stand down*!"

A heavy wind drowned out Fenstorm's orders, Catherine's sobs, everyone's shocked screams. Wings beat the air, fire blazed, and Paffos kicked off the ground in a cloud of dust. Faces turned up to the sky as the dragon flew dizzying circles over their heads, his screams soaked in fear and pain.

"I have to go after her!" Emily strained to catch a glimpse of a pale face against the inky dragon hide, a pink sweater, any sign of the girl still holding on fast, but they were too high. Too far away.

Ozzy choked on his own scream. "Are you insane?"

"Fenstorm's lost control!" Sure enough, the Flight Master was down on his knees, eyes closed in silent prayer. "I have a dragon! I can do something!"

Ozzy spluttered incoherent arguments, but there was no time. Emily reached beside her and found Ozzy's arm. *The ground,* she thought, struggling to wipe her mind clean. *He's on the ground…*

Heat flooded Emily's palms. Titan held still, his breathing slowing in time with hers. Ozzy's arm tensed but she held on, her mind whirring with images of him safe on the grass, at Fenstorm's side with Elliott and Finn.

"Emily, what—" Ozzy said with a surprised gasp. With a final surge of energy, her hand gripped open air. "Emily!" The scream came from way below her, Ozzy's familiar voice high but not in pain. Safe. Out of the way.

"Sorry!" Emily called down. "Okay, Titan. Uh… how do I do this?"

Her question was enough. Titan kicked off the ground and launched into the clouds with one powerful push. The cold wind bit into Emily's face, making her eyes tear, but she didn't dare close them. She was weightless, bound by no rules but her own. Titan cried out, a sound of triumph that Emily echoed, her screams audible to only her and her mount. She dug her fingers into his neck, squeezed her heels, and Titan levelled out as they circled the tallest turrets of the castle. With a downward shift of her body, Titan dipped, threatening to unhook her precarious grip. Instead of screaming, Emily ground her teeth and peeled her eyes wide, trying to counterbalance every unexpected shift in Titan's body. She could be bucked off at any moment, but it didn't matter. This was freedom.

Emily searched the sky with sharp eyes. *Snow. Blood. Pinecones in the mud. A wounded animal, a deer, I think.* Each gulp of air registered a new movement to consider, another animal nearby to avoid. A meal to be had and the scents pulling her to it. Not her—Titan. The dragon's head bobbed up and down through the clouds, and Emily was sure he was testing the waters, his senses channelling into her mind. *Okay, let's focus. How far could they have gone?*

Navy wings veined in red pumped on either side of her, bringing them into an easy glide around Black Mountain. Shadows played in each crevice and nook of Selwyn castle while the cold still frosted the tall, peaked windows in a film of white and grey. *Is that...?*

Catherine's scream was easy to pick out from the cry of dragon fury from a distance. On the north side of the castle, Paffos clung to the stone wall with talons like brushed steel. There, hanging off the edge, the beast reminded Emily of ink pouring out of a full bottle, staining a page with permanent black. Titan pushed on, his neck straight, Emily's fingers curled under the rough side of his scales, locked into place.

"Get close, Titan. Can you do that?" As soon as Emily formed the words, they rocketed toward a wide balcony jutting underneath the tower. Faces peeked out of windows, and a small group converged on the ground below, but Emily sat upright on Titan's neck and shielded her eyes from the glare of Paffos's back. "Catherine? Are you okay?"

"Cammy?" Catherine's voice was shaky and thick, choked by tears and terror. "That you?"

"It's Emily!" She waited, but there was no sound except for the crunch of rock as Paffos hung from the upper wall like a squirrel in a tree. "I can't get up there or Paffos'll take off again. Can you get him to come down?"

A pause. "Are you kidding me?"

Emily closed her eyes, willing Titan to stay still. "Okay, then you have to jump!"

"*You* jump!" Catherine called.

"I'm not the one who can't handle my dragon!" Emily took a steadying breath and composed herself. "Look, we'll catch you. I promise!"

"No!"

Emily sighed. "Can you get right under her, Titan?" A short snarl vibrated in the dragon's throat, and Emily grinned. "Yeah, I know she's a pain, but we can't leave her here." A grunt, a stream of smoke blanketing the balcony like thick smog, and Titan crawled to the base of the tower. Pink flashed out from behind a wing, and Catherine's tear-streaked face tilted down in agony.

"You're insane. I can't jump!" Catherine's arms constricted Paffos's neck. "I'll die!"

"You're stuck on an angry dragon," Emily said with impatience. "You really want to talk about dying now?" She straightened her back, and Titan placed his two front claws on the tower, lifting her higher off the ground. "Look, I can't get closer to you without making Paffos nervous. You're going to have to help me out here."

Catherine squeezed her eyes shut. "What if you drop me?"

"What if I catch you and then yell at you for wasting so much time?" Titan's jaw opened in a fanged smile, but Emily huffed with impatience. "I'm counting to three."

"No!"

"One!" Emily stretched her arms. "Two!"

"I'm not letting go!" Catherine warned, her curls sticking to her wet, pale face.

"Three!" Titan beat his wings and jumped into a semi-circle underneath Paffos's spiked tail. A wail made Emily's ears ring. Whether it was Catherine's or hers, she couldn't be sure. The world tilted, and the sky rushed forward at an angle as Emily clung to Titan with all the strength she possessed, her legs and arms throbbing, burning with fatigue.

Thud.

"Catherine?" Emily peered over her shoulder to catch a flash of brown hair and a glint off her glasses before Titan sped up into the sky. "It worked! Are you okay?"

"Just make sure this thing doesn't kill us!" Catherine clambered higher onto Titan's back and gripped Emily's waist, her hands shaking and cold.

Emily kept her eyes level. A laugh bubbled in her chest, and Titan howled in triumph, tittering in short bursts as though they were one. They banked a hard right, circling the last corner before Fenstorm and the rest of their group materialized on the grounds.

"That was amazing!" Elliott called as he ran to greet them.

Finn followed close behind on shaky legs. "Stupid. So stupid. You almost gave Ozzy a coronary."

"Call it a *heart attack*, for Elders' sake!" Elliott reached up, offering Catherine his hand, but the girl disentangled herself from Emily without hesitation. She swatted Elliot's hand away, toppled off the dragon on her own, and marched through the group of initiates, clipping as many as she could with her shoulder as she headed back to the castle.

"She seems fine," Elliott snorted. "How did you learn to do that?"

Emily ignored the question, sliding off Titan with regret. "Where's Ozzy?"

"Right where you left him." Finn jabbed his thumb over his shoulder with a hint of a smile. "Go see for yourself."

She gave Titan a pat on the neck and raced across the lawn to where Ozzy was sitting beside Fenstorm, face green around the edges. "Ozzy, what happened? I didn't hurt you, did I?"

His lips quirked into a grin, and it took some effort for him to focus. "I've been better. Threw up a little in the bushes over there. Could have done without that."

Elliott leaned in close, giddy with happiness. "I don't think Ozzy and dragons mix. I mean, you couldn't see much from where you were sitting, but he looked like he was going to pass out even before you transferred him onto the ground. He's been sick ever since you left."

Ozzy scowled and turned to Emily. "You look like you survived, though."

Before she could answer, Fenstorm spoke up, his voice strained and grainy. "Rathburn, what were you thinking? Aren't you an Elemental?"

"I only wanted to help. And yes, sir, I am," she said under her breath.

Fenstorm shook his head. "Rathburn, Paffos and I are bonded. He might have needed a minute to himself, but I was with him and Miss Bonner the whole time." Shame made Emily pause, her cheeks hot and her palms clammy. "I asked him to settle on the nearest tower and wait for me to get to him, but then you had to complicate the mess."

Shame deepened to regret. Of course, Fenstorm would never have let an initiate die; he was a member of the Guard, bonded to Paffos with years of practice. Emily bit the inside of her cheek, wishing she could somehow disappear.

"I didn't think of that." Flames licked at the back of Emily's neck. "I'm sorry, sir."

Silence and eager smirks surrounded Emily, and the message was clear; she was out. She had to be. Fenstorm exhaled in a loud huff, noticing their audience for the first time. "Look, I understand this can't be easy, but you might want to keep a lower profile until all this . . . blows over," he said, nodding over his shoulder. "Why don't you take Shinkle here inside and make sure he doesn't trip over himself, hm?"

Emily nodded, ducking behind a sheet of frazzled black hair. "Yes, sir." Titan wound his long tail around his sinuous body, fine rivulets of smoke feathering the charred earth. She offered him a smile, fingers itching to pat his neck once more before leaving his side. "G'bye, Tite," she said, pulling Ozzy away.

Titan trained large, watchful eyes on Emily and Ozzy until they disappeared into the castle.

A Graven Mistake

"EMILY! OZZY! OVER HERE!" WILLOW waved them over from the first row, books already laid out in order of size.

"Really?" Ozzy sank into the seat beside her with a groan. "The front of the class?"

"I'm too small to see from the back."

The news of Emily's identity spread like a brushfire, but the snarls and snaps biting at her heels were a whisper against her hardened skin. The orange glow of the setting sun filtered through stained glass windows, casting pools of watercolour across the grey walls. After a day of suspicious talk around her encounter with Titan and Catherine, sundown meant the torture was almost done.

She rubbed her arms against the growing cold. The

promise of a hot meal and sleep kept her afloat, dragging her through their last lesson of their first day. She sat, her muscles aching, as Ozzy unpacked his things beside her.

"Ow!" A young man with dishevelled brown hair stumbled through the door, rimless glasses teetering low on his nose. Gloved hands clutched a stack of books to his chest while a wrinkled suit pooled in strange folds over scuffed shoes. "Good afternoon, everyone—ow!" he repeated, tripping on a crack in the flagstone. With a bashful smile, he recovered himself and made straight for the podium at the front of the room. "I'm Master Ward, and I'm here to dive into magical ethics and laws for as long as you'll have me." He paused and waited.

"I heard about this one," a girl said without any effort at a whisper. "Total embarrassment. Gets weirder and weirder the longer he's here."

"Right." Ward shuffled his books around. "Can anyone tell me why ethics are important to consider in our careers as Empaths and Elementals of the realm?" More silence followed by a few light coughs scattered throughout the room. He cleared his throat, and a thick fog obscured his glasses. "Uh, well, not all abilities are formed equal. For example, one Elemental might be limited to helping one specific type of plant grow and thrive while another can create large amounts of plant matter out of sheer will."

"Both are pretty useless, if you ask me," Camilla said, earning her a round of giggles.

Beside Emily, Willow lowered her eyes to her book.

"However," Ward says, "does that mean one Elemental is better than the other? Do they have the right to grow plants wherever they like or manipulate shared lands for their own benefit?"

"If they can, why not?" came a question from the back of the room.

Ward smiled. "That is the question of ethics, isn't it? Should we be able to do something simply because we can?"

Camilla snorted. "What's the point of having magic we can't use? You might as well send half of us to the Commons."

Someone hit her. Hatred rose inside Emily's chest. *Please, please, please.*

"You raise an excellent question, Miss Kirby." Ward's smile was wide and bright and much too happy. *What?* "Take myself, for example. Does anyone know why I wear gloves?" The conversation had taken a strange turn, and no one could venture a guess. "I'm an Elemental with quite a . . . controversial ability. I can absorb the ability of anyone I touch for a very brief period of time and use it. And even though I have never taken advantage of my magic and the High Council checked into me thoroughly before allowing me to live freely, I am always met with revulsion."

The response was immediate. Chairs creaked with uncomfortable shifting; gasps and hisses flew around the room like arrows soaring towards their mark.

Catherine cringed away from Ward. "You're a *leech*?"

"That's the derogatory term for it, but yes," Ward said, not disturbed by the comment in the least. "The moment my skin touches another's, I am able to borrow and manipulate that Elemental or Empath's ability until the effect wears off." He peered around the room, eyes resting on every face in turn. "Are you offended?"

Elliott shrugged. "As long as you don't touch me, sir,

I'm fine with it."

"Thank you, Mister Fitzgibbons. As for the rest of you," he continued, "I can imagine you're not quite sure about how you feel. Which, I promise you, is a common opinion. After all, I don't have any true power of my own except to steal it from another. That's why I can't teach you spells or magical brews or anything truly impressive. I'm here teaching *ethics* because, really, what else can I offer?" He stood behind his podium, alone, both in person and in ability. Emily sat up straighter, the surge of respect for the man sudden and surprising. "So, what does that mean for me in terms of ethics?"

Ozzy raised his hand. "You have the right to use your ability, but since your magic invades the privacy of others, should you use it at all?"

He smiled, a row of straight white teeth brightening his haggard appearance. Kind, warm. "I couldn't have phrased it better myself, Mister Shinkle. Much more astute than your brother, I see."

Ozzy beamed. "Thank you, sir."

"Now," Ward said in a low voice, "who here believes the Commons should be abolished and the realm mixed?"

The small room exploded into mutiny.

"Is he joking?"

"Completely insane!"

"What'd he say?"

"Enough!" Ward's voice boomed over the noise, and the initiates quieted at once. "Empaths and Elementals evolved from non-magical people long ago. While we are different today and even live in different realms, they are our brothers and sisters, are they not?"

"Well, sure," Elliott said, "but they're in another realm!"

Finn nodded. "Yeah, they don't know we exist. They can't hurt us anymore if they don't know where we are. Those people in the Commons have no magic, and they know where we are!"

Ward shrugged. "So?"

"So, they can hunt us down if they think we're keeping it for ourselves!" Camilla slammed her fist onto the table. "They can steal what we have!"

"Much like I can steal your abilities if I simply touch your hand, Miss Kirby?" he asked. Camilla floundered, her mouth opening and closing in mute rage. "The difference," Ward said, "is that mine is an ability and therefore more socially acceptable than someone non-magical taking advantage." The room grew quiet and remained that way until the sky turned black and their faces paled with the appearance of moonlight, Ward firing questions off one by one and reading from a weathered textbook every so often.

"I think we can leave it there for today." Ward shuffled his papers and collected his book as chairs scraped against the ground. "Miss Rathburn, may I have a word?"

Emily smiled as Ozzy hesitated beside her. "You go save me a seat."

He nodded and joined Willow out the door with the rest of the class. What could she have already done? Her stomach growled, and her head ached.

Ward stacked his books, biding his time in silence until the last initiate shuffled out the door. "I hope I didn't bore you too badly," he said with a faint smile. "I tend to get passionate about arguing the controversial."

Emily clutched her bag to her side. "Passion and arguments are fine with me."

"Good. That's very good." His eyes were a deep sea-green, flecks of gold glinting in the low light. "You know, Miss Rathburn, I came to live here, too. Everyone in my family was a huge success and went on to do great things."

"That's . . . great." The Gallery would be full, the food warm. And her bed warmer.

"It is." He paused, drumming his fingers on his books. "I was different, though. A little bit . . . odd. It may be difficult to see it now, but standing out from the pack can be a gift."

Ah. "For some people, maybe," Emily said, thinking of Victor and every single face like his that looked down on her. "I usually find blending in makes things less complicated."

"That's true." His smile was soft. "But remember, not everyone will judge you harshly. It might be worth keeping your head up and your mind open."

"I'll keep that in mind." Emily shifted from toe to heel, back and forth. Outside, a loon wailed in the growing black. "Is that all, sir?"

Ward's eyes grew wide. "Oh yes, I'm so sorry! You have a lovely evening. And I have no doubt you will do well here, Miss Rathburn. Your blood expects it."

My blood can give me a break. Emily scurried out the door to find some supper and an end to her day.

When Emily woke the next morning, Catherine's and Tina's beds were already empty. Their first lesson on brewing was in a dank room at the top of the eastern tower with too many windows leaching cold into the air.

Catherine sat on her own, pruning herbs and pulverizing insects with so much force her glasses slipped down her nose. Emily considered checking in on her—after all, if a hostile dragon encounter didn't qualify as some sort of icebreaker, she didn't know what did—but what would be the point? An awkward conversation? A thank-you, or an apology leaving them both embarrassed? Neither scenario seemed likely.

Emily lingered after the lesson, relishing the silence in the winding halls as the initiates travelled down the narrow stairs to gather in the Gallery for lunch. Alone with her thoughts, she breathed deep, her bag swinging off her shoulder with every step as she dipped into a mental state of peace, taking the winding corridors at a stroll while sunlight filtered through clear windows. East Tower was a good distance from the Gallery, giving her enough time to herself before the chaos of the lunchtime crowd.

"Penny for your thoughts?" Victor trotted up beside her, his good mood pushing her down a black hole.

"You can afford more than a penny," she said without a second look.

"True." He pushed his hair out of his eyes and unhooked the bag from her shoulder, hoisting it onto his own. "But I'm not greedy."

She sighed. "What's with you and bags?"

"I was raised to be a gentleman," he replied with a shrug. "I know we're a rare breed, but you can't tell me your standards are that low."

"Gentlemen don't turn innocent girls into live statues," she countered. "Especially girls who didn't have a chance to defend themselves."

He gave her a sidelong frown. "I'm surprised you're defending her. Anyway, Camilla's hardly innocent. She was being rude, and I didn't like her speaking to you like that."

"You don't think I need a hero, do you?" Emily rolled her eyes. A group of three older girls slowed down as they passed, watching her with naked envy. "Because that's how it sounds, and I'd rather not lose my appetite before lunch."

Victor laughed. "You might be right. From what I hear, you can take care of yourself just fine."

She screwed up her nose. "You heard about the dragon?"

He stepped aside to allow her through a doorway and nodded. "Everyone heard about the dragon. I'm impressed. It's hard to have that kind of control under stress, especially on a first attempt."

"It happened to work out." Emily fought the rush of pride his words incited, remembering he was everything she hated. "And I didn't control Titan. He picked up on what I needed him to do and did it." They wound down the stairwell and, finally, voices wafted up from the Gallery. She picked up speed, eager to be rid of him. "Look, I've gotta go. Nice chat."

Go away now, go away.

"Actually, I wanted to know when you were free for your extra credit work," Victor called before she was out of earshot. Emily turned, Victor's eyes burning liquid under the low torchlight, making her shrink on the spot. "No better time to get ahead than the first week."

"What are you talking about?"

"Didn't you tell Magdale that you wanted to help around the castle?" he asked, inching closer.

"Well, sure, but—"

"And she told you that you'd be working with another initiate to show you the ropes?" Victor faced her head-on, and she could smell his soap, spicy and clean.

Lie. "Yeah, but I haven't—"

Victor grinned. "I'm a house favourite around here, so when Magdale mentioned it to me, I had to accept."

Emily groaned. "You can't be serious."

He jabbed a thumb into his chest. "I'm one of the best Elementals my age in this place. Plus, the High Council likes to see public assistance on an applicant's record. It's a win-win."

Public assistance. Emily took a firm step back and shielded her chest with her arms. "Can't you find someone else to torment? I mean it, *anyone* else."

"No. So, does tonight work for you? After dark, the Gallery entrance? It'll be like a date."

Emily chewed the inside of her cheek, hating the way her face burned when he spoke. "I won't be going anywhere with you if you talk like that."

He raised his hands, the picture of innocence. "I can deal with that. Only a little harmless flirting, then."

Emily pressed her thumb and forefinger to the bridge of her nose. She'd promised Magdale to do the work, to pay her way; her pride depended on it. And yet, backing out sounded like a much better option. Victor could have been tricking her, but how would he have known about Emily's arrangement with Magdale if he hadn't been told? There was no way out unless she chose to go back on her word, and that wasn't a possibility. Or ask Magdale for another initiate to guide her. And that would be admitting weakness, being precious. Another impossibility.

"Fine," she said, hating the flare of triumph in his face. "But I'm warning you, Graven, if this is a trick—"

"No tricks," he promised, surrendering her bag. "Just some good, old-fashioned learning by moonlight. Romantic, right?"

"You're pushing it."

He laughed. "See you later, Rathburn." One last smile and he sauntered away, hands jammed into his pockets.

Ozzy waited for her at what was becoming their usual table. His hair stood on end, Willow trying to smooth it down for him with little effect. Horus suppressed laughter behind a forkful of potato, eyes dancing. "Where've you been?" Ozzy asked, sharper than his usual tone.

Emily dropped into her seat and dragged an empty dish toward her. "Got held up. What happened to you?"

He huffed, swatting Willow's hand away. "Turns out my brew had a delayed effect. I sat down and then *this* happened." He gestured to where a crown of thorns made from his own hair twisted around his head.

Horus's eyes watered. "This is the best day."

"Be nice," Piper chastised. "Do you remember your first brew?"

Horus beamed, unfazed. "Sure—it was a disaster. I couldn't stop talking for two days, just non-stop blabbing. By the end, I couldn't stand to be around myself."

Piper stifled a giggle. "Then maybe you should be a bit nicer."

"Maybe, but I'm happy to watch when this stuff happens to someone else. It's a rite of passage." He shovelled another helping into his already full mouth. "It ge's wo'se, too."

"Thanks, Horus," Ozzy muttered.

Old Gwendolyn was in good spirits; her roots twisted into the ground, the fairies happy to make camp in the patches of forest-green moss painting the delicate tentacles. Emily glared at the endless happy faces. "Have any of you seen Catherine Bonner?"

"In the corridors, once or twice," Piper offered with an indifferent shrug. "Why? She make off with another dragon?"

"That wasn't her fault," Finn countered, joining them with Elliott. "It was Fenstorm's responsibility to stop that from even happening. I'm surprised he hasn't lost his job."

"The man was just trying to make a point!" Elliott countered, already heaping shepherd's pie onto his dish. "Serves her right for being such a raging lunatic. Camilla, though, I feel bad for."

Piper rolled her eyes. "That wouldn't be because you asked her out on a date and she rejected you, would it?"

"You what?" Horus asked, face screwed up in mock disgust.

Elliott shrugged. "I thought she could use a friend after what happened."

"Catherine hasn't come back to our dorm," Emily explained. "She might be horrible, but I saw her face up there. She was terrified."

"Who cares," Horus said. "She's awful—they all are. If she's moping around somewhere because she's embarrassed, it serves her right."

Ozzy nodded. "He's got a point. I'm sure she'll perk up soon and you'll be wishing she'd stayed gone a little longer." He gave up on his hair and glared at the growing pile of books beside him. "I know it's our first day, but

I have a ton of work already. We should get a head start tonight."

Emily buttered a roll, dread creeping into her throat. "Uh . . . I can't tonight."

"How come?" Ozzy asked.

She sighed. "I have to do some extra work for Magdale. You know, catch up since I have no idea what I'm doing."

"Sounds like a pain," Horus said. "What's she making you do?"

"Honestly, I'm not sure." Emily put down her bread, no longer hungry. "But she decided to stick me with Graven, so it'll be painful no matter what."

The effect was immediate; Ozzy's eyebrows scrunched up, Horus coughed on his thousandth piece of steak, Piper and Elliott made a soft whistling sound, and Willow sat in dazed silence.

"Going for the big fish, eh?" Elliott nodded, wearing a lopsided grin. "Respectable."

"It's remedial work. I have to do it." Everything about the conversation made Emily want to disappear into the floor, and she stared at Ozzy, eyes pleading with him to talk about anything but Victor Graven.

"Graven's a legend around here," Finn said with a hint of jealousy. "You're lucky he's helping you out. He never takes on a new initiate if he can help it."

"Graven's a nightmare." Horus jabbed the air with his fork. "Every girl in here's secretly in love with him. Some of the boys, too. And he knows it. I'd keep your date to yourself unless you want Crazy Camilla scratching your face off in your sleep."

Piper frowned. "Victor's really not that bad."

Horus grinned. "You're only saying that because he's pretty in the face and his father knows almost everyone with a private security box at Blintwoods."

Ozzy leaned in close, as the rest of the table continued their debate on Victor's eye colour. "I just had an idea. It might be worth asking Victor on your date tonight if he knows anything about the Blintwoods robbery."

"It's not a date," Emily countered. "And why would I do that?"

Ozzy tapped his fork on his dish. "You heard Reinhold. Victor's father owns the box beside the one the thief wanted. He might know who owns the box or what's in it, especially if he's got his skin on the line. At the very least, he'll know if they have any leads on the real thief."

Ozzy had a point. Emily couldn't be blindsided again if another member of the Guard came sniffing around, threatening her place at Selwyn's. And, if she was honest with herself, the chatter around the Blintwoods security box had her a little more than curious about what was inside it. If Victor had any information, there was no harm in asking him for it.

There weren't enough stragglers left behind in the Gallery to have too many witnesses, but Emily's insides squirmed, nonetheless. The torches lit one by one by the front doors as moonlight glowed in the windows, her feet finding the growing shadows with ease.

"Hey, there." Victor appeared beside her, silent as a whisper. "You look nice."

Emily frowned. "This is the same thing I wore today."

"And you looked nice today, too. So, are you ready?"

No. Emily wished she could race back up the steps with her pride intact. She sighed. "Just tell me what we're doing."

He led the way to the door and pulled it open for her with a dazzling smile. *I could kick him.* "We have some choice," Victor said. "There's some bucket scrubbing in the dragon den that we can do."

The night was frigid and crisp, but she was more concerned about the words *bucket scrubbing* than the darkness painting the grounds. "What's in the buckets?"

"Mostly rotten meat and dried blood left over from the raw hides we feed the dragons."

"And what's that supposed to teach me?" Emily asked, glad for her light dinner.

"Not to leave meat in the feed buckets." Victor grinned. "Plus, no one wants to do it."

"No kidding," she muttered. "Next?"

"We can get rid of the bats in the upper towers. They've formed a pretty big colony up there. Or..." He trailed off, stopping in his tracks.

Emily shivered. "Yes?"

"We could do some light gardening."

They were squarely in the middle of the courtyard, the choice floating in the clean air not a choice at all. And Victor wanted it that way. Emily stared him squarely in the eye. "I feel like I'm falling into a trap here, but let's do the gardening."

"Good choice." Victor took off at a brisk walk around to the back of the castle, where the fog curling over Black Mountain filtered down to the grass. Emily followed close behind and willed her heart to slow. "Have you been here yet?" he asked, indicating a large building with tall, glass walls and a domed ceiling at the edge of the forest.

"Nope."

"It's a greenhouse." He opened the door, and they slipped inside.

The result was immediate. The air was fragrant and warm, sweet and heady with the rows of shrubs covered in flowers and berries coloured deep red and pale green. Large petals in pink and gold feathered out over their heads, leaning in toward them as they moved deeper under the dome. "Master Murray has a bit of a Thorny Truth problem. The things are deadly but useful, and they're growing too fast. He can't keep up with the pruning."

"So, we're trimming some bushes?"

They stopped at a long stretch of green potted plants no higher than her knee. "In a way. Thorny Truth can't be cut like any other plant, or Murray would have gotten this done a long time ago." He found two pairs of shears and a large bucket, handing one of the hefty blades to her. "Full-grown Thorny Truth is unpredictable. See, they look like plants when they're young, but as they grow, they get stronger. They can possess other plants, animals, people even. Like a parasite. And they're . . . particular."

Emily peered into the pots at the innocuous vines curling their way skyward. Up close, a smattering of fine thorns ran the length of the stem, hiding under the veils of delicate leaves like predators in waiting. "What happens to the thing being possessed?"

"They attack and kill anyone with a dark or immoral purpose." Victor laughed at her stunned expression. "Don't worry, Rathburn. These little guys are still pretty young, so they'll let you touch them as long as you reveal something true about yourself whenever you do."

Emily recoiled, the idea of revealing anything to Victor Graven more alarming than a plant with a mind of its own. "I don't want to tell you anything personal about myself."

"You can do what you want, but they bite." He crossed his arms over his chest, smug. "And you're not telling me, exactly. You're talking to the plant."

"This can't be the only thing in here we can do," she grumbled.

Victor looped the shears through his finger, spinning them around with a casual flick of his wrist. "It needs to get done, and you need some exposure to magic. If I learn a bit more about what makes the dragon girl with the homicidal father tick, then that's a bonus. So, you want to start? Because I could go on arguing all night."

She sighed and held up the shears. "Tell me how this works."

He grinned. "Yes, ma'am. Tell a truth and snip a branch. It's as easy as that. The truer the statement, the easier it is."

They worked in near silence, the only sounds to break the soothing calm in the greenhouse the snip of their shears and their muttered truths.

Victor positioned the blades around the upper stem of the vine. "I have brown hair."

Snip.

"I'm wearing a blue sweater," Emily said.

Snip.

The hour ticked away, snip by virtuous snip, the knotted, twisted vines receding to neat stalks of tiny blooms as the night slumbered on.

"How much longer do we have?" Emily asked, brushing a wayward strand of hair from her eyes. "I'm running out of things to tell the bloodthirsty bushes."

Victor tracked the movement of her fingers with a spark of interest. "We could make it more interesting, if you want."

Emily's hands paused over a new pot. "Meaning?"

"Meaning, I'll ask you a question and you answer it truthfully. Then you can have a turn."

"Pass," Emily said. "I don't like games."

Snip.

"Well, unless you want to spend the next hour thinking of more garbage trivia about yourself, it might be fun. And I like having fun."

Snip.

"Fine." She stretched her back and winced. "But if I don't like the question, for whatever reason, I don't have to answer it."

"You can have three vetoes, no more than that, or it's not fair. Same goes for me." His smile shone in the moon-washed light, the flicker of interest bright in his face. "But there's no subject off the table. That's my rule. Agreed?"

Emily turned it over in her mind, irritation flaring at how eager she was to agree. If she played her cards right, she might be able to find out what Victor's father knew about Blintwoods and the box. Victor's interest in toying with her like a dog with a liver treat might not be the worst fate after all.

"Deal."

He looked down at her, and a wicked smile spread across his face. "I'll start you off easy. Where did you grow up?"

A toe in the water. Revealing, but not so much so she resented him having the information. "The Commons."

Snip. The end of an overgrown vine fell to the floor.

Victor's eyes widened. "How did an Elemental end up living down there?"

"You can ask the question on your next turn." She smiled despite her better judgement. "Do you have any siblings?"

He placed his blade around an unsuspecting branch. "An older sister." *Snip.* "Come on, Rathburn, that wasn't even interesting. Do you know your parents?"

She pursed her lips. His eyes met hers, challenging her to pass, to refuse to answer. "No." *Snip.* "Did Magdale ask you to work with me, or did you volunteer for this?"

A grin. "Pass." *Of course. He doesn't want to admit to choosing this so he can spy on the Rathburn traitor first-hand.* "How did you find out you were an Elemental?"

Memories, fast and uninvited. The cold ground underneath her, a doll, ragged and worn clutched in her small hand. It was the only thing she owned aside from the heavy gold necklace. She wanted her doll—her *friend*—to be safe. Not to suffer like she suffered. "I got upset when I was a kid and ended up taking something that didn't belong to me." *Snip.* Not a pleasant memory, and the answer was vague. The vine fought back as she pressed the blades together. A thorn lashed out and scratched the inside of her wrist before collapsing to the ground, defeated.

"Better not hold too much back, Rathburn. Lying stings, even if it's a lie of omission." His smirk reeked of satisfaction, of a boy used to getting his way.

"Are you having fun torturing me?" she asked.

"You're cute when you're upset, but that does count as a question." He raised his shears, toying at the end of a vine with the edge of the blade. "I don't consider this torture. I'm only trying to get to know you a little better." *Snip*. "What's the deal with you and the Shinkle kid?"

Whiplash would have caused less of a jolt. "Ozzy? We're friends."

He assessed her, scrutinizing every inch of her face. "That's it?"

"That's enough for me. Why's it even relevant?"

He pointed at her hand. "We'll see. If you're lying, I'll know."

She rolled her eyes and, without looking, took another vine clean off the plant. "What's the deal with you and Camilla, then?"

He grinned. "Jealous?"

"No. It's just tit for tat." Emily flexed her hand, and the cramp eased from her thumb.

"Fair enough." Victor paused, staring up at the glass dome framing the smattering of stars far above. "I've known her since we were kids. She might annoy me now, but she wasn't always so . . . difficult. It's hard to give up on someone you know so well." He frowned at the potted Thorny Truth at his feet and angled his shears along a thin, inconspicuous branch. The vine circled back, scratching Victor's palm deep enough to draw a thin trail of blood before falling to the ground.

"Lying stings, huh?" Satisfaction swelled in her chest. "Your turn."

A truth, but not the full picture. What are you not saying? Instead of asking the questions distracting her from her goal, Emily focused on the plan. "Why'd you agree to come here with me?" he asked.

She considered the question. "I guess . . . I want to know how far I'll go."

"That's evasive." He peered at her, eyes dark in the low light, but probing. Insistent.

"Maybe, but it's also true." *Snip*. "See?" Emily nudged the new addition between her feet, and the branch skittered away. "My turn. If you had to choose between saving a Commoner's life or money, which would you choose?"

A dozen emotions played across his angular face, and his jaw clenched. "Pass. Have you ever loved anyone other than yourself?"

Anger now, at knowing the choice he refused to say out loud, at the sting his return question left behind. Emily glared. "Pass. What does your father know about the Blintwoods robbery?"

For the first time, Victor floundered. His eyes narrowed, and colour bloomed in his pale face. "What?"

Emily grinned. "You heard me."

"Why do you want to know that?"

"You need to answer the question, not understand why I'm asking it."

Victor tossed his scissors on a nearby table and faced her, shoulders squared. "Actually, I don't."

She stared at him, baffled. "Yeah, you do. Those are the rules, remember?"

"Sure, I do. I also remember I have one pass left."

Emily dropped her own shears to the ground. "Why won't you answer the question?"

"Because people who don't have what I have always want to know, don't they? You people always want a piece of the high life. Of what it's like. Well, I won't bite."

"You people . . . " she repeated, the words like barbs in her mouth. "You mean poor people?"

Victor had the sense to look embarrassed, shaking his head in denial. "You know that's not what I meant."

"Right," she said. "I don't have to ask you to cut away at your little killer shrub there to know that's *exactly* what you meant to say. You think you're better than me—"

"I didn't say—"

"You don't need to! Pick up your scissors and let's have a look!" Anger, quick and undiluted, pulsed in her veins. She was back where she belonged, back to where she was most at home. Alone, in her own corner. And focused on what was most important.

He shook his head, sadness breaking across his face. "Look, can we start over? We were having a pretty good time before both of us lost focus."

"I think I learned enough for tonight." She crossed her arms across her chest and kicked a withering branch with her toe.

"Right," he muttered. "I'll walk you back."

"I can find my own way. Thanks for the lesson." She made for the door before he could stop her, breaking out into a quick walk around the side of the castle. The night was silent except for the crickets singing their predictable song to no one in particular.

CHAPTER THIRTEEN

Grey Coloured Glasses

HEAVY WINDS HISSED THROUGH THE trees carpeting Black Mountain, mirroring Emily's sense of doom. She and Ozzy trudged across the courtyard for their first meeting with Master Grey, the sheet of steel sky overhead more ominous than any of the stories Horus could have scared them with.

Ozzy eyed the trees as though they might come alive wielding an axe. "How'd it go with Graven last night?"

"Worse than I expected." Emily picked up her pace. The mountain peaks, so dark the previous night, glowed in the daytime without the oceans of fog choking it.

"Did you find anything out about the Blintwoods box?"

Guilt washed over her. "I tried, but he wasn't exactly in a sharing mood." A squat stone cabin materialized around a bend in the trees. She frowned, disliking the way the ivy clung to its crumbling walls, alive, choking it in eerie beauty. "You're sure this is where we're supposed to go?"

"That's Blackwood Cottage," Ozzy said. "Look." He nodded to a pair of initiates disappearing through the dark shadows and shuddered. "The place looks like a prison."

On the outside, Blackwood Cottage was falling apart. Gaps in the mortar allowed light to escape from the cabin while the forest grew around the stone as though embracing it with a thousand crawling fingers. But on the inside, souls crumbled quicker than the walls. The silence was thick in Emily's ears as they tiptoed up the aisle, the frozen panic on every face doing nothing to allay her own fears. Willow sat alone in the first row, ready with books and ink and a canyon of space between her and the others. Taking their places near the back of the cabin, Emily and Ozzy unpacked their books.

And waited.

It wasn't long before heels clicked outside the door, a latch turned, and the cold billowed in like a passing frost. The figure was slender, tall, gliding to the center of the room without the slightest glance at her rapt audience. A heavy travelling cloak masked most of her face in shadow and scratched at the flagstone floor as she ghosted to the hearth at the top of the cabin. With a flick of her wrist, flames erupted behind the grate, throwing her in shadow.

"Good afternoon." A velvet voice, rich and soft—and familiar. She lowered her hood around her neck, and the waning light reflected steel-white on her cropped hair. "I am Master Sable Grey. Your presence here, as mildly aggravating to me as it is, is still a privilege to you granted at my discretion. Remember that every time you set foot in my cabin." She arranged her books on a desk in the corner, but Emily couldn't take her eyes off Grey's face.

Each movement was sharp, practiced, efficient, like one of the stray cats lurking in the Commons' least travelled side roads. *That voice.* Emily leaned forward.

And then Grey looked up. Surveyed the room. And hooked her gaze onto Emily a beat too long.

You've got to be kidding.

Silver hair with matching eyes. Empty eyes. Emily's windpipe throbbed, remembering the bodiless hand reaching out of the rubble, out of the smoke, and squeezing . . . *The Blintwoods thief.*

Grey roamed the aisles, her words clipped and monotonous. "Incanting a spell takes presence and precision of both mind and body. You must connect your will to your ability and your ability with the outcome you desire. Only when you become practiced in the basics of control can you hope to expand your ability past the manifestations you show right now."

There was that word again: control. And while Emily cringed away from it, Grey's lips twisted around it like a lover's kiss. Her heels clicked in the complete silence, punching a beat in time with Emily's racing heart. "Open your books to the first chapter. Miss Colray, begin reading from the top."

Willow cleared her throat as pages rustled, and read: "'*Incanting and spell casting is the most ancient and pure manifestation of magic for Empaths and Elementals, calling upon the natural abilities of the individual to—*'"

"Louder," Grey said.

"Um . . . '*to manifest and influence the outside world. Simple tasks, such as—*'"

"I said *louder*, Miss Colray. Are you hard of hearing?"
Click, click, click.

Someone cleared their throat, and Willow's tiny shoulders hunching in silence. She looked up from her book, a young fawn in the crosshairs of a hunter's bow. "Could you please pass the reading to someone else? I . . . I think I'm too nervous to do it."

It was painful to watch. Grey towered over Willow like a bird of prey as they locked eyes. "Spells can be basic or complex. I'm sure you know not all Empaths or Elementals are good enough to live at this castle and be mentored here. The reason for which is that some abilities never progress past the fledgeling state. Not to say those individuals are useless—we need those to tend our horses and help serve our food. But they'll never be more than the Empath who can commune with slugs . . . or weeds."

Emily found herself gripping the tabletop until her fingers throbbed. Grey's eyes flashed and Willow never moved, her back as straight and fragile as ever.

"So, you see, talent and ability are not the same," Grey continued with a smile dripping with poison. "And then we must consider circumstance. Miss Colray, where were you born?"

Willow's voice was small, a whisper on a high wind. "The Commons," she answered without any hesitation.

Grey nodded. "The Commons," she repeated. "You see, just as Empaths and Elementals can be unfortunate enough to have a child without an ability, the inverse can happen as well. Miss Colray's birth parents lived in a ditch, and when their precious daughter showed signs of Empathic control, they sold her to a barren couple in the city. So here she is, a nobody from the Commons who got extremely lucky. However, Miss Colray's luck runs out now. Because ability. Is. Not. Talent."

"Master Grey, I'd like you to stop." Willow's voice was small but clear, her head bowing over her book.

Grey ignored her, straightening herself further. "With me, there will be no privilege or luck determining whether or not I recommend you to the High Council. You are all as equally low as Miss Colray."

Willow's shoulders began to shake, and the trees outside twisted, their branches *tap, tap, tapping* against the filthy cabin window. The room went green, and Elliott and Finn exchanged bewildered looks, but no one spoke up. No one.

"Stop crying," Grey demanded, fingers clenching into fists at her side. "It is a reality, Miss Colray. You should be relieved that despite your tainted lineage you get to—"

Crash. The sudden noise pulled everyone away from the slow torture at the front of the room, and Emily exhaled, thankful for the excuse to look away.

"What was that?" Grey demanded, her eyes molten in her hard face.

"Sorry, Master Grey," Catherine apologized from over a pile of fallen books.

For the first time since crossing the doorway, a hint of colour pooled in Grey's pearlescent cheeks. "Would you be more careful with your things?" Her eyes darted to the left and right as though in search of a hidden threat. The branches retracted, the pale daylight piercing the green once more.

Catherine's eyes flashed to Willow's curved back. There it was—a flicker of empathy, of humanity. For the remaining few hours, no one spoke unless asked to.

The wind howled, trees rustled against the dirty windowpanes, and Willow's tears dried on the pages of her notebook. When Grey dismissed them, Emily tried to catch Catherine's eye, but the girl sped out the door alone, Willow close on her heels.

Emily and Ozzy braved the cold night winds, making sure to stay close together, her heart too heavy to carry without help. They bolted for the castle, taking the stairs back up to North Tower two at a time. Emily never thought she would be happy to find the lounge full of rowdy initiates, but it was perfect for not being overheard. She sank into an armchair, the fire crackling between them as though it belonged in a different world, a happier place.

Grey.

"What she did to Willow . . . " Ozzy raked his fingers through his hair until it stood on its own. "I mean, I heard she was bad but—"

"It was Grey!" Emily blurted.

He blinked, nonplussed. "I know. That's what I was saying. She's a cow."

"No, you don't get it." Emily shook her head as the vision of cold, steel eyes sent a dagger through her chest. "The Blintwoods robbery. The hooded woman—it was *her*!"

"What?" Ozzy's voice cracked. "That can't be true."

"I'm positive! I told you I'd recognize her if I saw her again, and I'll never forget those eyes."

Ozzy frowned. "But you heard Horus. They watch her way too closely for her to do anything illegal."

"Whatever's in the box must be really important, then." Emily sagged into her seat. "She's one of the best

Elementals out there. She's a criminal, Ozzy! She helped my father murder all those innocent people, and she's still doing things behind the Masters' backs!"

He shook his head, eyes lost in the fire. "Okay, calm down. Let's talk about this. How did no one notice she was gone from the castle? Don't you think someone would have figured out she was running around Gildenveil City?"

There was an answer—she knew it. Then, realization struck like a hammer. "Grey was supposed to chaperone the Skytrain! She does it every year, but Master Fogg took her place."

Ozzy's eyes grew wide. "If you're sure about this, we should tell someone. Magdale seems to trust you."

Emily surprised herself by laughing, a short bark that was more animal that Elemental. "Oh yeah, they're really gonna take my word for it. I told you before, no one will believe me, Ozzy. Magdale might like me, but she knows I have a bit of a patchy history, and Grey is a Master. I can't win."

"Okay, then what? We let it go?" He chewed on his thumbnail, gnawing it down to the flesh.

Emily lowered her voice. "Victor."

With a groan, Ozzy reached into his bag and pulled out a small, cloth-bound book. "You told me Victor wouldn't tell you anything," he pointed out. "What makes you think he'll change his mind?"

"I wasn't talking about asking *him*."

"Look, you know I'll help you any way I can." He flipped through pages while his eyes remained unfocused. "But you're getting in deep here. If Grey's involved in something, we can't be caught anywhere near it."

The flames in the grate flickered, throwing burning confetti into the air. Orange and yellow and burgundy heat ate away at the old logs.

Selwyn castle was the answer to avoiding punishment for her previous life, it was true. How could she go back to the Commons to fight for those she left behind if she made no progress at the castle? But those silver eyes were on the path to destruction of both her past and her future. Leaving Grey alone went against every instinct she had. But worse still, letting Grey get away with whatever she planned meant watching her father's legacy continue to plague her for the rest of her life. She couldn't let that stand.

"I need to do this, Ozzy." She stared into the flames as though they held the answer to the sudden anger gripping her chest. "I won't ask you to take the same risks. But I can't stay out of this now. Grey is breaking the law and might actually get away with it."

Ozzy rolled his eyes. "Yeah, I figured. I'm in, whatever you need. Except if it involves dragons," he added, blanching. "No dragons, please."

Emily smiled. "Let's call that Plan B."

The rest of their first week passed in a flash, ending with an afternoon in Blackwood Cottage as the poisonous cherry on top. Emily and Ozzy stepped around the corner of the castle and made their way across the courtyard against the blustering wind. Beyond the trimmed lawn dusted with the first fallen leaves of the season, autumn was in full possession of Black Mountain; orange and yellow and red smattered the tops of the trees, setting the peaks ablaze.

"Whoever thought an afternoon with Grey in that stuffy cabin was a good way to end the week should be dragon food," Ozzy muttered. He cast a dark look at the edge of the trees where Blackwood Cottage lurked in the shadows.

"Don't remind me," Emily groaned, pulling her sweater higher over her ears. "Did you talk to Willow at all this week?"

Ozzy shook his head. "She's been pretty quiet. I can't get much out of her when I do see her, and she's been disappearing into her dorm a lot, anyway. You?"

"Same." Emily sighed. "I think she's still pretty shaken up."

"Well, I have some good news that might cheer you up," he said, fishing in his jacket pocket. A flash of navy against cream caught the afternoon light, and Ozzy waved the letter with a look of satisfaction. "Looks like you were right."

"What's that?" Emily asked.

"Proof Grey should have been the chaperone on the Skytrain. Here, have a look."

Emily took the paper with stiff fingers, a smile creeping across her face. "How did you get this?" she asked, looking down the list.

He beamed. "Every Master at the castle gets a schedule with things they need to do to prepare for a new year. This was Fogg's schedule."

Grey's name leapt off the page, inscribed in black ink next to the entry: '*September 29th, Fenvale Clearing, Skytrain, Incoming Initiates.*' Beside this was a handwritten note in sprawling letters reading, '*Replacement: A. Fogg.*'

Ozzy took the list back and shoved it back inside his coat. "I went by Fogg's office early this morning to ask about the Empath coaching we had this week, and she was asleep at her desk." He shook his head, suppressing a laugh. "Honestly, I don't think it's coffee in that mug of hers. Anyway, this was on her desk when I went to wake her up." He opened the door to Blackwood Cottage and exhaled with relief at Grey's absence. "Everyone had something to do, so it explains why no one noticed her missing. Murray was on a supply run in Black Mountain, Ward was cataloguing the library, and Magdale was off on a personal errand."

"So, I'm a *personal errand.*" Emily rolled her eyes. There were two empty seats left in the room; Willow hunched in the back corner with the vacant seat beside her holding her bag. With a pointed look, Ozzy sidled up next to Willow, leaving Emily to endure Catherine's glare of hostility in close range. Because getting close to Catherine was Plan A.

The door opened, and Grey prowled inside. "Veiling spells," Grey announced by way of greeting, "are simple enough to perform given the right level of concentration on the object you are trying to disguise. For an Elemental, they may focus on disguising an object or themselves, and for an Empath, shielding one's thoughts from others is a valuable skill. These are not to be confused with Transference, which causes an object to disappear. Veiling makes something invisible and is a necessary step to master before Transference."

Catherine sat bolt upright, a frown of concentration creasing the narrow space between her brows.

"The spell is *Concelium,*" Grey continued. "Focus your mind on the object you wish to conceal. If you are an Elemental sitting beside another of your kind, remain in your seats and work together. Empaths, Mister Shinkle, has the unfortunate ability to get into anyone's mind." She scowled in disgust, and Ozzy's cheeks flared. "He will be attempting to manipulate you in the most invasive way possible, and it is your job to try stopping him." She glanced around the room for the first time and closed her eyes as though meditating. "Did I say to take your time?"

Chairs scratched the dusty floor, books flipped open, and Ozzy staggered to his feet with a final look of sympathy from Willow. With a throbbing pain in her stomach, Emily grabbed her notebook and placed it on her desk. Catherine paged through her book, already mouthing the spell.

Say something, say something, say something. "I can make anything disappear and reappear somewhere else. I hope that makes things easier for me."

"*Concelium.*" A funnel of sand swirled under Catherine's hand, the tiny particles scratching against the wood. She repeated the spell once more, and the small cyclone twisted and danced but did not disappear from view.

"So you can manipulate dust?"

Catherine glared at the miniature tornado. "I can manipulate *air*. And this cabin is filthy, so my ability can be visible for once."

"Right." *Right? That's all you can say?* "I mean, that can be a really powerful ability to have." When Catherine continued to ignore her, Emily placed her hand onto the cover of her book and breathed deep, her pulse steady and her fingers electric. *Right, just focus on your own work, then.* "*Concelium,*" she muttered. The book flickered in and out of sight but remained solid under her fingers.

Catherine glanced at her sideways. "Showing off again?"

"I'm not showing off," Emily said, affronted.

"Then what do you call jumping on a dragon and playing hero on your first day?" Catherine retorted, her eyes stormy behind her glasses.

"You're not seriously throwing that in my face. How about a 'thanks, Emily' instead?"

Catherine threw her a scathing look. "Thank you? For humiliating me? I don't think so."

"Maybe you should try being mad at Camilla since she's the one who got you into that mess," Emily hissed as Grey tossed Finn's bag to the ground. His uncle would have been terrified.

"Trust me, I'm not thrilled with her either!"

It was becoming harder to keep her voice down. "Look, you don't like me because I'm a Rathburn. I get it. Can we practice before Grey turns us into snails or something?"

"I didn't like you at first because you're a Rathburn. I don't like you now because I just don't like you." Catherine lifted her hand over the desk once more. "I can be better at this magic stuff than you with some practice, you know."

Emily rolled her eyes. "Then stop yelling at me and focus on your windy dirt."

Catherine scowled but moved her arm in a smooth, calm motion through the air. "*Concelium*," she said, the words slow and clear. The sand faded from view for a full second before reappearing beside Emily's right hand. Catherine's jaw hinged open, her cheeks turning pink.

"That was good," Emily said, surprised the compliment was sincere. "Okay, my turn."

After a half hour, Emily had managed to veil her textbook for a full minute before losing hold of the spell, and Catherine had performed well enough to prevent any other outbursts. They slipped into an easy rhythm, moving back and forth, offering pointers to the other.

Catherine lifted her eyes from the sand cyclone and broke the heavy silence. "Why did you do it?"

Emily frowned. "Why did I do what?"

"You know. Help me. I've been a bit . . . tough with you."

"I hadn't noticed," Emily mumbled. She rested her hands on her lap, flexing her fingers to release the tension. "I didn't plan on helping you, so don't get any ideas. But if I had known how much you'd still hate me, I probably would have let the dragon eat you."

Catherine's lip twitched. "You're not so bad."

Emily grinned. Progress—it was small, but it was there. "By the way . . . thank you."

Catherine's brows pulled low. "For what?"

"Dropping your books to get Grey off Willow's case." Emily turned to where Willow patiently waited her turn for Ozzy to test her, hair pooling around her heart-shaped face. "She's my friend, and what you did for her was nice."

"It was an accident," Catherine corrected her, a wayward spell throwing her cyclone into an impressive somersault. "I'm clumsy."

"Right." Emily's answering smile was genuine. "Well, thanks for being accident prone."

It was now or never.

"So . . . you said you're mad at Camilla?" Emily weighed and measured her words, her tone, her expression. *Nice and slow*. She waited for Catherine's response, her breathing shallow.

"She almost got me eaten by a big lizard, so yeah." Catherine's face darkened, bitterness creeping back into her voice.

"Want to talk about it?"

"With you?" Catherine asked. "Not really."

Emily gathered herself, bracing for the hit. "Her and Graven seem close? Aren't you friends with him, too?"

The result was instantaneous. Shutters slammed behind Catherine's stormy eyes and any semblance of warmth between them evaporated. "Why?"

Back up—slow down and back up. "Well, you don't seem to like him, either. Did something happen?"

"Camilla and Victor can do what they want. If she wants to follow Graven around like a baby dragon, she can go right ahead." Her eyes flashed. "I hear she might have some competition."

That's new. "Huh?"

Catherine rolled her eyes. "Don't pretend you didn't notice. Victor likes to think he's everyone's gift to the realm, but he finds you *extra* special. It's driving Camilla crazy," she finished with a sly grin.

"That's probably why he's trying so hard to be my friend," Emily reasoned, hoping she sounded as casual as she could. "You must know his parents, then, if you were all so close. I heard his father was at the Blintwoods robbery."

Catherine whirled in her seat, and Emily recoiled at once. "Look, let's get this straight," she said, voice calm.

"We aren't friends. I don't know what you're getting at, but I won't be talking about Camilla or Victor or anyone else with you. Why isn't this stupid spell working properly? *Concelium!*" she bellowed, slashing her hand through the air.

A wall of air rushed out of Catherine's hand, splintering their desk and sending the pieces soaring. *Oh no.* Tina Lee screamed in surprise, her hands jumping out of her lap. *No, no,* no! Tina's desk burst into flames, sending a blast of heat around the cabin. Initiates flew from their seats, and tables squealed out of the way as the fire began eating away at the room, bit by combustible bit.

"*Enough*!" Grey snapped her fingers, and the flames vanished, Tina's charred desk giving off a defeated hiss. Grey breathed hard, her cheeks high with colour and her eyes like flint. "Who did this?"

Catherine floundered, tears pooling behind her glasses. "I didn't—"

"It's my fault," Emily interjected. From the corner of her eye, Ozzy gawked at her. "I was distracting Catherine, and she lost control."

"You." A statement, not a question. Emotions played across Grey's twisted face. She pressed her lips into a fine line and glowered at Emily with naked hate. "Of course it's *your* fault."

Emily nodded. Waited. Unspoken words passed between them, Emily's memory of what happened at Blintwoods reflected in Grey's flat eyes.

"Miss Bonner," Grey hissed. "You'll be coming back here tomorrow morning to summarize the importance of proper technique in veiling spells for me. And you won't be leaving until I'm satisfied you will never be distracted again. And *you*, Miss Rathburn, will be joining me tomorrow evening to clean this place up. Sundown. Don't be late."

"Yes, Master Grey," Emily muttered. Catherine retreated into her books, but Emily didn't have the energy to keep pretending to be interested in veiling spells or Catherine's secrets. It was time for Plan B.

Grey in a Corner

SATURDAY MEANT REST AND LATE dinners and casual parties back in the dormitories, but Emily's first weekend at Selwyn's was set to kick off with a date with Sable Grey. Ozzy, Horus, and Piper were huddled with mugs of hot chocolate and a glittering display of rainbow waterfalls trickling over the spitting fire, courtesy of Piper. And, although it pained Emily to peel herself away from them for the inferno of Blackwood Cottage, catching Master Ward in his office on the way out of the castle was a welcome distraction.

"A little early to be getting into so much trouble, don't you think?" Ward chuckled as he crammed various books and stray bits of parchment into his bag. His office was bare, the walls a plain brown stone, the one window behind him no bigger than a peephole. Every flat surface of his desk held a quill, candies wrapped in translucent paper, scraps of parchment with words scribbled in a rushed hand, or a bottle half-filled with ink. His gloved hands fumbled through the pile with little grace.

"Think you can get me out of this thing with Master Grey tonight, sir?" Emily slumped under the weight of her bag and the upcoming evening. Her clothes fit well, for once, but that meant they were too tight, too *stiff* for her liking. "I'd appreciate the help."

He laughed. "I wouldn't attempt to go against Master Grey. You'll have to take the punishment, I'm afraid."

Her heart fell. "This has to be some record. I didn't mean to get on her bad side so fast."

"I can't be sure, but I think your father would have had you beat." He chuckled. "He had a rather large mouth and a difficult time keeping it shut."

Emily looked up, startled. "You knew him?"

Ward smiled at some memory, eyes staring into the distance. "We were schoolmates, and he was one of my best friends."

"Was he . . . I mean, what was he like when he was here?" Her father had always been a blank face in her mind; first, one of kindness, of love to make her long for the man she never knew. But recently, he'd become a menacing shadow threatening her entire future, and she couldn't long for that.

"I didn't see any sign of what he would become, if that's what you're truly asking," Ward said. "He was charming, intelligent, big-hearted, and, despite being an absolute pain, loved by everyone. No matter how things turned out, there *was* good in him."

Emily's thoughts turned dark. "Apparently not enough of it."

Ward locked eyes with her, clear pools of green. "You're strong, are you not? Compassionate? Resourceful? Do you think you'd be any of those things had you grown up differently?"

Emily crossed her arms, refusing to feel anything other than resentment for the faceless man in her mind. "Guess we'll never know."

The sun set outside their window, shadows creeping down Ward's face. "There are beginnings to every end, Emily. It only takes a bit of time and distance to realize sometimes, the best way to start new is for something we cared about to leave us." His eyes grew wide, and he jerked his arm too quickly, toppling a stack of notes to the floor like a dozen helicopter seeds from a maple tree. "If I don't stop talking, you're going to be late!"

Emily groaned as Ward bent to pick up his things. "Master Ward, you can take your gloves off around me. I don't think you're going to sneak up on me and steal all my power."

Ward smiled, but his eyes were distant. Sad. "I've gotten quite used to the gloves. I'd rather be safe and have them on, just in case. And, as for your night with Master Grey, I daresay it won't be pleasant, but a punishment isn't supposed to be. Come on," he urged, picking up his overstuffed bag and ushering her toward the door. "I'll walk with you. I've been meaning to have a word with her for some time, anyhow."

Gratitude rushed over her as she shouldered her bag and made for the courtyard. They walked in companionable silence, the echoes of laughter and the warm scent of dinner—lentil soup and braised lamb—bidding them a cheery goodbye as they marched to Blackwood Cottage.

Ward's gaze settled, transfixed, on Black Mountain lurking underneath the burning sky and fog.

Emily followed Ward's gaze and ignored the unsettling noises rustling the bushes behind the cabin. "It's a shame we can't go up there."

"It is," he agreed, his tone light.

"I wonder why they're scared of the fog." Dark twigs littered the pristine lawn, crunching under her sneakers as she walked.

"As do I, Miss Rathburn." Ward considered the sharp debris on the ground. "I wonder that very much indeed."

The door of Blackwood Cottage creaked open, and Ward smiled at Emily with bleak encouragement. "She's not that bad. Do what she says without argument. But," he said with a small smile, "don't be shy to take a poke around. I'll bet she has more than a few interesting things to pass the time hidden away in that cottage of hers."

"Did you say something, Master Ward?" Grey stood in the shadows, her figure materializing through the doorway.

"Sable! I was telling Miss Rathburn that tonight is going to go smoothly. Selwyn's is quite punishment-averse, after all." Ward beamed at Grey, and Emily fought the urge to jump in between them.

Grey eyed him with open dislike. "A little *too* punishment-averse, if you ask me. Sometimes a tighter fist is needed to crush the weak from the masses."

"Ah, well, maybe one's definition of weak needs to be adjusted." He smiled despite the heat in Grey's cheeks and the sharp edges of her jaw.

"Speaking of fists," Grey said, "it's a bit warm for gloves. Are you feeling all right?" She advanced, and

Ward took an automatic step back. Her eyes flashed, a small smile pulling at her thin mouth.

"You know the stigma I face because of what I am." His words fell flat, his fingers clenching. "I'd rather avoid the trouble altogether. I suppose you see that as weakness as well."

"I do indeed." Grey rolled her eyes and stepped aside. "As riveted by this conversation as I am, I do have some menial labour to supervise which, contrary to what many may think, is not the way I enjoy spending my time."

"Of course," Ward said. "As long as we're getting straight to business, you wouldn't mind my coming inside to take a peek at your stores, would you? I've heard you have quite the assortment of spell books, and I'd very much like to have a look." He craned his neck, but it was pitch black inside the cottage with little to see.

"I do mind. I'm sure you can find what you're looking for in the library. You seem comfortable there."

"Maybe some other time, then," he replied, bowing his head. "Well, Miss Rathburn, I bid you an excellent evening."

Emily waved a weak goodbye. "Thanks for the walk."

"Remember," he said under his breath. "Don't argue and keep your head up." With that, he trudged back to the castle, the shadows swallowing him.

Emily slid past Grey, careful not to let any part of her touch the woman's heavy cloak. Tina's charred relic of a desk stood like a solitary lump of coal in the middle of the floor, a slopping bucket and brush sitting beside it.

"You are to clean and arrange the contents of my storeroom." Grey indicated the open cupboard with a small glint of pleasure in her cold eyes. "When you are done, you will clean the desk you vandalized until I am satisfied."

Emily registered the heaps of tattered furniture and books overflowing from the supply room. "But that'll take all night!"

"I daresay it will," Grey replied with a satisfied smile.

Seething, Emily dropped her bag by the fire and marched across the room. A mess of old, dusty spell books and grimy odds and ends poked out of the mess. She pushed back her hair, ignoring the feel of Grey's eyes on her back.

"Is there any particular order you want this in, Master Grey?" Emily asked.

"Just do the work, and I'll let you know if I like it."

Hours passed in slow torture. Emily's hands burned with fresh splinters, her feet and shoulders throbbing with the effort of shifting what appeared to be decades of clutter. The moon was high by the time she had managed some semblance of order and could move on to the desks. She scrubbed away the soot with a stiff brush, knuckles cracked and peeling. When the first rays of dawn fought their way into the cabin, Grey pushed her chair away from her desk with a screech.

"I think that's enough." Grey yawned loudly, her own features dirt- and sweat-free. She tossed her keys on the podium at the front of the room and stretched. "You might be able to get in a quick nap before breakfast, but be sure you're not late for your first lesson. We wouldn't want to have any more missteps on your record." Grey threw open the door and moved toward the forest, head held high.

"Miserable hag," Emily cursed under her breath. She tossed her brush into the black, muddy water and pushed herself up to her feet, knees throbbing. Emily swung the storeroom door shut with a distinctive slam, relishing the noise.

The morning air was a relief as she stormed across the courtyard, the idea of food and sleep keeping her feet moving, but only just. Bushes rustled and cracked behind her, but she was too tired to care if an animal attacked her; at least that would mean some recovery time in bed. Selwyn's glistened with fresh dew like a mountain encrusted with diamonds—beautiful if not for the heavy weight of sleep threatening to take her down where she stood.

With a gasp, she stopped moving. *You've got to be kidding me.* While her body moved closer to North Tower, her bag was back at Blackwood Cottage. The temptation to leave it behind was overwhelming, but she couldn't abandon her things.

She raced back, all hopes of sleep tossed aside. The cottage door was still ajar when she poked her head inside the musty room. "Hello?" she called. Her bag sat in a lump by the hearth with no sign of Grey.

Emily hurried inside, shuddering at the sight of the open storeroom taunting her. In the growing dawn, the desks and chairs arranged in neat rows cast predictable shadows across the flagstone. One slice of darkness cut the room on a diagonal, running from the edge of the fireplace, across her bag and over the floor. She ran her free hand down the length of the stone. *Is this a door?* Narrow, wide enough to wedge her fingers behind.

The morning was quiet, peaceful.

I should go. Emily tugged on the mantel.

A low groan sounded as the gap widened. Another tug. Her heart kicked like a mule against her ribs.

Pull harder.

Emily's palms slipped over the rough, cool stone. The wall crept open. She glanced over her shoulder, expecting to see Grey looming over her and finding nothing but her guilt. *Ka-thug, ka-thug, ka-thug.* Her pulse bumped in her ears, the air gusting out from behind the hidden wall cold. Musky.

With one last look at the door, she slid behind the fire.

The room had no windows; four moss-covered walls stared back at her with a loneliness that echoed in some deep part of her heart. A singular torch burned above a narrow bed frame made of plain steel. An old dresser stood in the far corner, piled high with books and yellowed sheets of parchment. No pictures, no colours, no personal touches. And yet, the bed, the dresser, the collection of books . . .

Does she live *here?* Power thrummed in even currents down Emily's arms, and she tiptoed into the room, hands pressed to her side. The spell books were peeling, the parchment dotted with handwritten notes and faded ink. Familiar words sprung out from the pile, and Emily knew she couldn't turn back—not yet.

"*Blintwoods Under Fire, by Elie Quinn.*" Emily leafed through the rest of the stack with a sense of satisfaction: articles, handwritten spells, and clippings detailing disappearances, murders, or both. The books were equally strange: "*A History of Selwyn Castle—Dark Beginnings,*" she muttered, reading through the titles. "*Migellus—An Autobiography, Binding Spells Through the Ages.* What's she got all this for?"

A branch cracked outside the cabin, and Emily jumped. She stumbled back to the open wall and peeked into the cottage. Alone—for now. With her exit clear, she edged out, pushed the wall shut, and grabbed her bag.

Grey was involved in something bigger than one attempted theft. *Disappearances, murders, spells . . .* It all led back to whatever was being kept at Blintwoods. Something in Zaphira's old shop was important enough to jeopardize Grey's future at Selwyn's.

Whatever was hidden in the city was big enough to murder for, to bring back a past that had evaporated with the disappearance of Baxter Rathburn. But Grey wouldn't get what she wanted. Emily wouldn't allow it.

Days turned into weeks, and neither Emily nor Ozzy had managed to make anything of Grey's collection of notes. The chilly drafts of autumn seeped into the cracks of the castle like a poison, and winter whispered through the shivering trees like a promise. To make matters worse, Catherine and Camilla had rekindled their twisted friendship, the two girls inseparable once again with one small difference: Catherine was taking her incompetence with spells seriously, spending more time with a book in her hands and her backside in a library chair than with her nose in the air.

"Don't you believe in breaks?" Ozzy moaned. He cleared the last step up to North Tower with a huff, arms laden with yet another haul of library books. "We looked at all the books you remembered from Grey's room. There's nothing important in them."

"C'mon, Ozzy." Emily tried to sound cheerful over her own ominous stack as they melted through the door to North Tower, the effect like passing through a pool of cool water, but the effort was exhausting. "It's not so b— ouch!" The toe of her sneaker snagged on the carpet, and she stumbled, her books teetering in her arms.

"What happened?" Ozzy threw his stack onto a vacant table in the lounge with a huff.

Emily scanned the ground and sighed. "I'm so tired I'm tripping over my own feet." She settled into her favourite chair by the fire while the faint sound of dragon cries shook the windows, the voices high and playful and much too soft to be anything as large as Titan—hatchlings. *Cute.*

"Another reason to take a break," Ozzy said with a dark look at his bag. "What did you end up taking?"

Emily thumbed through the titles. "I've got volumes three through seven of the *Migellus Chronicles* and *Ancient Spells for Ancient Minds Who Can Still Remember That Far Back.*"

Ozzy slumped in his chair. "Migellus has been all over the world and discovered too many magical artefacts to count. We'll be here all year trying to pinpoint what Grey was after if it's got to do with Migellus. And I've already been over binding spells. They link you to an object, but you have to see and touch what you're binding yourself to. Not useful to us."

Emily frowned. "One thing is still bothering me, though."

He snorted. "Only one?"

She tossed a book from hand to hand. "I know I've heard of Migellus before, but I can't remember where."

"He's famous. You probably read his name some-where." Ozzy pulled the Scroll out of his bag and began flipping through headlines with a practiced hand. "Have you spoken to Catherine at all lately?" A loud *thump* across the room cut them off, a book falling off a shelf or a door slamming shut. "You know, since that day with Grey and the fire."

Emily shook her head. "She's talking to Camilla again, so I think Catherine's a lost cause."

Ozzy rolled his eyes. "I don't get you girls—enemies one day, swapping first kiss stories the next. Didn't you say Catherine wasn't so bad on her own?"

"She isn't," Emily said. "I think I'd even like her if she wasn't so determined to hate me. Anyway, Victor was our only lead, and he hasn't spoken to me since the Thorny Truth incident. So, get comfy with the books."

Ozzy's eyes flew wide, and his fingers gripped the Scroll tight. "There's something here about Blintwoods! Listen to this: *'Where Is Zaphira?', by Elie Quinn. On September the 29th, local safe-shop and rare supply dis-tributor, Blintwoods, suffered a rare and worrisome breach. An explosion, now confirmed to have occurred in order to gain access to a mysterious security box on the property, marked the shop's first attempted robbery in nearly a millennium. While it seems the box in question remains intact, further inspection of the scene by Guard Official Gideon Reinhold and witness to the explosion, Christopher Graven, report a fair amount of damage to the premises.'"*

Emily gripped the edge of their table. "Christopher Graven. There's Victor's father again."

Ozzy nodded. "According to this, he was in Blint-woods when the thief set off the explosion, and he's been involving himself with the investigation."

"Anything about what was in the box? Or about me being there?"

"No," Ozzy said, and Emily's relief was bittersweet. While no news about her in the Scroll was good news, she still needed to know what Grey was after. Ozzy ran his finger across the parchment, and the letters grew larger: "'Shopkeeper Zaphira, who has been entrusted with the welfare of the realm's most valuable goods and possessions, is now considered a missing person. The Blintwoods Empath has not been seen for approximately one month, a length of time unusual for her character and position within realm security. While Zaphira's magical safeguards are seemingly still operational, one must wonder for how long that will remain true.'" Ozzy scanned the rest of the article. "It looks like they're launching a full investigation into Zaphira's disappearance."

"This is crazy!" Frustration exploded from Emily's fingers in shocks and waves. "There's nothing about Grey, either?"

Ozzy shook his head. "I think they're focusing on Zaphira since nothing was taken."

"But it could happen again!"

"I know." He gripped her hand, fingers warm. "I'm sure they're doing everything they can."

"It's not enough," she groaned. "Every day that we don't find proof of what Grey's doing is another day she gets away with stuff like this! And now I can't even ask Victor what he knows because he already shut me out."

Ozzy's gaze drifted to the fire, the flames dancing across his pale face. "What if I have a way to crack him?"

"You?"

His face fell. "You don't have to sound so surprised." He fished through the stack of books with a crooked smile. "I have an idea."

Emily soon discovered Halloween was a huge affair at Selwyn castle. The last days of October brought a decrease in concentration and a drastic uptick in the awkward social habits Emily never understood; girls flocked down the halls in droves, discussing costumes, dates, and plans for a big celebration, while the boys wandered around with minds full of hope and not much else.

Emily and Ozzy, however, had other priorities. The week of Halloween was filled with nothing but plotting the small details of Ozzy's idea until both of them were certain they could do nothing more but wish for some luck. North Tower was quiet as the initiates drank in the last snow-free days by Black Mountain, but Emily's mind was a storm of worry. If they failed, would Grey do worse than kidnapping a defenceless Empath from the city? But if they succeeded . . .

The idea of being the one to erase her father's stain on her life was a temptation she would never admit was just as important to her as justice. With questions flowing through her mind, she left Ozzy in the lounge, exhausted and nervous, and pushed open the door to her dormitory.

Tina sat cross-legged on her bed, a spell book open on her lap and a quill tucked behind her ear. She smiled as Emily walked in, her hair blue under the low light of a candle. "Hey, Emily. I thought you'd never get back.

You have a visitor." She nodded at the open window, eyes shining.

A shadow shifted at her windowsill, a torso leaning on her ledge. "Victor?" she asked, bewildered.

"Hey there, Rathburn." Victor's smile was a bright spot in the darkness. *Ugh, why does he always have to look so . . . happy?* "Bad time?"

"Well, it's not a *good* time. What are you doing here?" She dragged her feet across the floor and stuck her head out into the cold. Left, right. She squinted at the tower wall, aware of his eyes on her, the smell of him up close. "How did you get up here?"

"Levitation, Rathburn. I'm pretty good, right?"

With a frown, Emily backed away until there was enough distance between them. "What's wrong with you? Why are you out here so late?"

"Shhh!" His face contorted in mock anger. "Your voice carries. How are you going to explain this if people come to see what's wrong?"

"Same way I'll explain how you ended up maimed if you don't leave," she retorted.

He grinned. "I love it when you get mad. It's like a kitten with claws."

I'm too tired for this. "Goodnight, Victor." Emily reached over to close the window, but he raised his arm across the open frame to stop her.

"Okay, okay, I'll be serious." With an easy push, he hoisted himself onto the sill and sat facing her. "Magdale wants a progress report on how you're doing, and I don't like looking bad with the Masters around here. We need to schedule another meeting."

"No thanks."

He raised his hands in defeat. "You're right, that was a pretty bad pitch. Let me try again. Please, oh please, join me in a serious and completely innocent activity after hours."

Tina buried her face in her book, eyes not moving over the page, and Emily sighed. "Victor, it's late, and there is no way I have the energy for this right now."

"Then don't fight me on this, for a change." He nestled into the frame as though the wood and steel were comfortable. "You still need to work, and I'm still assigned to help you. So can you let me tell you the plan before you shoot it down?"

If there was anything Emily had learned about Victor Graven, it was that nothing was ever cut and dry. "Look, if I agree to another meeting, you'll leave? Right now?"

His eyes were wide, innocent. Untrustworthy. "I'll let you get to bed and won't bother you until I see you next. Deal?"

She exhaled. It was as good as she was going to get, especially when she was too tired to spar with him. "Fine."

Victor's eyes crinkled, and a small dimple formed in one cheek, something she'd never noticed before. "Good. I'll be in touch with the details."

"*Fine.*"

He didn't leave.

"Are you going to the feast tomorrow?" he asked, inspecting a patch of dirt on the heel of his shoe.

Emily pressed her nails into her palms to keep from screaming. "I thought you said you would leave."

"That's a yes, then." He nodded, thoughtful. "You have a date?"

"Goodnight, Victor."

Victor turned to Tina, who had abandoned all pretence of minding her own business and was watching them both with rapt interest. "Do *you* know who she's going with?"

Tina smirked. "If I did, I wouldn't tell you."

Emily closed the window on his nose with a satisfying snap, forcing him out into the dark. The last thing she needed was to let Victor Graven into her mind when getting into *his* was more important.

Chapter Fifteen

Tricks and Treats

THE NEXT MORNING, THE ENTIRE castle woke in a buzz of excitement. Streamers and pumpkins decorated the halls, live bats hung upside down in the classrooms, and even the wind got into the Halloween spirit, shaking the castle windows with its frigid breath. Emily sat in the Gallery among a sea of distracted initiates, Old Gwendolyn swaying overhead with the hum of excitement.

The fairies were in full form, too; thousands of vibrant white lights darted overhead, nestling deep in the ruddy tree roots until the entire Gallery glittered. Emily couldn't appreciate any of it. She had tossed and turned most of the night, a comfortable position impossible to find despite the thick mattress and down blanket. Catherine looked no better than Emily felt; dark circles bruised her eyes as she struggled to pay attention to Victor and Camilla, who were much too involved in their own conversation to notice anything but themselves.

"I'm going to vomit," Ozzy moaned over a full dish. As though hearing him, Old Gwendolyn's roots snapped to attention and slithered out of dodge.

Emily stifled a yawn. "Is it the nerves or the fact that we have Flight in fifteen minutes?"

"Ugh!" He dropped his face into his hands and began to hyperventilate. "Please tell me this is a bad idea. It's a bad idea that's going to get us nowhere with Victor, and we'll get kicked out of the castle. Why can't you ask him again? I'm sure if you're nice to him . . . "

Emily threw Ozzy a sympathetic look. "I can't start asking questions and pretending I'm his friend. Look, I know it's not the best plan, but it's the best we've got. And if it works, we're going to get some information out of Victor. If it doesn't . . . well, I'm used to living on the streets." She chuckled at Ozzy's bewildered expression and got up with a satisfying stretch. "Come on. We can't be late."

Today's lesson was important; not only had Fenstorm banned live dragons from their lessons since their first day, but Emily's entire plan hinged on getting access to Titan. She led the way out of the castle and let the brisk wind jolt her awake. Each step was outlined in her mind like every important plan always was, but none of it mattered if she couldn't fulfill her part. The initiates huddled together against the cold, but no one minded the weather with the promise of a party that night.

"Welcome, everyone." Fenstorm's breath came in small puffs, his face redder than usual. "You all must have your minds on the celebration tonight, so I'll be sure to keep this light. Just some basic body positions today, okay?"

Ozzy nudged Emily in the ribs, and she raised her hand. Cleared her throat. *Breathe.* "Sorry, Master Fenstorm?"

"Yes?" Fenstorm squinted against the wind, perplexed.

"Since today is a special occasion, I was wondering if, maybe, we could try riding a dragon again." Her tongue was dry in her mouth, her fingers numb.

Everyone but Finn and Ozzy sparked with excitement. Finn teetered on the spot and, despite knowing the details of their plan, Ozzy turned the exact colour of congealed oatmeal.

"I don't think that will be necessary," Fenstorm muttered to a smattering of disappointed groans. "What? You all remember what happened, don't you? I didn't sleep for a week after that!"

"But don't we need to know how to handle an actual dragon at some point, sir?" Emily pressed. "Or else, what's the point of even having us here. The Guard won't take us because we can read a book, will they?"

"Yeah, please, sir," Ozzy said, his voice an unimpressive monotone.

Their group broke out into nods and pleas of agreement, the loudest being Elliott, who had grown to double his size from enthusiasm. Emily let it all unfold, her fingers cold and her heart racing.

"Fine, fine!" Fenstorm boomed, and the day grew quiet. "I'll get the dragons, but I want no funny business, understood? You follow my orders, you stand where I tell you to, and you step away when I say so. Miss Rathburn, since this was your idea, you'll stay after class and help me round up the herd."

That's even better. Excitement made her heart pound, but Emily nodded, serene.

Fenstorm closed his eyes, his worn features smoothing over. The air around him rippled, undulated, waves like sonar strong enough to bend the trees to his will rippling the grass. Within seconds, dragon song broke out from the sky. The air shattered into music, and it was no longer cold; the confusion of flapping wings and excited clicks broke out over the courtyard like an oncoming battle. Titan's red and navy stood out from the sea of green and grey, and something inside Emily relaxed.

One by one, the dragons landed with a quaking thump. Their nostrils flared, tongues lapping at the sky, tasting the wind. Titan tucked his wings to his side and crawled over to Emily, the rest of the initiates giving him a wide berth.

"Hey, Tite." Emily smiled as he snorted smoke into her face. "It's good to see you, too."

"Well, it looks like Rathburn's on the right track." Fenstorm nodded, one quick movement of the chin. "See what she's doing?"

"Playing with a deadly lizard?" Finn said. Emily laughed and patted Titan again.

"No, Dashwood," Fenstorm continued. "She's letting her mount smell her. That's how they get to decide whether or not they want to eat you. Go on, you all asked for this!" Each of them chose a dragon, Ozzy and Finn both remaining a safe distance away from their own small mounts. "Now, if they sniff you and start blowing smoke in your face, you can go ahead and climb on.

They're still young, so the predator instinct isn't strong, and none have an established bond, so it shouldn't be too difficult. But," he continued, his mouth disappearing into a thin line, "if they rear up on their back legs . . . well, you lot look like you can run fast."

Paffos curled up on the ground by the trees as though asleep, except for one yellow eye swivelling over them. One by one, the dances began; smoke blanketed the grass, and the initiates grew quiet. Catherine's dragon wriggled with impatience, its pale blue talons clawing tunnels into the ground while Ozzy hopped in circles around a smaller grey dragon teetering on the edge of sleep. Emily stroked Titan's strong neck, the low thrum of happiness in his throat sending vibrations through his entire body.

"Okay, Tite," she said with a final stroke of his head. "I'm coming up."

Her foot found the familiar groove under his wing. She gripped one of his scales and pushed off the ground, swinging her other leg over his neck. It was easier this time; the planes of his back and the grooves in his scales were familiar and warm. "Let's show off a bit. What do you think?"

Titan growled and unfurled his wings, flexing them beside him. With a delicate snort, he launched them skyward, high enough to leave the world behind but still close enough to see the courtyard tracing the outskirts of the castle up to the cliffside.

Emily knew their plan was risky, but up in the air, none of it mattered. Despite a few rocky turns where Titan's enthusiasm had her slipping dangerously low on his back, they sailed the skies as one. Soon, they were joined by the rest of their group, and the clouds were peppered with dragons. The remainder of the morning passed without any tears or loss of limb. So, when Fenstorm ordered them back down to earth, it was with disappointed groans.

"All right, settle down!" Fenstorm called. "That wasn't too bad. Shinkle, Dashwood—let's work on maybe touching your dragons next time, please?" Ozzy and Finn stood shoulder to shoulder, both ashen. "Dragons go back to their den," the Flight Master continued. "Rathburn, I'll show you how to change their stone nesting and feed them. The rest of you," he finished with a hint of a smile, "nice job."

Emily gave Ozzy a small wave as he headed off with Elliott and Finn. Without a word, the dragons took off in one giant flock, Paffos leading the charge. "Where are they going?" Emily asked, following Fenstorm across the courtyard.

"I like to let them fly back to their den on their own after a training like this," Fenstorm said, his voice a low grunt. "Lets them feel like a family without us humans getting in the way." He blew into his large, calloused hands for warmth and led Emily down the tree line. "Now, when we get there, don't get close to their snouts—they'll be hungry, and I don't want any accidents. You can Transfer things by touching them, right?" Emily nodded, and Fenstorm's features relaxed. "Good. That little talent'll come in handy with changing their nests."

The dragons' den was a deep cave carved into the northern base of the castle. The reek of sulphur mixed with the thick ash to form a haze billowing out of the cave, obscuring the iron bars that caged in the animals.

Fenstorm walked through the open gate first, heading for the rows of miniature caves punched into the rock on either side of the cave.

"Each of these little alcoves is a den for one dragon. Kind of like a large beehive. And every alcove is occupied, so it's a big job. Food's here." He kicked the side of a large metal bin overflowing with slimy red meat. "And the fresh stones are here."

Emily glanced at the tall pile of grey granite blocks stacked in the middle of the cave. "You usually do this yourself, sir?"

"It doesn't have to be done too often," he grumbled. "Nest needs changing a few times a year, and the feeding part goes quick." He lapsed into silence and clapped his hands once. "Get to it, then! Oh, and Rathburn . . . you have a real skill with that dragon."

"Thank you, sir," she said, the first twinges of guilt twisting her stomach.

Just as Fenstorm had predicted, tending to the dragons was easy work for her. Emily's fingers hummed over every boulder until they disappeared into the alcoves. After a while, the smoke thickened to a soot black as the rumbling grew louder. Emily coughed, moving to the bucket of raw animal hide. The horrible snarls of ripping flesh dripped a chill down her neck. Titan peered out at her from one of the miniature caves and she smiled, tossing him the largest piece of meat she could find.

"I'll see you later." Emily backed out of the den and closed the gate behind her, the lock dangling free.

The sun set on Halloween day, but the night stretched ahead. Emily and Ozzy put the final touches on their costumes and made their way through a maze of carved pumpkins, real spiderwebs, and flickering candlelight. The Gallery doors stood wide open, orange light from the roaring fires pouring into the entrance hall. Masked and painted faces prowled inside, bodies swaying to the eerie music. Tables covered in rich, black velvet formed a horseshoe around the room, and Old Gwendolyn's roots curled around the legs of the furniture as though they would be dining off the old tree herself.

Emily stood in the doorway, colourful dresses flitting around her in a blur, and smirked at Ozzy. "Did your mother know how ridiculous that costume would make you look?"

He adjusted his large hat shaped like a lizard's head, pulled down the sleeves of his green unitard, and shrugged. "Sometimes I think she does it on purpose. I mentioned *one time* that I thought lizards were cute, and she makes me a giant reptile for Halloween. She even gave it a tail!" He turned, flipping the long, scale-covered rope attached to the back of his costume with a groan of disgust.

Elliott pushed through the crowd with Finn in tow and smiled at them. "I think it suits you!" He winked, red metallic breastplates jangling across his chest.

"What are you supposed to be, Fitzgibbons?" Ozzy asked.

Elliott puffed up his chest. "Isn't it obvious? I'm a dragon!"

Ozzy peered down at his tail and frowned. "I should have said I was a dragon instead of a stupid lizard," he muttered. "So, Finn, what happened? Didn't want to dress up tonight?"

Finn, however, wore plain linen pants and a collared shirt. "Costumes are ridiculous. Parties are a perfect way to communicate all sorts of diseases, but Elliott made me come. Looks like Emily and I had the same idea," he added, appraising her with a nod of approval. "You didn't dress up either."

Emily grinned, pointing to her black headband decorated with two black circles over her greyest and shabbiest outfit. "Sure, I did. I'm a rat."

Elliott clapped Finn across the shoulders. "See? Everyone's getting in the spirit. Look at those girls over there. Or there." He pointed randomly into the crowd, scanning the room for eligible targets. "Don't they look like they might like a little communicated disease? Eh? Ha!" He nudged an unwilling Finn over to the closest cluster of unsuspecting girls. "See you later!"

With a quick wave, Emily released her breath. She scanned the room once, then again. "I don't see them."

"They'll be here," Ozzy reassured her. "Just keep looking."

"Hello, you two!" Willow's pale face erupted from an enormous unicorn's head. "Great party, don't you think?"

"Yeah, it's fantastic," Ozzy said, torn between watching the room and gawking at Willow's elaborate outfit.

"Nice costume, Willow." Emily grinned. "I didn't even recognize you."

"Thanks!" She beamed. "I made it myself. Oh, by the way, Victor Graven's looking for you, Emily. Are you dating him?"

"Huh?" The mention of Victor's name in casual conversation threw her, the heat in her face making Ozzy's eyes roll. "Oh, no, never. At all. Ever." She adjusted her costume ears and crossed her arms over her chest.

"Oh, okay. That's a shame though—he's really nice to look at." She peered around the room and pulled her headpiece over her eyes.

Emily offered the girl a warm smile. "Grey's not here, Willow. You don't have to be scared of her. She won't do anything to you, especially not with so many of us around."

"Right." Willow blushed, toying with the bright tassel hanging off the end of her tail. "I know. She wouldn't even show up to the party anyway. But I'd avoid her all the same, especially right now."

"Why?" Emily asked.

"She's on the warpath." A worried look pinched Willow's eyes, and she lowered her voice. "I saw her pulling initiates aside, asking them if they took her keys and her old textbook on veiling spells. She doesn't like you very much, Emily, so I'd stay out of her way."

"Right." Emily sighed. "Thanks for the heads-up. And, uh . . . you won't tell Victor you saw me, right?"

Willow shrugged. "Not if you don't want me to. Oh, and we all saved you a seat—usual spot. I have to visit the ladies' first and I . . . um . . . might be a while. Costume's a bit complicated." With a final wave, she flitted away as fast as her hooves would allow, tipping over a display of carved pumpkins with her impressive tail.

Emily couldn't tell what she was eating or drinking; the food was too heavy in her constricted chest, the drink too cold on her flushed lips. The music blared. Their plan would never work. Horus and Piper laughed, and Willow mentioned her parents, the Commons, something about plants. The lights dimmed, and Emily shifted in her seat, eyes straining to stay on target: Victor and Camilla.

Focus.

Once the dance began, it was easier to spot the pair wearing matching costumes of red velvet and frills—something too formal for a Halloween party but elaborate enough to mirror their embellished egos. Couples and small groups filtered onto the dance floor, obscuring her view of Victor's table until Emily was ready to crawl out of her skin.

"Yes, I love this song!" Horus announced, pulling Piper to the center of the floor. "You two coming?"

Emily shook her head. "Sorry, I don't dance."

"Plus, I think my head's too big," Ozzy added, pointing to his drooping green hat. Horus stifled a laugh, already twirling Piper on the spot, and Ozzy groaned. "How are we supposed to keep track of Victor and Camilla in this mess?"

"Just keep your eyes open for a really snotty girl dressed in frills throwing rocks at defenceless animals and you'll find Camilla," she grumbled. "Have you seen Catherine?"

"Nope. One less person to worry about." Ozzy looked at her, pleading, as Victor rose from his seat. "Maybe we can do this another night. You know, when there's less of a mess and I don't have a five-pound embarrassment on my head."

"This was your idea, and it's a good one." Emily's breath caught in her throat as a dark head moved through the crowd, a figure drowning in pink taffeta trailing close behind.

Victor stopped at the far side of the Gallery, a bronze goblet in one hand and an animated Camilla hanging off his other arm. He scanned the room in silence, light and shadow playing across his sharp features.

"I've got them," Emily said. "Come on, Ozzy, we'll be fine." Three new initiates came into the Gallery, and Victor eyed the door, his attention elsewhere. It was now or never. "Ready to get your head bitten off, lizard boy?"

Ozzy squared his shoulders and picked up a full goblet from their table. "Wish me luck." He set off across the dance floor, swaying as he walked. "Sorry! Oops, that was your foot, wasn't it? Tina, how are—oh, I'm so sorry, I didn't see your dress. I think I need glasses, I can't see too well."

Bump, slap. Ozzy moved closer now, a few feet away, leaving a trail of irritated initiates behind.

Emily edged through the crowd after him, careful to stay out of sight.

"Sorry, sorry!" Ozzy's voice carried over the heavy beat, the fairy lights glittering off his raised goblet. "I can't see with this big hat on. I've lost my—*whoops*!" In one quick motion, he tripped and crashed into Camilla, his drink leaving a deep red pool down her ruffled bodice.

"My *dress*!" she shrieked. "This is a family heirloom!"

"Calm down, Camilla." Victor brushed away a few wayward drops off his smoking jacket. "It was an accident." His eyes darted into the crowd, and disappointment flashed across his face. "I'm sure it'll be fine once you clean yourself up."

"*Clean myself up*?" Camilla stomped a foot like a petulant toddler. "My dress is ruined!"

"I'm r-really sorry," Ozzy stammered. "I—I can help you get the stain out, if you want. Or maybe you should go change?"

Camilla rounded on Ozzy with a look of deep and pure loathing. "Don't even think of touching me, Shinkle."

"It's just a dress, for Elders' sake." Victor sighed. "Shinkle's right. Let's head back to the dormitories and change. I want to get out of this stupid outfit, anyway." He pushed past Ozzy without another glance, Camilla close on his heels.

"Perfect," Emily murmured, stepping out from behind a boy dressed as a large teacup. "You looked like you really tripped."

"I did!" he said, wheezing. "I can't see where I'm going with this stupid costume!"

Emily unhooked the tie on his lizard head and tossed the monstrosity to the floor. "There—we'll tell your mother someone stole it. Come on, we'd better move fast, or they'll be done mopping each other up before we even get there."

By the time they snuck out onto the grounds, the party was in full swing. They tore across the courtyard, following the faint smell of ash and charred meat to the northern edge of the castle. The dragon den loomed like a black pit in a cloud of oily smoke.

"You're up." Ozzy coughed over the dust and ash. "No way I'm going in there."

Emily pulled open the gate, the lock still swinging free, and cringed at the screeching hinges. The low hiss of steady breathing grew louder the deeper she went into the den, a coiled tail or a claw dangling outside of the dark alcoves. Her heart kicked up its pace, growing heavier with every step, the air thicker. Hotter.

Titan was awake when she stopped at his den. "Hey, Tite. I need your help." She stretched out her hand, and the air thrummed with warmth. Titan's tail slithered out from under him, and his nails crunched on fresh rock. One foot, then another, out into the open, his wide eyes bright. "Thanks," she breathed, relieved.

Titan lowered his snout and thumped his head once on her palm. Emily led the dragon—*her* dragon—out into the night and was certain in his presence they wouldn't fail.

"I must be insane." Ozzy took an involuntary step back as Titan stretched his neck out into the night. "Are you sure you can handle this, Emily?"

"He's harmless." Emily patted Titan's side. Mounting Titan was second nature already, and Emily was at peace between his wings, his heartbeat moving life into her with every one of his breaths. "Just hold on to me, okay?" she called, lifting Ozzy behind her.

He gripped Emily's waist and buried his head in her back. "Let's go before I change my mind!" he said, voice muffled.

At his request, they were off.

They launched toward the stars and looped around the castle, weaving between the low clouds for a bit of cover. Emily cleared her mind, and Titan took over, his powerful muscles guiding them around the turrets and high walls of crumbling stone and thick ivy. Somewhere during their take-off, Emily lost her costume ears, and she laughed into the wind.

Camilla and Victor would be in the East Wing, a branch of the castle overlooking the sea and stretching high up onto the cliffside, but Emily had never been there. Trusting Titan to take her where her heart desired, they plummeted out of the sky where a row of windows sent orange light into the mist steaming off the water below.

"Do you see them?" Emily called. They dipped lower, circling the east wall in a steady glide as the flickering lights of empty rooms whizzed past.

"Are you kidding me?" Ozzy's voice cracked. "My eyes are staying shut until this thing slows down!"

Emily squinted through the icy wind, and a swatch of pink stood out in the sea of grey and navy. As though sensing her shift in attention, Titan struck out for the ground, landing at the base of the wall with a muffled thud. Strong claws hooked into the stone, and he scaled the wall with rapid precision, the crumbling and grunting drowned out by the moan of restless waves.

The window was open a crack, and Emily sat upright, hiding in Titan's shadow for an uninterrupted view. She slid one finger behind the pane to widen the gap, wincing as the hinges protested. Camilla scrubbed at her dress with a cream-coloured rag, blood high in her cheeks with little attention to give the window at the end of the room.

"Stupid boy! That traitor-loving idiot!" Camilla spat, the venom thick in her voice. "My mother's going to kill me for ruining her dress."

Victor sighed, leaning against the fireplace like a statue. "Lay off, Camilla. That dress is horrible, anyway."

Camilla's face fell. "You said you liked it."

"I said I think girls in ball gowns are beautiful, not that I liked *this* dress on *you*. And be careful what you say. Calling people traitors up and down the halls isn't winning you any favours."

"But she *is* a traitor," she whined, the sound grating in Emily's ears. "Everyone thinks so—except for you. I don't understand why you're so fascinated with the Rathburn trash."

"Watch it." Victor's rich voice grew much too even. "You want me to turn you into a tree stump again?"

"What *is* it about her?" Camilla crossed her arms, petulant. "Is it pity? Because she's not even that pretty."

Victor stared through Camilla as though she were a mirage. "Rathburn's interesting. Unlike pretty much everyone else in this castle."

Interesting. Like a forgotten object at the back of a closet you don't quite know what to do with. *Interesting.* "Ozzy, come on!" Emily said, trying not to let Victor's words give her too much of a complex.

Ozzy peered over the windowsill. He steadied his breath, and his body relaxed. Silence fell over them all, and Emily held her breath as Victor tilted his head to one side, noticing the faraway look in Camilla's eyes.

"Camilla? Did you hear me?" Victor asked.

"Sorry, yes, I heard you." Camilla's apologies echoed off the walls, and Emily exhaled in a low, steady hiss as Ozzy's mouth formed the words first.

Victor detached himself from the fireplace and paced the room. "Did it ever occur to you that getting on Rathburn's good side might be useful?"

"How?" Under Ozzy's influence, Camilla's voice was calm. Too even, much too kind. Ozzy focused on the girl, a film of sweat making his forehead shine.

"Because traitor or not, old man Rathburn was a powerful and well-placed Empath on the High Council. If you can't be nice to Emily for my sake, then do it out of self-preservation. Making enemies with his daughter could be a nightmare for you if he ever finds out."

"I hear he's dead," Camilla said after a brief hesitation. Emily pursed her lips, willing herself to focus on Victor.

Victor's eyes grew hard. Guarded. "I wouldn't be so sure about that. They never found him. Anyway, Emily's got real, raw talent and something . . . something like . . ."

"Like what?" Camilla prompted.

He hesitated, his brows pulled low over his eyes. "Like fire." Victor cleared his throat. "Maybe she could help us figure out what's in that Blintwoods box my father seems so interested in. That is, if you ever quit being rude around her."

Emily's heart hammered, and she kicked Ozzy's shin with her heel. "Ow." Ozzy grunted, massaging his leg. "I know, I know!" Camilla's protests echoed out the window, and Ozzy shook his head. "I mean, sorry! What about the Blintwoods box?" He mouthed an apology, and Emily patted his knee.

"I told you already." Victor shook his head. "Father hasn't stopped hounding the Guard for information, and he's *never* cared that much about anything."

Almost there. Emily leaned in closer. *Come on . . .*

Camilla's voice faltered, and Ozzy slumped lower on Titan's back. "Does your father know what's in the box?"

Victor laughed. "You're asking me that *again*?"

"I'm not very smart," Camilla said.

"Smartest thing I've heard you say yet." Victor raked his fingers through his hair, his ruined jacket forgotten. "Father keeps more gold in his pocket than the average person in Gildenveil earns their entire life. Whatever

Migellus is hiding is more valuable than anything he already owns, and that's saying something."

"Migellus?" Camilla's voice rang out in alarm.

Victor stopped in his tracks. "Yeah, Migellus, remember? It's *his* box. Seriously, how much did you drink?"

"Like I said," she continued, "I'm not too bright. I'm sure you have some ideas about what could be hidden in there. Or if they know who broke in."

Victor screwed up his nose. "Not a clue. But I want to know *badly*. And if I find out before him, all the better."

"It's . . . too . . . much," Camilla grunted, and Ozzy lurched to one side. Titan's claws crunched into the wall.

"Did you hear something?" Victor asked.

Camilla's response was automatic. "No, nothing."

He frowned. "Look, no one's asking you to do anything." Victor picked up a glass and took a long sip. "Just keep Grey off my case—I don't know what she's so interested in all this for, but she's getting annoying. Snooping around my dad, sending spies around the city to find information on the investigation. It's pathetic."

Ozzy was breathing hard. The rock cracked.

Victor turned. "Okay, I definitely heard something that time."

Emily held her breath and gripped Titan harder. With a final groan, Ozzy collapsed into Emily's back, and Camilla's usual haughty voice took over once more.

"What was what?" Camilla asked. "What were you saying?"

"I heard something outside," Victor muttered. Emily hunched as low as she could, but the sound of footsteps was growing louder. All Victor had to do was get to the window. Look outside.

Don't come closer. Emily's fingers went numb, and she closed her eyes, willing Titan to stay still. *Please…*

"What are you doing here?" His outrage forced Emily's eyes open, and she braced herself for whatever was coming.

But Victor wasn't talking to her.

"Catherine?" Camilla asked. "I thought you said you were sick."

"Catherine?" Emily chanced a peek over the windowsill and, sure enough, Catherine stood frozen beside the fire, her body flickering in and out of focus.

"Are you spying on us?" Victor's face contorted with anger, and he took a step closer to her, his shock thick enough to touch.

"Victor, that's not—" Camilla started, but he cut her off at once.

"Why else would she be in here?" Victor's anger rattled the windows. "She veiled herself to listen to our conversation!"

Catherine stood in stunned silence with her arm above her head, hand dangling limp with defeat. Like a caged animal, she surveyed the room and cast a pleading look at the window.

"Oh no," Emily groaned, as Victor approached the helpless girl. "The idiot tried veiling herself."

"What?" Ozzy came back to himself long enough to glance over Emily's shoulder. "Why's everyone yelling?"

Emily's hands prickled, sharp sparks of energy dancing across her palm at the mounting tension. Her stomach churned and her head whirred. And then Catherine's eyes slid over to the window again, her eyes locking with Emily's.

"Catherine's in there. And she knows we're out here." Emily's vision sharpened into focus while Ozzy ducked behind her, uttering curses into her back. *Catherine saw me. If I don't do something, she'll give us away.* Molly's face replaced Catherine's, and something dormant inside Emily shifted. *I have to help her. A distraction.* As soon as she made the decision, the current rushed through her body like a storm, the waves crashing through her veins and down to her fingertips. Her vision blurred, and her necklace grew warm around her neck, too warm . . .

Crash.

A glass hit the floor.

The arguing stopped.

Catherine stared around the room, bewildered and alone. Then screaming erupted from the ceiling.

"Catherine, *put us down*!" Victor's legs pushed against the ceiling where he hung like a bat, his face filling with blood.

Camilla's back pressed against a rafter, her shrieks incoherent as her dress billowed out from under her.

For a moment, Catherine's mouth hung wide as her eyes swivelled back to the window. "What did you—?"

"Run!" Emily commanded as quietly as she could manage. The last thing she saw in the window before she jabbed her heel into Titan's flank was Catherine racing from the room, and both Victor and Camilla still trapped in the air like two livid chandeliers. Titan spiralled into the clouds where Emily could no longer hear the rage, the screaming, the protests. And that was good. *That* meant freedom.

For now.

Ozzy lifted his face from Emily's sweater and called out over the wind. "Did you do that?"

"I—I don't think so?" If she was honest with herself, she wasn't sure. Her ability had never behaved so strangely before; she could never influence something she couldn't touch. But the surge of energy that had taken over her body was new, too. Stronger, somehow. It couldn't be a coincidence . . .

"Are you sure Catherine saw you?" Ozzy asked.

Emily paused. "Yes. She looked straight at me."

He groaned. "That's it, we're done!"

"I couldn't leave her there!" Emily pressed herself lower onto Titan's neck and he dove, leaving the stars behind. "I'm sorry, I just couldn't. She seemed so . . . trapped."

Titan thudded onto the ground behind the cover of the dragon den, sending ripples through the trees. With a low grunt, he bucked them off, tail swishing behind him.

Emily's adrenaline was fading fast. Her hands and legs ached from holding onto him for so long, and a headache began to bloom somewhere behind her eyes. Without hesitation, Titan crawled through the open gates and disappeared into the den. Arms heavy, Emily closed the door and secured the latch, her hands shaking by the time the deed was done.

"Do you think Victor and Camilla saw us, too?" Ozzy asked as they trudged back to the main castle entrance. "What am I saying? Catherine saw everything, so the other two will *definitely* know what we did. We're done for. Mother's going to hang me!"

The faint sound of music wafted out from the Gallery, but Emily had never wanted to join a party less.

"Catherine can't give us up without admitting to breaking the rules herself." She patted Ozzy on the shoulder as they climbed the stairs back to North Tower. "She was trespassing in that dormitory. We're going to be fine."

Ozzy's feet thumped over the carpet, his agitation echoing up the stairwell as Emily refused to take the hidden corridor and chance another strange vision. "Trespassing isn't the same as stealing a dragon." He sighed. "At least it wasn't for nothing. Now we know all of this has something to do with what Migellus has in his Blintwoods box."

They cleared the landing in silence and stepped into North Tower, eager for some rest. But the lounge was full. Worried faces turned to the door as Emily and Ozzy crossed the threshold, the tension palpable.

Tina waved them over to where Horus, Piper, Elliott, and Finn huddled close together. "Thank Elders you two made it back." She threw her arms around Emily's neck and squeezed before releasing her to attack Ozzy next. "We got worried when you two didn't come up right away."

"We're okay, Tina. What's going on?" Emily asked, unsure her heart could take much more.

Horus slumped down in an armchair and threw his feet on a nearby table. "They stopped the party early. Just my luck they decide to be *careful* on Halloween night."

Piper threw him a dark look from under heavily painted eyes. "Do you even hear yourself sometimes? That psychopath could still be out there!"

Emily frowned. "What psychopath?"

"Someone broke into Chief Master Millendorf's office," Tina said. "I was passing his door, and it was open. It's *never* open. Grey, Magdale, even Ward—they were all trying to make sense of the mess. It's completely up-side down!"

Ozzy paled in the orange glow of the fire. "Who did it?"

Horus snorted. "Who knows? But they really screwed up my night."

Piper rolled her eyes. "The problem is *how* they got in. The place is a fortress—no one gets in there unless Millendorf lets them in." She stared into the fire and shivered. "I wonder what they were looking for."

Emily's stomach twisted. "Me too."

CHAPTER SIXTEEN

The Lost Ring

THE WEEKS FOLLOWING THE HALLOWEEN feast were a blur of rumour and mistrust. Every whispered theory and suspicion, no matter how outrageous, had one thing in common: Emily. Most of the initiates refused to eat in the Gallery around her and countless more gave her a wide berth in the halls. She wasn't sure she would have ever admitted it out loud, but the silent rejection was worse than the constant name-calling—at least when they insulted her out loud, they were speaking to her. It was better to spare herself the headache and eat outside where the trees couldn't judge her.

Emily prodded her cold beef stew with her fork and sank deeper into her jacket. "I'm really sorry about this. I didn't think everyone would assume *I* broke into Millendorf's office."

Ozzy gulped. "Forget them." He patted his seat of yellow and orange maple leaves and wiggled deeper into the pile. "I like the change. It's better than finding bark in my food and watching Horus eat half the table."

Emily offered him a small smile. "Thanks, Ozzy. And maybe you're right. At least no one's kicked us out." Emily picked out a sharp, black thorn from her own cushion of leaves and tossed it into the trees. "I mean, if Catherine was going to say something, it would have happened already."

"Speaking of the devil," Ozzy said, mouth going slack, "look who it is."

A long mane of chestnut curls billowed out from under a thick jacket across the courtyard, Catherine's familiar square glasses glinting in the sun. Her eyes landed on Emily and Ozzy, but instead of heading in another direction, she picked up her pace.

"What the Elders is happening?" Ozzy asked, horrified. "It looks like she's coming over here."

Was the other shoe about to drop? Could Catherine have been biding her time until she'd found a way to nail them to the wall without putting herself in harm's way?

Emily and Ozzy looked up, their lunches forgotten. Dressed from head to toe in purple and draped in silk scarves, Catherine stood before them like an enormous grape, her expression unreadable. The silence was heavy. Awkward.

"Isn't it cold, sitting on the ground like that?" Catherine adjusted the flap of her purple bag, then moved it from one shoulder to the other.

Ozzy blinked. "You came here to ask if we were cold?" He wrinkled his nose against the sunlight. "Yeah, it's cold. Bye now."

Catherine fiddled with her hair, the tight curls snaking around her plum nails. "Right. I figured this wouldn't be easy." More waiting. More silence. She sighed and dropped her arms to her side. "Look, I wanted to say thanks, okay?"

It's a trap. "You're . . . you're thanking us?" Emily asked.

"Yeah."

"Seriously?" Ozzy threw Emily a sidelong glance. "She's serious?"

"I'm serious, all right!" Catherine blurted. "Look, I'm just gonna put it out there, okay? I've been spying on Camilla and Victor, and if you two hadn't been outside that window when you were, then Vicky-dearest would have probably reported me."

"He still might," Emily pointed out. Her stew was cold sludge in her bowl, but she wasn't hungry, anyway.

Catherine's eyes glinted. "If he says anything, he'll have to explain how he ended up hanging off the ceiling with Camilla's skirts around her shoulders." She smirked. "I hate him, but the idiot's got pride. And that doesn't look good any way you swing it."

Ozzy snorted. "Please. You've been glued to Victor and Camilla since we got here. You're probably up to something right now and that's why you're being nice. What is it?" His sneer contorted his round, kind face. "Is Camilla hiding somewhere in these trees about to dump a bunch of toilet water on our heads?"

"Actually," Catherine said, her thick eyebrows pulling together, "I only hung out with Victor because Camilla's obsessed with him for some reason. And Camilla..." Her eyes shifted to the ground, regret thick in her voice.

"Camilla's been dead to me ever since she let that stupid oversized turtle carry me off."

For the first time, a twinge of sympathy made Emily forget the cold. "So, what? You were using them?"

Catherine exhaled in a puff of white mist. "I heard Victor talking about that robbery and how his father's been after whatever was in that box at Blintwoods or whatever. It's none of our business, but Victor and Camilla wouldn't stop. Even when Grey started getting involved. If I know Victor, he's dragging Camilla into something she can't handle, especially if Grey's interested." She took a deep breath, the colour high in her cheeks.

"Why didn't you ask them what they were up to? Talk to Camilla about it?" Emily asked.

Catherine scowled. "That moron thought she and Vicky had their own little secret, so she wasn't talking. And neither was he."

"So, you decided to spy on them," Ozzy said with begrudging admiration. "Why would you want to help Camilla if she's become such a nightmare?"

Catherine shrugged. "She hasn't always been like this. She used to be nice—have some common sense, you know?" She sighed. "Even though she's turned into Victor's lapdog, I couldn't abandon her like that."

Understanding dawned, and Emily groaned. "Ugh, the veiling spell! I've never seen you try so hard to get something right!"

Catherine nodded. "When Grey had us practicing a few weeks ago, the idea of veiling myself so I could listen in on Camilla and Victor seemed pretty good. So, I..." She cut off, her square teeth digging into her bottom lip. "I might have snuck in when you left Grey's cottage the night you had that punishment for her and grabbed one of her spell books. You know, to give me a little more help."

The door—Emily had slammed it shut after organizing Grey's stores but had found it open after going back for her bag. "*You're* the one who stole Grey's book?" Emily asked, her blood rushing to her ears. "Did you ever stop to think that you would be putting me in Grey's sights by doing that?"

"Yeah, I didn't really care about that before." Catherine shrugged. "If it makes you feel better, the book helped me out a lot."

"Well, I'm glad," Emily said, oozing sarcasm. "But what did you need her keys for?"

"Keys? I didn't take any keys."

'Course you didn't. Emily shook her head. "You don't have to lie."

"I think I know what I stole." Catherine dug the toe of her leather boot into the ground, the soft earth fanning around her shoe. "I needed to do something, okay? I think you two can understand that."

There it was—the other shoe dropping. "We had to check in on Victor for our own reasons," Emily said, a slight edge of defensiveness in her voice.

Catherine arched a brow. "And the only way you could do that was to steal a dragon and possess Camilla? At least all I did was take a stupid book and trespass a little." Her lip pulled into a hint of a smile, and she shrugged. "Your way was cooler than mine, though."

Emily crossed her arms. "Thanks, I think. But we had no choice. You . . . well, you wouldn't understand."

"It's because of Grey, right?" Catherine abandoned the small hole she was making in the mud and floundered.

"Okay, don't get mad, but I overheard you two talking about it a couple times. I didn't mean to."

"We're dead," Ozzy moaned, burying his face in his hands.

"I was practicing a lot in the lounge, and I overheard you two talking about Blintwoods and Grey. And then I was *really* happy I was gonna get to the bottom of things because if Grey's still going around doing illegal stuff, that means big problems for everyone. By the way, you two need to talk lower if you want to keep things a secret."

"You were veiled!" Ozzy cried out, exasperated. "Was that *you* we kept tripping over?"

Catherine had the decency to look embarrassed. "Yeah. But if anyone should be upset about that, it's me. You scuffed up my good shoes."

"Unbelievable," Ozzy said. "Well, since you can veil yourself now, maybe it was you who raided Millendorf's office."

"Oh sure, and I got the door open how?" Catherine asked, her voice sharp and oozing contempt. "I was too busy running away from Victor and Camilla when the office got turned over. But if that's how you want to play this, maybe it was you two and your big dragon who turned his office upside down."

Ozzy tossed his empty dish to the ground and glared at her. "You think no one would have noticed a fire-breathing monster running around in the castle?"

Catherine's hands balled into fists. "It could happen!"

"Enough!" Emily cried. "This is insane! Ozzy, Catherine didn't break into Millendorf's office. She wouldn't have had time to do it and, sorry Catherine, but you're not that good." She turned to the scowling girl before

Ozzy could manage a retort. "Catherine, yes, we spied on Victor and Camilla, and we borrowed a dragon to do it. Either report us or forget it happened!"

Catherine scrutinized Emily's face for a moment. "Why'd you do it?"

Emily blinked slow. "I told you, it's our business."

With a small frown, Catherine nodded. "You don't trust me, I get it. I've been treating you like dirt up to now. I'm . . . I'm sorry about that, too, by the way." She clutched her bag to her side and pushed her glasses higher onto her nose. "I wanted to apologize in person and . . . and to thank you for saving me. Twice." She turned on her heel, head held high, and then stopped. "And you should know I won't say anything about what I saw. So don't worry about that, okay?" Her words came out rushed, thick with emotion. She marched off to the castle, thick soles chewing up the frozen grass.

"Incredible." Ozzy shook his head. "She's got nerve."

"That did take guts," Emily agreed. Catherine was getting farther and farther away, her shoulders hunched and her head bent against the onslaught of cold coming from the sea below. "Hey, Catherine!"

Catherine stopped, turned. Took a few deliberate steps closer. "What?"

Not many people had ever changed their minds about Emily; for most of the realm, she would always be a Rathburn first and an Elemental, a girl, a person, last. And she hated it.

"Want the rest of my stew?" Emily asked. "I have extra."

Despite the good-natured bickering, Catherine fit into Emily and Ozzy's world as though she'd always been there. For the first time in weeks, thoughts of Grey and Victor and the Blintwoods attack didn't consume Emily's heart and mind. Together, she and Ozzy brought Catherine up to speed on their suspicions about Grey. And without Camilla around, Catherine was kinder, more open to talking, and less prone to insults.

Saturday morning in mid-November was a day for late breakfasts and lazy hours by the fire. Initiates flooded the Gallery, the frosty drizzle outside pattering against the windows and driving everyone indoors. Ozzy helped himself to his third muffin and flicked through the Scroll, his emerald sweater dusted with crumbs and stained with coffee, while Horus, Willow, and Piper played cards farther down the table.

"Still nothing in here about Millendorf's office." Ozzy frowned over the parchment. "The top Elementals and Empaths in the realm live here, and someone breaking into that office has never happened! How can no one have reported this?"

"Who cares?" Emily wrapped her fingers around the steaming mug of cacao in her lap. "We know Grey did it."

Catherine rolled her eyes. "Grey's evil, but she's not stupid. She wouldn't break into the Chief Master's office under everyone's nose."

The cold weather had quieted even the fairies nesting in Old Gwendolyn's roots for warmth and shelter. They burrowed into the walls, a muted glow like faraway stars on a clear night. Emily frowned into her cup, the brown liquid swirling, and ignored the hoots and laughter around her that belonged to a different world.

"Who else would do it?" Emily asked. "No one expects to see her at big events, and she's one of the best Elementals there is. She could have easily gotten into Millendorf's office without being seen."

Catherine brushed a wayward crumb off her sleeve and pushed Ozzy's dish further away from her to avoid any more food from getting onto her cerulean sweater. "If she's the one who tried robbing Blintwoods, then she's capable of getting into Millendorf's hidey-hole. Don't count her out, Em."

Emily's temples throbbed. "Ozzy, did you find anything else on Migellus at the library?"

Ozzy scowled. "Don't mention that name to me when I'm enjoying my muffin. Between researching him and trying to keep up with practices so I don't get kicked out of this place, I might lock myself in the dragon den and hope one of them gets me."

"Never repeat this, but the nerd is right," Catherine said, ignoring Ozzy's hostile expression. "We've been researching this every day, and that's just since *I* started helping you out. Unless there's some rare magic book that Ozzy hasn't already read, I'd say we need a new plan."

A memory clicked into place somewhere at the back of Emily's mind. Images and words escaped the box she kept tucked away for random information and pieced themselves together in perfect harmony. A thin journal with golden letters and a staircase winding up to the sky with books in orbit. What was the name of it again? "Rare book," Emily repeated. "I can't believe I didn't remember up until now!"

"What's happening?" Catherine asked.

Ozzy groaned. "She's got an idea."

"But that's good, right?"

With a sigh, Ozzy abandoned his breakfast. "Honestly, it could go either way."

"Ozzy, do you remember the day we met?" Excitement coursed through Emily's veins, the first light of hope waking her up from a slumber she hadn't known had taken over her. Overhead, the fairies buzzed with excitement.

"Sure," he said at once. "You saved me from my mother."

Emily grinned. "The shop owner put a book into the private collection when I was there."

"He does that all the time." Ozzy shrugged. "Sometimes he gets threats, or someone tries to bribe him for one of the rare editions, so he locks them away."

Emily closed her eyes, imagining the navy cover and delicate golden letters, willing the words to come back to her. "You told me your dad heard someone was trying to get into the private collection, remember? I got a look at one of the books he was carrying up the stairs before he locked it away. It was about Migellus and something else . . . a ring, I think."

Ozzy grew pale. "Do you mean the *Lost* Ring?"

"That's it!" Emily exclaimed, earning her a few dark looks from the initiates at the next table. "You know it?"

"Listen," Catherine interrupted, "I know I'm new to the gang and all, but can you please bottom line this for me?"

Ozzy stared at them both in bewilderment. "There's only one Lost Ring in our history, and no one's seen it in at least three centuries!"

"You're getting all worked up about some ring?" Catherine said, nonplussed.

"*Some* ring?" he croaked. "I can't believe you never heard about this, Catherine. I mean, Emily I get—she grew up in the Commons. But you live in the city!"

Catherine glared at him. "I might not know about special rings or talking magical spoons, but I get things done. Now can you explain what's got you all worked up?"

Ozzy sighed. "The Lost Ring is a legend. The first person to ever manifest an ability was an Elemental but, since Masters didn't exist yet, he had no idea how to control his magic. Some people in his village witnessed what he could do and attacked him and his family for it."

"Bunch of savages," Catherine grumbled. "I hope he let them have it."

"That's exactly the problem." Ozzy's eyes grew sad, his voice subdued. "He went into such a rage when they captured his wife and son, he ended up accidentally killing them all himself."

"What happened to the wife and son?" Emily asked, fearing she already knew the answer.

Ozzy stared down at the table. "They died, too. All that was left of his home and family was a crater of dirt and rock."

"Well, there goes my breakfast." Catherine wrapped her arms around her stomach and glared at her half-empty dish. "So how does this Lost Ring come into all this?"

"Apparently, that Elemental was so traumatized by what he did that he slept in the rubble where his family died for two whole days," Ozzy said. "No one knows exactly how the magic happened, but all that emotion pushed his ability out of him and into the earth."

"He lost his magic?" Emily asked. "I didn't even know that could happen." Her ability had always been a part of her, both mind and body. The idea of it being gone, of existing separate from it, had her gripping her seat until her fingertips hurt. No matter how long she'd spent pretending to live without it.

Ozzy nodded. "It has to be really strong emotion, and the timing has to be right, but it can happen. Anyway, one of the pebbles he had been lying on absorbed his power, but he never wanted it back. Instead, he forged it to his wedding band as a reminder of his pain and wore it until he passed it on to someone else."

"So, there's a ring out there with this Elemental's ability?" Emily asked, perplexed. "I mean, that sounds weird to me, but not horrible."

"Not only him." The whites of Ozzy's eyes were visible all around. "I don't know how it happened, but that ring took on the abilities of every owner it had. It's been passed down through generations."

It took a moment for the idea to settle. Thousands of years of Empaths and Elementals, abilities both small and epic spanning the realms, were contained in one place. Emily's next question flickered into her mind along with Grey's face, and her heart fell, her fingers going numb.

"Ozzy, what happens to the new person who owns the ring?" Emily asked, her tongue dry, her muscles coiled and pulsing.

"I mean, it's just legend at this point," he said at once, the blood leaching into his collar. "No one's seen the Lost Ring for centuries. It could be anywhere, if it even exists at all."

"What happens?" she repeated. Ozzy frowned at her, and the answer was written in his wide eyes, his hunched shoulders. Still, he didn't speak, and Catherine stared at each of them in turn, not daring to say anything herself. "Ozzy," Emily pressed, "if someone finds the Lost Ring with all these abilities in it, what happens?"

Ozzy's shoulders grew rigid. "They take on the abilities of every single person who's owned the ring before them. They would become the most powerful person alive."

CHAPTER SEVENTEEN

Fairies in the Trees

GREY WAS AFTER THE LOST Ring—the truth of that fact was absolute. Late fall sped by, the days growing darker and shorter, the shimmer of frost glazing every bare tree and blade of grass. Winter break raced toward Emily at an uncomfortable rate, and every time she laid eyes on Grey, a new set of anxieties added to the growing list: Did she find the Lost Ring yet? Would today be the day she turned the realm upside down? Where was Zaphira?

Baxter Rathburn was long gone, but Grey was still alive and well enough to continue his legacy. And that possibility was more terrifying than anything Emily could have imagined.

The rest of the castle, however, was concerned with one thing: bi-annual eliminations. The library and North

Lounge burst with Empaths and Elementals studying to secure their place at the castle, the stress in the air thick enough to squeeze.

None, however, suffered more than Master Ward. As the weather grew colder, so did the initiates during every lesson. Terrified of being in the same room as a man capable of weakening their abilities, many had stopped attending his lessons. Worse still, the few who did decide to show up were only interested in ridiculing him for the slight stammer he'd developed and his trembling hands. Each day brought a darker shade of purple to the bruises under his eyes and, while Emily faintly worried whether or not he would crack, her focus on Grey wouldn't be shaken.

North Lounge was quiet despite every armchair and stool being occupied. The page open in Emily's lap blurred with fatigue, and her quill hovered midair, a small ball of ink quivering at the tip. "Ugh, not again," she sighed as a black dot pooled across her brewing notes. "Now I can't see what ground moonstone does to dragon blood."

"That's easy." Ozzy added a note in the margins of her page. "It's lethal."

"I thought it became *more* powerful." She rubbed her eyes, the fire too hot on her face.

Ozzy shook his head. "No, that's wolfsbane."

"Right." Emily tossed her things onto the table with a resigned sigh. "I'm going to start packing my things."

Ozzy smiled, dark circles framing his bloodshot eyes. "You know your stuff. Just relax. Catherine should be back any minute now, so let's take a break and figure out how to make her feel better when *she* fails."

On cue, Catherine materialized through the door in a frantic tangle of mussed curls and unlaced military boots.

She bounded toward them, a maniacal grin plastered to her face. With a sigh of relief, she dropped herself into a free armchair and hoisted her feet up on Emily's notes. "Veiling spells!" With a flourish, she dug a pastry out of her jacket pocket and took a ravenous bite.

"Huh?" Emily stifled a yawn and kicked Catherine's feet off the table.

"My evaluation! It was veiling spells!"

Ozzy shook his head. "Of course it was. Only you would get that lucky."

Catherine took another bite, her eyes bright with relief. "Hoooo, you should have seen Grey's face when I disappeared right in front of her snotty nose. Probably disappointed I didn't blow up my desk again. I feel bad for whoever has to go see her next." She beamed, not looking the least bit regretful.

"Hope you feel good enough to do some brewing next." Emily cringed at the mess of notes scrawled on the page, lines crossing out unwanted words while Ozzy's corrections hovered in the margins. "Because I'm about to throw up."

"Oh, I'm definitely going to bomb that one." Catherine's grin widened as she tossed her bag onto the ground and attempted to smooth Ozzy's hair. "I can't make a salve or a serum to save my life, and I've accepted that. The Masters in this place are gonna have to accept it, too. You don't have to be good at everything to earn an education."

Ozzy shook his head. "It doesn't worry you that failing anything can mean you're out of this place after January?"

Catherine shrugged. "It's good to know one's strengths

and weaknesses, Oswald. As long as I don't melt the tower down to the ground, I'm calling it a win."

Emily stared at her with wide eyes but, to her surprise, Ozzy crumbled into a fit of laughter. "I envy you, you know that?"

"Everyone does, my friend." Catherine closed her eyes with a look of absolute bliss. "So, did you two find anything on . . . you know...?"

At the mention of their extracurricular studies, the pit in Emily's stomach grew wider. "Sort of, but it's not much to go on. Ozzy, do you still have the book?"

He rummaged through his bag and dug up a heavy, leather-bound volume. "It's not a huge lead, but it's something. Here, listen: '*The Lost Ring is the foundation for magical tradition as it is known today. Passed only from father to son, it is embedded with the magic of its creator through a form of binding spell and an intense emotional state to activate the magic.*'" A sketch at the top of the page showed a pale gold band with a roughly cut stone embedded into the metal like a diamond fresh from the mines.

"Binding spells," Catherine repeated. "Emily, didn't you say Grey had a book on binding spells in her sad little room?"

Emily grabbed her bag and stood, legs like lead posts. "She did, but binding spells are only good if you *have* the object you want to bind yourself to, remember? She was probably interested in the magic behind it, but it won't help her actually find the ring."

"That's not bad," Catherine said, leaning in closer, "but I have something better. On my way back here, I overheard some gossip. Apparently, Ward caught Grey going through a stack of his old books in his office. She didn't ask permission or anything. It totally freaked him out. The two of them got into a huge argument that Magdale had to get involved with and everything."

"Ugh, no wonder Ward looks so terrified all the time now," Emily muttered, the fire throwing menacing shadows across their faces. "Is there no one who's going to put that woman away?"

Ozzy shouldered his bag and lurched to his feet. "Well, the holiday break should help us out."

Catherine snorted. "Why? Think you'll get a map to the Lost Ring from daddy for Christmas?"

"Think about it," Ozzy said, ignoring her jab. "Everyone's off their guard, no one's in the library, and there aren't any schedules or rules. You'll have a ton of time to yourselves to go through more books."

"You two are such mood-kills," Catherine complained. "I swear, if I have to spend my holiday in that dusty library, I'll—"

"Make us invisible?" Emily asked.

"Set us on fire!" Ozzy exclaimed.

Catherine scowled. "I hate you both." She gave her armchair one last, longing look before picking up her things. "Oh, before I forget! Magdale pulled me aside when she caught me spying and told me to give you this." She dug in her pocket for a crumpled piece of parchment and handed it to Emily.

Emily flipped open the note, her mood darkening with every neat, looping word she read.

"What's it say?" Ozzy asked, already halfway to the door.

She tucked the note in her pocket and marched after them. "Nothing. Come on, let's get this over with."

While Emily should have been relieved after leaving the smoking air of the brewing tower, the note from Magdale beat with its own pulse in her back pocket, refusing to be ignored. By the time the castle had succumbed to the darkness of nightfall, Emily's nerves were writhing in her stomach like grass snakes. She padded down the main stairwell leading out of North Tower, both eager to get the night over with and regretting every step forward.

The first true snowfall of the year blanketed the Selwyn courtyard, small piles of glitter shifting and climbing with the indecisive mood of the wind. Emily's boots crunched into the frost, and she rounded the castle at a brisk pace, her path trailing behind her like a ghost. Her breath crystallized in the air, leaving a soft dusting of ice on her lashes.

Black Mountain was once again covered in thick, impermeable fog, and any remnants of her good mood evaporated. With a scowl at the shadows hiding in the trees, she stepped onto a narrow path at the edge of the grounds and followed the fallen pine needles nestling into the powdery white drifts to a fallen oak deep within the forest.

"Hello?" she called, her voice much too loud in the unnatural silence. The territory was unfamiliar, the first tendrils of fog trickling through the trees and reminding her how far from the castle she'd traveled.

Magdale would never have allowed her up Black Mountain as the fog pushed through the trees and held the chill to the earth; and yet, the forest path was where the instructions had led her, approved by Magdale herself.

Victor stepped out of the trees, the collar of his thick blue sweater high and his hands pushed deep inside his thick tweed coat. "Right on time." His black hair had blown away from his face, highlighting the red patches of cold colouring his cheeks. "I was sure you wouldn't show, but I'm glad I was wrong."

"The note came from Magdale, so I couldn't ignore it." Emily tracked every movement he made with practiced eyes. "I'm sure you did that on purpose."

"Nah, I'm not that manipulative." Victor frowned at her coat, a plain black layer of wool without a hood or scarf shielding her from the elements. "Aren't you cold in that?"

"I'm used to it." And it was true—the Commons weren't generous in providing supplies for the winter, so she'd grown a thick skin after years of going on supply runs in the worst months of the year. But Victor didn't know those details, and she was determined to keep it that way. "So, what are we doing here?" *Keep it light. Stick to the point.*

"It's a surprise," he said, a mischievous grin lighting his flushed face.

"Ugh." Emily rolled her eyes. "Why do people say that like it's a good thing? I *hate* surprises."

"Even presents?"

She crossed her arms. "Especially presents. No one gives something for nothing. The biggest way to owe someone without ever having asked for a favour is to accept a gift from them."

"That's a pretty bleak way to live." He pondered the ground, making deep tracks with the sole of his leather boot. "Okay, it's not a surprise, then. It's a . . . training drill that I haven't explained to you yet."

"Better." The stress constricting Emily's throat eased a fraction. "We're near Black Mountain. Let me guess—more gardening?"

He laughed. "Not exactly. You ready for a hike?"

Without meaning to, she found herself suppressing a smile, a genuine flicker of enjoyment at the idea of physical exercise. She followed him over a fallen log and navigated the rocks and sharp bends with ease. Her muscles worked hard, the familiar discomfort in her legs a relief. They pushed down the path, deeper into the mountains. Together.

"This place is hard to get to when the trees are in bloom because there's so much blocking the path," Victor called over his shoulder. "But in the winter, the way is clear."

"You're seriously not going to tell me where we're going?" She hopped over a patch of ice, fingers tracing a low-hanging branch caked in snow, releasing white confetti into the air.

"Nope."

The moments passed in easy silence, their heavy breathing marking the time. No birds sang, no creatures skittered across the snow. The night was a perfect, eerie picture of winter peace, with white flakes and Victor and thinning trees giving way to more light in the distance.

Without warning, the path opened ahead of them. Branches and shadow gave way to brightness glittering off the ground in blinding prisms and pale blue snow drifts. Millions of small, white lights swarmed above the clearing like fallen stars, and Emily drank them all in, breathless.

"I'm guessing we're here," she said, not daring to take her eyes off the strange lights looping through the air. "Are those fairies?"

Victor's face flickered with brightness and shadow. "Yep. It's not as impressive in the day, but I think they like it better at night, anyway. Something about this stretch of land must attract them."

"Fairies," she repeated. "It's beautiful."

He smiled, warmth rolling off him in thick waves. "It is."

Her nerves were gone, her worries and fatigue and stress all left behind somewhere in the trees. No one could touch her where she stood. Emily inhaled, letting the cold expand her lungs and give her blood new life. So, when the unwanted thought occurred to her, she turned to Victor in a panic. "You didn't bring me here to trim fairy wings or something, did you?"

He laughed, the sound guttural but soft. "Weird first guess, but no. I wanted to show you their home outside the castle where they're free." Victor's meaningful stare brought the blood rushing to her cheeks. "And I thought it would be a good place to practice."

Emily glanced around the clearing once more. Apart from the fairies, there was nothing there warranting a journey so far from the castle. The land was naked, untainted, and pure. But unremarkable. "Practice what?"

"Well, I remember my first year. There's not much that goes on outside of standard spells and Masters reading at you from textbooks. We didn't get to push ourselves harder than we could handle. You know, prove what we could do before the Masters made their first round of cuts. I didn't want that to happen to you, so I thought you could use some help."

She frowned at him. And lied. "I'm doing fine with my magic."

"You're powerful, Rathburn," he agreed, turning his face up to the sky. "But you've got so much potential you're not tapping into. See, I can only make things stop or go faster, manipulate things to physically do something I want them to do, but the object has to be there already. I can only work with something in front of me, and I have limits. You," he said, hunching his shoulders against the cold, "*dissolve* matter. Make something go wherever you want. You have no idea how much harder that is to do."

Emily tried to read past the thin lines and brief flickers of emotion on Victor's face to find the joke. Victor Graven, admitting a shortcoming, a weakness, wasn't something she thought him capable of. But his eyes were open, admiring, even. Emily tried her best not to grin with pleasure at the compliment.

"So," he continued, turning so they faced one another, inches apart, "let's see how far you can take this talent of yours."

She stared up at him, unflinching, and the words spilled like water from a full cup. "Where I grew up, I had to push myself a lot or I didn't survive. I had to think on my feet. Work under pressure. I'm used to it, and I've only ever gotten this far." Except for one accident on Halloween night, but she wasn't about to be *that* honest. "What makes you think I can be anything more than what I am now just because you're asking me to?"

She was speaking about her magic, but it was so much more than an ability. She had given up her life—a sad, lonely life as an outcast, to be sure—but a life she *knew* and was good at. She left Molly and the Commons under threat of punishment, but underneath the excuse she told herself, she knew she wanted more. To be *bigger,* to make a real difference outside of the shadows. To let people know her. But what if all she'd ever be is an outlaw from the Commons with tainted blood and a criminal past?

Victor hesitated, his hand hovering between them, and pushed a strand of her hair out of her eyes. "You answered your own question. You're a fighter, Rathburn. And fighters don't settle for less than they deserve. If I learned anything about you so far, it's that you toss the rules in the trash and make up your own. Even if it's a bad decision."

Her breathing grew shallow, her heartbeat too fast. Her palms raced with heat, and her necklace hummed under her jacket. She nodded, and he smiled back at her. "So, what's this assignment?" she asked.

Light flickered in his eyes like shards of gold. "I want you to catch a fairy."

Huh . . . not what I expected. "I'm sorry, I thought you said you want me to *catch a fairy.*"

He laughed low in his throat. "You heard right."

"One of them?" Emily pointed up at the sky. "Up there."

"Yup."

Emily chewed the inside of her cheek. "Do you have a really long net?"

He took her elbow and led her into the middle of the clearing, the canopy of lights like a shattered sun. "If you can make something disappear when you touch it, I'll bet you can do it without physical contact, too."

She considered the idea. His logic was sound, a perfect explanation for how he and Camilla had ended up straddling their ceiling on Halloween night. But accidents were one thing; pushing her magic to do something it wasn't used to doing was a beast she'd never tried taming before. "You mean, make something far away come to me or go somewhere else?"

"Or both." He nodded.

"I have no idea how to do that."

"That's why we're here." Victor's gaze bored into hers. "What do you feel when you use your ability? What do you focus on?"

She thought for a moment, letting the cold air clear her mind and push away the nauseous feeling in her stomach. "I concentrate on my hands. It's hard to explain, but I think about how they feel in that moment and how I *want* them to feel. Then it just . . . happens."

He nodded, pulling her hands between them and turning her palms skyward with gentle fingers. "What do you feel now?"

Like throwing up. Like you need to stop touching my hands. She took a deep breath and forced herself to focus on anything but Victor and the wind and his touch on her skin. "Nothing."

"Impossible. Come on, close your eyes."

Despite his warm fingers at the back of her hands, he made no other move to approach her, gave no sign of his request being a trick. He focused, his intent pure, and a large part of her thawed. She wanted to trust him. She needed him to *want* to help her.

Her eyes slipped shut.

"Okay, now are you cold?" he asked.

"A little. I can feel the breeze on my fingers."

"That's good." His voice dropped to a low hum. "Is it a strong breeze? Do you not like it?"

"It's . . . soft," she said. "It reminds me of the winds high up near my room, right when I'd be climbing out my window. It's freedom." Her mind was a box, and the lid was creaking shut, blocking out the extra, unwanted noise. Her hands existed in the nothing, and Victor's voice guided her through the dark.

"What else do you feel?" His voice was low, controlled, but his words were brimming with power.

She allowed the night to wash over her, let the wind shift the hair around her cheeks and tickle the soft padding of her fingers. "There are animals moving in the trees. They're not alive, but not dead, either. They live in the forest. They know we're here." Her palms prickled, and the trees fell away, the world a backdrop to the storm building inside of her. "The wind is coming from the east, and the fairies like it because they can taste the fresh pine from high up on the mountain when it blows their way."

Victor's next words came from a distance. "What did you feel when you saw the fairies?"

Her mouth twitched into a soft smile as the image of lights bursting through the dark tangle of branches shocked her. And then there was Victor's face, gleaming, bright, and open. "Stars. Millions of stars. I'm warm. I'm . . . safe." The humming was electric, a fire kindling hot, battling the cold outside her body.

"Are your hands getting heavier?"

Her mind focused, and she frowned. "No. The fairies are light. Small. I can't feel them at all."

"But they're there."

"Yes." The storm was raging around and within, Emily's ears full of the sound of water rushing against boulders, her hands no longer part of her body but an extension of her mind. The energy peaked in her palms, and she welcomed the heat and everything it offered. And then it all faded to nothing.

"Open your eyes," Victor said. The box opened once again and the forest crashed around her, the stillness of the night a shock after the whirlwind of power coursing through her. Heat rolled between her and Victor, enveloping them, different than the heat of her magic. Their bodies nestled safe in the aftermath of the storm. "Rathburn, open your eyes."

For once, she complied without argument. The fairy was bigger than she'd imagined, its round cheeks and delicate skin glowing with life. It nestled into her palm, staring around in mild interest, too curious about its change in location to fly away. There were no visible wings— only the beautiful face of a child with strange, intelligent eyes and a glow, a burning white under its skin.

"I did that?" she asked. She cupped the fairy in gentle palms, twisting her head for a better look.

"With some help."

She grinned up at him. "Only a little." The fairy rolled onto its side, noticing her for the first time and, with a small smile, zoomed back to its family above. "Thank you. That was the most amazing thing." And she meant it.

"If I didn't know better," Victor said with a wink, "I'd say you were being nice to me."

The clearing was empty, and the fairies buzzed low overhead, drowning out the doubt in her mind. "I might regret saying this, but you do have your decent moments. Don't let it get to your head, though."

His breath mingled with hers. "I'm not so bad, you know. If you give me a chance."

She met his gaze. "I'm not the best at giving chances. My gut is usually right."

"But not always." He frowned, eyes never leaving hers as his hand, warm and hesitant, hovered over her cheek like a warm blanket. "Getting hurt isn't always bad, Rathburn. If you're lucky, other people might even take a chance and let you in, too."

His lips grazed her forehead, and she shivered. "I'm sorry," she said, taking a step back. The connection was broken at once, his warm lips disappearing from her skin. "I've seen a lot of pain come to people who don't get to choose how they get hurt. How can someone *let* themselves get caught up in something that might cause them pain? To let themselves be so vulnerable?"

His eyes burned into hers, his voice rough. "Because Empaths and Elementals and those people you left behind in the Commons . . . we all need someone to care about us. We can't always be powerful. And you can't expect someone to care if you don't offer it back to them."

She took a bigger step back. His arm fell to his side, and she stared at her boots, the cold creeping into her bones. "I think I'm ready to head back now," Emily said.

He nodded and cleared his throat. "Okay. I'll walk you back to your dorm."

"Actually, I want to think about everything that just happened. On my own." She fought the urge to tell him she was sorry, to explain she had no idea how to reach out to him when her life had been spent on the run. Instead, she hitched a small smile to her lips. "But I'm looking forward to what you have planned for next time."

He shoved his hands back in his pockets and his shoulders relaxed. "One of these days, you're going to have to let me walk you back to your dorm. I have a reputation to keep up, and this whole walking away without me thing is really hurting my ego." His smile was soft, his eyes shrouded in darkness.

"One of these days," she agreed, turning for the trees. "G'night, Victor."

"Happy holidays, Rathburn."

She walked away, both hating and relishing the distance. The trees welcomed her back into blissful loneliness.

CHAPTER EIGHTEEN

Deck the Halls

OZZY LEFT TWO DAYS BEFORE year end to spend the holidays with his parents. Snow fell on the castle like down, large cotton feathers building in the corners of windows and drifting into the entrance hall. The fires in North Lounge crackled, working hard to bat away the frost seeping into the walls.

The initiates who stayed behind filtered in and out while the scent of chocolate and peppermint clung to their clothes. Catherine and Emily settled into their favourite armchairs with nothing to do but melt in the warmth of the nearby fire. Emily tucked her feet underneath her and imagined Molly in their old room without any decorations or rich food and doubted she would ever enjoy herself like the other initiates did.

"So, what are the holidays like in the Commons?" Catherine took a sip of hot coffee and nestled into her chair with a small sigh as the pale afternoon light filtered through the snowy tower windows.

Emily stared into the fire as logs jumped and cracked behind the grate. *Bracelets, freshly baked bread, the rare sparkle of laughter.* "They weren't so bad." She let the memories wash over her like a worn but favourite blanket. "We got to wear our nicest clothes and eat together in the kitchen. There wasn't much food, and we didn't get big presents or anything, but I'd usually make an extra supply run so the kids could have something special. Like a surprise, you know?" She laughed and her heart bled tears. She lived for surprises once. Now, she hated them.

"Sounds nice," Catherine muttered. "You ever miss it?"

The memories flooded back faster now. The world was painted in grey, and supplies from the city were scarce. As a child, she'd trudged down dirty, sludge-covered roads looking for leftovers to snatch. Once, a mother walking her child down the opposite way had huddled against the biting winds, giving her mittens to the young girl. *I'm not cold*, she'd said, handing the shabby rectangles of worn fabric to her. *You take them.* And the woman had smiled while the backs of her palms reddened. That was Emily's job; shouldering the pain so others could feel the most joy was a sort of happiness, but a burden, nonetheless.

Emily blinked fast, the fire coming back into focus. "It was lonely sometimes, but it wasn't all bad. How about you?" she asked, eager for a subject change. "You didn't want to go home?"

Catherine snorted. "Haven't you noticed that most of us in here don't go home? There's a reason for that."

Before Emily could ask why, Elliott dropped himself on the arm of her chair while Finn pulled up his own seat, fine hair sticking out at odd ends. "Nice to see you both stayed," Elliott said. He offered Emily a sugar cookie, and she took it, grateful for something to do with her hands. "I was hoping you two would stick around."

"We didn't have much choice," Catherine pointed out. "Emily's got nowhere else to go, and my dad's on a long holiday with his new girlfriend."

"Why didn't you go with him?" Finn asked.

Catherine's face hardened. "I mean, he mentioned going with me alone—you know, the two of us—but he decided to kill my cheery spirit by taking *Mireille* instead." She swirled the deep brown liquid around and around in her mug. "I'm better off here where I don't have to walk in on him playing 'pin the tail on the dragon' in nothing but an apron."

Elliott screwed up his nose. "Mine forgot to book me a spot on the Skytrain," he said with a tone so casual Emily looked up from the fire. "They're having the entire family over and got so busy with invitations they completely passed me over."

"And mine told me not to come home until I could light a torch without matches," Finn said in a dull monotone. "So here I am."

"You're telling me you all have families to go home to and none of you are seeing them?" Emily asked. The idea was baffling. "I thought the whole point of the season was suffering with the ones you love."

"I like staying at the castle during breaks," Elliott said with a shrug. "The food's amazing."

"You know, we can try helping you out," Emily said, handing Finn her uneaten sugar cookie. "With your magic."

"Elliott's tried everything, and nothing's helped," Finn moaned. "Maybe I have to accept I'll be working as a blacksmith for the rest of my life." He set the cookie on the table and slumped into his seat.

"There's nothing wrong with that," Emily said at once, but the misery on Finn's face softened her tone. "What about asking one of the Masters for extra help?"

Finn looked up from his hands. "I didn't think of that. But I don't know any of them well enough to ask for something like that. And this is embarrassing."

"Magdale would do it." Emily smiled, hoping her enthusiasm would brighten his mood. "Or Master Ward. He's been having a bit of a hard time because of how everyone feels about his ability. It might even help get him out of his funk."

"That doesn't sound like a bad idea." Finn's eyes shone with hope. "Thanks, Emily."

The knot in her stomach eased. Molly was far away, but Emily had come to Selwyn's to make a difference. To do some good.

Finn relaxed by the fire while Elliott and Catherine began tossing tree ornaments to one another, flashes of gold and cherry soaring overhead while the afternoon took a nap under a blanket of white. Their chatter lulled her into a comfortable haze, and the day trickled away until sleep found her. Dreamless, fitful sleep.

Emily awoke on the eve of the new year to the smell of brown sugar and molten butter. Her window was painted white, and the snow was still falling like dust on the grounds. She inhaled deep and stretched, her bed warm and soft and the dormitories quiet.

She eased out of bed and placed her palm on the cold window, her fingertips leaving a hazy outline on the glass. "Happy New Year, Molly," Emily whispered.

She reached into the drawer of her bedside table and pulled an oversized sweatshirt over her head. Turning to her silent room, a hint of crimson at the corner by the door caught her attention. "Hey, Catherine, wake up!" she called, jogging to the small stack of shiny packages on the ground. "We have presents!"

"Mmm," Catherine groaned. Two hands gripped her covers and pulled them over her ears.

A large box of homemade candy sat beside a small envelope from Ozzy. She peeled the wax seal apart and grinned as a sheet of white parchment fell onto the floor. "Ozzy got me a copy of the Scroll."

"Mmm."

Some chocolate from Magdale and a generic card from the Chief Master came next, the first going on her bed for later and the second straight into the trash. But the last package was small, wrapped in thick, gold paper glittering in the dull light of the room. A cream-coloured card was folded on top, and she peeled it open to reveal a note written in neat cursive. Her heart kicked into gear, and she cursed at herself for getting excited as she read: *'Thought you could use a surprise you might actually approve of - V.'*

Emily peeled the wrapping away, careful not to tear the beautiful paper. Tucked inside a wooden box was a glass figurine, refracting light onto the walls in shards of multi-coloured diamonds, its beauty as close to the real thing as she could have imagined.

"Is that a fairy?" Catherine muttered, scowling over the edge of her duvet.

Emily grinned. "Yep. I think it's a tree ornament."

"Ugh, Victor's a beast." Catherine regarded the crystal fairy with distrust. Throwing her covers to the floor, she dragged a comb through her nest of knotted curls and pulled on a heavy knit sweater in muted brown.

"Hey, Catherine," Emily said, unable to suppress her happiness. "Guess what?"

"Don't say it."

"Happy New Year." Emily ducked out of the way of a large book hurled at her head.

"Gah, I said don't say it!" Catherine pulled her boots on in a huff. "I need coffee before I can deal with anything *happy*."

Overnight, the castle had been transformed. Reds, greens, and golds glittered in the corners of every room and from every bannister and doorframe. Garlands of holly and cranberry twisted around torches and over windows while low candlelight flickered from the branches of a dozen fir trees scattered around the castle.

Emily and Catherine moved down the hall from North Tower to the Gallery and Emily drank in the warmth. She stared in awe as warm cookies wafted overhead, trees and snowmen made of vanilla dough and frosted sugar following an invisible path. "This is fancy," she said, plucking a snowflake cookie from the air, the sharp taste of warm gingerbread making her stomach growl.

"Camilla used to love the holidays." Catherine scowled and swatted a cookie away from her cheek.

"She used to say it was the one time during the year she could bake and relax and not feel like she should be doing something else. And that everything . . . glowed. *Blech.*"

Initiates trickled into the Gallery, where Old Gwendolyn was dressed in all her glory. Twinkle lights wound like golden filigree through her roots and down to the floor while the fairies vibrated in a tight knot at the top of the room like a pulsing light fixture.

Emily's jaw went slack. "Glowed, huh?"

"Camilla might be a lovesick idiot, but she was right about that."

Emily smiled up at her. "You miss her." It wasn't a question—the sadness trembled in Catherine's voice.

"Sometimes," she admitted. "She's my oldest friend. But I can't pretend I like who she is now."

"No," Emily admitted, "but it's okay to miss something, even if it isn't good for you anymore."

Catherine's smile was slow, but sincere. "C'mon, let's go before Horus gets to the cake first."

Brunch was a quiet affair. The regular round tables were swapped with long, oval buffets covered in red and gold tablecloths. Bowls of sweet oranges dotted in cloves served as decoration, adding to the heady fragrance of pine and baked apples, platters of waffles, bacon, French toast, and fruit.

The meal extended well into the early afternoon and, by the time the eggnog and cider were being served alongside the strawberry cakes and chocolate pudding, Emily was fit to burst. Leaving Catherine with Horus and Piper, she crossed the Gallery to where Ward was deep in conversation with Willow.

"Happy New Year, Master Ward." Emily dropped into the empty seat beside him. "Hey there, Willow. How are you doing?"

"I'm okay," she said, her voice more nasal than usual. "I'm getting over a pretty bad cold, but at least my nose stopped bleeding."

Emily resisted the urge to stare at Willow's nose. "Er . . . that's great, Willow."

"Happy New Year to you, Emily." Ward's smile was a shadow of his former cheer, his clear green eyes sunken, darting, rimmed in red and surrounded by the dark skin of sleepless nights. "Miss Colray was just telling me about some research she's doing on the Commons."

Willow grinned, her eyes shining. "After what Master Grey said about my parents, I got to thinking about where I came from and who they are. Instead of being embarrassed about it, I guess I find it fascinating."

"Aw, Willow, that's great news," Emily said. "Find anything good?"

"Not yet, but I think I'm getting close. My parents don't know who my biological parents are, but I've been looking through old records on my own. Master Ward even helped me get some of the more private books the Masters use because of his connections with Ms. McKibbons, the librarian."

Ward ran his fingers over the curling gold thread in the tablecloth. "It's not a problem, Miss Colray. I'm only too happy to help."

"Actually, Emily, I wanted to ask if it would be okay to talk to you about the Commons sometime." Willow twisted her fingers into a tight knot across her chest. "I don't know much about it, and maybe you could tell me about the people you knew. I wouldn't ask if it wasn't important and—"

"Sure," Emily said at once. "I'll help any way I can."

Willow beamed. "Thanks, Emily. You're a good friend." She got to her feet, red cotton balls dancing off her plaid skirt. "Anyway, I'm going to swing by the greenhouse to check on the Thorny Truth. Master Murray can't get away to do it himself, and they're taking over the other plants."

"Have fun," Emily said as Willow bounced off toward the exit.

"Strange girl." Ward toyed with his untouched piece of salmon. "But I'm happy I could help her. She's had to endure quite a bit of unpleasantness."

"I don't think she's the only one." Ward's hunched shoulders and gaunt face made Emily tense. At once, Grey was back at the forefront of her mind. "Has Master Grey been after your books again, sir?" she asked.

He reached for his goblet, knocking it over in the process. Cider spilled onto the rich tablecloth, the deep velvet bleeding. "Word does get around in this place, doesn't it?" He mopped up the wet spot on the table with a napkin, his gloves shining. "I've been a little bit preoccupied, but I'm probably wrong. Everyone thinks I'm insane, anyway."

"I don't."

His face crumbled, and his fingers clutched the tabletop. "You may be the only one, I'm afraid. Master Grey is talented, and everyone here seems to think she's being properly held in check. I wish I knew what she wanted so I wouldn't have to worry any longer about my safety." Ward shook his head, eyes trained on the table, his ribs visible through his shirt. "I'm so sorry, Emily. That's rather inappropriate of me."

Pity surged through her chest, chased by pure anger. "I might have some ideas about that," she muttered. Fear and curiosity flickered across Ward's face, and Emily backtracked at once. "I shouldn't be saying anything. She's a Master here, and I don't want to cause any more trouble that can get me thrown out. I need to stay at the castle. You understand, right?"

Ward leaned forward, voice low. "Emily, as much as I want to know what you're up to, I should warn you. You shouldn't be getting mixed up in anything involving Sable Grey. She's dangerous."

Emily bristled at the authority in his voice. "I know what I'm up against, and I'm being careful, sir. But the things she did with my father, the things people have caught her doing . . . it's getting to be too much to ignore."

"What things has she been caught doing?"

Don't say anything else. Just stop talking. "That's all right, sir. It's nothing."

He frowned. "You're hiding something. This sounds reckless. Have you spoken to Magdale about it? She's very fond of you, and I'm sure she can help." Ward peered around the Gallery and pushed his chair away from the table.

"No!" Emily grabbed his arm, and he flinched away from her touch as though burned. *His ability.* "I'm sorry, sir. But I can't tell Magdale anything. She won't believe me without proof."

Ward sat down, his eyes on hers. "Emily, what's going on? Proof of what?" When she didn't answer, *couldn't* answer, he pursed his lips. "I knew your father

and respected him very much. I can't let something happen to his daughter if I can help it. So, you either tell me
what you're up to or we go to Magdale. It's your choice."

Emily clenched her jaw, regretting the decision she'd
made to walk over to his table. Telling him about seeing Grey at Blintwoods, about breaking Titan out of the
dragon den and snooping around Grey's room, would all
put her at risk of getting thrown back to the Commons.
Ward liked her, that much she knew. But she couldn't be
sure it was enough. *The truth. Tell as much of the truth
as you need to.* "Sir, you've heard of the Lost Ring, right?
Super powerful, absorbs magic, and fathers pass it only
to their sons?"

Ward's pupils contracted, what little colour he had in
his face draining away to nothing. "Yes, yes, of course.
Why do you ask?"

Emily paused. "I think that Grey might be after it."

"Impossible," he said in a hushed voice. "People have
been looking for the Lost Ring for centuries. What makes
you think Grey wants it?"

"I can't explain it all now." Across the room, Horus
flitted from table to table, challenging anyone who would
listen to a cider-chugging contest. A thought crept into
her mind, and Emily's palms began to itch. "Sir, do you
know what book Grey was looking for when you caught
her going through your stuff?"

"Of course, but it's only a reference book on Selwyn
castle. There's nothing about the Lost Ring in there."

She brightened. "Do you think I could borrow it,
anyway?"

"If you like." Ward chewed his lip, the struggle plain
on his face. "On one condition."

"Anything." Finally, a lead. Finally, a step closer to Grey, who'd been miles ahead of her at every turn.

"You need to keep me informed. This is big stuff you're mixed up in, and if you're not comfortable going to Magdale or the Chief Master, then I need to be involved to make sure you don't get yourself hurt." Ward shivered, his gloves scratching together as he rubbed his hands for warmth. "Do we have a deal?"

Ozzy would be anxious a Master was aware of their plans, and Catherine would be indifferent at best. But what other choice did they have? Ozzy *did* say they needed to make some progress over the holiday break.

Emily nodded. "Deal."

The rest of the afternoon unfolded in an easy haze. Belly full and mind clear, the world stood still enough for her to slip into her dreams with no effort. Shiny, silver reindeers chased giant cranberries up Black Mountain while Catherine and Ozzy ran into the trees to catch them. Emily raced up the path on their heels, but the darkness inside the forest was blinding. They succumbed to the shadows, trudged through the snow and leaves and twigs sharp as ebony needles pricking their feet and slithering up their legs.

They ran from *him*.

It ends where it all begins.

Her neck was heavy, so heavy.

It begins where it all ends.

The mountain was her only hope. But she couldn't see. There was too much fog, her feet were like lead, and time was slipping away.

Still, he chased her.

And, still, she ran.

Chapter Nineteen

On the Wings of a Dragon

JANUARY USHERED IN BLIZZARDS AND Ozzy's return. The castle filled with bright-faced initiates trickling in from their family homes, happy to have survived eliminations. And while the return to a familiar routine was comforting, their second round of lessons quickly proved more gruelling than the first. Workloads mounted, Masters began spot-checking progress in the halls, and even Master Fogg had switched to coffee instead of her questionable tea.

Emily, Ozzy, and Catherine bent their heads against the wind, their Friday morning Flight lesson abandoned midway through because of the icy snow pelleting from the clouds. And, although cuddling with dragons seemed like a good way to combat the blustering cold, the growing beasts hated the snow more than any of the initiates.

"I almost miss eating chicken and broccoli at home if it means not having to go outside in this sludge," Ozzy complained, his cheeks patchy and red.

Catherine scowled over her violet scarf, snow sticking to her glasses and matting her curls into a damp, frizzy mess. "Quit complaining and walk faster. At least we can get some coffee now instead of dancing with monsters."

"Why can't they just cancel Flight until the spring?" Ozzy moaned.

"Because Flight is not a joke," Emily snorted. The castle loomed behind the blanket of flurries, its peaks blurred and whitewashed. Two snowy bodies still braved the storm but, instead of hurrying back to the castle, they headed straight for Emily. "Who's that?" she asked, eyes too watery to see their faces.

"I'd recognize that stupidly perfect outfit anywhere." Catherine groaned, picking up her speed with a sudden burst of effort. "Come on, let's move before they talk to us."

But it was too late. Victor and Camilla stepped into their path like two tall and immaculate ice sculptures. Camilla took shelter behind Victor's elbow, her eyes on the trees at the base of Black Mountain.

"Hi," Victor said, his usual grin competing with the glacial weather. "Talking about anything interesting?"

Catherine's smile was ominous. "The castle's infestation of rats, actually. Behold the king and queen."

Emily edged Catherine with her elbow. It was freezing—too cold to be fighting out in the open when a roaring fire waited for them inside. "We were trying to get back to the dorms. What do you want?"

"Is that how you greet someone who got you the perfect holiday present?" Victor asked, while Camilla pressed her lips together.

Catherine's answering glare scorched the air between them. "No, that's how you greet someone you want to throw in a ditch. Want a demonstration?"

"Maybe another time, Cat." Victor inclined his head. "Ms. McKibbons let me out of the library early, so I thought I'd meet Camilla after her Flight lesson." Victor's eyes locked on Emily. "There's been a ton of books vandalized or gone missing, so there wasn't much for me to do today besides listen to her rant about 'unruly children.'"

Ozzy blinked. "You work at the library?"

"Volunteer, actually." Victor turned and led the way back to the castle. "McKibbons needed the help. I needed the extra credit. And it's always good to have someone owe you a favour."

Camilla leaned into Victor's side, hair billowing out behind her. She tipped her chin in their direction and smirked. "You look miserable, Cat. Realize you picked the wrong friends yet?"

"Shut up, Camilla," Catherine grumbled. Emily linked her arm through Catherine's, earning her a small nod of thanks.

"If I had your ability," Camilla said, "I'd be blowing the snow away from me so it's not in my face. But I'm sure you tried that."

"Mind your business, Cammy!" Catherine called over the bluster. They reached the castle steps and tiptoed up the icy stone, avoiding the pockets of snow making the climb treacherous.

Camilla reached the top first and turned to face Catherine, eyes tight and cheeks blistering red. "I'm only trying to help you!"

"Little late for that, don't you think?" Catherine spat. "I survived being abandoned on a dragon, so I think I can handle some frozen water!"

The wind picked up, and snowfall turned into a proper squall, the day roaring with the rage of winter. Camilla and Catherine squared off, oblivious to the mounting chaos around them.

"You're being stupid!" Camilla's face pleaded with Victor for support, but he stood by Emily's side, letting the argument play out with an exasperated sigh. "It was one fight, and you leave me to go hang around *her*?" Camilla's eyes glazed with tears, the droplets glistening like chips of ice.

"That's not the only reason, Cammy. You changed." The pain was thick in Catherine's voice. "It's not the same anymore. Now can we go inside 'cause it's getting really bad out here!"

The sky was blurry with snow, the air pitching, screaming. *Screaming?*

"I'm not going in until you apologize to me for throwing away years of friendship. And can you calm down? You're blowing down the castle!"

"I'm not doing anything!" Catherine turned around, frowning at the blanket of grey and white hanging low overhead. "It doesn't even feel cold anymore."

Emily ducked her head under her arms as ice pellets burned her cheeks. Windows rattled, and the ground rumbled as an ear-piercing cry pummelled the castle walls. She coughed, spluttering over the flakes sticking to her tongue and choking her. *Burning* her.

Not flakes.

Ash.

"Get inside." Worry twisted Victor's face into someone Emily didn't recognize. He grabbed Ozzy and Emily by the shoulder and pushed them through the front doors, scooping Catherine and Camilla along the way.

"What are you doing?" Catherine complained. "Don't touch me!"

Initiates trickled out of the Gallery or hovered midway up the stairs, confusion etched on every face. Victor didn't slow, his eyes hard. "The Gallery is the safest spot in the castle. Stay as close to Old Gwendolyn as you can, and whatever you do, don't go back to your dorms until it's safe."

"Victor, what are you talking about?" Camilla asked.

A roar tore through the castle, and they all clamped frozen hands over their ears at once, the raw, bone-shattering cries vibrating Emily's ribs. The entrance grew dark as a large shape sailed across the window, blocking all light from the world. And then, the world exploded in a flash of hot, orange fire.

"Dragon!" The cry came from the growing crowd. The screams of terror erupted all at once, a wild chorus in the spreading heat. Faces blurred past Emily, feet clomping, stamping upstairs, hurrying for safety. Chaos. Panic.

Dragon.

Brady pushed through the crowd, face flushed. "Ozzy! Why are you still here?" A girl hurtled into him, and Brady grunted, struggling to stay upright in the roiling sea of bodies. "Never mind. Just get out! Graven, Fenstorm needs help outside!"

Victor's face was pinched with worry, but he nodded. "Right. I said *go*, Rathburn!" With one last pointed look at them all, Victor and Brady disappeared into the fray. Another cry ripped through the castle, and the initiates scattered in every direction like marbles.

Emily's teeth rattled in her head. Flames lapped at the windows and scorched the outside steps before someone forced the entrance door shut. Heat boxed them in on all sides and Emily coughed, her lungs seizing and her eyes watering.

"Let's move!" she cried, spluttered, coughed.

With her head bent against the mounting smoke, she pushed Ozzy and Catherine deeper into the castle, elbows and hands poking, slapping, shoving as she struggled to walk. Camilla was gone. Faces flew by. *We need to get away from the crowds.*

"What about my brother!" A coughing fit overcame Ozzy, and he doubled over, the smoke overtaking him.

"He'll be fine!" Catherine screamed. She and Ozzy pressed in close, their combined weight enough to boulder through the mess. Masters rushed in the opposite direction, calls for order swallowed by shriek after shriek from a massive dragon sailing above the castle. The walls rumbled, and the air shook with each beat of the dragon's wings.

They made it to the stairwell and ducked behind the climbing spiral steps.

"Where's Camilla?" Catherine asked, coughing into her sleeve.

Emily shook her head. The entrance hall flooded with initiates running for the Gallery, funnelling down the steps into a bottleneck of hysteria and fear. Among them, a halo of white curls flitted past, a path opening before her with a casual flick of her wrist. "Move aside!" Magdale called over the crowd. "Everyone inside the Gallery as quick as you can. Come on, Mister Fitzgibbons, you're holding up the line!"

"I lost Finn, Master Toth!" Elliott's wide, brown eyes shimmered and pooled, their depths scanning every passing face. His head swivelled on his neck, his arms and legs growing and shrinking in quick succession as terror took over him.

"Magdale!" Emily shouted over the roar. She stepped around the stairs, and both Ozzy and Catherine grabbed her sleeve. She turned to them, pulling herself free. "Go through the secret passage Horus showed us, Ozzy! The Gallery's a mess to get to, and the tunnel won't be so crowded. I'll be right back!" Before Ozzy could protest, she rejoined the fray.

The panic in Elliott's eyes called her, begged for help. Both Ozzy and Catherine would be fine, but Willow was nowhere to be found—even Camilla had disappeared, dissolved to nothing. How many were still outside in the courtyard fighting off the dragon? Five? Ten? Had everyone made it back to the castle, or were there still stragglers trapped in the blaze outside? The stampede took hold of her like a river's current, and she let it sweep her away.

She couldn't go back, couldn't move, couldn't stop.

A wave of heat rushed inside the hall like a raging bull as the doors creaked open once again and the wall of smoke knocked her back, the billowing, growling air eating away at Emily's nerve. The crowd was an animal all its own as it pressed in on her, pulsing, thrashing. She couldn't make Elliott out in the crowd or find Willow, or Horus, or . . .

Another cry, farther away, somehow, and she teetered on unsteady feet.

Am I passing out?

The drumbeat of wings flapped a faint rhythm, no longer causing the castle walls to shake in fear.

This doesn't feel like passing out . . .

The air was still so thick, the tar-like smoke worming into every corner of the hall. But it was no longer scorching hot, not a furnace but a hot summer day. The rioting slowed, and everyone scanned the room, the door, the stairs. The sky was a defeated, roiling grey.

It's too quiet.

And, from experience, that was never good.

Magdale's head popped into view at the door, her usual pink cheeks covered in soot and grime and . . .

No.

"Make some room!" Magdale cried.

More bodies entered the castle, but Emily couldn't see past Magdale's stern face. The mob backed away, giving her room. A sob, and then another broke out, but the tears were soft compared to the pandemonium of a moment before. Emily's ears rang, but her eyes remained level. Magdale bent over two dark figures sprawled on the ground, her hands working with buttons and collars, sweeping back hair. "Everyone, go back to your dormitories! The dragon is gone—go!"

But no one moved—not even the lifeless bodies on the ground.

The world lurched.

Undiluted power ran wild in her veins, begging to be used. Trees raced past, the moonlight filtering through the branches as he chased her.

The images came at her fast, bowling her over. An invisible arm wound around Emily's waist, and her legs moved of their own will.

Away from the bodies. *Bodies?*

Away from the crowd.

Up the first step, then the next.

Emily fought against the magical bindings, but her will was weak and her mind was in pain. Every nerve was alight, firing, sizzling in agony, and yet she couldn't move if she wanted to. Instead, her feet took over on their own, up and up and up. Away from it all. It was warm, and despite the thick scent of smoke and charred flesh, Emily welcomed the heat. Willed it to burn the images from her mind.

The sobbing grew louder, shaking her from her haze, and she tried to turn back. *Why can't I go back?* Emily leaned away from the arm supporting her and tensed her legs, willing them to stop moving.

"Emily." A voice beside her, calm and commanding. "We need to get out of here."

Those shapes on the ground . . .

"Emily? Can you hear me?"

Is he talking to me? She couldn't tell. She couldn't care. The ground must have been so uncomfortable.

"Say something."

"Victor?" Emily asked, her voice shaky.

"That's right," he said, relief thick in his hoarse voice. Her vision came into focus, and she peered up at his blackened face, a cut on his forehead oozing deep red blood down his temple. "Come on, nice and easy."

She shook her head. Master Ward's frail body lay broken and bruised on the ground below her, his already ragged clothes torn and caked with grime and gore. His face wore an unconscious mask of pain where his injuries didn't muddle it. Beside him, Finn Dashwood lay in a sagging heap, leaves matting his crumpled form. Emily remembered his anxious face the first time he had seen a dragon, a face now cold and blank.

Her stomach heaved. She struggled against the strange hold, but the act of staying upright was challenge enough.

"It's harder for me if you fight it." Victor grunted with the effort of steering her and guided her farther up the stairs. "Let's get you back to your dorm."

His words jolted her back into her body. "You're using your magic on me?" she asked, hysteria kicking her voice into a high pitch. "Let me go! I have to help them!"

"Someone more qualified than you *is* helping them." He chanced a brief look down the stairs. "Look, it wasn't exactly my first choice to force you out of there, either, but I don't think you would have moved on your own. There's nothing you can do for them." His dark brows pulled low over his eyes, casting shadows across his face.

"They're dead," she croaked.

"You don't know that."

"They weren't moving." Her eyes lingered on his profile, and her fingers stretched to his head. "And you're bleeding."

Victor bent his head away from her, and she let her fingers fall. "I'm fine. I've never seen anything like that—it was so . . . so *big*."

She couldn't think about the dragon. Not yet. "Is Brady okay? How about Fenstorm? Was there anyone else—?"

"Stop, Rathburn." Victor's eyes were intent on her face, roving over her like a floodlight. "Everyone made it out. Whatever the dragon was after, I don't think it was too thrilled hanging around with us for too long. It took off pretty quick. What about you?"

"Me?" The smoke thinned out, and she could breathe fresh air underneath the blanket of soot. "I'm fine. I'm not the one who went out to fight a dragon. But we lost Camilla, and I haven't seen Willow. And Elliott was looking for Finn."

And there are bodies on the floor.

A girl, her face lifeless and covered by a curtain of her hair.

Emily's heart constricted, and she couldn't breathe. "Stop."

Victor looked at her as though doubting her sanity. "Do you need a break?"

She pulled against him, and he let her go at once. "Didn't you hear what I said?" she asked, her hands growing numb. "Camilla could still be down there! And all my friends, all those people!" Emily pressed her eyes shut, hoping to squeeze out the image of Finn on the ground. Instead, his outline flickered behind her eyes, a permanent shape branded in her memory.

Victor rolled his eyes. "Camilla's going to be fine. I'll bet you anything that she abandoned the three of you to take care of herself. She's probably up in the dorms right now, changing her outfit to something less covered in dragon ash." He snorted, the sound one of contempt rather than amusement. "You, on the other hand, have the instinct to help, which is *really* annoying at a time like this."

"That's not your business." Emily took a purposeful step down. And away from him.

Darkness passed over Victor's impatient face. "I'm only trying to help you, Rathburn."

"If you wanted to help, you could be down there with Magdale."

"They don't need me," he said through clenched teeth. "I learned a long time ago that sometimes, the best thing you can do is back off."

"But you never do." Emily's fingers vibrated, and her fists grew hot. "I'm not some helpless little girl, Victor. I know you're trying to help, and in your own way, you *really* believe that's what I need. But what I *actually* need right now is to find Catherine and Ozzy and make sure they're okay!"

"Emily? Is that you?" Ozzy raced down the stairs, his expression a perfect mask of panic. Catherine stomped close behind, her fear contained, but only just. With a laugh, Ozzy threw his arms around Emily's shoulders. "We waited for you to come back, but you were gone!" he said in her ear.

"I . . . I wanted to help Elliott." The sob of relief bubbled up the back of her throat, suffocating her.

"That's what I told Ozzy." Catherine massaged a stitch in her side. "As soon as you stepped away, we lost track of you. We figured you'd go back to the dorms when the dragon finally took off, but when Ward and Finn got dragged in like that . . . " She exchanged a worried glance with Ozzy, who'd backed away, leaving one hand on Emily's shoulder. "Well, we got worried."

Emily frowned, and Ozzy hitched up a reassuring smile. "It's okay, though. We don't blame you."

"I don't get it," Emily said. Victor leaned against the banister, his eyes trained on the ground. "Why are you all so worried about me? I'm fine."

"Well, it's just that . . . it sort of looked like what happened when . . . " Ozzy wrung his fingers together, cheeks red.

Catherine rolled her eyes. "Ugh, she's fine, Ozzy—you can say it!" She turned to Emily, the haughty look on her muddied face not unkind. "It looked a lot like what happened when your dad attacked those people. We figured seeing all that might have triggered you or something."

"No one would have blamed you if it had," Ozzy reminded her.

Understanding, unexpected and brutal, dawned on Emily. But before she could thank them for caring, apologize for being so stupid, Victor cleared his throat. "I should go find Camilla," he said, trudging down the stairs with his chin tucked to his chest. "See you all later."

"Hope not!" Catherine called after him, then, under her voice, she cursed. "I'm starting to see a little too much of Graven if you ask me."

Emily offered half a smile and, together, they climbed the rest of the stairs in silence.

Quiet was never good—she knew that for a fact. But, right then, all she wanted was to drown in it.

Chapter Twenty

Ward Away the Evil

During the week following the attack, the entrance hall was given a wide berth, and the grounds swept for damage. Initiates avoided the large, crimson patch on the middle of the stone floor until a Master cleaned it out in the middle of the night, erasing any sign of the dragon's destruction inside the castle. The grounds were torched and many of the old trees burnt to ash. But while soot was still tracked into the castle daily, the loudest reminders of the rogue dragon were Ward and Finn.

Master Ward remained quarantined in the clinic's private wing for a month. Rumours of burns and scars and mutilated limbs circulated in hushed voices while initiates crept past the locked clinic door in the hopes of catching a glimpse of him.

Finn, however, had not been so lucky. No one spoke of the boy who kept to himself, whose burns had rendered him unrecognizable. And soon taken his life.

It was bad luck to speak of the dead.

Ozzy rubbed his bloodshot eyes and slouched in his armchair. "How many times are you going to read that book, Emily?"

"Until I figure out what Grey wanted in here." She turned the page and skimmed the heading of the next chapter, the familiar words taunting her. No matter how many times she'd combed through each sentence, she still came back empty-handed. Initiates filtered in and out of North Lounge, but she didn't see them—only more disappointment disguised as an old book sitting in her helpless hands.

"Ward won't sleep another day in his life when he wakes up and finds out we've got nothing." Catherine toyed with one of her curls and stared out the window. "Poor guy. He'll have to quit. Maybe change his name."

"He'll be fine because we're going to find something," Emily insisted.

"I say we take the stupid book and throw it at Grey's stupid head," Catherine muttered. "A concussion is a good backup plan."

Ozzy sighed. "I can't believe I'm saying this, but I agree with her." He threw a loaded look at Catherine and cleared his throat. "Not about the book throwing, but that we hit a dead end and need a break. Do you want to come check on Elliott with us?"

Emily cringed at the name. Elliott had disappeared for a few days after the attack and, in the weeks following his return, had kept to himself, quiet and pale. In a terrible way, Emily was thankful for his absence, both physical and mental; what do you say to someone who's lost his best friend in the blink of an eye? Anything Emily could think of was awkward on her tongue. Nothing could be enough to ease his pain, to stop Willow's sobs, to smooth the matching looks of worry on Catherine's and Ozzy's faces as they pretended to listen to Horus talk about his lessons in a flat monotone. All Emily could do was nothing, and nothing wasn't good enough. Not when she could do more.

Instead, she spent every waking moment with Ward's book, hoping to find a way to make things right again.

"Emily, some of the initiates are having a magic tourney in the Gallery tonight," Ozzy said in his softest voice. He leaned over, trying to catch her eye and failing. "They have booths and games to test us against each other, and there's a prize at the end. I thought it might be fun to go."

"Yeah, it doesn't sound too bad," Catherine piped in. "We even get to dress up and everything. If I try hard enough, I might be able to catch Camilla in a good tornado. Plus, Oswald told me I could help him with his outfit."

"I didn't say that."

Catherine grinned. "Hush now, you don't know what you're saying."

"I'll pass." Emily flipped the page. "You two go without me."

Ozzy sighed. "You need a break—we all do. It's not helping anyone to read the same thing over and over." He pursed his lips as though tasting something sour. "Finn wouldn't want everyone to give up on their lives because of him."

Emily's shoulders hunched in at his words, but Catherine rallied. "Besides, you look terrible." Catherine cast a pointed look at Emily's wrinkled clothes and frazzled hair. "Do we need to drag you in front of a mirror to paint a picture of how hopeless you look?"

In fact, they didn't; Emily hadn't slept for longer than an hour or two at a time in days, waking in a sheen of sweat, fingers searching for Ward's book. The tangles in her hair had made it impossible to brush without her usual patience to keep her going. Finn's death had sparked a fire in her belly refusing to be ignored. But, for the first time in hours, she let Ward's book fall into her lap and stared at Catherine.

Emily looked up. "Wait—say that again?"

Catherine frowned. "I said you look like you lost your mind."

"That's not what she meant." Ozzy pinched the bridge of his nose and shook his head.

Catherine blinked. "Yeah, it is. She hasn't changed her clothes in two days, and I'd like to head off the smell before our room starts absorbing it."

"That's . . . that's it!" Emily cried. She flipped through the pages with renewed energy. "That's what I was missing!"

"She's a goner," Catherine said a calm voice. "Think they have a cure for mentally unstable Elementals with really bad hair?"

Emily squinted down at the open book, a genuine grin spreading across her face. "There you are." She held the book up like a trophy so Ozzy and Catherine could have a look. "I know why Grey wanted this book and why Millendorf's office was broken into."

Ozzy squinted at the page and frowned. "'Art and Décor—A Selwyn Tradition'?"

"What do you see in the picture?" Emily tapped the faded image she had glossed over a dozen times before.

Ozzy read the caption out loud. "*'Alexander Mordredovich Selwyn, Founding Father of Selwyn Castle'.*"

Emily nodded, her excitement growing. "I've never seen this painting in the castle."

"Me either," Catherine said, "but this place is massive. It's probably hidden in a dungeon somewhere."

"Or," Emily continued, "it's in the room where every other item belonging to a Selwyn Chief Master is."

Ozzy's face slackened. "Millendorf's office."

Emily nodded. "Now, look at his hand."

Catherine and Ozzy leaned their faces closer to the worn page, where a small, faded band flashed on Selwyn's finger, a familiar stone perched at the center. "This looks almost identical to the drawing of the Lost Ring we saw in that library book!" Ozzy exclaimed.

Emily nodded. "Ward's obsessed with old books. He helps McKibbons in the library all the time and always has something to read with him. Grey must have figured that if anyone had information on the Lost Ring, it would be Ward. And," she said as another puzzle piece clicked into place, "Victor mentioned the library's been vandalized. I'll bet Grey's been combing through every book in that place and couldn't find a copy of this, so she needed to get Ward's."

"So, the hag saw this picture and decided to break into Millendorf's office to check it out for herself." Catherine's lips curled in disgust. "Figures."

Emily fiddled with her necklace, thumb tracing the edges with mounting anger. "We need to find that ring before she does."

Catherine propped her chin into her palms. "Well, that shouldn't be too hard now."

Ozzy turned to her, bewildered. "Empaths and Elementals who know the legends inside out haven't managed to find the thing. How do you figure it'll be easy for us?"

"Well," Catherine said, her tone the same she'd use to explain how to tie her shoes to a young child, "we know the ring got passed from father to son or whatever sexist tradition they believed in back then, right?"

Emily brightened. "And since not many people connected the ring back to Selwyn or had proof of him wearing it, they haven't managed to link it to him. Catherine, you're a genius! If we track Selwyn's family tree—"

"We find his last descendent and hope he still has the stupid thing," she finished.

Ozzy's jaw hinged open. "Amazingly . . . that makes sense."

Catherine stared at him and shook her head. "You insult me, Oswald."

The library was full for a Saturday afternoon. Torches burned low on the walls, and books staggered through the air as though too tired to do anything but weave through the aisles in search of their proper place. Emily peered around her tall stack of books as she led the way to the table at the farthest corner, careful to avoid Ms. McKibbons and any questions she might bring.

"What happened to carefree childhoods?" Catherine let her pile of spell books thud onto the desk. "I should have never opened my big mouth."

"Why do girls complain so much?" Ozzy pushed his hair out of his eyes. Slumping into the seat opposite Catherine, he picked out his first book without reading the title and glared at the cracked binding.

The pressure was getting to them all. Emily rubbed her eyes, wishing she could pour into bed and sleep for days. But rest was a luxury. She fanned her books across the dusty table, and a swatch of pale blue caught her eye.

"Hey, I'll be right back," Emily said. When Ozzy and Catherine waved her off, she slipped into the aisles, happy for a small taste of peace.

It was a sign. An omen. A cosmic reprimand for having waited so long. But she wouldn't wait any longer. Elliott Fitzgibbons sat in a far corner of the library, staring at his hands as his fingers grew longer, thinner, wide as spades and then back to their original shape. She still didn't know what to say to a grieving boy, but with a lead on the Lost Ring and a step closer to righting Grey's—and her father's—wrongs, it was time to give it a try.

"Hi." Emily's heart thumped behind her ribs, and her pulse hammered in her ears. She cleared her throat, aware of the tingling in her fingers and the weight of her necklace.

Elliott's shoulders tensed, and his eyes were bleary. "Yeah? Oh . . . hey, Emily." His voice cracked with disuse, and a new wave of guilt crashed over her.

Theft, she could do without batting an eye. Comfort, however, was out of her league. Emily stood too straight, too quiet. Her face was all wrong. "Are you . . . ? I mean, I know you're not okay." She sighed. "We haven't had a chance to talk since it all happened. I feel bad about that." Her cheeks grew warm, and her words were all wrong, too.

Elliott blinked, his face like chalk. "I'm fine. Just . . . getting by. I should have been there. I should have helped." He made no effort to conceal the fresh tears standing in his bloodshot eyes. "I was looking for him, you know."

"You couldn't save him from a dragon." Emily wished she could tell herself the same thing and believe it. Her guilt was mirrored in Elliott's tortured face, but she wouldn't let him see it. "There wasn't anything you could have done for him."

"Tell that to Finn." Elliott wore a mask of tortured pain. "He was having such a hard time with everything, and I made fun of him. I shouldn't have done that. Maybe . . . " His voice cracked, and he pressed his lips together before championing on. "Maybe if I hadn't teased him so much, he wouldn't have been out working so hard without me. I should have been better."

Emily reached out and placed her fingertips on his shoulder. "He was working hard because he was having trouble with his ability, not because of anything you said. I'm so, so sorry, Elliott. Can I do anything?"

He sniffed and stood from his seat. Elliott had no bag, no books. It was as though he hadn't been there. "I appreciate that, Emily. I think I just need a walk. I'll see you." He trudged off, head hung low, until he disappeared into the shadows.

Emily made her way back to her table, unsure if their talk had helped her or given her another reason to have nightmares. Elliott's face sent a bucket of ice water pouring down her back, and she ghosted back to her table, missing Molly and grateful for Ozzy and Catherine, who were still poring over textbooks on their weekend. For her.

"How's Elliott?" Ozzy asked without looking up.

Emily rubbed the back of her hand across her eyes and opened her book. "Not great. You two find anything?"

Catherine shook her head. "It's all so *boring*. Plus, I have pages missing in mine."

"Well, here's something." Ozzy opened *Life and Death and Life Again—Sometimes*. "*'Morenius Mordredovich Selwyn, Elemental warrior in the First Uprising of the Realm and distant ancestor of Alexander Selwyn, led his army into battle against magical oppressors, claiming victory in only four days and suffering the lowest number of casualties ever recorded. Selwyn retired to the remote countryside with his two sons, Xenith and Parsapian, and built Selwyn City in twenty-one days.'*"

"What's Selwyn City?" Catherine asked.

Ozzy frowned. "It's what Elementals and Empaths named their community before The Great Divide happened."

"He had to have the Lost Ring," Emily said with complete certainty. "No regular Elemental could do all those things without some extra help. At least we know we're on the right track. Now we just have to go down the family tree." They combed through the Selwyn family bloodline, moving from father to son, generation to generation, extraordinary accomplishment to the next.

Until they found him.

"*'Alexander Selwyn,'*" Ozzy read, his excitement climbing until he was perched at the edge of his chair, "*'founder of Selwyn castle, opened his doors to brilliant young Empaths and Elementals to much anticipation. Unfortunately, his success was short-lived, as he unexpectedly passed peacefully in his sleep days before his fiftieth birthday. Selwyn is survived by his two children.'"*

Emily frowned at the page. "He died? What about his kids?"

Ozzy lowered his head. "Alexander Selwyn . . . founder and father . . . here we go: *'Shortly after his death, daughter Beth Selwyn disappeared from the castle grounds and was found deceased. Investigations ruled her passing a suicide by Guard officials. Elder son, Xavier, disappeared soon after and was also presumed dead after an extensive search.'"*

Catherine glared at the book. "They *all* died?" she asked. "That's it?"

"That's all it says!" Ozzy leaned back in his seat. "I can't find anything else on Xavier Selwyn to show he got the Lost Ring before his father passed away."

For the first time since running into Grey at Blintwoods so many months before, Emily considered giving up. She rubbed her temples, afraid of how little time she had left before Grey reached the finish line, and glanced over to where Elliott had sat. This had been their final thread. And now, it was gone.

A shadow moved out of a tall stack of books and headed straight for their table. Emily sighed. "Now's not a good time, Victor."

No lopsided smirk, no flirtatious quip. "I'm sorry to interrupt."

"Then don't," Catherine muttered. "Take the hint, Vicky, and go."

His eyes were guarded, black in the low light. "I'm actually here to deliver a message. Master Ward is awake, and he asked to see you, Rathburn."

She jumped to her feet. "He's awake? How is he?"

Victor shook his head. "No idea. He woke up yesterday and has been asking to see you ever since, but they only passed along the message now."

"Okay, I'll be back soon." Emily grabbed her bag with trembling hands. Victor stepped aside as she made to run off, but the sound of chairs scraping stopped her cold.

Catherine slammed her book shut. "Hold on! We're coming with you!"

Emily glanced back at them, feet still moving. "I think it's better if I go on my own. He asked for me, and I don't want to give the nurses any reason to turn me away."

Catherine opened her mouth to argue, but Ozzy placed a restraining hand on her arm. "I think she's right," he said. "You go see Ward, and we'll keep looking through things here."

Emily smiled. "Thanks, Ozzy. I'll be back soon." She hurried to the door, the way to the clinic already mapped out in her mind.

"Rathburn, wait!" Victor called, rushing up behind her. "Why are you running? It's not like he's going anywhere."

"You wouldn't understand." She took a sharp turn down a corridor lined with tall windows glowing pink with imminent twilight. Outside, a few fairies floated away, their light bidding Emily a warm goodnight. "Why are you following me?" she asked, making no effort to hide her irritation.

The clinic door loomed ahead, a heavy slab of iron with a handle, and the only person she cared to listen to was Ward. She pulled the door open and slipped into the clinic, leaving Victor behind without so much as a thank-you.

"Yes?" The healer on duty clicked her way around the white reception desk with hooded eyes, bright red curls pinned neatly under a white cap.

"I'm here to see Master Ward. I'm Emily Rathburn."

The healer pursed her lips at once, distaste causing her to take a step back. "Fine. Follow me."

Both the reception and clinic were outfitted all in white; starched curtains hung around steel-framed beds covered in white linens, the simple iron frames lined into neat rows under the large windows. Emily walked down the row of empty beds in silence, every step bringing her closer to the truth.

"Fine, Miss Rathburn." The healer came to a stop beside a curtained-off cubicle. "No touching the patient, yelling, eating, drinking, levitating, or animals of any kind. Now, I know he sent for you, but keep it short and light. He's still a tad . . . frazzled." Her tiny black eyes sat close together above an upturned nose, lips curled in disapproval.

"Right." Emily exhaled in relief when the woman turned and clicked away. "Thanks."

Now what? Do I knock? It's a curtain, I can't knock.

"Please come inside before that dreadful woman comes back." Ward's voice was thin, scratching against his throat like sandpaper, but familiar and very much alive.

Magdale sat beside Ward's bed, a tray of cookies balanced on her lap and a steaming cup of coffee hovering at her elbow. A hint of a smile twinkled in her blue eyes as she rearranged Ward's blanket with fussy fingers.

"I know I'm breaking almost all her rules, but honestly, what harm will some food do?" Magdale complained. "Come, Emily dear. Have a cookie."

"Um, no thanks, Magdale." The knot in Emily's chest was making it hard to breathe, let alone eat, and the room was too small for the injuries held within it.

Ugly purple bruises covered Ward's face. Deep cuts leaked fresh blood from his forehead while a heavy blanket covered the thick bandages covering his torso. Ward smiled at her through cracked lips, his one good eye sparkling.

"It's better than it looks," he said with a weak smile. "No need to look at me like that—I'm not dead yet."

"Flavian!" Magdale chastised.

"I heard you wanted to see me." Emily's voice quivered, and she took a deep breath, reminding herself she had no right to be upset. She needed to be strong—for Ward. For Elliott. For Finn. "I can come back, though, if this is a bad time."

"Not at all," Ward said at once. "Magdale has been coming to visit every day since the attack. She's the only one the healers will let in without me having to beg, and while I very much appreciate her, it does get quite lonely."

"Well, visits help the healing process," Magdale said. "And the injured can't be choosy. Speaking of visits—Emily, you haven't been to see me in ages."

"I'm sorry, Magdale," Emily said. "I've wanted to, but things always seem to come up." It was a half-truth; visiting Magdale had escaped her mind, a fact she wasn't proud of. But there was also a large part of her that cringed away from the thought of having to lie to her.

The Elemental Master sat before her like she'd done in the Commons months before, and Emily's heart ached.

"Yes, with all the dragon-riding and extra work with Mister Graven, I'd imagine it's difficult to find the time." Magdale's eyes glittered, and Emily was overcome with shame. "How are you doing, Emily?"

Terrible. Awful. I miss the Commons. Emily glanced at Ward. Something inside her shut down. "I'm doing . . . better. Keeping busy helps."

"My understanding is you saw more than you should have during the attack." Ward scrutinized her with his one good eye, its iris a vivid emerald against his bruised skin.

"I did." Emily gathered her courage, using the space between heartbeats to steady her breathing. "Do you remember what happened, sir?"

"Pieces," Ward said, a slight tremor in his voice. "Mister Dashwood managed to scrape by eliminations once again but was worried he wouldn't continue to be so lucky. He came to me for some help at someone's suggestion, and we were taking a walk around the grounds to discuss the issue. But then this . . . this horrible *screeching* started and I . . . I just . . . "

A fresh wave of guilt crashed over her, threatening to drag her so deep underwater she would never resurface. Finn had been outside with Ward because she'd told him to ask for Ward's help. Had it not been for her suggestion—no, *interference*—Finn might still be alive.

Not yet. Emily pressed the pain far down. *You can't worry about that right now.*

Tears trickled down Ward's cheeks. "That poor boy. I hope his family finds justice for him."

"Flavian—" Magdale threw Ward a warning look. "It was an accident. We don't have to talk about this now."

Ward pushed himself into a seated position, wincing in pain. "Dragons don't materialize from nothing, Magdale." He turned to Emily. "I won't take up much of your time, but I do need to speak with you privately. Magdale, could you give us a moment?"

Magdale perched beside Ward's bed, pity warring with disapproval on her round face. With tight lips, she clapped her hands to clear the food away and got to her feet. "Five minutes," she warned. "I need to go check on the investigation into Zaphira's whereabouts, anyhow." As she stepped across the curtain, she addressed Emily alone. "He needs rest, Emily. Please try not to upset him."

Emily nodded and, before she could blink, Magdale disappeared in a flash of blue eyes and bright light.

Ward sighed. "Between Magdale and the healers, I haven't had a moment alone to think. Tell me that you found something useful in my book."

Straight to business. This I can handle. "I did. But I have a question for you that might save me some time. What happened to Alexander Selwyn's kids? I can't find much information about them."

Ward coughed, the sound like marbles in a tin can. "It's not a happy tale," he warned. "Selwyn was a highly regarded man. His son, Xavier, showed all the promise of following in his father's footsteps, but his daughter was not so gifted. But when your father is the founder and Chief Master, well . . . doors open to you that should otherwise have remained closed."

"So, his daughter wasn't very talented with her magic, but Selwyn got her a spot in the castle anyway. What about Xavier? What happened to him?"

Ward frowned. "He and his father had vastly different views on the world. From what I gathered through previous studies, they argued about their values until Alexander passed away." He paused, struggling for breath. "That family had horrible luck. Anyhow, it all happened quickly after that. Beth fled the castle when her father died, and Xavier disappeared soon after his sister's body was found in Black Mountain." Ward's eye slipped shut as he fought the pull of sleep.

Emily stood rooted to the spot, something about the story still nagging at her. "What was she doing alone on Black Mountain?" she asked. "I mean, especially if she was young and didn't have the best control of her magic. She would have known it was dangerous."

Ward's eye drooped. "I'm not sure anyone knows for certain—no one alive, anyhow. But Beth . . . Beth is a true mystery." He blinked and took a long, deep breath. After a moment, soft snores escaped his swollen lips.

Emily couldn't stand the confines of the room any longer. With Ward asleep, she rushed out into the sterile white hall, hoping she wouldn't run into Magdale or the healer on her way back to the library.

I did this to Finn.

Her stomach turned, and the lights outside the clinic doors were too bright.

It's my fault.

She needed to find Ozzy and Catherine, to make it all right somehow.

"Rathburn! Hey, slow down."

"I'm not sure anyone knows for certain—no one alive, anyhow."

"Rathburn!" Victor stepped into her path, and Emily stopped short.

"Not now, Victor!" she said, breathless. "I need to go."

"What happened in there?" When she pushed past him again, he didn't fall behind. Keeping pace, Victor's eyes burned into the side of her face as windows streaked by. "Why did Ward want to see you?"

"None of your business."

A strong arm swung out before her, forcing her to a stop, but he was sure not to touch her. "Something's off about this whole thing. Can you tell me what's going on with you?"

Emily glared at him. She stepped further back, her patience finally run dry. "Is that why you came to tell me he was looking for me? So you'd have an excuse to be there and harass me when I got out?"

Victor sidestepped the question. "I think it's a little weird that he asked for you as soon as he woke up," he spat. "You're mixed up in something you shouldn't be. I can feel it. Let me help."

Something in her crumbled. Heat pulsed down her arms and into her fingertips. "You want to help? All you've done is play around with me like I'm some brand-new toy." Across from her, a wall torch vanished, the light in the hall dimming at its disappearance. "I'm tired of you following me like you actually care what happens to me."

"I do care."

"Well, unless you can tell me what happened to Beth Selwyn, I have no use for this conversation or your concern," she said. "What's going on between me and Ward is my business, got it?"

"Beth Selwyn?" His face screwed up in confusion. "What do you need to know about her for?"

A low hiss of frustration escaped Emily's lips. "Leave it alone, Victor."

She turned to walk, to run, to never look back, but he spoke, voice soft and even, infuriating as it carried down the corridor. "I might have a way to get you what you need."

She stopped. Forced as much distrust into her face as she could manage and turned to him. "Why would you do that?"

He shrugged. "Because I can. Meet me at your usual table in the library Monday at sundown. I should have something by then." The air between them crackled, and she ignored the dip in lighting as another candle disappeared into thin air. He nodded a wordless goodbye, tucked his hands into his jacket pockets, and took off in the opposite direction of the library.

Emily stared at his back, breaths coming fast. Another game, another trick to get her to confide in him.

Did he ever really trick you, though?

She swatted the thought away and waited for the crackling in her fingers to disappear before leaving Ward and Victor behind. She knew what to do, and she hated herself for the small part of herself yearning to do it.

How to Catch a Ghost

"MISS LEE, PLEASE TRY *NOT* to turn anyone in my cottage into a living torch," Grey instructed, her silky voice strained. "You're trying too hard with the spell. It's terrifying."

"Yes, Master Grey." Tina's lower lip trembled. "Sorry."

As news of Ward's improved condition made its way around the castle, Grey's mood deteriorated. And, although Emily had begun to lose hope of ever making it through another elimination, there was one good thing about Grey's horrible attitude—it was proof she hadn't found the Lost Ring yet, either.

"She's insane!" Catherine hissed, mimicking a rather violent stabbing with her quill as the rat on her desk scurried off to safety.

"Shhh!" Ozzy kicked Catherine in the shin as Grey stalked past. "Just focus on the spell before we're stuck scrubbing her toilet for a month. C'mon, Cathy, let's see what you've got."

"Don't call me Cathy!" she complained, eyes darkening.

"You have to learn to focus even if there are distractions!" he said. "Remember, there is empty space between the cells of the rat. Focus on moving air through those empty spaces, and you can't go wrong." Ozzy rolled his eyes. "Don't make that face, you look like a troll. Ready?" He picked up their rat before it jumped off the desk and plopped it beside Catherine's open hand.

Two desks down, Willow had abandoned the small sprout of Thorny Truth she was to make grow and was immersed in a large journal bound in faded cloth. Elliott sat beside her, staring at his clasped hands, struggling with fingernail growth.

"Poor guy hasn't been himself since the attack," Ozzy mumbled, watching Elliott with pity in his eyes. "I wish we could do something."

Outside, the sky was a deep magenta, faded pink light dancing around the edges of the world and streaming through the windows like living, moving crystals. "We can," Emily muttered. "Ward thinks Grey was behind the dragon attack, and I believe him. Probably another distraction to get to the ring. We need to take her down."

"I take it back." Catherine pulled her hands away from the rat with a grunt of dislike, and it scurried across the desk. "Grey's insane, but *you're* suicidal."

"It's sunset," Grey announced, voice clipped. "You can leave. But I would suggest you all practice because today's performance was rather pathetic. Miss Colray, please see me after you pack your things. The rest of you . . . good luck."

Emily peered over at Willow, who was packing her things without a trace of fear. "Do you want us to wait for you, Willow?" she asked. "We can stay outside until you're done." She cast a worried glance at Grey, who stood by the fire, her back to the room. Silver flashed off her spiked hair, and Emily resisted the urge to throw something.

To Emily's surprise, Willow smiled. "I asked for this meeting with Master Grey. It's okay, I'll see you three at dinner." She trotted to the front of the room and waited at Grey's podium for the room to clear.

"Wonder what the Elders that's all about." Catherine was pale as they left Blackwood Cottage, her eyes wide behind thick glass frames. "I feel like I should be throwing myself between them."

"We can ask Willow later." Emily led the charge back to the castle. "We'd better hurry or we'll be late."

"Right." Ozzy rolled his eyes and picked up his pace. "Graven's waiting."

The path to the library was growing all too familiar. Emily's legs moved out of sheer muscle memory, her heart pounding with anticipation. The heavy mahogany doors opened with a dusty sigh.

"Why does Victor even need to be involved in this?" Catherine frowned at the rows of books as they passed. "You didn't tell him anything, did you?"

"'Course not. But he thinks he can help get some information," Emily said. "At this point, I'll take all the help I can get."

Catherine seethed, navigating the stacks with practiced steps. "He just better not have brought Camilla."

Victor leaned against their favourite table by the far window, arms crossed, hair mussed, face serious. "I didn't bring Camilla," he said in a low voice, and Catherine had the sense to blush. "But she says hi, if that helps."

"Shut it, Vicky," Catherine muttered.

"Right. Follow me." Without wasting any time, Victor strode to the end of the library, past windows and shelves and tables of initiates with bent heads and sagging shoulders. "I told you I've been volunteering here for a little while and McKibbons owes me a favour."

"So?" Catherine hung back, her eyes trained on Victor's shoulders with naked hate.

"So," he continued with a hint of annoyance, "when Emily mentioned Beth Selwyn, something clicked. For some reason, Beth seems to be a popular topic around here."

Emily frowned. "You're talking about the vandalized books. Did you find the missing pages?"

Victor took a sharp left down a corridor Emily had never travelled down. The air was cool but heavy, as though the dust had gathered undisturbed for years. Portraits lined the stone walls, and unlike the rest of the library, there wasn't a book or window in sight. He stopped at a set of tall double doors with steel bolts dotting their edges. "Those are long gone. But there was a pattern to the vandalized copies—something they all had in common."

Emily's heart stuttered. "The Selwyns."

Victor nodded. "Someone around here has been interested in their family tree, and I'm guessing you three aren't the ones who've been tearing pages out of old books."

"But if the pages are gone and you don't know what was on them, what are we doing here?" Ozzy asked.

"I've gotta agree with Oswald," Catherine said. "No offence, but I trust his book know-how over yours."

Victor placed his palm on the aged wood door, and a small hum filled the corridor. The hinges squeaked in the silence as the next chamber opened before them with a sigh.

The room was wide but shallow, with walls of cracked and mouldering stone lined with glass cases. A single table sat in the middle of the floor with a stack of books resting on its dusty surface where a pair of wide, pale grey eyes peered at them from around the pile.

Victor inclined his head. "Thank you for letting us in, Ms. McKibbons. I realize how rarely you do this for any of the initiates, and no one knows this library's secrets better than you do."

McKibbons's furrowed brow softened, and a tinge of colour bloomed on her wrinkled cheek. "Not at all, Mister Graven," she said, her voice like gravel. "I'm glad I can help you in some small way. You didn't tell me *these* were the friends you were talking about, though." McKibbons straightened herself and stared up at Ozzy, Catherine, and Emily with unmasked confusion. "Don't you three ever want to get some fresh air? I would, if I was your age again."

"A question I ask myself all the time," Catherine muttered.

Victor threw her a silencing look, but his voice was soft. Encouraging. "Ms. McKibbons, would you be able to show my friends what you found on Beth Selwyn?"

The old librarian pursed her lips, her blonde curls vibrating with a sudden tremor. "I haven't shown it to anyone in years. Not even the Masters who've asked for my help on the subject in the past have gotten a look at this particular book." Her eyes moved from face to face, her knotted fingers twisting until the skin turned pink. "But you've been so nice to me, Mister Graven. No one is ever kind to me."

Victor's eyes were molten fire. "I appreciate that."

Catherine screwed up her face. "Blech."

McKibbons got to her feet, her old shoes crunching on the cold stone floor. "The Selwyn history is a rather dark thing. Why would you young bunnies be interested in that?"

"Research project," Ozzy replied, not missing a beat. "For Master Ward's class."

"That so?" McKibbons flushed crimson. "Master Ward has been rather kind to me as well. A big help this past year, what with all the missing books and rowdy initiates." She sighed, eyes misting over. "Fine, but you can't tell anyone I did this, or I'll hunt you all down. Except for you, Mister Graven. I trust *you*." She puttered over to one display case and ran a crooked finger over the glass. At once, the gleaming surface turned gauzy, molten, liquid.

"You're an Elemental," Catherine said as McKibbons reached into the case to retrieve a slim, red book no bigger than her hand. "I always thought you were an Empath."

"Most book lovers are," McKibbons said with a wry smile. "They can hear the books, commune with them, you see. I still love every page in this castle even though I can't speak with them, but my talents lie with protecting the barrier around these precious tomes instead." She thumbed through the book, caressing the words with the lightest touch. "The stories in this room carry the realm's most powerful and destructive spells. I haven't been able to protect the others as well as I should have, but I still have these. That is until Chief Master Millendorf gets wind of all that's happened under my nose and tosses me out."

Victor stepped forward, sympathy clear in his eyes. "Everything's going to be all right. This wasn't your fault." And, with the kindness in his voice so thick, Emily could almost have believed what he said was true. Almost. "Is that the book you wanted to show us?"

McKibbons sniffed. "The smallest stories often get so little credit. Poor children, lost and long forgotten." A second passed before the woman spoke again, each word as careful as the last. "Beth was beloved to all who met her but was painfully shy and very, very afraid of the world. Strange, don't you think?"

"What is?" Ozzy asked.

She paused, her chin quivering. "That a timid, terrified little girl would climb up a cliff on a dangerous mountain in the middle of the night for no reason. Anyhow, here." She handed the book to Victor, her outstretched fingers drifting in midair after he plucked the leather-bound volume from her hand.

Ozzy peeked over Victor's elbow to read the title. "*Tell-Tale Tales of Dreamland*. This is a basic book of sleeping spells. My mother reads this when she's having trouble going to bed."

"This copy is a rare edition," McKibbons explained, her voice taking on a defensive edge. "It has an extra story that's been out of print for ages. Page thirty-eight is what you're looking for." She shuffled off toward the door. "I never saw you—understood?"

Victor bowed his head. "Perfectly. Thank you, Ms. McKibbons."

"Yes, yes, fine." Her low muttering faded down the corridor until they were alone.

Ozzy took the book from Victor and flipped it open to the right page:

> *"The King of all Kings is where it begins,*
> *With terror and love attached by a stRing.*
> *Great, powerful men, wonders of one kin,*
> *'Till he of that line imagined Selwyn.*
>
> *He worked, and he fought, his efforts rewarded.*
> *Through strength of his heart, he*
> *naught could be thwarted.*
> *The king had a prince and princess to follow.*
> *The man loved them both, but one turned out hollow.*
>
> *Of present and past, darkness battles light,*
> *The dark wield power, good steals to the night.*
> *The prince lays his claim, the king has his doubts,*
> *But who would have thought the weak could win out?*
>
> *With terror and love wrapped up in one Ring,*
> *The King of all Kings is where it begins.*
> *As princes collapse, fall prey to their greed,*
> *A lonely, small princess, doomed to a Black deed.*
> *In eternal death between blood and bone,*
> *Moon shines her full face; Black won't fight alone."*

"What the Elders is this garbage?" Catherine asked. "You think we needed to read a poem?"

Ozzy, however, held the book to his chest with blood

pooling in his cheeks. "Victor, do you think we can we take this with us?"

"McKibbons won't mind as long as she thinks it's for me." Victor turned to Emily with a grin. "See? Told you I'd deliver."

"Get over yourself, Vicky," Catherine said. "You'll give yourself a migraine. Ozzy, you really think that poem will help?"

The rhyme somehow dredged up Emily's nightmares, the visions that had assaulted her when entering North Tower for the first time clearer than ever. She turned to Victor, her throat tight. "Yes."

"I can't believe you doubted me," Victor scoffed. "Apology accepted, by the way."

"I didn't apologize."

"That's right, you didn't." The planes of his face were smooth and calm, but his eyes alive. "So maybe you can repay me now. I wonder what I'd like in return—"

"Hey, buddy," Catherine interjected, jabbing his shoulder with a long, square nail. "If you think this earned you some kind of favour in this little group of ours, think again." She grabbed the book and tucked it into Ozzy's backpack. "Membership is full. Try again next year."

"Actually, I was thinking more along the lines of a date." Victor crossed his arms over his chest, eyes glinting. "With Emily, I mean. I like you both, but you're not my type."

Emily's neck grew warm. "I'm busy."

"I didn't mention a day yet," he pointed out.

"I'll still be busy." Emily couldn't believe his audacity and, worse still, her own stupidity. She should have known—she *did* know Victor wasn't selfless, and yet she'd accepted the help anyhow. "I'm not currently in a dating mood."

"You tell him, Em," Catherine said, face smug.

Victor grinned. "One date, Rathburn. With me. Alone. And if you hate it, I won't ask again."

Now, that *I'm interested in.* She hesitated, relishing the way her pause commanded his attention, kept *him* on his toes. He stood still and composed, but she could see a vein pulsing in his neck as though his heart were racing. "One date and you leave me alone?" she asked.

"One proper date, just the two of us, that I get to plan, and you get to approve, if that's what makes you comfortable." He was leaving nothing to chance, his grin smug.

Emily smiled. "Deal."

"You're joking," Catherine spat while Ozzy's face went slack.

"Nope." She marched to the door, motioning for Ozzy and Catherine to follow. "Victor, you can have a date."

He grinned. "Perfect. I'll come pick you up around eight tonight."

She sighed. "Can't. Busy."

"Okay." Victor wouldn't be discouraged. "Tomorrow night, then."

"Still busy."

He frowned. "Why am I sensing a problem here?"

Emily glanced back at him, his brows pulled tight on his broad face. "No problem at all," Emily reassured him. "You said I could approve the date, and I didn't say *when* I'd be free. Little warning: it might be a while because this book you helped us find is going to keep me really, really busy." She slid out of the room, the corridor louder as her heart *thump, thump, thumped* against her ribs.

"What a chump." Catherine trotted beside her on an invisible cloud. "Emily, I want you to tell me this story every night before bed so that I don't forget it."

"He did help us, though," Ozzy countered.

Catherine threw him a dark stare. "That's debateable. It's still only a weird poem until you can prove it helps find the Lost Ring. Don't you take his side, Oswald."

Ozzy shook his head, clutching his bag to his chest as they made their way out of the library. "It's also brilliant. No one would think to look in a common book like that! It's important information hidden out in the open. And there's something about those words that make sense, you know?"

Catherine threw him a sidelong stare. "You sound as loony as McKibbons looks."

"It's all here!" Ozzy ran his fingers over the poem for the third time. "A king, a prince, and princess? That's got to be Selwyn and his two kids. And the *r* in the word 'string' is capitalized, which can't be a mistake because—"

"—that spells Ring." Catherine rubbed her bleary eyes. "It's a clue. We get it. Can we go to bed now?"

The sun was climbing up the window in the lounge, but they were the only ones to see it. Early mornings were for sleep, but neither Ozzy nor Emily could rest until they understood the poem promising an end to the constant threat of Grey.

Ozzy ignored Catherine's pleas. "According to this, Xavier was filled with darkness and evil."

"Aren't they all?" Catherine grumbled.

"But if I'm reading this right," he continued, "Selwyn might have broken tradition by giving Beth the ring. Listen to this: *'the prince lays his claim, the king has his doubts'*? I think Alexander knew his son wouldn't use it for good."

"Okay, say Beth *did* get it," Catherine reasoned. "Do you honestly think her dear older brother would let her have it without a fight?"

"Not at all." Ozzy's tone went sour, and his bright eyes narrowed. "If I know anything about talented older brothers, it's that they don't take rejection well. If what the poem says is true, then Xavier didn't take his father's decision well at all."

"So, Beth gets the ring," Emily said, "and, somehow, they find her dead on a cliff on Black Mountain? That's not a coincidence."

Ozzy tapped a line in the poem. "*'Doomed to a Black deed.' Black* is capitalized in the middle of a sentence." His eyes went round. "That's Black Mountain, and we know that's where Beth went. It's this part that I can't figure out." He pointed to the last verse. "Something about eternal death, living between blood and bone…"

"What was she doing alone on Black Mountain?"

"I'm not sure anyone knows for certain—no one alive, anyhow."

Emily's head throbbed, but it had nothing to do with a lack of sleep. "Ward said something about no one alive knowing what happened to Beth. Is it possible that she's a . . . ghost?" *I sound insane.*

Ozzy propped his elbows on his knees. "I mean, sure. There are stories of people coming back from the dead in that form. Some say a ghost guards North Tower, you know."

"Who says that?" Catherine asked. "I've never seen a ghost around here, and I've lived in the city my whole life."

"They probably find you too loud," Ozzy said. He turned back to the poem, ignoring Catherine's withering look. "It makes sense, Emily. And ghosts are usually bound to the place they died, so that would mean she's still up on that mountain somewhere."

"Hold on." Catherine raised a hand to stop Emily from vaulting out the door. "We can't take a stroll up to Black Mountain looking for a ghost that might live there."

"Why not?" Emily shrugged. "I've been past the treeline. It's not that bad up there."

Catherine balked. "Everyone's snuck past the trees, Em. Actually *going* up the mountain is something else. Do you know what's up there?" She shook her head, pushing the curls out of her face. "I'd rather not get eaten by some horrible monster or get lost in a fog. And what's your plan, hm? Take a nice hike when you're feeling up to it, call out Beth's name, and when she pops out for a cup of coffee say: 'Hey there, little ghost girl! Please point us in the direction of where you hid your daddy's ring before a psychopath finds it.'?"

"Not *when I feel up to it*." Emily's excitement grew as the path to her goal sprawled out ahead of her. "A specific day."

Ozzy turned back to the page, brow stitched together. "The moon shines her full face . . . you think the full moon is somehow connected to Beth and the ring?"

"It makes sense," Emily said. "It might have something to do with the ring or the protection around it. Anyway, when's the next full moon?" Catherine and Ozzy sat in heavy silence, neither one moving. The fireplace gave off sparks, and Emily frowned. "What is it?"

"Look," Catherine said, raising her hands in defense, "you know I'm all for a bit of rule-breaking. But this sounds like a bad idea."

Ozzy released a heavy breath. "Yeah. I mean, I know Grey needs to be stopped. But ever since the dragon attack, Mother's been a mess. And Brady's been reporting back to her, too. I don't think I can put my family through more worry if something goes wrong."

Emily nodded, and her heart sank. "I get it. You both have people who worry about you." The admission left a ragged hole in her chest and an acidic film on her tongue. There was no one to worry about her or make sure *she* was okay. But that didn't mean Ozzy and Catherine should be punished for it. "I'll go on my own, then."

"Em, that's not what we meant!" Catherine said at once. "I just think all our body parts are perfectly nice where they are."

"It's okay. Honest." A strange calm settled over Emily. It had been this way since the beginning, operating in the shadows, the risk on her shoulders and hers alone. It was the only way to make sure no one else got hurt. But she'd gotten comfortable and become careless. Let people in. Let people take some of the burden. It was enough. "This is my mess. Grey was my father's accomplice. I *can't* let another disaster happen when I know how to stop it. And I won't let her bring me down by hiding behind my bad name."

Catherine propped her boots up on the table and pressed her eyes shut. "Listen, if you're still going to do this, then I'm coming with you. What's the fun in living if you can't say you survived a ghost attack?" She toyed with a stray curl and gave Emily a withering look. "Plus, maybe if I get dismembered or something, my dad'll come visit."

Ozzy let out a tortured groan. "Neither of you have a chance without me, so I *have* to come now. Ugh, Brady's going to kill me when he finds out. Then he'll tell Mother . . ." He trailed off, eyes lingering on the fire. "You know what? Let them worry. I'm in."

Emily cleared her throat. "Thank you—honestly, thank you. But you can change your minds, you know. I won't be mad."

Catherine pursed her lips. "When's the next full moon?"

"Way ahead of you." Ozzy rummaged through his bag for the Scroll. "According to this, the next full moon is in . . . three days." Blood drained from his cheeks, and his skin turned the colour of old lemons.

"Three days?" Emily repeated, her own anxiety spiking.

"Oh, would both of you get over it?" Catherine said. "Three days or three months, something's always going to try eating us up there. All we can do is practice some basic magic and have a solid plan."

"You're right." Ozzy's cheeks were pale. "We should go to the library for some extra spell books. Maybe ask Horus for some help, too."

Catherine threw him a pained stare. "We've combed that entire library, okay? No way I'm going back there to look at more basic magic we could learn on our own. We need something more . . . specific. Leave the spell stuff to me and keep your eyes open if I need help." With a sigh, she leaned into her chair. "It's kind of a shame, though. Part of me doesn't want this to end. Nothing like the fear of death to make you feel alive, right?" She ducked at once, avoiding Ozzy's copy of *Magical Mysteries and Mysticism*, as it soared straight at her head.

CHAPTER TWENTY-TWO

Even the Best Laid Plans

THE DAY OF THE FULL moon brought with it gloomy skies and a crackle in the air promising a loud, satisfying storm. Emily, Catherine, and Ozzy crossed the grounds in heavy silence, the plan for the evening looming over their heads like one of the many silver clouds above. Emily's eyes lifted to Black Mountain, where the fog had crept back over the green surface in a thick haze. In a few hours, the fog would be all around Emily, pressing in on every side.

A tall shadow hobbled toward them, waving a dark hand. "Hello, you three!" Ward called, puffing with exertion.

Emily focused with some difficulty. "Master Ward!" she said, stopping in her tracks. "I had no idea they released you!"

Ward's frayed suit hung off his narrow shoulders, and his cheeks had become mere hollows in his face, but his smile was familiar and kind. "The healers said it was time, and I have to agree. Ms. McKibbons was kind enough to set some things aside for me, so I'm jumping back into my work." He indicated the short stack of books tucked under one arm and offered a shy smile. "Anyhow, I wanted to apologize to you all."

"Apologize?" Emily said, stunned. "For what?"

He hunched his shoulders against a strong gust of wind. "I had a lot of time to think in recent days, and I quite regret putting you in the middle of all this Grey nonsense. No matter how keen you are to help, you are initiates and have enough on your plate without any extra pressure put on you."

"That's okay, sir." Emily's smile hurt her cheeks. "I offered to get involved. Apparently, it's what I do."

"Well, I appreciate that," Ward said, "but I've decided to confront her on my own. Tell her I know she's after the Lost Ring and that I'll be turning her in to the Guard. I'd prefer not to alert her ahead of time, but as a colleague, I feel it's only fair to give her a chance to defend herself."

Emily's stomach bottomed out. "But you just got out of the clinic."

"Yeah, no offence sir," Catherine interjected, "but you look awful. Grey'll turn you into a cockroach, or worse, as soon as you tell her you know everything."

"Maybe you should rest on it?" Ozzy offered.

"I doubt she'll make that much of a fuss." Ward chuckled. The scars on his face shone silver in the weak daylight. "Anyhow, I need to put this to rest. And this is the only way to move forward."

Emily glanced at Ozzy and Catherine. "Can you two go on and save me a spot? I want to talk to Master Ward for a minute."

Ozzy made no motion to move, but Catherine linked her arm through his and tugged. "Don't be too long, Em," Catherine advised with a tight smile. "You know how testy Grey gets when you're late . . . or breathe. Or cough." Ozzy glanced over his shoulder but allowed himself to be pulled off to Blackwood Cottage, leaving Emily alone with Ward.

"Sir, you're going to tip her off," Emily said, stress making her hysterical. "She's going to know that her secret's out, and then all this would be for nothing."

Ward smiled, but his green eyes drooped. "I appreciate your concern, but she won't stop until she either gets what she wants or is forced into the open. I need to take this to Magdale and the Chief Master, too."

Emily ground her teeth. "If you knew I was close to finding the ring so Grey could never find it, would you wait?"

"Emily, that's impossible. What good would that even do?"

"Grey has gotten away with crimes in the past. If you call her out, she'll cover her tracks or change course, or move even quicker. Please, sir." The lilt in her voice, the wideness of her eyes; she was begging, and yet she didn't mind. She needed to be the one to expose Grey and put an end to the chaos she and Baxter Rathburn had brought to her life. "I have a plan that's going to work. Wait until after tonight before you make a decision, okay?"

Ward's face went blank. "Tonight?"

She nodded. "We might not get another chance. I *need* this. Please."

Indecision twisted his scarred face. "Will you be safe? Is there any danger? I could help; I'm feeling much better."

Emily shook her head at once. "The less you know, the better. Especially with Grey lurking around." In truth, she had no idea what they would face up on the mountain, or what sorts of things they would need to do to find Beth. Ward was kind but would always be a Selwyn Master, upholding the rules and too weak to help. Even if he wanted to.

Ward lowered his eyes to his hands. "Then I can at least offer you some protection. The dragon attack might have weakened me, but my ability is intact. When I touch someone, I retain their ability for a short time without needing to be near them. It's temporary, but useful. Allow me." He raised one gloved hand, and his lips began to move, too fast for her to understand. Warmth spread through Emily's body, and she was grounded, tethered, her feet planted in the right place. "Ms. McKibbons is quite good with protective spells. No harm will come to you now."

"Thank you." Emily didn't trust her own voice.

He bowed his head against the gathering storm and shuffled off, leaving her alone. Emily hurried off to Blackwood Cottage, an inexplicable pit of mourning making every step forward a special kind of torture.

The lesson dragged on longer than usual. Grey prowled the aisles while they all bent their heads over a bland text. Catherine's leg jiggled beside Emily's, their table vibrating with her movement, but it was too dangerous to talk. Were there really monsters on Black Mountain? Was the fog dangerous, or would they be able to see and breathe? Questions bounced off one another in her mind, her eyes reading the same sentence for the third time.

A light knock on the door tore Emily out of her daydream.

Grey's eyes flashed, equal parts fire and ice. "What?"

The door opened a crack, and Piper peered inside the room, her hair a wild crown of curls after the wind. "Sorry, Master Grey. I have a message from Chief Master Millendorf."

Grey let fly a stream of curses Emily had never heard used in one fluid sentence. "Read to yourselves and do *not* perform any spells before I get back." Her heels clicked against the floor, and she disappeared outside in a whiff of cold air.

"Hear that, Camilla?" Catherine glanced over her shoulder with a lopsided smirk. "Don't do anything stupid. I know it must be hard."

Camilla scowled. "Shut up."

Catherine rolled her eyes. "What's the problem? Not so mean now that you have no friends and precious Vicky likes Emily better than you?"

"What are you doing?" Emily muttered. "Leave her alone."

"Let it go, traitor." The colour rose in Camilla's cheeks. "I don't need you to come to my rescue. Why can't you two mind your business?"

"Funny, I used to think that about you all the time." Catherine nudged Emily's leg with her knee and lowered her voice. "Get ready."

Emily and Ozzy exchanged bewildered looks as the girls stood up, old friends facing off across the cabin.

"Don't talk to me like that!" Camilla warned.

"Do you think Victor keeps you around because your stupidity makes him look good, or does he just feel sorry for you?"

"*Ugh!*" Camilla's scream filled the cabin, and a flash of blue light crackled in the tiny room. Catherine lifted her hands like a shield, and a strong current of air pushed past Emily to knock Camilla to the ground. Initiates scattered as chairs and tables soared into the walls. Catherine's hair twisted around her neck like a noose at Camilla's command, wrapping itself against her skin. Back and forth it went. Forces collided while the rest of the initiates panicked or cheered.

"Go!" Catherine cried, nodding in the direction of the storeroom.

The door was open.

Emily leapt over fallen chairs, cut to the edge of the room, and raced down to the open door. Somewhere, a stack of parchment exploded, sending clouds of confetti sprinkling down on their heads like snow. The row of spell books sat on the shelf in the exact place she'd left them. Heart hammering, she placed her hands on as many covers as she could, focusing on her bedroom until her palms stung and fire was in her veins.

Emily slipped out of the dark, dusty room and rejoined the fray.

Grey wouldn't find out her books were missing amidst the wreckage of her cabin until it was too late.

Emily found Ozzy hiding behind half a chair. *Catherine, you're insane, but I think you're also a genius.*

Emily lay awake while the sky turned black. She turned her necklace over, listening to the even breaths around her. Visions of leaves and wooden horses and perfect braids flitted around in her head and in the shadowy corners of her room. The Commons were far away, but every soul she had met sat in the dark with her, waiting. Watching.

It was time.

She and Catherine moved as one, pushing off their covers and tiptoeing past Tina, whose light snores were a comfort. Not long ago, it was Molly who had stayed behind, and the thought made Emily's heart splinter. With a silent goodbye, she slipped out of the unlocked door and into the hall.

Ozzy waited for them in the shadows. "What took you so long?" he complained, hands vibrating at his side.

"Relax." Catherine rolled her eyes. "I don't think Beth is on a schedule. Couldn't you at least have combed your hair?"

Ozzy bounced on the balls of his feet, ignoring the jibe. "This is a bad idea. Did I say that already?"

"You say lots of things I ignore," Catherine said. "Look, Oswald, we'll be fine." She took his hand and gave it a squeeze. "We're in this together, so if you get killed, I'm probably not far behind. I can't die this young and this pretty. Get what I'm saying?"

Ozzy nodded and gripped Emily's fingers with his free hand. They linked hands until the circle was complete. Emily took a steadying breath. With her eyes closed, the electric charge stung her palms, the force of their combined magic dazzling.

Gone. Emily focused on the fire building in her heart. Their magic surged, scorched, crashed into her over and over again. Her lips moved, mouthing the familiar veiling spell while her mind remained focused.

You don't see us.

Her head collapsed into a pool of cool water, the droplets trickling down her head, her face, her shoulders, her knees submerging into nothingness.

We're not here.

The water disappeared, and the fire was snuffed out. The buzz in her skin dropped down to background noise, and she opened her eyes.

"Did it work?" Catherine appraised her legs with a twist of each ankle.

"I can still see you." Ozzy's fingers were slick with sweat. "But I think that's because we're linked."

"I felt the magic work," Emily said. "It's as good as it's going to get. Let's go."

Fast feet, down the quickest path to the exit, past locked doors and familiar corridors. The windows creaked, and the walls groaned with the sounds of night-time, and the wind called their names. If Emily closed her eyes, she was back at Saint Barth's, weaving through the Commons while everyone slept. Every so often, the rusty hinge of a door squeaked or the echo of another set of footsteps nearby would pull her focus, but not enough to break it.

It took an eternity to reach the entrance hall and escape into the cool, dark night. The stone and grass on the way from the castle to the courtyard were still scorched in some places, but the shadows and moonlight masked the damage well. They dropped their hands, and a weight was lifted from Emily's shoulders, making it easier to navigate the pockets of darkness along the castle wall.

Black Mountain waited for them. Jagged peaks loomed over them in the distance, the fog thick and suffocating across it like a disease. The trees meant safety from prying eyes but the beginning of something much more dangerous. As they stepped past the first row of firs dotting the edge of the courtyard, Emily's necklace grew heavy and warm against her already heated skin. A thin tendril of pearl-grey fog lingered over the narrow path she and Victor had navigated together. With Victor, her nerves were based on something else entirely.

Emily stepped onto the path with Catherine and Ozzy close beside her. Somewhere inside the trees, a branch snapped, and leaves slithered across the ground like a thousand hungry insects.

The fog called out to Emily like an old friend.

And she followed.

Chapter Twenty-Three

Into the Black

GO BACK. DON'T LEAVE ME.

"Stay close together, okay?" Emily tiptoed through the mist, her mind at war with her heart. And wasn't that always the case?

Their sneakers squelched through the soggy earth. Branches on either side of the path reached out, clawing at them with twisted fingers. Moonlight, dreamy and cool, danced off the natural twists and movement in the forest, giving Emily too many places to watch and fear.

"We're going to get lost," Catherine complained, swatting a moth from her hair. "Is anyone here a nature expert? Or maybe has some werewolf battle training I don't know about? 'Cause I know I said this would be fun, but I'm pretty sure I was out of my mind."

"Shhh." Emily stepped over a fallen log. "I've been down here before. We're not far."

"From what?" Ozzy wiped sweat from his forehead.

The path spun out ahead of them until the wide clearing she and Victor had visited another lifetime before yawned open. Bright pinpricks of yellow light reflected off Catherine's glasses as they turned their faces skyward. While the fog was a thick, roiling carpet across the wild grass, the fairies above were a stream of sunlight. Except, instead of drifting in a loose, lazy cloud, the tiny beings had formed a path in the sky—an airborne road pointing them in the right direction.

Ozzy's eyes were wide. "Are those fairies?"

Emily nodded. "They're attracted to magic in the mountain, apparently. I figured if there was something powerful going on tonight, they'd be the best way to guide us."

Ozzy grinned. "I think you're right. This is amazing, Emily!"

"If you say so." Catherine marched into the clearing. "Less sightseeing, more moving. The longer we stay here, the bigger the chances of getting maimed."

Relief swept over Emily, and she grinned with renewed purpose. They crossed the clearing under the brightness of the fairies and found a narrow but still discernible path on the opposite side.

Progress was slow but steady, the fog growing thicker, the path harder to see the deeper they traveled. They climbed higher into the cloud, the trees wilder. Angrier.

The cloud cut out ahead of them.

With no mist to refract light through the trees, the moonlight returned to the hovering orb in the sky. Emily took a reluctant step forward, and the ground crunched, crackled, as though the leaves had turned into a bed of eggshells. A dull pulse thudded through the air, beating in time with her heart, and she squinted, searching for the source. Somewhere in the dark, a thousand tiny nails scratched on a thousand stones, the high-pitched shriek mounting in urgency.

"Can you hear that?" Catherine asked.

"It's like a heartbeat." Ozzy covered his ears with his hands. He searched the ground for an opening in the path, but there was none. "It looks like this way is blocked off. Maybe we took a wrong turn."

"No," Emily said. A cloud shifted, making room for more moonlight to filter down through the forest. The fairies swarmed close.

Barbs. Endless vines crawled across the ground, covered in sharp, gleaming spikes. Black ropes climbed over rocks and invaded the earth, snaked up trees, and into the mud like a puddle of spilled blood.

Emily took a step back. "It's Thorny Truth. I've never seen one this big, but the plants taking over the greenhouses look like smaller versions of this one."

"Okay," Catherine said, "so all we have to do is tell it something true about ourselves so we can go, right?"

The rustling grew closer, the metallic screech louder. Trees pressed in all around, the branches longer and more twisted than before. Victor's voice echoed in Emily's mind: *"See, they look like plants when they're young, but as they grow, they get stronger. They can possess other plants, animals, people even. Like a parasite."*

The trees. The scratching. "We need to get out of here." Emily stumbled backward.

Catherine snorted. "It's a stupid plant, Em. I can blow it out of the way."

"You don't get it." The soft slithering grew louder, and Emily's skin crawled. "Fully grown Thorny Truth takes over living things. Regular plants, animals, *anything*!"

The fairies scattered, throwing them into near darkness.

Catherine lifted her boot, hovering it over a patch of thorns. "So, what you're saying is this giant bush is going to try murdering us?" Rolling her eyes, she thrust her foot into the ground.

Hard.

Thick, black liquid spilled over Catherine's foot and splashed across her leg.

A branch snapped.

Hooves beat the ground, the sound like metal on metal closing in.

Antlers soared through the air and bucked Catherine onto the ground, the back of her head connecting with a dull thud.

"Ozzy, get out of the way!" Emily screamed.

The deer doubled back, tramping across the path, its breaths coming in putrid, white tufts. Its eyes glowed a vivid green from behind its matted fur while brambles and vines twisted into its coat like armour. Emily and Ozzy pulled Catherine to her feet and backed away from the animal into the body of an old oak.

"Did you ever figure out what to do if you found an animal possessed by Thorny Truth?" Ozzy asked, his breathing ragged.

Emily shook her head, hair sticking to her neck and cheeks. "We didn't get that far."

Above them, a low-hanging branch swiped down on them with a series of cracks and splinters. Emily dove onto the ground, pulling Ozzy and Catherine with her. The ancient tree loomed over them, twisting and pulling at the earth until rubble spilled from its roots.

"Trees aren't supposed to do that!" Catherine shrieked. "Ozzy, what do we do?"

"Why me?" Ozzy cried. "I didn't know this could happen!"

The deer ran a spiked hoof across the ground, and more vines crept toward it, twisting around its four legs like a soft caress. In the darkness, two more pairs of vibrant, green eyes flickered into existence, the trees and bushes along the path quivering in excitement.

"Okay." Emily's heart pounded in her chest. "If Thorny Truth can possess things, it'll probably try to take over us, too."

"How does that help?" Catherine asked, trembling.

"We can either try to outrun it, or make it think it doesn't want us," Emily cried. She dodged to the left, a vine grazing her shoulder. The screeching of thorns on rock made her ears sing, but there was no place for distraction. "Keep moving!"

Ozzy and Catherine leapt out of the way of another swinging branch, and the animals in the forest lowered their heads, their growls sending vibrations into the earth. Shapes emerged from the shadows, and vines hissed against the fallen leaves. Black Mountain was alive—and they needed it dead.

"The wind!" Emily called as she threw herself onto the ground once more. Her clothes ripped and pulled, the snarls of Thorny Truth clawing at her ears. "Catherine!"

"What?" A fir tree ripped free from the fragile ground, and Catherine stumbled to her knees to dodge a cascade of needles raining down on her head. Ozzy pulled at her, yanked at her arm, but the vines were closing in, attacking from all sides. Catherine's eyes flew wide, her hair fanning her face in a chaotic mane. "Oh! Right!" She closed her eyes and pulled her palms up from the thick coils climbing her arms.

A low rumble built behind the trees. Emily crawled to a spot on the ground far from the deadly plant and laid herself flat. The storm was building, the leaves lifting into the air in a spiral of cold air. The wind pitched around them, and Emily pressed her face into the virgin mud with one eye still on Catherine, her serene face guiding the air. Trees leaned into the onslaught as though bracing themselves, but the hurricane was too strong. Dirt lifted into the sky as plants and animals alike were thrown backward, away from the path.

A narrow trail shook loose in the nest of Thorny Truth, the fog free to filter through the obstacle. "Ozzy!" Emily shouted, getting to her feet. "Catherine! *Run!*"

There was no telling how long the opening would last. Catherine dropped her hands, chest heaving, and the windstorm came to a groaning halt. Ozzy staggered upright and grabbed a stunned Catherine by the elbow, pushing her toward the infestation of Thorny Truth. The trees were sprouting upright again, lumbering back to the path. Emily's sneakers pounded the ground, fists pumping the air as she sprinted after them.

Almost there, almost there, almost there . . .

The fog trickled ahead of her, calling her to the other side. Ozzy passed through the knot of thorns first, Catherine close on his heels.

Ten feet . . . eight . . . six . . .

Something heavy slammed into Emily's ribs. With a low grunt of surprise, she tumbled sideways onto her right shoulder, pain lancing through her neck and arm. Wasting no time, she rolled onto her back and rammed her heels into the solid, broad chest of a rogue deer. Its rotten breath was suffocating, the flat green eyes peeking out of a face covered in thorns.

"Emily!" Catherine's screams came from somewhere far. Somewhere safe.

"Go!" Emily called back. She blocked another attack with her arms and turned in time to see Ozzy and Catherine clear the thorns. *"Go!"* She struggled and shoved, but the deer was everywhere, its thorns digging, searching. Antlers raked her side and tore through her sweater, the trickle of blood immediate and slow.

Consciousness slipped away until she was groggy. Alone. Colours flashed in her mind's eye: the greys and browns of old stone mingled with the shine of buffed metal gleaming in the strong midday sun. Instead of dirt and gravel, a wide path slicked in black tar cut the tall buildings in half, gleaming boxes arranged in neat rows end on end. It was hot. She peered down at her feet, and her shoes were soaked in red.

She blinked and the pitch-black road was crumbled to pieces, boulders and metal spikes protruding out of a deep hole in the center. Emily gasped, shutting her eyes, unwilling to see the blank faces on the ground. What had happened here? Where was she? Her chest throbbed, empty, and a sob escaped her lips. *I did this. I caused this.*

Regret, bitter and crippling, brought her to the brink of agony. Tears slid down her cheeks, and she rubbed her hands on her thighs, willing them to be clean. But they would never be clean. She hadn't wanted to be her father's daughter . . . but maybe, somehow, that's exactly who she'd become.

She let the darkness have her.

Black.

Everything went black.

"Hey, are you dead?" Catherine's voice pierced her heart, jarring her awake.

Emily's eyes flew open, expecting those tall buildings and smooth paths to be staring back, finding Catherine's concerned face instead. "What happened?" she asked, her voice sticking in her throat. Panic fuelled her, and she launched off the ground in one fluid motion. She expected thorns, green eyes in the darkness, but the forest was silent. "Catherine? You're okay?"

"Yeah, but *you* don't look so great." Catherine ran her dirt-covered hands through her hair. "And I thought you had bad hair before. You're a mess."

"Thanks." The relief was overwhelming. "Where's Ozzy?"

Catherine smirked. "He's in the trees over there throwing up. I don't know if it was the killer bushes or the rabid deer . . . or maybe the ten minutes he thought you were dead, but he's not handling it too well."

Ten minutes?

Ozzy stomped out of the trees, his cheeks smeared in dirt and tears. "It was all three, I think." He eyed Emily from head to foot, lips pressed into a tight line. "We thought you were a goner."

"Me too," Emily admitted with a grimace. "Was I really unconscious that long?"

Catherine nodded. "I don't know what you did to

get that thing off you, but it worked." Catherine threw a nasty look back at the unmoving growth of Thorny Truth. "One second you were under that demon animal, and the next, everything disappeared. The trees went back to normal, and the creepy deer disappeared. We pulled you across, and the vines didn't even try to stop us."

Ozzy rubbed his palms up and down his shaking arms. "We don't know if they're gone for good, so maybe we should keep moving." He pointed up the path where the blanket of mist was thick and oily. "Something tells me Thorny Truth isn't going to be our only problem tonight."

They huddled together, the closeness more for comfort than warmth. Low-hanging willow trees lined the uphill road, each branch of gauzy cotton a threatening figure in the mist. What had she seen when the thorns had pierced her skin?

She tried to remember the details, hoping repetition, like with dreams, would keep the memory alive. But just as dreams did, the memory of the strange road crumbled to pieces and slipped farther and farther away with every passing second.

They followed the fog deeper into the mountain until Emily's body ached.

"We should be getting close, right?" Ozzy was breathing hard, his face shiny and blotchy with effort.

"Close to what?" Catherine complained. "We don't even know what we're looking for. For all we know, Beth Selwyn isn't up here anymore and all we're doing is getting some exercise."

"Catherine." Ozzy's wide eyes were fixed ahead, and he stopped walking.

She crossed her arms and faced him. "Don't '*Cath-erine*' me. Can we all entertain the possibility that we're doing this for nothing? We've been at this for hours!"

"Catherine," Emily echoed. She couldn't breathe. She didn't dare try.

"You're against me too? Listen, I'm trying to be realistic."

"Catherine, *shut up*!" Ozzy rested his hands on her shoulders. Before she could unleash her outrage, he turned her to face the crest of the hill. "Look!"

"Look at wh—*oh*!"

At the top of the road, in a narrow shaft of blue-white light, a box floated in midair. Its dark shape twisted around an invisible axis, the mist hugging it close. They approached the case slowly, the distressed leather and wood giving off an earthy scent while a large, intricate brass lock rusted shut on its face.

"It's a chest!" Ozzy leaned in to inspect every scratch, every curve of the lock and frame. He lifted his hand to touch it, but Emily rested a hand on his arm, stopping him with a silent warning.

The chest reflected in Catherine's eyes. "Maybe the ring is in here."

Emily shook her head. "Seems a bit too easy, doesn't it?"

"Easy?" Catherine's voice was shrill, too loud in the stillness of the mountain. "You call escaping death by homicidal bush *easy*? We must have passed some kind of test by escaping that stupid plant and that's why this box is here."

"Emily's right," Ozzy said. "Why would the Lost Ring just be hanging out here in the open?"

"Who cares?" Catherine stepped toward the chest, hand outstretched.

Something wasn't right. Emily turned, ready to reason with Catherine, to pull her away. "Maybe we should think this through before—NO!"

Catherine plucked the chest out of the air, a smug smile playing across her lips. "See? It's just an old box. You always worry for . . . "

Her words evaporated. A thick cloud of blue smoke spurted from the chest's keyhole. Thick clouds pooled around their ankles, crawling across the ground, but a good amount wafted into Catherine's face as she inhaled deep. Her eyes rolled to the sky, and she fell with a *thump* to the ground, the chest tumbling from her limp arms.

"Cover your face!" Ozzy exclaimed, and Emily obeyed at once. Catherine didn't move. Curly hair covered her face until there was nothing but blue smoke.

You're alive, you're alive, please be alive...

It took too long for the smoke to clear. When it did, there was nothing but pale white mist once more and Catherine's lifeless body on the ground.

Emily dropped beside her friend, body numb. "She's still breathing! Any idea what happened?"

Ozzy shook his head, eyes fixed on Catherine's still face. "She needs to see a healer, but how are we going to drag her back to the castle like this?"

"We won't have to." A large gust of wind rippled through the trees. Emily pushed Catherine's hair back from her face, banishing her terror to the darkest corner of her mind in the process. *My fault, my fault. Just like Finn. My fault.* With her palms on Catherine's shoulders, she closed her eyes and imagined the clean, white drapes, the beds with sheets tucked into its two bottom corners.

Her hands grew warm, hot, the familiar surge of power reassuring.

And then Catherine was gone.

"I sent her to the clinic." Emily regained her footing with some difficulty. "We can't trust this chest. Maybe . . . maybe we should bring it back with us and try next month." *Good, that's good.* "I mean, I don't know if it'll even let us take it, but this isn't worth anyone else getting hurt."

No one answered.

"Ozzy?" She turned, afraid he had disappeared, too. But Ozzy stood in the same spot, bewildered eyes turned to the sky. "What is it?"

A low snarl shook the willows and rumbled through the mountain.

And then she saw it.

The dragon crouched low on its haunches, blocking their path back to safety. Its crimson scales absorbed the light, so they shone like rubies. Its bloodshot eyes met theirs with an intense hunger, pupils constricting to slits, claws flexing in the soft earth. Titan was big, but this dragon towered over the trees with a head as large as an old fir and teeth like swords.

"Emily?" Ozzy asked, eyes tracking the forked tail as it swished across the moon. "You see the big dragon, right?"

"Don't move," she warned, creeping upright, little by little.

The beast exhaled, and a thick cloud of hot, dry smoke furled from its snout. Saliva dripped, cloudy and thick, from a massive jaw pulled up in a grotesque smile made of a thousand yellow fangs. Emily took a tentative step closer to Ozzy, and the dragon's snarl turned into a roar of outrage. It reared onto its hind legs, sending flocks of birds scattering into the sky. In a flash, its long neck snapped down on them like a viper, teeth turning the ground to sand.

"Run!" She pushed Ozzy down the path, the chest forgotten by the edge of the road. Another growl, another cloud of tar blackening the night. Emily dove behind a fallen tree trunk as the dragon's snout thundered against the earth mere feet away from Ozzy racing off to safety.

They'd been separated. This was it.

Keep running. Ozzy's footsteps faded away. *Keep running and get help. I'm so sorry.*

My fault, my fault, my fault . . .

"Hey!" Ozzy called from his place within the trees. "Over here!"

Emily peeked over the trunk, and terror clutched her heart. Ozzy waved his arms above his head, scrambled away from the dragon, pulling it away from her hiding spot. The dragon's snarls of hunger and rage vibrated in her bones, but it followed Ozzy, pupils focused on the boy with the terrified face.

The chest lay forgotten at the edge of the forest. In the mud, in the dirt. The key to finding Beth—the entire reason for jeopardizing her future and both Catherine's and Ozzy's lives—and stopping Grey sat in a pile of dust, ready to be trampled or set aflame.

It's heavy. Emily focused on her hands. *Rough. The leather and wood are soft, the brass is scratched but smooth. My hands are empty, waiting, the wind is coming from the north, I'm going to die . . . no, the wind is blowing from the north.*

Victor would have smiled as the power washed over her. He would have caressed her face and taken her hand.

A hand that was no longer empty. The chest was a wonderful weight in her arms, and she tucked it into her side before leaping out from behind the fallen tree.

"Ozzy!" she cried. "*Run!*"

Ozzy reacted at once. He scrambled up the hill, kicking up dirt and rocks as he pounded the ground, speeding past the dragon's hind legs. Stunned, the beast let fly a roar that frothed the clouds, a stream of fire scorching the sky into an inferno.

Emily grabbed Ozzy by the elbow, and they vaulted up the hill, the dragon's enormous claws raking trees free by the root, unearthing tunnels and caverns of destruction as it lumbered after them. Another burst of fire missed them by mere feet, the heat of its breath so close it stung the back of Emily's neck.

"I can't . . . keep . . . going!" Ozzy sobbed, his face caked in dirt and blood. He stumbled to the ground, pulling her down with him in a heap of aching limbs and tears. They clutched one another and hid their faces in their arms, fear stealing their voices and their last brief moments of life.

Another cry, farther away, different somehow. Emily pressed her eyes closed and waited for the end while a fresh quake shook the mountain.

Please be quick, please, please . . .

It was taking too long. It *shouldn't* have taken so long—at least not with all the noise and fire, the gnashing teeth and steel tearing flesh. Emily opened her eyes and stifled a sob of terror or relief, or maybe both.

A second dragon crouched before the first, its black shape hunkered low on the path between them and the red dragon.

"Naglar!" Emily's words were strangled as she shook Ozzy, willing him to look up.

Red and black circled one another, around and around in a deadly dance. A roar of frustration, of warning, another slash of teeth and a crunch of bone. Naglar beat back the blows, avoiding his opponent's claws and sinking his teeth into the long, red neck instead. Fangs pierced the tough hide, and the red dragon shrieked in pain and outrage as fresh blood poured onto the sodden earth. A barbed tail swung out from the left, burying itself in Naglar's ribs, and both dragons collapsed in a ferocious knot.

"No!" Emily screamed, pulling against Ozzy's restraining fingers. "Don't hurt him!"

"Are you insane?" Ozzy asked, his face contorted in horror. "Those are full-grown dragons. They'll kill you!"

Ozzy was right, but Emily couldn't blink. Reaching out, her heart ached as Naglar offered another sharp bite.

That did it. The red giant's eyes rolled, and its legs twitched before slumping to the ground. The air was choked in smoke, the ground a mess of black blood and dirt. Naglar swayed, his yellow eyes swivelling in their sockets. He locked eyes with Emily while sparks flew from his flared nostrils and collapsed onto his heaving belly.

She pushed herself to her feet and took a step forward, Naglar's eyes like beacons in the night.

The red dragon took its last breath. The sparks and grunts stopped.

Black Mountain was quiet once more.

"Let's go," Ozzy insisted, pulling at her sleeve. "Come on, let's get out of here. *What are you doing?*"

"He won't hurt me." Dirt and sweat stung her eyes, but the dust was settling. She left Ozzy and the chest behind and picked her way down the path, the air cloying with the metallic tang of blood. Naglar breathed in shallow bursts, kicking up debris with every exhale, his wings draped on either side of him.

"It's okay, Naglar." Emily reached her arm out between them. The pleasant warmth of his smooth scales filled her palm, earning her a low groan of contentment. "Thank you."

Naglar closed his eyes and leaned into her hand. With an enormous effort, he turned to the body of the red dragon, nudging it with the peak of his wing before turning back to her. He did it again, and then once more.

Ozzy tiptoed down to investigate, the chest cradled in his arms. "What's he doing?"

"No idea," she said, mystified. "It's like he wants to show me something." Emily let her hand fall to her side and walked around to the unmoving scarlet body. Up close, the dragon's jagged teeth shone a dull yellow against the black, slippery gums. Rows and rows of spears packed tight in its open mouth like hundreds of deadly spikes threatened to shred her to pieces, even in death.

Except for one small gap in the dragon's jaw, the fangs were uninterrupted.

Naglar grunted as Emily leaned into the yawning mouth for a closer look. A brief glint of metal protruded from the gums in the place of a tooth, its sheen dull but visible enough.

"There's something in its mouth!" she called.

"What?" Ozzy cast a wary look at Naglar. He hesitated, fear warring with curiosity. Curiosity won out; he gave Naglar a wide berth before craning his neck over Emily's shoulder. "There's something metallic in there. What is it?"

She squinted into the hot, putrid jaw. "See that rounded top at the end? It kind of reminds me of an old key." Naglar made a pleasant clicking sound, and she turned to the chest in Ozzy's arms. "I'm right, aren't I? You don't think it could be the key for that chest?"

The idea was enough to turn Ozzy green. "I mean, it's possible." He screwed up his face against the foul smell coming out of the dragon's mouth. "But I can't see how we're going to get it."

The solution was simple enough. Emily focused on her hands, on the feel of the heat and smoke on her skin. Every ounce of energy funnelled into her hands, searching for the small metal object in the dragon's mouth. The key would come to her, just like the fairy and the chest had.

Except, it didn't.

Ozzy rolled his eyes. "You can't use magic on a mature dragon, even if it's dead. Their hide and skin are completely impenetrable, remember? The only way we're getting that key out of its mouth is if we yank it out. And there's nothing you can say to get me in there."

Emily grabbed onto the edges of the massive jaw. "Fine. Give me a boost." With Ozzy's reluctant help, she pushed off the ground and hoisted herself into the dragon's mouth.

A wall of humid breath hit her like a brick wall. Her sneakers slipped over the smooth flesh, the key peeking out from behind a large canine. Careful steps, slow and easy. Everything was sticky and hot, the smell of charred meat and copper overwhelming, but she needed the key. She'd come this far . . .

The key was within arm's reach. With a triumphant grin, Emily grasped the hot, slippery metal and tugged. Her stomach lurched, but she couldn't back down. The gums squelched, and she pulled harder, bracing herself on a nearby tooth. "Come on," she grunted. The metal gave another inch, and, with a final surge of energy, she tugged it free.

Ozzy bounced on his heels, arm outstretched to help her down as she picked her way back to him. "You smell horrible!" He eyed the blood-smeared object with a groan of disgust. Naglar gave a final grunt and spread his wings, slicing a nearby willow in two before leaving them behind in a cloud of dust. "Okay, let's have a look," Ozzy said, the relief at having Naglar gone softening his tone.

Emily wiped the slime on her sleeve and handed the key over. The handle was large and elaborate, but the end was small and brass . . . identical to the fastenings on the chest.

Ozzy inserted it into the chest and turned, the tumblers clicking over one another in quick succession. They kept the chest at arm's distance, ready for whatever would come, and Ozzy flipped open the lid with one long finger.

Emily peered inside. "It's empty." *Huh, not what I was expecting.* Moonlight caught on a bright spot within the dark wooden interior, and she took a second look. "Hold on, I think there's something stuck to the corner." She reached into the chest and came back with a yellow square of parchment.

"What is it?" Ozzy asked.

The cramped handwriting had faded to a ghostly scrawl, the ink pale but legible. Jagged lines and uneven loops moved across the page as though put there by a rushed hand, and Emily moved the parchment closer to her nose for a better look. "It's that poem McKibbons showed us." She read through the text a second time, to be sure. "This one is written by hand, though."

Dark woods, frantic running, tripping over fallen roots…

It begins where it all ends.

Her necklace grew heavy.

"It's *almost* the same," he corrected, reading over her shoulder. "Here's something that never made it to the book." He pointed to the bottom of the page and squinted at the blurred words. "I think it says *Sanguinis Vivocopsus*, but I can't be sure."

And then the world disappeared.

Chapter Twenty-Four

Beth

The wind kicked up in Emily's ears as the ground beneath her feet dropped away. The trees swam; colour rushed past them. There was no air, there was no gravity, no ups or downs. A dizzying sense of being everywhere and nowhere at once enveloped her in a tight cocoon, and she fell into it kicking and twisting for freedom. In the madness, a girl screamed, and Emily couldn't block out the noise. They spiralled into nothing until gravity found her again and threw her to the ground.

Emily's foot folded beneath her as they hit the damp, sodden earth. Pain spiked through her ankle like a hot poker, and she gasped before crumbling to her hands and knees. They had been transferred somewhere else, somewhere at the heart of the thick fog. Grey mist poured in on all sides like air gone solid. Impenetrable and cold.

"Emily? Are you okay?" Ozzy crawled over to her in the gloom, his hand finding hers.

"I'm fine." The words pushed through her gritted teeth, the pain shifting her focus. "I came down on my ankle too hard." She ignored the pulsing in her foot and pushed herself up to her knees, biting back a cry of pain. Ozzy's arms shook as he pulled her to her feet. "Did you Transfer us?" she asked.

He grunted under her weight. "No. I wouldn't even know how."

Emily nodded. "Me either."

"Can you walk?"

Good question. "I don't know—I think so." Emily shifted her weight so her injured foot rested flat on the ground, and she suppressed a cry of pain. Ozzy looped an arm around her waist, and she let him take the burden, towing her deeper into the cloud. "Where are we?"

"Black Mountain." The thin voice was a shock in the night.

Gooseflesh erupted over Emily's body, and her heart hammered. "Who's there?" she called. There was only mist and darkness and nothing. Pure nothing. The fog shifted, swirling tighter around them as though attracted to their panic.

"Why have you come here?" the voice asked. A girl. Young . . . much younger than Emily, from the sound of it.

"Emily's an amazing Elemental, and I'm a pretty decent Empath," Ozzy warned, voice unsteady. "It's two against one, and people know we're here!"

"No, they don't, silly boy." A soft giggle echoed through the trees. "And your magic can't hurt me."

"We can try." Emily blinked away a bead of sweat. They took another step, and the mist closed in, hugging them close.

"You cannot hurt the dead."

A beat of silence. *We made it.* "Beth Selwyn." Another round of giggles answered her, and Emily focused on the sound, straining to pinpoint it in the haze.

"We don't want to hurt you." Some energy crept back into Ozzy's voice, but Emily could still detect the undercurrent of fear. "We came to help you."

"No," Beth countered, voice sharpened to a point. "You want what's mine."

"Yes," Emily answered. The truth was better. "We're looking for the Lost Ring, but it's not what you think."

"And what do you know of what I think, Emily Rathburn?" Beth asked mildly.

A fresh sheen of sweat broke out over Emily's body. The pain lapped at her calf like an infection, and her necklace stung with heat, pressing into her skin. "How do you know my name?" she managed over the ache.

"Your name has been whispered through these trees for quite some time," Beth said. "I thought you might come for me one day; the hungry always do."

Emily stumbled through the mist with Ozzy by her side. "We came to warn you. Someone knows you have the Lost Ring, and they're coming to take it. She was in league with my father—and if you know who I am, then you know that Baxter Rathburn wasn't a great person."

A high-pitched laugh echoed off invisible trees. "You came to help *me* protect the ring?"

"Yes!" Emily's vision blurred. "It's not safe anymore. You need to hide it or give it to us so we can bring it back to the castle. We can use it as proof to put away the person threatening you."

"Lies!" Beth screeched, the sound needles in Emily's skull. "Power is all you want. It's all they *ever* want! My poor father knew, and he died for it."

"We don't want it for ourselves!" Emily protested. She broke away from Ozzy and took a painful step forward. "Grey is after the ring, I'm telling you!"

"Sable Grey? From the castle?" Beth said, a new edge to her voice. "Selwyn castle is sworn to protect me and mine. More lies!"

"No!" Emily coughed on the damp air. "Your father gave it to you instead of your brother because he trusted you more. Am I right?"

A beat of silence. Emily waited while the mist pulled back to reveal wisps of tall grass and crumbled earth at her feet. The shadows of grey boulders and curved branches flickered into view for the briefest of moments before being swallowed by the smog once more. Emily and Ozzy pulled greedy breaths as clean air crept under their noses, and a tiny shadow, smooth and effortless and so heartbreakingly small, advanced on them.

Beth Selwyn peered up at them through unfathomable eyes, long hair and tattered nightdress floating out around her like a protective veil. Her translucent face was drawn. "My father was a wonderful man. He always said he loved us both equally, but how could he when I was never any good with magic? I tried hard, of course, but it was never enough."

"It was enough for him," Ozzy said. "He gave you the Lost Ring for a reason."

A sad smile played across Beth's narrow face. "When the time came to choose the ring's next wearer, the decision was obvious. I was an embarrassment, an Empath with no chance at bettering herself, but Xavier..." She trailed off, features softening at the memory. "Xavier was everything a Selwyn heir was supposed to be. He was handsome and strong, and everyone loved him. *I* loved him."

Emily was rooted to the spot. "But your father saw something else in him."

Beth's eyes were dark. "His nature was not his fault. The ring was supposed to be his, after all. We both knew it." Her lips pinched together at the sour memory. "He was so *angry* when Father passed it on to me. Xavier tried to convince him that I had no use for it, that I didn't even want it, but Father wouldn't be swayed." She paused, her voice cracking. "My brother didn't mean to do it."

"Do what?" Ozzy asked.

Beth's eyes shone with tears of pearl and opal, and Emily knew the answer before it could be spoken. "Xavier killed your father, didn't he?"

The mist surrounding Beth closed in. "Father came to me in secret one day," she said. "He told me I was his wonderful girl and that it was time to break tradition for the greater good, that the ring would pass to me instead of my brother. He told me I would have a long life and more power than I could ever ask for. But I wasn't to give it to anyone—not even Xavier. Not even if he begged me."

Her form rolled, quivered, not solid, not gas. "I didn't understand any of it then; I was a girl who couldn't even hear the flies think, let alone be a proper Selwyn heir." Tears spilled down her sunken cheeks. "I wasn't special like my brother. Xavier went to Father's chambers one night when everyone was sleeping and..." She trailed off, and the wind kicked up in violent protest of the memories being tugged loose in her mind.

"So you ran," Emily said. The images of a forest, of a chase, of someone following right at her heels. She had known Beth's story all along. And yet, nothing could prepare her for the truth spoken out loud.

Beth nodded, a minute jerk of her chin. "I had to keep the Lost Ring safe, like Father told me to do. When Xavier came for me, I took the ring up into the mountains. I made sure no one would ever find it. Not even my brother."

"I'm so sorry." Emily took a step closer.

Beth's eyes flickered back into focus, twin black pits growing hard with anger. "Enough! You pretend to care about my story when all you want is to destroy my father's last wish. You are *all* the same!" The mist closed in, a wall meant to choke them, smother them so they couldn't scream.

"We're not!" Emily protested. Ozzy grabbed Emily's arm as her ankle threatened to give way. She ground her teeth against the pain and stared Beth in the eye. "My father did awful things to innocent people. No matter what I do, people hate me because of my last name. That's *my* burden to live with!" The dam around her heart buckled, and every drop of self-loathing poured into the air between them. She took a steadying breath and, for once, let the tears flow unchecked. "I can't be like him. I won't hurt you or anyone else. You can trust us."

Beth's smile was sad. "You may believe your intentions are pure, but realities change. Greed lives within us all. The one they call Mordred knows that." She shivered, a rattle of bones sending chills through the air.

"Mordred is dead." There was a new edge to Ozzy's voice, a spark in his eyes. Fear.

The wind died away, Beth's eyes darkening until there was nothing but their terrible, liquid depths. "Perhaps." She studied their faces.

"Please." Emily's shoulders shook. They were so close to the end—to redemption. None of this was her fault but, somehow, she wouldn't rest until the molten hot twist of guilt in her gut was quenched. "Beth . . . please."

Beth's eyes flashed to Emily's, settled there until they were the same girl. Emily pushed every ounce of disappointment and hurt, every instance of self hatred she could muster into the space between them, willing Beth to understand. She *had* to understand.

Beth spoke after a long moment. "I could tell you where it is, but it may be best if I show you. Once you see its burden, you can decide your fate." She stood silent and unmoving as a corpse, her fine hair lank. She raised her palms to the sky, and the fog spiralled around them, pulling them into the abyss.

When Emily opened her eyes, they stood on a dark path surrounded by full branches that danced and swayed in the wind. The sharp scent of earth and rotting leaves stung her nose, the moon swollen and low overhead. It had rained.

A very solid, very real Beth Selwyn clambered up the hill behind them. She hunched under a heavy cloak, her feet navigating the uneven terrain with awkward, hesitant steps. Emily tried to step out of her way, but it was as though her feet were buried in wet sand. With a breath like a whisper, Beth passed through Emily's body, dragging them all along after her.

"Beth!" a boy called. "The mountains are dangerous. Stop running so we can talk!"

Beth crossed a circular clearing that Emily knew would one day be home to thousands of fairies. The woods whizzed by, and the ominous threat behind them followed. She tripped over a large root, sending her crumpling to the ground. *I've seen this before.*

Beth sobbed into the damp earth and curled her fingers into the mud, a soft gold band shining on her thumb. Blackness spewed from her fingertips and coiled into the leaves and tree roots, spreading like wildfire. Within seconds, the delicate vines had grown into a living, writhing pit of thorns curling out to the trees, searching for its first victims. Beth leapt across the garden of Thorny Truth without any trouble, her face ashen.

The chase in the woods. The moonlight.

Laughter boomed through the trees. "Sister! What powers you have! Do you think this plant will slow me down?" Beth ran faster, but she couldn't outrun her brother's taunts as they rumbled through the mountain. "I would hate to see you give your life for a dream that can never be reality. Give me my ring, and everything can go back to how it was!"

Beth clambered up the path while Emily and Ozzy raced after her, connected by the memory. The distant crack of thunder sent a shower of thorns raining down on them, and Beth cried out, shedding tears of blood that tracked down her soft cheeks. The thorns kept coming, and she lunged for cover under a tall willow tree, knees pulled up to her chest.

"She has to move." Emily's voice was hollow. "Why isn't she moving?"

Ozzy's eyes glistened. "Look at her hands."

Beth pulled the Lost Ring off her thumb while a new wave of tears cut clean tracks through the dirt on her cheeks. She traced a finger across the softness of her palm, leaving a deep cut in its wake. With unsteady hands, she placed the gold circlet into the wound, kissed it with trembling lips, and clenched her fist shut.

The parchment came out next from a pocket in her cloak. Ink spilled from her index finger, and Beth scribbled down the words now so familiar to Emily. A poem— and a map.

Tears crept into Ozzy's eyes. "She wrote the poem herself. She knew he was going to kill her, but she still wanted someone to find the ring one day. Someone worthy."

The hail of thorns came to an end as Beth scratched the last words on the page. Her lips worked fast, muttering an incantation Emily did not recognize. Beth added the poem to her injured hand, kissed the bit of parchment just as she had done the ring. A strange glow in her closed fist threw her haggard face in sharp relief until both poem and ring were gone.

"Blood magic." Ozzy pointed to the last words on the page: *Sanguinis Vivocopsus*—blood and body combined. "That's what created the ring in the first place, and she used that same rare magic to hide the ring permanently. That's why no one could find it."

An object she wanted to hide from her brother and a poem to map its final location. The existence of the poem meant Beth never wanted to hide the ring forever; she only wanted to hide it from the wrong person.

"Sister!" Xavier cried, closer now.

Beth flinched, dashing the tears off her face with bloody knuckles. With a grunt, she pushed off from the ground and took to the cover of the trees, far off the beaten path. They fumbled their way through the brush, the low-hanging branches snagging on Beth's ragged clothes, but she didn't slow. With every snarl of an invisible creature or roar of frustration vibrating through the mountain, she pushed on faster.

"You cannot hide, sister! Won't you make this easier on us both and surrender?"

Beth pushed on, but her movements were becoming sloppy, clumsy. She couldn't catch her breath and she slowed, cheeks bright with fatigue. A tree root looped out of the earth, and she went sprawling on all fours.

He was gaining on her.

And she knew it.

She brushed branches aside and stumbled through a wall of leaves opening into a second clearing: bigger now, the sky a canvas of navy and green, a rocky cliffside lurking beyond the flat ground like a slumbering giant. There was nowhere to hide.

"*Beth*!" he cried, voice manic. "I want to talk to you!"

Beth crossed the clearing at a full sprint, Emily and Ozzy close on her heels.

"Stop!" Emily cried, but Beth couldn't hear. Because Beth was already dead.

"Strange, don't you think?"

"What is?"

"That a timid, terrified little girl would climb up a cliff on a dangerous mountain in the middle of the night for no reason."

Emily could do nothing but watch in horror as Beth began to climb, dragging her and Ozzy up the sharp edges.

Xavier breached the boundary of the clearing when Beth was already well into her climb. He was young and blonde with broad shoulders and a wide stride. "There's nowhere left for you to go, sister!" he called from below.

Beth let out a tortured gasp as her fingers slipped over the rock. "Xavier, please—stop this!" She leaned her heated cheek on the cliff's cool surface, fatigue draining her of all colour.

"Not until you give me my birthright!"

"No!" Her sobs were muffled by the rock. "You know I can't do that!"

The ground rumbled. "Have it your way!" Xavier raised his arms. "Want to see my new trick? Father taught it to me before he died. Ironic, isn't it—that his teachings are what will get you killed when all he did was *adore* you?" Jaw set, he leapt up into the air, invisible hands propelling him up the side of the cliff.

Beth regrouped and forced her shaking arms to work faster. She stumbled and bled. Still, she climbed.

And still, he laughed.

"I can't watch," Ozzy moaned.

Emily's visions. Her nightmares. They all led back to Beth and her fate up on the cliff. With a shudder, Emily knew she never had a choice; she was destined to be here. To watch. To *see*.

Beth cried out in relief as her fingers discovered a flat ledge. She pulled herself up with a loud grunt of effort, and her fingernails split from her fingers as she hoisted herself onto solid ground. She crawled to safety on her belly and leaned her back up against the rock face. There was nowhere left to go, and she sat on the wide ledge and waited for her fate to find her.

"Hello, sister." Xavier flicked the air, and a smoking hole crumbled into existence by Beth's ear. The loathing in his eyes twisted his handsome features into something inhuman. "Give me the ring or my aim will improve."

"No." Beth's chest rose and fell with her panic. "He told me never to give it to you. Please understand, brother. I cannot betray his request."

"*Where is it?*" Spit flew from Xavier's chapped lips, and his dirty nails raked the hair away from his forehead. "This is not a game, Beth!"

Beth looked up at him, pleading. "What has happened to you?"

"What do you mean?" He towered over her, his brows pulled together. "I'm only taking back what is mine by right. Something that you have stolen from me."

"He loved you." She pressed her back into the rock. "Father *adored* you. Even with all your fights and your pride, you were always his son."

"Our father was a fool," Xavier said. "So much power in his reach, and what did he do with it? He turned our home into a tavern for the riffraff of Gildenveil."

"They're not riffraff."

"They are unworthy!" he roared, eyes like flint. "Empaths and Elementals who think they are equal to our family have no place in our halls. They would have us back in the Dwalind realm, hiding in fear."

"The Great Divide is an embarrassment," Beth cried. "That we need to create a separate world for ourselves to stop the slaughter is awful. You must see that. Without this ring, I'm no better than a Commoner. And yet, because of my name, I am favoured?" She shook her head in disgust. "We should be learning from the past, not repeating it."

Xavier sneered. "You sound like Father. You were always so jealous of me, of how talented I am."

"I *love* you!" she cried. "You were always the better choice to carry Father's legacy, but you would destroy everything he has worked for with that power! How is that just?"

"I would make it *better*. I would bring dignity back to our people. The Lost Ring was created from destruction, and only through destruction can it be used to its full potential!"

"You're wrong." Her knuckles shone white against the slate grey stone. "It was created out of love and can be used for good. It *will* be used for good."

"Enough of this. Give it to me. *Now*."

Beth ignored him, a quiet smile playing across her glistening cheeks. "When we were little, you told me you would always protect me." Her fingers dug into the dust around her. "You were so kind when everyone else was so cruel."

"Where is it?" Xavier lifted his hand, and the air shimmered.

This is it. Despite knowing how the story ended, seeing it unfold brought a fresh wave of dread to Emily's heart. *This is the end. And I have to watch it.*

"And today," Beth continued, "it is my turn to protect you."

"Protect *me*?" he howled, eyes wild. "Protect me from what?"

Beth's face shone with the force of her love. "From yourself."

She lifted her hand, a jagged rock clutched in her fist, and slashed her other palm clean open. For the second time, a stream of blood ran down her wrist, and she tossed her weapon to the ground.

"What are you doing?" he asked, a shadow flickering across his face. "Beth?"

"I love you. Forever." Beth lifted her trembling fist to the rock, a warm smile illuminating her face. "It's love that created the ring, brother—not destruction. Love and blood. And that is the only magic powerful enough to keep you away."

"NO!" He charged, speed making him sloppy, panic making him stumble. But he was too late.

Beth pressed her injured palm against the rock at her back and closed her eyes as red smeared across the stone, a sigh of relief so sweet escaping her blue lips. She muttered a spell under her breath as Xavier lifted his hand to strike.

The edges of the scene blurred away to nothing, leaving Emily with Ozzy and the memory of Beth's spirit.

"Now you know the truth," Beth said. "Is it everything you imagined it would be?"

The pain in Emily's ankle was a dull throb compared to the vise around her heart. "That was terrible." The words were inadequate. Weak. "I'm so sorry, Beth."

"Do not pity me. I've fulfilled a great honour by protecting my family's legacy from poor souls like my brother."

"What happened to him?" Tears trickled down Ozzy's face, his breath hitching in his chest.

Beth's pain seeped into the air they breathed. "He searched for the ring for years after that. Every full moon I would come here and wait, ready to protect my father's legacy. Xavier tried deciphering the spell I cast to bind the ring to Black Mountain, but my sacrifice was too powerful, as most blood magic is. He died many years later. That is all I know."

"*Sanguinis Vivocopsus,*" Ozzy said. "The spell you wrote at the end of your poem. You exchanged your life blood for the ring's protection."

Beth nodded. "Binding with blood and emotion is very powerful. Using the power of the Lost Ring to cast that spell made it unbreakable by anyone but me and my will. And only the worthy could make it through the safeguards. That night was a full moon, limiting the threat to my ring to nights such as these."

"But Xavier could find your poem and track you down like we did," Emily said. "Why would you want it found at all?"

Beth smiled. "Were you not listening? The ring was created with magic and love, the twin pillars of my father's beliefs. Something like that should always exist. I did not want to make it an easy task to accomplish."

"Well, we got this far," Emily said. "You have to know we're worthy of it after all we've been through to get here."

"You've come farther than most, it's true. But I also know that you are a Rathburn. And you," Beth said, turning to Ozzy, "have a drive to prove yourself that can end many ways. I cannot be too careful—not after everything I've given up. If you want my ring, then you must earn it." She lifted her arms, and the fog receded to nothing.

They stood in the same clearing as the one in Beth's memory. The cliff towered over them in silent expectation, the sky brightening to a sea with dawn fast approaching.

"What are we doing here?" Emily asked, fear turning her blood cold.

"This is where it all began." Beth's voice was an echo in the clearing. "Where it all ends." She gazed up at the steep incline as the first flickers of orange and pink leached into the sky.

"You sealed your spell when you put your hand on that rock," Ozzy reasoned. "So does that mean the ring is somewhere up there?"

Beth nodded, her body already fading. "I sealed my fate, and you have sealed yours. See it through to the end or leave my legacy alone. The choice is yours."

"What does that even mean?" Emily asked. Her ankle throbbed, and her eyes burned. When Beth didn't answer, Emily stepped closer, determined to hear the truth. But Beth was gone with the rising sun.

A large branch appeared over Ozzy and fell, thumping him on the back of the head. His eyes rolled to the brightening sky, and he folded to the ground, unconscious and pale.

"Ozzy?" Confusion paralyzed Emily. In her shock, she didn't look over to see what was making the sound of footsteps behind her.

"Well, now that *they're* gone, shall we get on with it?"

CHAPTER TWENTY-FIVE

A Rock and a Hard Place

DAWN TICKLED EVERY BLADE OF grass, every twisting branch and crevice of rock. But the new sun hovering on the edge of the horizon could not reach Emily. She dropped to her knees beside Ozzy, her mind a chaotic mess. Her breathing came fast and shallow, her throat dry. She didn't look up when she spoke. "What are you doing here?"

"Hello to you, too, Miss Rathburn."

But we were so careful. It can't end like this.

A vacant smile. A step forward.

A dream. I'm dreaming.

Those eyes. She knew those eyes.

A nightmare . . . this is a nightmare.

Those eyes were empty.

Cold.

Familiar and still so bright. So piercing. So *green*.

"I don't understand." Emily curled her fingers into the earth, willing the ground to stop spinning. None of it was real. It couldn't be.

"Well, that's to be expected, I suppose." Master Ward closed in on her, dark fingers playing with the charred bits of skin at the base of his wrist. The darkness of his hands wasn't coming from gloves but from the blackened skin of his naked fingers.

Emily's stomach roiled.

Ward's smile was soft. "If you were going to run into anyone, I assume you were thinking of Sable Grey."

Emily huddled over Ozzy's still form, refusing to hear Ward's words. "We need to get Ozzy to the clinic."

Ward cocked his head, looking Ozzy over with clinical indifference. "We? Why would I do that?"

Emily shook her head. "Because he needs help. Please."

"What I *should* do is tie up all loose ends, but I suppose there is no point in leaving a larger trail of bodies behind me if it isn't necessary." He frowned, his voice light. "It was close, though. If he would have seen me, I'd have had no choice."

"Sir, I don't think you're well." A hundred emotions bubbled up inside her. "You don't know what you're saying."

"Denial is so pathetic." Ward studied her from behind a pale mask of disgust. "Look at you, cowering over that boy like a fool. You're better than that, Emily. You're a *Rathburn* . . . and my partner. I should like to finish what we started before you fall to pieces."

"Partner?" she croaked. "What are you talking about?"

"Well, as competent as I am," Ward said, "I couldn't have gotten this close to the Lost Ring on my own. It was a long road getting here, but we did it together. I had to do some rather distasteful things, mind you, but sometimes you must take lives to advance your own."

"You're telling me Grey was never a threat?" The idea was ridiculous and, somehow, so fitting. His interest in her, staying so close, offering his help; it was all so obvious, and yet, she was so blinded by her version of the truth.

"Not the threat you were expecting, no."

She giggled. It was ridiculous. But the idea that she'd trusted the one person who would betray her was so perfect it was laughable.

Ward flicked his hand, and the heavy branch beside Ozzy's unconscious body disappeared, re-materializing at her waist. With a grunt, Ward shoved the rough bark into her body, driving her backward and trapping her under its weight. She cried out and pushed at the tree, but it was no use. It weighed her down, pressing the air from her lungs as it squeezed her into the ground.

He crouched low, eyes glazed and unfocused. "No one expects much from me. They all hate me because of my ability. They think I'm an abomination."

"It's not because of your magic." Her words were hard, brave, even. But inside, she was dying. She had trusted him, thought of Ward as a friend.

He drew closer, close enough for her to see the flecks of shadow in his green eyes. "You know, it's your ability that's allowing me to do this to you. It's quite a practical sort of magic. The irony is so sweet." He curled his fingers into a fist, and Emily screamed as the branch bore down on her. "There was a hole in my glove when I saw you outside Blackwood Cottage. You gave me such a lovely gift, and as long as you're alive, I can get what I need. Any sudden movements, and I shall have to reconsider my position. Understood?"

She winced. "Yes."

He nodded, his breath warm and sticky and coming in short bursts above her face. "Good." He extended his charred fingers, and the weight on her chest was gone.

She sprawled out into the mud and soggy leaves, pulling in long, deep breaths. "Why are you doing this?"

Ward shrugged, circling Ozzy's body. "I've been searching for the Lost Ring for years. I travelled everywhere, *looked* everywhere, done so many things." He flexed his hands, and his face darkened, the scarred skin shining black and crimson where it stretched across his knuckles. "I took the post at Selwyn's years ago to access the library archives. I hate children, you know."

The headlines in the Scroll from Grey's room. The rumours Horus had mentioned at the beginning of the year. "Did you make all those people disappear?"

He nodded. "I couldn't let them go once I'd interrogated them. McKibbons finally proved useful when she pointed me to Migellus's old book at Wick, Wax, and Wane after months of helping catalogue that library, but that ridiculous shop owner refused to show it to me. Before I knew it, that lead was locked away and lost to me." He wrinkled his nose. "That vulture of a librarian guarded her best books just as fiercely, but it was easier to manipulate her."

"She liked you, you know." Emily's ankle pulsed and her legs were weak, but she found the ground more solid under her as she got to her feet.

"Like I said, I had to do some distasteful things to get what I needed. And everything comes with a price." He glared at his hands, turning the blackened fingers over with a hiss of disgust.

She followed his gaze. "The gloves . . . you don't wear them because of your ability." Not a question. "What did you do?"

"Catching on, are we?" He scowled. "About time, too—this little game was getting tiresome. I'd received some intelligence about Migellus's box containing the Lost Ring through a few contacts of mine. The only way to get into a secure box that wasn't mine was to use Zaphira's ability against her. It was genius."

"Zaphira's been missing for months." Bile rose in Emily's throat. "What did you do to her?"

"I tried to reason with her, but of course she wasn't having it. So," Ward continued, eyes blazing with delight, "I *convinced* her." His smile spread like blood from a wound. "When Zaphira refused to see things my way, all I had to do was brush an innocent finger across her hand. It was a power like none I'd ever encountered; to manipulate the images everyone can see is invaluable! So, I crafted a world around her to trick her into opening the box for me."

Emily stared at his hands. "Too bad it didn't work."

Ward's face turned bitter. "Zaphira resisted. I had to lock her up in her own basement, to push her harder, and leak a story about her taking a well-deserved vacation. But the old crone caught on to my trick and fought back with tricks of her own. Before I knew it, I was breaking into the secure box and causing an explosion that destroyed my hands."

Emily pulled up the memory of the explosion at Zaphira's shop. Crowds of people swarmed the building while sparks and smoke poured out of every crack. And then, there was the encounter that started her obsession. "But I saw Grey there, not you. I'm sure it was her."

Ward walked a half moon around them. "Sable Grey has never liked me. She probably fed that false information about Migellus's box to lure me out into the open, hoping to catch me and redeem her own reputation."

All this time, Emily was chasing Grey for a wrongdoing she didn't commit in the hopes of clearing her own name. And Grey was doing the same for herself. "There's one thing I still don't get."

"I'm sure there are many."

Emily ignored him. "You had access to everything we did—books, information, whatever magical ability you wanted. Why did you get me involved with you?"

"Have you not been listening?" Ward's throat quivered, and spit flew from his twisted mouth. "Grey was always watching me! I couldn't just walk around turning over stones to find the Selwyn heirloom. Plus, you involved yourself, so leading you to the answers I needed you to find was simple. But I must admit, a part of me was simply curious."

Her nails bit into her palms. "About what?"

"I wasn't lying when I told you I knew your father," he said. "I'm a huge fan of his. I was curious to know his daughter—to see if you were like him. But you turned out to have so little ambition." His words were an unexpected blow to the heart, but Ward persisted, unfazed. "I eventually found a portrait of Alexander Selwyn wearing the Lost Ring itself in a rare book. I needed to see that painting in person. And that's when you proved your use the first time."

Emily glared up at his pale face. "What *use*?"

"When I heard about your late-night punishment at Blackwood Cottage, I thought it would be the perfect way to get a hold of her infamous skeleton key. I hid in the forest until you were done."

"Well, you got what you were looking for."

"Yes. I saw the portrait confirming Alexander had the ring. But it wasn't there as I'd hoped. He did not receive my failure well." Ward shuddered.

Emily's gaze narrowed. "He?"

"Never mind!" Ward clenched his fists, opening old wounds so they shone a deep, obscene pink against the dark flesh.

"Is someone else making you find the ring?" Emily asked. "Who is it?"

"*Enough*!" Emily clamped her mouth shut as Ward trembled with rage. "I still have your ability. I would not test my limits if I were in your position."

Emily didn't care. "After ruining all those innocent people's lives, you're just someone else's puppet? Pretty pathetic, if you ask me."

Ward shook his head. "No one is innocent."

"*We* are!" she protested, pointing to Ozzy's motionless form. "We looked up to you, tried to *help* you! Look, can't you let Ozzy go?"

Ward paced back and forth, each step leaving a deep imprint on the soft earth. "I didn't want things to go this far, but sometimes life doesn't give you a choice. You of all people understand that." His face crumbled, a peek of his former vulnerability shining through the terror.

Emily squared her shoulders. "If you're going to kill me, get it over with." The guilt was numbing. "You got what you wanted, anyway."

"Elders, why the rush?" Ward's eyes grew wide. "There could be more safeguards up on that mountain I may need you for. I need us to be on the same page so we can move forward together. Once I have the ring in my hands, yes, I'll have to kill you. But not a second before."

The back of her neck dripped with a nervous sweat. "If you let Ozzy live, I'll help. And you need to leave Catherine and Willow alone, too."

Ward grabbed her by the elbow and pressed her forward with surprising strength. "You're not in a position to negotiate. But maybe we should go before Oswald wakes up, just in case I do decide to be generous." Together, they marched toward the cliffs, the faint sound of birdsong coming alive far into the forest. "I am curious, however. Why would you need me to promise not to hurt Miss Colray?"

Emily forced herself to avoid Ward's eyes. "You promised to help her find her parents. I'm thinking you had some kind of plan for her, too."

Ward nodded. "Unfortunately, appearances matter. I was merely trying to be kind to a sad soul. But that sad night reminded me that inspiration can strike at the most unexpected times."

"What *inspiration*?" Emily asked as she dragged her feet across the grass. The sun snuck its way up the sky, its pace slow and steady. *Hurry up and find me. Someone...*

"You made a point of mentioning that the ring passed from fathers to sons. Something about how you said it . . . I had never considered the possibility of a daughter as an heir, but it seemed like something Alexander would do. After that, I just needed to encourage you to investigate Beth Selwyn and validate that suspicion."

The cold seeped into Emily's bones. "You were lying in a clinic bed wrapped up in bandages most of the year. Too bad the thing didn't finish you off."

He grinned. "Do you know why poor little Finn Dashwood died?" Ward waited, enjoying the flickers of emotion toying with her composure. "I knew that dimwit Beth Selwyn had safeguards around the ring. I came up here on many occasions to test them out, and I wasn't pure of intention enough to get past the Thorny Truth. But when Mister Dashwood came to me for some help on *your* recommendation, it was as though fate smiled down on me." He never blinked, and neither did she. "You shouldn't be so judgemental, Emily."

The knife sank into her gut and twisted. She knew her own guilt. But Ward knew it, too. Despite her best efforts, Emily's control slipped as her breathing sped up and her cheeks flushed. She didn't trust herself to speak, but Ward didn't seem to expect her to.

"Poor boy didn't question me at all when I told him that Thorny Truth was the best way to get over his fear of his own magic." Amusement played across Ward's face as the shadows from the overhanging cliff washed over him. "The infestation is quite impressive, but once it tastes its victim's blood and determines them worthy, it becomes as harmless as a house plant. The dragon, however, was quite the surprise."

"*You* killed Finn. And I helped." Hate boiled like molten steel, slow and thick, in Emily's veins.

"Technically, the dragon did." He shrugged. "After I

escaped, I knew that I needed someone with a little more stamina to make it to the end. And you fit the description beautifully. So, I linked us."

The rock glittered before them. Emily stopped in its shadow and turned to Ward, frowning. "You what?"

"You thought I was casting a protective spell on you earlier, but I linked us. That is how McKibbons guards her precious books, you see. She links herself to the books so she can sense when they're in trouble. I went to see her with the excuse of picking up my books, borrowed her ability, and linked us so that I was allowed anywhere you went."

"What about Naglar?" Her voice shook, and her chest was tight. "Did you get him to help me, too?"

Ward smiled. "Actually, no. That was a happy coincidence. Sometimes, things work out even for the worst of us."

There was nothing happy about that moment.

Ward had won.

"We're here. Now what?" she asked, the venom thick on her tongue.

Ward frowned. "Because I linked us, I saw most of what Beth showed you. We recreate Beth's final moments exactly. Every detail counts. If Beth climbed, that's what we're doing, too."

The will to resist left Emily's body. She filled her thoughts with the climb ahead and let her mind drift outside her body. Without a word, she pulled herself up, thinking of nothing but the grooves in the rock that Beth had used to pick her way up into the sky so many years before. Sharp edges of stone bit into her flesh, grating her hands raw. The wind pulled at her torn clothes, and the sun blinded her. Somewhere in the recesses of her mind, the knowledge that she would never see Ozzy or Catherine again threatened to unhinge her. Instead, she focused on the pain and pulled herself higher with Ward struggling to keep up.

She considered turning back. If she planned it well, she could launch herself off the rock and take him with her. Catherine and Ozzy would be safe, and so would the rest of the realm.

She wished she was that strong.

Instead, she pushed on, like a coward.

Instead, she climbed higher.

Her hand searched over her head and found nothing but open air. A landing. *The* landing.

Emily boosted herself over the lip with difficulty. Her bloodied fingers stung from the dirt and sweat pressing into her fresh wounds, but she didn't care. The flat rock face that Beth had leaned into before her death greeted her. It was the last thing Beth had touched, and Emily would suffer the same fate.

Ward pulled himself up after her, chest heaving. "She was sitting right there." He stood, shaky but focused, and pointed to the tall expanse of grey rock. "Go on."

Emily stared at the rock and waited. There were no dragons to save her, no ghosts to show her the way. She was alone in the end as she was in the beginning. "There's nothing here!" she cried over the wind.

Ward pushed her with a growl of frustration, and her head cracked against the stone. Lights swam across her vision and her knees buckled, dropping her to the ground. *Look at that,* she thought as warmth bloomed on her forehead. *I'm bleeding.*

Ward was a blur against the pink sky. "You're not trying!"

Emily clutched her head, stemming the flow of blood. Leaning back into the freezing rock, the world slowed and then stopped. As she opened her mouth to tell him it was over, that there was nothing left for her to do, her shoulders grew warm where they pressed against the stone. Her necklace burrowed deeper into her skin as though searching for the heat at her back, and an overwhelming sense of loss and desperation flooded her.

"Get up." Ward laced his fingers into her tangled hair and ripped her back, tossing her to the side. At once, the heat on her back disappeared. With Emily's ability still in his blood, Ward transferred loose bits of rock away from the cliff, clearing a hollow into the mountain. There was no ring, no Beth, no clue—except for a glowing hand etched into the stone no matter how much destruction he inflicted. Ward continued working, his movements erratic, power biting away at the hand but doing nothing to dull the glow.

He can't see it. "Maybe this isn't the right spot." Emily's palms were damp, her eyes stinging with sweat.

Ward was breathing hard, his hair matted to his head. "It's the *exact* spot. I don't understand. I did everything right!"

"I really don't—"

Ward's index finger swivelled in Emily's direction, and his lower lip trembled. "One more word and your heart will exist outside your body. Is that what you want?"

Emily recoiled. He couldn't kill her if he thought she was the key to finding the ring, but accidents happened—especially if he lost control. She crawled over to him, to the strange, shimmering hand still taunting her. The magic in the mountain pulled her forward, and she let it take hold. She longed to touch the rock again, to feel its warmth against her skin. She was so cold.

"Well?" Ward asked.

Emily sat back on her heels and tipped her face to the sky, letting the warmth of new daylight seep into her skin. "Beth didn't tell me what to do, and I have no idea, either."

Ward's body stiffened. "Pity you still feel you can lie to me." His face was nothing but sharp lines.

But Emily wasn't afraid. Not anymore.

With a sigh, she collapsed against the mountainside and pressed her shoulders into the rock. Her necklace hummed, and her body filled with pure energy—like a star on the brink of supernova. Somewhere in the distance, screams of pain and despair ripped through her head, and she let the tears come. "I'm ready to end this, now."

A guttural roar escaped Ward's lips. He raised his palm, and a patch of skin peeled away from her arm, leaving a raw, aching gash behind.

Emily screamed.

Her skin turned to flames, exposed and bleeding.

Another curse. He used her magic against her, and she was too weak, too tired, to fight back.

She screamed louder.

Ward lost all control, and the heat on her back grew, becoming as hot as the pain. He raged and threw curse after curse at her, peeling both skin and dignity away in small, torturous pieces. Despair ravaged her heart, the unfamiliar voices calling to her from somewhere in her mind.

Emily's vision flickered, and the world fell away. Half-conscious, she dropped to the ground and screamed over and over, wishing for death.

Ward panted, eyes swivelling back and forth, searching for a way out of his own personal prison. "I can stop. I *want* to stop. All you must do is trust me. Help me find my ring, and I will end this for you."

His words were so much like Xavier's: promising relief but delivering a fatal blow.

Emily lifted her eyes and fought to focus on Ward's face. She carved her fingers into the dirt, feeling the cool sand and sharp pebbles under her fingernails, just as Beth had done. She smiled. "No thanks."

He lifted his hand.

The pain welcomed her home.

She drifted in and out of consciousness. Somewhere in the place between life and death, she heard herself speak: "I feel sorry for you." The blackness pulled her under, and she drifted for a second or an eternity; she didn't know.

A strong voice whispered in her ear. *"The hand."*

Emily blinked away the lights peppering her vision. Ward and pain and the promise of a new, beautiful day she would never live through stared back at her. Taunting.

"Emily, the hand!*"*

Ward's fist swung out from somewhere in the abyss, and a crack of pain splintered her head. She heard herself grunt and kicked out hard. A loud, satisfying crunch followed by a howl of surprise pierced the quiet morning as her sneaker connected with his ribs.

"Get to the hand!"

She didn't have enough energy left to question it. *I'm trying…*

Did she speak out loud? So much pain, so much yelling. Not long now until it would all be over.

But she had to get to the hand first.

Ward clutched his ribs and took a few laboured steps toward her. With a burst of energy, Emily twisted around and raised her arm.

This is how Beth died. The thought was unwanted, unprovoked, and somehow brought her peace.

Beth. Her sorrow. Her pain.

Where it all began . . . where it all ends.

And Emily finally understood why Beth had led her here, to an end of her very own. She waited for the fear to paralyze her, but it never came. Her fingers reached while Ward pinned her to the ground, ready to deliver the final blow. The way to ensure the ring's safety was a sacrifice.

A *blood* sacrifice.

"Touch it!"

Someone called her name, but there were too many voices, too much sadness all around, pressing in on her. Ward's foot crunched into her ankle, and some distant part of her conscious mind registered the new burst of pain. She didn't care. It all ended where it began, anyway.

"Emily!"

Her fingers grazed the glittering outline of Beth's hand in the rock before she collapsed. Ward screamed, a roar of outrage shattering the last bits of consciousness she clung to. The air around him roiled, and a shadow enveloped him, holding him tight until his eyes rolled in his head.

Her body exploded.

It was over.

And that was fine.

"Emily?"

"Emily!"

Strange sounds called to her from the edge of nothing. Emily flexed her fingers and toes. She should be in pain but couldn't remember why. The details didn't matter.

"We're too late!"

Why wouldn't the voices leave her alone?

"Nice, isn't it?"

But she wasn't alone at all.

Emily squinted at the shadow in the distance but couldn't quite make out his face. He stood under a wide stone archway surrounded by pure emptiness. Nothingness.

The other voices were still there, but farther away, the texture of their panic lapping at the edges of her mind. *"Get her inside."*

Emily ignored the frantic echoes twisting her heart into a knot. "What is this place?"

"You tell me." His smile was bright, easy, a source of light in the darkness surrounding him.

Mind games. Perfect. "I don't know." The harder she focused, the louder the voices became and the greater the pain in her head. She pushed the thoughts away with haste.

"Bad place to get lost." He chuckled, the small movement of his broad chest sending a glint of something metallic out into the void, blinding her. New shadows joined him, silent, writhing shadows with eyes burning like small embers.

"*Am* I lost?" she asked.

His eyes were warm, dollops of coffee cream in a broad face. "Do you want to be lost? I mean, you can go back, or you can take a walk with me. But you *definitely* can't stay in this place. It's pretty depressing."

The voices behind her pitched higher, clawing at her mind. "I . . . I'm not sure. Maybe if I knew what happened I could figure out what I want to do." Emily rubbed her temples. Her limbs were no longer weightless but heavy rods of lead cementing her to the ground.

"You hear the voices, kid? Yeah, I guess you do. It's been so long . . . " He sighed.

She focused on the man, ignoring the pain in her skull. The object at his throat shone like a star, like the very sun. "You can hear them too?"

"If I try hard enough."

Emily waited for him to say more, but he only gave a half-smile, his stance relaxed. The voices buzzed louder, forcing unwanted images into her mind: mountain peaks covered in a white blanket, dark forests, so many lies. So much betrayal. She pressed her eyes shut, her mind a puddle too murky to see into.

And there was more.

A boy on the ground, hiding behind a book. A girl with a will of iron but a heart that had become home . . . home...

Home?

"Yes, there was some good with all the bad, too," the man said. "Funny how much good you can find in the worst places."

"Or how much bad you can find in the good." Another shadow—a woman, tall and slight, her left arm missing.

"Do I know you?" she asked the man. Colour and sound assaulted her, the frantic cries behind her threatening to pull her away. And she wasn't ready.

He shrugged. "It's possible."

Emily wrenched her eyes open. "What do the voices mean?"

He sighed. "That you have to choose."

The glint of metal on his neck caught Emily's eye once again. "You're wearing my necklace." She reached up for her own, only to find it gone.

"It's our burden, kid. You're just keeping it safe for a while."

Emily shook her head. "I don't understand."

"You will."

"Pass me that salve."

"I don't know how she could—"

"It doesn't matter. Hurry up."

"He sounds like he cares about you." *He?* The man closed his eyes, took in a deep breath, and the restless shadows fidgeting beside him grew still. "It isn't over until you decide."

"Decide *what*?"

"Whether you're ready to stay or go." The sadness was raw in his voice.

Something inside her shifted, and the voices now had faces. Images flooded back to her in fractured pieces, scenes and emotions coursing through her. *Catherine . . . Ozzy . . .*

A sob of joy escaped Emily's lips, tears blurring the stranger's dark outline. "Funny how much good you can find in the worst places," she whispered, the words feathering her lips.

He smiled. So did the others.

"See you, kid."

She closed her eyes once more and let the voices pull her back.

Chapter Twenty-Six

Moving On

"SHE CAN'T HAVE *CHOCOLATE*!" Ozzy protested.

"It's better than *flowers*!" Catherine's voice oozed sarcasm. "What's she gonna do, smell herself to recovery?"

Emily groaned. "Would you two be quiet? My head hurts."

A chair scraped across the floor. "Emily! How do you feel? Magdale, she's awake! How are you?" *Ozzy. He sounds worried.* Emily forced her eyes to open and immediately regretted it as the dim light assaulted her.

"How do you think she is, you moron?" Catherine's smile was warm as she leaned over Emily's bed. "Seriously, how bad do you feel?"

Emily's vision was blurry, and her temples throbbed. "I'm okay, I guess." She tried to sit up, but a shock of pain, sharp and hot, surged through her ribs. Memories came pouring in: the mountain, dragons with keys for teeth, Beth . . . *Ward*. She tore at the duvet, panic flooding her veins. "It's Ward! It was him the whole time, not Grey! Did you get him?"

"Slow down!" Catherine pressed her hands on Emily's shoulders, forcing her back to bed. "Everything's fine. I mean, we're a bit bruised up and annoyed we missed all the real action at the end—"

"Speak for yourself," Ozzy muttered.

"—but we're *fine*. Turns out that leather chest was rigged with a sleeping gas, so apart from a couple bumps on the head, we both got lucky." Catherine turned to Ozzy, worry flashing on her face. "And we know about Ward."

Emily settled into her pillow. "You do?"

Ozzy nodded. "I woke up after you started climbing, but it was too late to stop you. Victor showed up with Magdale after you got to the top, so they were able to get to you and get me out of there before anything worse happened."

Catherine frowned, face stormy. "I can't believe I owe Graven for rescuing us. This is the worst day of my life."

Victor. Of course. "I guess it's a good thing he can't mind his own business sometimes." Emily peered around the room, taking in the burgundy walls with deep wood trim and the wide fireplace giving off its blissful heat. Her muscles tensed. "Where are we?"

Another meaningful look, and Emily suppressed her annoyance. "You were in the clinic for about a week, but it was a disaster," Ozzy said. "People were trying to break in to see you and making so much noise, rioting and throwing things . . . " Catherine threw him a dark look of warning, and Ozzy backtracked at once. "But, uh . . . this is much nicer than the clinic, anyway."

Of course, everyone would find out and, *of course,* she would be the first-choice villain of the story. It was the other unexpected revelation that had her blood hammering in her skull. "I was out a *week?*" Emily asked.

"You were in pretty bad shape, Em." Catherine patted Emily's hand. "He did some real damage. They healed your ankle and most of the cuts pretty quick, but the ribs and collapsed lung took a little bit more work."

The door creaked open, and a round face framed in white snow peeked inside the room. "She wakes!" Magdale called, eyes reflecting firelight.

Unwanted tears burned Emily's eyes as Magdale made her way to the bed, and she averted her eyes. "I'm sorry, Magdale. I shouldn't have . . . I mean, I know I wasn't supposed to do what I did." She peered up at Catherine and Ozzy, the words sticking in her throat. "I'm so sorry for everything."

"Oh, Emily," Catherine sighed. "Shut up."

Emily grinned, her relief helping somewhat with the pain. And yet, she still couldn't rest. Not yet. "What happened to the Lost Ring? Did he get it?"

Magdale gave her a withering look. "I guess I shouldn't be surprised that even injured, you won't let things go." She sighed. "Ward did not manage to get the Lost Ring, dear. In fact, he never had a chance, given how deranged he was. We needed to catch him in the act of trying something illegal, and we got what we needed . . . in the end. Not that the ends justified the means, however."

Wait. Emily frowned. "It sounds like you knew he was after it all along."

Magdale sat on the edge of Emily's bed, the springs creaking under her weight, while Catherine and Ozzy settled into their chairs with matching looks of shame. "We've known that the Lost Ring was on Black Mountain ever since Beth Selwyn put it there. Every senior Master at the castle is tasked with protecting its whereabouts. And we've also known that Flavian Ward has been after it for quite some time. We simply haven't been able to prove it."

An uncomfortable silence hung between them. "But why didn't you say anything sooner?" Emily asked, bewildered. "You heard me talking to Ward about it in the clinic. You could have told me something!"

"Emily, it is not my role as Master Elemental to inform an initiate about the inner workings of sensitive magical issues." Magdale gazed down her nose at her, but her smile was gentle. "We had been waiting for him to show his hand, but when I overheard you speaking with him and saw how involved you were becoming with the ring's story, I knew we had missed our window. With Sable's interference and then yours, it was inevitable Ward was going to be more careful. It would have served no purpose to tell you the truth except to interfere with your relationship with him. And that would have *really* set us back."

The room was too hot. "So, if I hadn't stuck my nose in this, you would have caught him anyway." Emily's heart sank. First Finn, then Ward. "I'm an idiot."

Magdale's smile was reassuring. "Your intentions were good, dear. I shouldn't have expected anything less from someone who grew up the way you did. And, in the end, your intervention wasn't the most harmful obstacle in our way."

"What do you mean?" Emily asked, her guilt making it hard to imagine anyone else doing worse damage.

"Despite what you think, you're still only an initiate. I don't think Ward ever saw you as a true threat or a means of getting the ring. I believe he always imagined you would fail—at least until you made it to Beth's resting place. Sable, however, was a bigger issue."

"Grey?" Ozzy asked.

Magdale nodded. "Because of her previous . . . *issues*, Sable Grey had not been entrusted with the ring's location, nor with the plan to catch Ward in the act. We planted the seed that Migellus had found the ring to entice Ward to go after it. Zaphira knew the risks; we thought he might try to get into the security box outright but never expected him to *kidnap* her. It became impossible to find her once he had control of her ability." She lowered her eyes to her hands. "Grey sensed something was amiss and went down to Blintwoods herself. I believe she spotted Ward during his attempted theft and, from then on, couldn't let it go." She sighed. "So many mistakes all around."

"I guess Grey and I have some things in common," Emily said, hating how sour the words tasted. "We can't mind our own business."

"Nah, don't say that," Catherine interjected. "You might both be nosy, but she's a *horrible* person on top of it all."

Magdale rolled her eyes but didn't protest. "Sable Grey has her own interests at heart and quite a strange way of behaving, it's true. But she's earned her place as a mentor at this castle. Anyhow, the Lost Ring was, thankfully, never recovered. On the next full moon, I will be asking Beth what new protections we can provide for it."

"So, Emily didn't get it after all?" Catherine asked. "Even after all that trouble?"

"The ring was never hers to find." Magdale's eyes warmed. "But of all those who tried, something about Emily brought her quite close."

The logs in the fire popped and glowed a deep, vivid red in the low light. "How long do I have to stay here, Magdale?"

"A few more days," Magdale answered, getting to her feet. "Your mind has suffered as much trauma as your body, so I think a bit more rest will do you some good. And now I think it's time for a nap."

Emily's eyelids slipped low, the knowledge that Ward didn't manage to get the ring in the end a burden lifted from her heart. "He's working for someone, you know," she said, groggy. "Ward wasn't trying to find the ring for himself."

Magdale, Catherine, and Ozzy hesitated halfway to the door. "Are you certain?" Magdale asked, her question an echo, a dream.

"He told me so," Emily muttered. The fire continued to throw wavering shadows across their faces, and Emily wished she were alone. Her last moments on Black Mountain were a blur of images both real and imagined, and she wanted to forget. "He looked pretty scared about it, too. What happened to him?"

"The Guard has taken care of Flavian Ward," Magdale said. "You needn't worry about him any longer."

Good. That's good. But there was one more thing to say before she could sleep. And she so wanted to sleep. "Thanks for saving my life."

Magdale closed her eyes for a moment. When she opened them, her face had aged a decade. "Of course, dear. Your intuition about Beth's blood magic binding the ring to the mountain was impressive enough to get you out of any trouble, so please try not to worry. Also . . . how did you get Naglar to help you with the other dragon?"

Emily shook her head, dreams mingling with reality until she wasn't sure which was which. "I didn't. He just showed up." She pulled her covers under her chin, her bandages pulling.

Magdale nodded, body half-hidden in the doorway. "And how did you know to touch the mountain in that precise spot?"

"I didn't." Emily yawned, eyes slipping shut. "The shadow man told me to touch the shiny hand on the rock."

She must have drifted off before Magdale could say anything else. Sleep claimed her, hooded figures and dragons wearing necklaces chasing one another over and over until there was nothing left.

Spring crept up on the castle before Emily was allowed to step foot outside. By the time the ground had fully thawed, and new life bloomed all around, her wounds had healed to raised, pink scars, and her worst bruises had faded to a soft brown. But, although her body was on the mend, her mind was damaged beyond healing.

Emily pushed her scrambled eggs across her dish as the whispers circulated around her. Months before, she might have minded. She may have even worked to prove them wrong in their assumptions about her and resented their judgement. As it was, there could be no one who judged her with more contempt than she judged herself. And, because of her guilt, she endured the hissing and name-calling with an open, black heart. It was a punishment for which there could be no redemption.

"I can't believe you won't help me study," Catherine complained, stabbing her potatoes with more force than necessary. "I still have a concussion, Ozzy!"

"It's not a concussion." Ozzy dug into his pancakes with renewed appetite. "You were always this hopeless." He grinned as Catherine flicked a blueberry at his head. "Honestly, Catherine, it's not that bad." Syrup leaked down his chin and onto his shirt while he flipped through the Scroll.

Catherine pushed her own plate away. "I don't really need your help anyway, Oswald. I was only asking to give you something to do. And, seriously, when will you learn how to eat like a person?"

"When you learn how to study without complaining," he retorted.

Emily smiled, the movement of her face unnatural. She let them talk—the busier Catherine and Ozzy were, the less time they had to exchange worried or pitying stares.

"Do you want some of my waffle, Emily?" Willow asked. "I took too much, and those eggs look like they could use a break."

Smile at her. Come on, move your face. There you go. "Thanks, but I'm pretty full."

"Huh. I didn't see you eat much." Willow pushed her waffles aside, and Horus helped himself to them without a word. "Are you nervous about the cuts coming up? I think I'll do okay since Grey's not the one doing my evaluations this time and I've managed to make a connection in Master Murray's greenhouse, but you never know."

Grey's suspension for investigating Ward had been an unforeseen perk to her interference, but no one spoke of it. The initiates didn't question their sudden luck, which was just as well for Emily, who was in no mood to talk at all.

Catherine grinned. "Oswald is gonna be helping me make the cut. If I'm not too much of a lost cause."

"Oh, that's nice." Willow rested her chin in her palms. "I wonder who's going to take over Master Ward's evaluations."

"I liked him," Elliott interjected from down the table. "He didn't seem as perfect as all the other Masters." With new colour in his cheeks, Elliott helped himself to a small breakfast, his appetite making a comeback.

Emily stiffened. No one had mentioned Flavian Ward since his disappearance from the castle. His influence had been minimal, and the gap he left behind was really a crack easy to overlook. Everyone was replaceable in the end. Except his memory haunted Emily's every thought. Even when his lessons were cancelled for the remainder of the year, the empty time slots in Emily's week were a reminder of how a criminal had operated without boundaries under her nose. And she'd helped him.

"Hey, look at this." Ozzy set down his fork and jabbed an excited finger into the middle of the Scroll: "'Developments around last year's mysterious explosion at the renowned magical supply and vault institution, Blintwoods, have surfaced,' reports Elie Quinn, special

Guard Liaison. 'Shopkeeper, Zaphira, has been found and admitted into critical care at the Gildenveil Rehabilitation Glen for repeated psychological trauma.'"

"At least they found her." Catherine peeked over Ozzy's shoulder, her curls covering half the text.

"Zaphira always had the best stories," Willow said with a faraway look in her eye. "And I liked her missing teeth."

Ozzy blinked. "Uh . . . right. There's more, though: *'Despite Zaphira's inability to communicate coherently with Guard officials, it has been strongly suggested the Blintwoods explosion and her own prolonged torture was the work of the elusive bounty hunter, Holly Malchan. Ms. Malchan is linked to multiple disappearances in both the Commons and Gildenveil City and is suspected to have associated with Baxter Rathburn during his later years as Void Gatekeeper.'"*

All eyes turned to Emily as she set her fork down. "Don't worry, I'm not going to have a breakdown. I know my dad was a bad guy. It's not a surprise anymore. Keep going, Ozzy."

He turned back to the Scroll: "*'Guard officials have organized with High Council Empaths and are confident Ms. Malchan will be apprehended shortly. An anonymous source has provided reliable intelligence regarding her whereabouts and, if successful in aiding with her capture, will be this decade's greatest hero.'"*

"Well, that settles it." Catherine scowled. "I officially can't trust anything I read. Hey, Horus!"

Horus swallowed the piece of waffle clogging his mouth. "Kitty-Cat! Need me to polish off some food for you?"

"Call me that again and I'll have you eating spinach

for a month." Catherine's smile dripped with acid. "You ever hear of Holly Malchan?"

"Nope." Horus shrugged and turned to Piper. "How about you?"

"I don't read the Scroll," Piper said, nonplussed. "Media garbage isn't for me."

Emily lowered her eyes to her dish and picked up her fork for something to do with her hands. *Eggs go left, eggs go right, then left again.*

"She's a bounty hunter, apparently." Ozzy turned his attention back to the Scroll and picked his way through previous articles. "A good one, according to this."

"Do those really exist?" Willow asked. "I mean, bounty hunting is illegal."

"Yeah, but they get the job done." Horus winked. "The Guard's all tripped up in politics, but bounty hunters do what they need to to. I'd love to meet one."

Emily had had enough. She eased to her feet, her ankle throbbing. "I think I need some air."

"Hol' on, I'm a'mof done eating!" Ozzy's fork became a blur as he worked to finish his breakfast.

Catherine frowned. "Is that even possible?"

"I just have to let Brady know where I'm going." Ozzy rolled his eyes. "Ever since . . . well, you know . . . he's been reporting back to Mother to make sure I'm okay. I thought it'd be nice when they started paying attention to me, but honestly it's annoying."

You don't say. "If you don't mind, I think I want to go alone. I'm a slow walker these days." She kept her voice level, clear of any pain. Inside, she was dying.

Ozzy opened his mouth to protest, but Catherine cut him short. "Sure, Em. We're gonna be going over some spells and teaching Ozzy how to use a fork if you need us. Just be careful."

Be careful. Be careful. Two words to remind her she hadn't been careful at all. Emily made her way out of the Gallery as fast as her sore leg would take her.

Time alone was like taking a sip of water after days of dehydration: insufficient and ineffective, especially after being stifled for weeks by Catherine and Ozzy, but necessary to stay alive. The entrance hall was quiet, safe from the dark looks and high expectations.

Except she wasn't alone.

"Hey, dragon whisperer. Still here?" The voice was bitter and familiar and so, so unwanted.

Emily's heart fell, and she tried to stifle the flare of anger in her chest. "Need something, Camilla?"

She sat on the lowest step of the stairwell, her long auburn hair drawn back into a ponytail. "You're walking," Camilla noted. With a burst of speed, she cut into Emily's way. "I guess whatever tried to kill you didn't manage it, huh?"

"Too bad, right?" Emily tried to step around her, but Camilla blocked her path. "Look, I'm tired. I don't want to fight with you."

"Me either." When Emily snorted, Camilla hugged her stomach. "I'm serious. You took away two of the closest people in my life. Catherine might not be speaking to me anymore because of you, but Victor's still around . . . for now. I don't want to upset him anymore, especially over you."

"Sounds like a healthy relationship."

"It's not." Up close, Camilla's cheeks were pale, her brown eyes small and puffy, rimmed in red. *She's been crying*. Emily couldn't find it in herself to feel sorry about it. "But he's all I have left. Because of you."

"It's not my fault your friends got tired of you." Emily's patience was dwindling; her stiff muscles were screaming at her to move, to walk away and never look back. "Look, I was on my way out."

"How do you do it?"

Emily blinked, her sluggish mind trying to keep up. To care. "Do what?"

"Get people to like you when you're *you*." Despite the snarky words, Camilla's face was serious. Sincere.

Emily laced her arms across her chest, willing as many barriers between her and Camilla as possible. "I don't know. I'm not perfect. No one is, but maybe you were right about me all along. Maybe the bad Rathburn blood really does run deep."

Camilla nodded. "Maybe."

"So, we agree that I suck, then?" Emily pursed her lips.

"We do." A bitter smile played across Camilla's lips. "But I have no real friends, so maybe I suck a bit, too."

"Maybe." Emily shifted her weight, the conversation veering into uncomfortable territory. "You could try to be a bit nicer, you know. It would help."

"And you could stop stealing everyone I love."

"I deserved that one." Emily needed air. The grounds waited, and there was nothing more she wanted than to stop talking. "If that's how you feel, then I'm . . . I'm sorry. I guess we'll never really like each other."

"I don't think we will." Camilla swiped the back of her hand across her nose and sniffled. "Stay off that leg." She sauntered back toward the stairs. "And Emily?" Camilla's eyes watered, but she jutted her chin in the air, making no motion to hide her tears. "Catherine's the best. If you hurt her, I'll hunt you down. Yeah?"

Emily nodded. "Yeah. And if you could take Victor off my hands, I'd owe you one." Sensing the end of their interaction, she trudged to the doors, the promise of a headache gathering like a storm behind her eyes.

Emily stepped onto the spongy lawn and pulled her hood over her head as she broke away from the castle. Her legs moved without conscious encouragement, taking her around the outer wall, across the courtyard, past the tree line, and down the familiar path into the forest. She wasn't sure why she was heading there—the forest had plagued her nightmares since her near-fatal encounter with Ward—but her feet kept moving, and she didn't have the energy to question her instincts.

The air was heavy with the scent of wet earth, and varied shades of green crept into the expanse of brown and grey. She expected fear to grip her, to make her stop. Instead, when she stepped into the clearing, she was numb.

And she wasn't alone.

Victor stretched his legs and pushed himself off the ground. His smile was easy, his hands tucked away in his jacket pockets as he strolled toward her. But his face was guarded. Wary. "Nice to see you walking around again, Rathburn."

Emily clenched her fists by her side. "Only reason I came is because I wanted to be alone." *And to punish myself, apparently.*

"Sorry to disappoint, but I did find this place first." His eyes moved over her face without reservation. "So, how'd you do it?"

"How'd I do *what,* Victor?" She wasn't getting rid

of him, and her skin prickled at the idea of being around him much longer.

She walked into the center of the clearing and combed the skies for the fairies. Perfect blue, unaltered by clouds or birds—or fairies—stretched overhead. Her heart plummeted into her gut, and her eyes stung.

"How'd you lose your guard dogs?" Victor asked, joining her. "I thought Ozzy and Catherine were magically chained to your hip."

"I didn't lose them." *Are the fairies hiding? Victor did say they prefer coming out at night . . .* "I came out for a walk to be *alone*. Some people know how to take a hint." Her head throbbed, and she was in no mood for the verbal sparring.

"How can I forget when it's the second time you mentioned it in under a minute?" He exhaled. "But I don't think you'd have come here if you wanted to be alone."

Her head jerked in his direction, and she was immediately disoriented by how close he stood, his elbow grazing her arm. "I had no idea you'd be here."

Victor's eyes were warm, teasing, but his mouth formed a pout. "That hurt my feelings, Rathburn. Deeply." Their breathing was even and matched. "I meant that maybe you came to see the fairies. That's why I come here, anyway. And why I assume you're looking up at the sky like it's done something wrong to you."

Ugh. "I did, but I should have figured they'd be gone during the day. I'll come back later."

"No point." His eyes traced the contours of her face. "They're gone. Disappeared about a month ago."

Emily glared at the sky. "Everything moves on eventually, I guess," she muttered. "Especially when someone comes along to screw up your life." *Someone like me.* She'd jeopardized Ozzy's and Catherine's lives, her own position at the castle, not to mention Magdale's reputation, and the futures of everyone in the realm. Scaring off a few hundred fairies was an unexpected item to add to her growing list.

He nodded. "Is that why you stay away from me? Because you think I'll move on, too?"

She laughed, the sound bitter even to her own ears. "You give yourself way too much credit, Victor. I stay away from you because I don't like you."

"Ouch," he gasped, his right hand clutching his chest while his left hovered between them, the heat from his hand warming her cold fingertips. "That was harsh."

"I won't apologize for being honest."

"No, tact isn't your style," he agreed.

She glowered at him. "*That* was harsh."

"You know that's not what I meant." His voice was light and easy, but there was an undercurrent of something else, something urgent, that made Emily want to run, want to hide, want to never come back. "You do whatever you think is right, no matter the consequence. It's admirable. Stupid, but admirable."

Just as they had done a lifetime before, they stood in the clearing facing one another, their eyes locked, black on black, challenge with challenge. The anger, so close to the surface, bubbled up the back of her throat. "Watch it, Victor."

"I am watching, Rathburn. And what I see scares me."

He rested his palm on the shoulder still aching from the collision with the ground, an impact she couldn't recall. His warmth spread down her arm and into her fingertips, easing the tension there, willing her body to heal. She could have shaken herself free, but every ounce of fight left inside her was focused on staying upright, on not showing the cracks threatening to split her apart.

"I don't have time for this." Her voice trembled. "I want you to either stop talking or go away. Please."

Victor, of course, ignored her. "I know you better than you think. To you, I'm just annoying and full of myself—"

"And selfish."

"—okay, and selfish. And you'd be right most of the time. It doesn't help my case that I brought Magdale in on whatever you were doing . . . but I'd do it again."

"Yeah, because you're annoying, full of yourself and selfish." *And a lifesaver, and not so bad sometimes . . . even a little fun, maybe.* But she couldn't tell him those things. That particular box in her mind needed to stay closed. She had no idea what to do with herself if it should ever open.

He shook his head, all trace of humour gone. "How can you say that? When I got there with Magdale, you were unconscious. We thought you were dead."

"I know." Her words, so carelessly spoken, broke him.

"You *know?*" he asked, his voice climbing. "You probably have some idea of how bad you were tortured, since you can barely walk straight and your side hurts when you laugh or move too fast." Emily's eyes grew wide, and Victor gave a short, mirthless laugh. "Yeah, you think I don't notice things, but I do. Ward lost all control of himself—it was the worst thing I've ever seen."

"Victor—"

"And there you were, lying on the ground *bleeding*." He frowned at her, seeking the truth in her eyes and finding the tallest and strongest of stone walls instead.

Emily stood straight, even though it made her ribs ache. "I lived, didn't I?"

"You almost didn't. You *shouldn't* have." Victor's jaw flexed. "If I had known that helping you could have cost you your life, I would have never shown you that poem."

Emily latched on to the only argument she had, a bright spot in the darkness to fuel her anger. And anger was what she needed to keep herself together. "Now I get it. You feel guilty for helping me." She shook her head. "Don't worry, you're off the hook for that. I'm not angry that you told Magdale or that you got me that book from McKibbons."

"I don't want to be *off the hook*."

She shrugged off his hand and glared at him. "Then what is it, Victor? What do you want?"

"I want the truth about why you were up there."

She laughed. "Why? It's done! It's over—it's all *over*!" The wall crumbled, and her cheeks grew hot, the first sign of emotion she'd shown in weeks creeping into her sensitive skin. "Finn's gone, Ward's probably in a prison or dead. I even scared away the fairies!" Her breathing came fast, the anger going from orange, to yellow, to bright white. And still, she fanned the flame. "Why can't you just let me live with all that in peace? Elders, you're annoying!"

"You'll get over it," he muttered. The corner of his lip twitched as she fumed inches away from him, her chest heaving. "By the way, you said 'Elders.' I've never heard you use a city expression."

The crackling storm within her shifted long enough for Emily to blink in disbelief. "You irritate me, Graven."

"You're probably right," he said, grin flashing. "And you didn't scare away the fairies."

The change of topic was like whiplash. "Huh?"

"The fairies," Victor repeated. "Little known fact about them: fairies aren't attracted to magic itself. They like darkness and mischief. And since magic involves both of those things, that's what they're most attracted to."

"Why are you telling me this?"

"I thought you might like to know that you made Black Mountain a little less dark. No idea how since you won't give me any details, but I know better than to ask." Victor peered down at her and lapsed into easy silence.

No more darkness. No more mischief. "The fairies left because I . . . helped?"

He nodded. "Yep. No more bad intentions for them to feed on."

A little bit of good, even with all the bad. The idea stirred something in her, some memory she couldn't quite place. Instead of poking at it, trying to uncover it, she left it alone. Sometimes good things were better left untouched.

"You know," Victor said, "I like our chats."

Me too. "Too bad I've got to cut this one short, then." To her astonishment, she meant it. But she was still raw, still buried under too much sadness to see the sun. Victor might have given her a glimmer of hope, but it wasn't enough to chase away the darkness. "Ozzy and Catherine are expecting me back."

"Then let me say it again." Victor's eyes bored into hers. "Next time you get mixed up in something like that again—the next time you're in trouble—you come to me."

Her response was automatic. Practiced. Robotic. The storm shifted once more, the storm clouds rolling back in, always so close to cracking together and releasing thunder onto the world. "There won't be a next time." *Please don't ruin this. I was just starting to feel better.*

Victor rolled his eyes. "Sure there won't. Just come to me before getting up on a cliff again, okay?"

She was five years old again. The bowl of freshly picked apples was up on the counter—a rare treat the Chancellor decided to share. She had stretched her fingers as far as she could, caressed the tender skin of the deep red fruit, and somehow ended up with the entire bowl in her hands. The Chancellor had locked her in the basement for a week. Careless, he had called her. Selfish. In addition to her own starvation, the other children had suffered meal rations because of her mistake as well. And she hadn't even been sure how it had happened. Only that it was her fault.

In the clearing, she was five years old again and had come into possession of a very valuable bowl of apples. But the voice in her mind told her she was careless. Selfish. And all she would do was destroy the precious thing she held because she wasn't worthy of it.

Victor's voice was soft. "It's okay to need help, Emily. You're only one person, but you're an important person. At least to me."

When she was five, she had been alone and terrified. Confused when the Chancellor scolded her. Belittled her. Starved her.

Now, she was older. And now, she was allowed to be angry.

"Which is it, Victor?" she asked, and her low, even tone caused his brows to pull together. "I'm special and powerful or I'm a silly girl getting into trouble who needs help?"

"That's not—"

"Do you know what I almost ruined?" Tears burned her eyes, and she made no effort to clear them away. "There's a girl in the Commons, at the place I lived before coming here. I was the closest thing she had to a sister. Her name was Molly, and she was happy and pretty and wonderful." More tears, more rage. "And I left her. I ran away so I could come here and maybe make a difference. And all I did was put her and everyone else in danger by trusting the wrong person." Blood coursed through her veins for the first time in a month, her outrage giving her purpose. Her eyes bored into Victor's, bold and unapologetic.

"You didn't do that on purpose, Rathburn."

"How do you know? I'm a Rathburn. All I'm good for is destroying things." Her eyes stung as something inside her kicked loose, and a blockage in her chest dissolved. She could breathe.

"Anytime you think that," Victor said, holding firm, "remember the fairies. Remember that there was some good that came from you being a Rathburn."

She would not let the tears fall. And she didn't trust her own voice. Victor's eyes were deep and free of hate or accusation, and she clung to that like a girl drowning in the sea.

"I guess I have a point," he said, ignoring the emotion playing across her face. "You stopped yelling at me for once."

Emily smiled and, for a moment, her face didn't hurt from the effort. "Sorry for all the yelling."

"If you want to make it up to me, you could take me up on that date you promised."

She laughed, and the sound was strange but welcome to her ears. "I hate you, you know that. I tell you something personal, scream at you, and you ask for a date?"

"Hate and love are siblings, Rathburn. I'll take what I can get. Plus," he added, inching closer, "I asked for the date weeks ago, so technically, this is just a reminder."

Emily turned back to the trees. The path to the clearing appeared smoother, brighter, the budding leaves a deep jade. They'd been here before: Victor offering a hand in the dark, and her, returning to the darkness on her own. "I have to get back."

But she didn't move.

Without a word, Victor brushed his fingers against the back of Emily's hand, then the inside of her wrist. His touch set her skin on fire but, still, she didn't move. "I wish you'd stay longer."

Her own fingers curled around to meet his, the soft brush of skin on skin giving her heart a jolt, pulling her away from her nightmares. The pain that had taken over her life ebbed away, trivial somehow in the safety of their small circle of trees.

Not much had changed since leaving the Commons; she was still a Rathburn, burdened by the shadows it carried. But, for once, the world held whispers of colour to replace the never-ending grey.

"I guess I can stay a few more minutes." Emily's cheeks filled with heat, and she let herself step into his arms, let him brush his thumbs against her hands. "You know, since this place is so nice. Not because you asked me to."

"You don't do *anything* because someone asked you to." Victor stood still, his chin resting on the crown of her head while the heat from their hearts pulled them closer.

Tomorrow, the pain would still be there. She would face her suffering, the hate, every mistake she'd made. But for the first time in her life, she was certain she wouldn't face any of it alone.

She pulled away from Victor, and he nodded, understanding. Releasing her hand, they walked the path back to Selwyn castle together. Back to Catherine and Ozzy and the other people she loved.

Back to her life.

Learn more about the author

WWW.VANESSARACCIO.COM

Facebook: @vraccio

Instagram: @authorvanessaraccio

Goodreads: @138301805-vanessa-r

TikTok: @authorvanessaraccio

ACKNOWLEDGEMENTS

While writing a novel is challenging and often soul-crushing, thanking those who made the process easier takes comparatively little effort. First, to my two babies, who are an endless well of inspiration: You are the driving force behind all my efforts, both sleep-deprived and caffeinated. I love you forever and always. To the mother who fostered my love of books and taught me how to read my first words, and the Papa whose faith in me never wavered, I owe you everything, including and especially my innate stubbornness. Natalia Leigh and the Enchanted Ink Publishing team, I thank you for bringing together all the design elements of this novel, lending your eyes to perfecting the final manuscript, and all the patience and professionalism you showed this newbie author. You gave me the confidence I needed. My editor, Fiona McLaren, asked all the right questions to bring my work to the next level—thank you for the flawless balance of encouraging praise and constructive criticism, even when a new round of edits brought me to the edge of tears (note: Marketing copy is the bane of my existence). Thanks to Cathy and Sabrina, who not only served as inspiration for my favourite characters in this book, but who cheered me on when I was ready to give up. Also, now you know I am, in fact, writing about you. And lastly, the greatest thanks goes to my amazing husband. Any way I write this will either sound gushy (which I hate) or cliché (which detracts from my sincerity), so I'll settle for this: Thanks for not divorcing me. Seriously. The days—no, *months*—of shop talk, telling me the brutal truth, even when I didn't want to hear it, watching the kids so I could work uninterrupted, making me coffee when the cups ran dry, and believing this thing could make it to the end, would have made any other man I know run. I know because I asked. Thank you for it all. Especially given that I named my villain after you. So sorry about that.

Vanessa Raccio,

author of *Lost Rings and Other Things*, has a bachelor's degree in psychology from Concordia University and a certification in personal training. After years of balancing "the jobs" with "the hobbies," she decided to pursue "the dream." Vanessa lives in Canada with her husband, two children, and a chihuahua who is both fierce and afraid of spiders in equal measure. When she is not writing, she can be found singing nursery rhymes, exercising, or baking something delicious.